SUNRISE

Sequel
to

A Dry Patch *of* Skin

SUNRISE

Sequel
to

A Dry Patch *of* Skin

Stephen Swartz

MYRDDIN PUBLISHING GROUP

UNITED STATES · UNITED KINGDOM · AUSTRALIA

ISBN-13: 978-1-68063-027-5

ISBN-10: 1-68063-027-X

Myrddin Publishing

www.myrddinpublishing.com

Cover design by Iris Schaeffer

Ich bin der Geist der stets verneint! Und das mit Recht; denn alles, was entsteht, ist wert, dass es zugrunde geht.

I am the spirit of ever denied! And rightly so; for all that is produced is worth perishing.

Johann Wolfgang von Goethe, *Faust* - Part One

Part One

1

. . . AT THIS POINT A CONFESSION SHOULD BE IN ORDER: I AM A VAMPIRE. Everything will make more sense now. Those who hear the words cannot see my appearance and may decide it is all mere boast. Indeed, you may think it pretentious to declare outright such a unique identity, yet I assure you that I have much experience upon which to base this conclusion. I bear all the gruesome traits, all the genetic curses, all the unpleasant *sensations* of this form.

First there is the papery skin which flakes at the slightest touch or the faintest flicker of sunlight. Hideous dry patches cover my body from head to toes; they crust over then split open and ooze a putrid pus. My skin is pale, sickly white yet not quite albino hue. The flesh on my head and face has pulled tight, causing my eyes to protrude from their sockets and my teeth to hang long from my gums. The point of my nose has withered away, the cartilage flattening. The hair upon my head has mostly fallen out; what remains are errant strands that seek to live on when the rest of me has died. I sweep them back and, on good days, gather them into a braid. That touch of fashion is solely for my convenience; no reason to put forth any effort affecting a proper appearance. No one will see it.

Indeed, I have seldom ventured far from this castle, and when I did go past its wooded precincts, it was only to surreptitiously observe the villagers living their happy lives or the occasional lost tourist wishing to see the Plitvice Lakes nearby. I craved a view of a very different life; indeed, a life I can no longer have.

You see, I died on October 31 in the year 2014. Yes, on Halloween (laugh, snicker). When I did visit those places, the village or the lakes, a few people perhaps saw me but didn't turn away; curiosity, I suspect, kept their eyes fixed upon me. Yet once satisfied their eyes operated properly, they quickly averted their gazes. I choose to believe it was out of politeness, but who can say for certain? I am, after all, a creature of the forest now—

"Who are you speaking to, dear?" asks a woman's voice.

"No one, Mother."

I glare into the shadows bleeding down the far corners of the long room, a hall of stone with long medieval tapestries covering the walls and a pair of lofty stained glass windows at one end depicting a band of hunters with horses and hounds in pursuit; then, the slaying of their vampire prey. A warning we best remember, Father states nearly every day.

The old gentleman occupies the opposite shadowy corner from the old lady. He reads a history tome as thick as his fist—volume three, I think. She embroiders, yet her boney fingers can scare hold the needle and thread, withered away over the years. The years have not been kind to them, though they are kind enough to others and prudently keep to themselves—as they did for many years between the days of my collegiate bliss and the subsequent completion of my own shocking transformation into this family fashion.

"Yet I hear you speaking," the woman insists. "Is it the visions once more?"

"No, Mother." I purse my lips—dry, cracked but not bleeding. I am short of blood. As usual. *Parents!* "They are not visions. How many times must I explain to you? No, I am merely thinking aloud—thinking loudly. You know I do that from time to time. It's how I maintain my sanity."

"Yes, dear, and yet I can hear you."

"Your thinking aloud disturbs your mother's sewing," says the man in the corner, turning his thick book upside-down, folding it over his knee.

"Embroidery," says Mother. "Not sewing."

"It's all the same to me, Love."

"You two have your hobbies," I say, adding a deliberate grunt. "You are happily occupied. My hobby cannot be performed here."

"And what is your hobby?' asks Father. We've had this discussion nearly every day for the past thirteen years, yet it is never resolved. We recite our scripts like actors on stage. The days pass like centuries in this house, an hour like a week, and nothing ever changes.

"What can you not do in this villa?" asks Mother.

"*Live!*"

I cannot stand that I shouted. I hate the echo. They push me to it two or three times a week now.

Shaking my head, I throw a dismissive hand at them. They never understand. They have been dead too long to remember the way life was before. Can anyone make sense of their parents? It must be similar in every family. However, in a family 'blessed' with vampirism genes, it can be particularly annoying. In a normal family, I could await their certain infirmity and eventual death. However, we are not normal—

"I'm going out," I announce, more to the stone walls than to my parents. What I have is a fate worse than death: to be dead, yet stuck with my similarly dead parents.

"Wear a coat," says Mother.

"And a hat and scarf," Father adds. "The autumn is upon us."

ᘓ

Outside the main entrance of this villa, I put my shoulder into closing the pair of monstrous wooden doors that separate us from the world. I stand on the gravel drive which leads down the hillside into the valley. Autumn comes early to higher elevations. It is barely October. Already a cloud of brown leaves blows across my path. Above, the yellow moon is hidden behind the half-bare trees that crown our hilltop, branches like a devil's fingers grasping the last glimmer of hope. The air, crisp like old biscuits, clears my head, raises my blood's ire. I catch the scent of a kill somewhere in the forest. A deer perhaps. Numerous wolves here. Sniffing the wild scent, I turn down the gravel drive, my old boots crunching the older rocks.

It is the season of the undead.

I have no one to talk to, none to converse with—what use are my parents? So I have taken to speaking with my alter ego. That's how I call my former self: a man once named Stefan Székely. It's a Hungarian name, although I was born in America. He and I still share the name, legally, yet I feel he is different from me. He lived, and also loved, in a far off land known as Oklahoma. For a while. That place was not for him; he began life in the northern tier of New York. Indiscretions there forced him to flee to that western state, settling into a city where he might continue making his living in the only trade he had learned: phlebotomy. Yes, I know that seems especially ironic now: a job where he works with blood, runs various tests, and so on. That keeps a supply of the red close at hand. Until you get caught sneaking a sip. Then you must run.

Actually, the running part was more a desperate attempt to find a cure for the incurable. That was his curse; mine, as well, for we are one. It crept upon me just as I fell in love with a woman who I met there in Oklahoma City. I was ready to settle down with her, make a family, have a long, happy life . . . even there in tornado alley. It's not for everyone. As for the tornado—

It was a tornado coming through the city that made it possible for us to meet. On social media, of course. She was a new reporter for one of the local TV stations. I manned the blood bank for the emergency. She asked people online to post their experiences. I commented about the blood supply—well before my transformation began. We got into a long chat—hours. Eventually we agreed to meet in the café of the Barnes & Noble by the Quail Springs Mall, near my apartment and on the way to her TV station.

I cannot say much more on that score. It was so brief and so long ago. Things progressed wonderfully from that first meeting. We had our ups and downs, getting used to each other, but finally everything was perfect. Then she noticed a dry patch of skin on my face and she suggested lotion. I needed more than lotion, as it turned out. I sought medical help, holistic remedies, alternative treatments, weird things, with no success. I did not know then what I know now: My body was slipping into what it should be, following the family curse.

You can imagine what a woman's reaction to that kind of situation might be. She remained as kind and patient as anyone could be. Being a gentleman, however, I knew I had to do what was best for her. I had to bow out, had to save her from my horror. I still held out hope for some cure. I fled all the way to Hungary, my family's ancestral home, then to Zagreb in Croatia. I arranged to receive cutting-edge stem cell treatment there which should cure me. Instead, it was the nail in my coffin. The experimental procedure assured I would forever more be one of the undead.

No, the procedure did not work. I was too desperate, too ravaged by then to think clearly. I should have suspected it wouldn't work. I would continue to devolve into this . . . this hideous creature strolling about on a night's lonely hillside.

I wonder about her sometimes: Penny Park, ace reporter for OKC News, who I called My Beloved. The urge is strongest in the evening, as the happy villagers below settle into their warm beds, holding each other, perhaps making love. Staring up at the moon, I see her face, her white cheeks and dark eyes. She was Korean, by the way, though born in Denver, fully American of Korean parents. She had problems with her parents, too. I see the smile that usually leaned to the side of her mouth, as though she struggled to hold back a smirk. She had the most delightful smirk. She would blink and I could not resist her.

A long story. A sad story.

A story that has ended. The new tale is how a man with so many years yet to endure can endure them living with his parents.

"It's impossible," I mutter to the breeze. My fetid breath startles a fox nearby and it dashes away through the brush. Animals can smell my death stench. And yet I am not dead. I shall never die.

Oh, I suppose there is not really any truth to that old superstition. The immortality thing. Long time, to be sure, but not immortal. Father said his brother made it two-hundred years, the longest in his family. Mother's aunt existed a hundred-fifty-two years. To those caught up in normal accounting, those years would seem like forever. Indeed, to me, might as well be forever. I'm not ready to be immortal. Not like this; not stuck in this crippled form with constant thirst, the nagging need for love, the desire for connection. And a good draught of blood.

Everything I left behind when I escaped to this forest in Croatia is forgotten now. They tried to protect me from the curse. When I was about ten, they sent me to live with a woman in Pittsburgh. My parents were doctors who cared for the deformed and deranged in the upstate asylum in Utica, a place they did not want me to experience—not after the first few years of my childhood. Kids at school teased me about living there.

They could not hold back the family curse. It arrived, swept them along. I discovered it in the letters Mother wrote. Only after their fake funeral in Makarska did I come to possess the letters. The funeral was only a formality, after years of retirement and seeking after their own treatments and cures, all in vain. It was a way for them to break free of society's curiosity, no questions asked.

I gaze up at the windows of our villa, dark in the night, nothing to signal to the curious to come up the hill and explore. It is not quite a castle. It has eight bedrooms but no dungeon. My parents call it a villa, perhaps a more modest label than castle. Castle is so pretentious, after all. Who would live in a castle? Cold and drafty. A fortune to maintain.

But I digress . . . .

A chill blows against me yet I feel nothing. My heart is cold. I do not shiver, do not pull my coat tighter. All I wish for at this moment is another chance to live again. Yes, pity me. If I could, I would find a way to return and live one impossible year, or even a full week, with Penny Park, then die as a mortal, clean and handsome, an open casket. That would be enough for me.

ೞ

With a rustle of leaves from the nearest tree, my thoughts jump to the little Hungarian girl I met long ago. Alma Jónás, a waif dressed in Goth fashion, helped me navigate through Budapest. When one of my spells overcame me, she got me emergency treatment. Then she insisted on accompanying me to the spa where I'd hoped to find a cure. What a bus trip! No cure. They would not let me in, as horrid as I appeared. We went on to Zagreb, to the clinic I had been trying to reach before I tried to switch to the closer spa in Sárvár.

God was playing fast and loose by then, teasing me, taunting me, challenging me at every turn. I thought I had wounded His pride at some point during my childhood. My 'aunt' in Pittsburgh never let me enter her church, knowing my curse. Revenge; I get it. A bit petty, I believe. However, I accepted the deal He offered: restore this unlucky waif, Alma, to full health, like she was before meeting me, and I shall go quietly into that good night.

The procedure I paid a lot for did not work, as I mentioned already. I awoke in the night, everything unhooked from me, lights off, a sheet over my face. When I arose from the bed and pulled on clothing from the closet, I had no plan but to check on Alma, back in the hotel. I was not sure at that moment if I had died or not. In the hotel room, I startled her; she no longer recognized me. And she was whole again, unharmed, no longer sick. So I said goodbye and departed—

The gravel crunches under my boots as I continue down the drive through the forest, down the hillside, the yellow moonlight full on my shoulders, broken only by the dark branches around me.

Leaving Zagreb after my death, I went to the only place left for me: the property my parents left me in the will. And it was here in this old villa that I found them—though not nearly as dead as I had assumed when I stood before their closed caskets in Makarska. It was an underwhelming reunion.

It may be that the transformation also takes away our emotions, our ability to be moved by circumstances. Not only can we no longer appreciate the jokes, we *are* the jokes—yet we do not notice. We enter a somber veil and are forever emotionless. Apparently, I have not yet traveled long enough down that road, for irony rains down like hail, pounding me into submission.

Ah! How morbid we've become strolling through the woods on an autumn eve! Are you happy now, God?

Reduced to a metaphor. I laugh.

My friend Milo descends from the trees, alights on my shoulder. He offers a tiny screech but I have no juice to share with him. He does not drink blood; what did you expect? There are no vampire bats in Europe. That's one of those ridiculous myths. Milo is one of those harmless *nyctalus lasiopterus*. Vampire bats exist only in Central and South America; they are named after the kindred of Count Dracula, as many know him. He is said to have lived across the valley, in a castle on the next mountain. Our neighbor. More myth—better for tourism.

Disappointed, Milo wings away, lost in the darkness.

If only I could fly away . . . .

My parents have found a balance. They keep to themselves, staying hidden in the family villa, turning it into a dungeon for me. Once in a while a visitor happens by to provide some drink for them. And me. I'd rather not, certainly, yet what choice do we have? The *heme* in blood keeps us going, restores some semblance of normalcy for a short time.

So I've become quite the student of blood disorders, diseases such as porphyria, and all manner of dubious legends collected into many mildewy volumes. Thirteen years of reading. I know everything about my condition. I understand my genetic history. Taken together, I still must defer to the popularity of sordid books and films of inaccurate, even silly, purport. That, too, is a kind of curse. The way people laugh at us, mock us, dismiss our condition as something Romantic. That is only further insult.

It's so clear now to me. I understand why my ancestors so hated the townsfolk, threatened their peace, and stole their bloody essence whenever they could. I can imagine how they were hunted. I can also imagine how they plotted revenge upon those townsfolk. The years fall away and I become aware of everything, past and present.

Now the future beckons . . . .

It has been thirteen years. I cannot continue living here with my parents. It is time for me to move out.

2

THE SLEEPING VILLAGE LOOMS BEFORE ME LIKE A SET OF TOY BLOCKS A child has arranged. Gazing out from the forest, I see the hovels, the houses, the three dozen structures containing humans, their tools and beasts, all quiet in the night.

Some evenings I stand watch over them, feeling much like a god— a protector. These are my people, my village, below the hill crowned by my family's villa. For many lifetimes we have drawn from this village the sustenance we needed. I must confess it is not always a voluntary offering. I choke a bit, thinking of that moral dilemma. I have never wanted to be evil.

Father has a way of putting it into a better perspective. We have a *symbiotic* relationship with our neighbors, he says. We give to them and they, in return, give to us.

What is it we give to them?

"Legend," my father replies. "Tourism. There's much money in the perpetration of legends. We grant tours. They get a thrill."

If enough tourists approach, I contemplate, there could be trouble for us. "Were not our ancestors harassed and driven out by these same people? The curious? The fearful?"

"The old ways," he mumbles, rubbing his chin as though whiskers still grow there. The affliction has robbed him of his infamous gray beard, once down to his waist. Still he strokes at it. "Over time, son, you see we've developed this propensity for amusement. The curious and the desperate flock to the mere mention of abnormality. And that is woefully us. So we stand as circus freaks. So be it. What of it? Pay us and stare as long as you wish."

I cringe at his honesty. Having spent most of my life apart from my parents, it seems as though I'm conversing with a distant ancestor rather than my own biological father. However, I fear he is correct.

The village is asleep beneath the yellow moonlight.

I step lightly. I do not step in any other way but light since my full transformation. I peer into dark windows. Often I can see the boy or girl of a family asleep in soft, downy beds. Often I pause to admire them, pondering the nature of childhood. What perfection, so ripe for corruption! Parents! They have a strange need to corrupt the innocent instead of letting them be. I am tempted to whisper a prayer; an old habit that is dying hard. I wish I could warn them.

You see, He who receives these prayers is an enemy of mine. We fought and I lost, yet that does not ingratiate me to Him. Trickster, I call Him. What entertainment must an immortal being call forth to fill the pointless days? No doubt playing with these petty pawns below the heavens provides sufficient distraction during the millennia. And me: I, too, have been played.

Look at me! Wandering among the homes of these people who so love life. I envy them. I hate them. Yet I adore them. They stand in as my memories, as reminders of days of pleasure and hope. Yet no more. He has cursed me; He has cursed my entire line for centuries. Whence came this gene? What purpose did it serve in the evolutionary plan? There is no sense to it. Surely, God is no scientist.

Too many questions come in the dark. In the light it is easy to sit within a room and read one of the many good books from the endless shelves we have. Without a good library, how could one endure?

Mother has her embroidery, her knitting, her crocheting, all the sewing and stitching crafts. She has a talent; so many years of practice will gain you that. She can sell her crafts at the market. For that, she has an accomplice from the village. Mother is unable to go herself. It is unfortunate, but social custom dictates she not frighten the children with her ghastly façade. Father is only slightly better off. He wishes to meet no one, although he would talk for hours about any history topic if someone were to ask a simple question.

I am able to prepare myself for public display. My Homburg's wide brim covers most of my face in shadow. The scarf and longcoat give me a solid form and these tall leather boots give me sufficient grasp while traversing over the gravel and loose clods. I am so dressed this evening as I make my way through the paths of the village, making my way to a secret destination. It is a place where I expose my shame.

Toward the north end of this collection of homes is an old barn. It is still in use, yet it would seem unusable to a casual observer. The roof sags, walls bend inward, wooden slats are weathered, nails loose, and the single window is broken out. It once housed a few hogs, then a lone cow that later died in the barn.

Tonight I find it occupied by Rósa, a woman of the village who knows me. Indeed, we met on the road one night and I, feeling thirsty and with a certain wild hunger in me, took her—as gently as I could, yet still taken.

"Good evening," I speak in a low, rough voice, my English words measured as her eyes open and she recognizes me. Perhaps I am late and she slipped into sleep as she waited. "Are you well?"

She responds in her native Croatian. I nod. She has been fighting a cold, not uncommon in autumn when the weather changes often and the moisture hangs about.

"I wish you swift recovery," I reply in the Croatian I have managed to learn these thirteen years.

She knows what to do. Standing, she comes to me and I hold her in my arms, a loose embrace. It no longer feels strange. It is something which feels cold, however, as though my temperature is transferred to her. A chill forms upon her flesh, her neck close to my lips. Her skin is cool. I breath in her motherly scent. My fangs reach for her.

"I think I'm with child," she whispers into my ear.

I pull back. "You deserve happiness."

"Please be careful from now on."

I nod, feign a smile. "Perhaps I shall need another to serve me next time. Can you recommend someone?"

"I will ask around," she says with a lustful moan.

Turning her head up, she gazes into my dark eyes. She becomes transfixed, hypnotized, frozen in my arms. She swoons and I hold her tighter. The sight of her bare throat triggers lust in me. My groin firms, presses hard against her. Her hand reaches down and grasps me as she moves herself into position. We come together.

My eyes close as I turn my face to her throat. My bite is quick, like a cobra's, yet less dangerous. The red essence spurts into my mouth. It's a good vintage; she takes care of herself except for too much beer. I swallow the stream as it spills, then lick the wound until it closes.

Her eyes are shut; she is weak so I lay her upon the hay, where she was napping before I arrived. I will never take too much of her, never enough to endanger her. Now that she and her husband are expecting a child, I must find another servant. After all, I am not a bad vampire.

I retrieve the fold of bills from my coat pocket and place it into her hand. Then I disappear.

Returning home, to the edge of the midnight wood and the gravel drive, my boots resist the slope. I am in no hurry. The dawn is far away. I need not fear the sunrise.

Sunrise is a metaphor, as surely as the sun is an eye to spy upon the world and the moon is a medallion of conquest. The sunrise is like the birth of a child, a life coming fully formed in a single breath. The sun appears, perfectly round, as bright as it will be, strikes us suddenly with its force as though attempting to destroy us in a single flash of fury. A single glance, they say, and we are no more. According to legend, an explosion of petrified flesh and calcified bone for those like me. Yet babies are born.

Another sunrise . . . .

Once upon a time those two, the parents I have, decided to make a child, even with the full knowledge of their genetic disposition. It was love, of course: that curse which makes people blind to reality, makes them ignore the odds and hope for the best . . . which seldom arrives. I understand. I was in love once.

And I was born, too. For that error, I learned to suffer. I lived my childhood mostly in the asylum where my parents worked. When their affliction became apparent, they sent me away. I saw my parents for the last time from across the parking lot, following my graduation ceremony. They dared not come closer. So I waved at them and they waved back. Then I went off to live my life.

I did not make much of it. I was dedicated to enjoying myself, to make up for the sacrifices my parents made for me. I felt I owed them that. In the end, it didn't matter. In fact, I fell in love and that changed everything. By the time I first noticed the affliction coming upon me, it was too late. I sought to resolve the problem. Nothing helped. So I said goodbye to my Beloved. I keep thinking through every step, trying to understand where I went wrong, for thirteen years now.

But I digress . . . .

My parents had prepared everything for me, it seemed. They left me money and property—the villa where we now reside. After twenty-two years, my parents were alive . . . looking worse than corpses in the ground for a dozen years.

I know young men cannot stand to live with their parents for more than a few years. Boys will hide in the basement, or make the garage into a private apartment. Secrecy will become the fashion of the day, parents the enemy. Boys long to escape as soon as they can, whether by transfer to a college, sleeping on a friend's couch, or entering military service. Some way to separate themselves from the parents. It is a rite of passage, the necessary break in order to enter adulthood. Time to become a man. And to enter adulthood is to claim one's manhood.

For me, the path is severely twisted. I was from the start separated from my parents. My aunt gave me free rein though it seldom occurred to me all the mischief I could be enjoying with that freedom. And so suddenly, at the age of graduation, I was put into the uncomfortable position of adulthood. With enough dalliances in upstate New York— my parents had retired and were traveling the world, it seemed by all the postcards—I might find some purpose in my life. Until I got into trouble; nothing criminal, just embarrassing.

So I took a new job in a state far away, expecting to get a fresh start in a different clime. Oklahoma. Tornadoes. TV news. Blood banks. I cannot help but say it again. It obsesses me. And there was Penny Park, my Beloved. And so, soon after achieving manhood, I began to devolve into boyhood. I became soft, romantic, unable to stand up for myself or hammer the world into my desires. I could not even make Penny understand my affliction. When it progressed to an unbearable degree, I swore to protect her by running away.

Yet not before one last tryst. It was an ugly affair and in the end it was she who fled from me, rushing out of my apartment with a piece of my skin in her hand, wretched from my wrist in her anger. I could do nothing but watch her drive away; that sight hurt more than the raw, exposed flesh on my torn wrist—

These woods are a fine place for such emotional outpouring. I let go a long howl, certain the local wolves laugh at me. This is my forest, my hill, and I do as I please!

So I indulge myself with long walks in the night.

"I need a place of my own," I declare to the moon, its fresh scowl showing through the autumnal branches. Then I could find some sense of accomplishment, to be an adult—again, a second adulthood. What else is there in life—or death, for that matter? More so a life that is, for all practical purposes, a death?

I have punished myself long enough.

The thought surges through me like a lightning bolt, unexpected and singularly powerful, halting me in my footfalls.

Punished myself for what?

I am not certain, perhaps one of several thoughtless acts. I have not always been a kind person. I have not always been moral or rational or displayed much altruism. There must be something I have done which is in need of retribution. And whatever it might be, I have accepted it.

Thirteen years living with my parents!

Surely that is a punishment. I cannot endure a hundred more years with them. Oh, their bodies would eventually break down and that would be considered death for those of us who are already dead. The body can no longer function. The bones cannot stand, the mind cannot calculate, and it all goes into a heap. A bundle of cells in a skin bag. Reduced to a slough of pus, then dried into dust. Having this affliction only puts us into a kind of hibernation, causing a drastic reduction of metabolism, the source of our longevity, our so-called immortality. But every organic thing will eventually break down through constant use, and so would my parents. So would I.

Yet a hundred more years of watching Father read his books and Mother stitching another piece of embroidery?

"I must go," I grumbled. "I must get away."

And so it is, in this pre-dawn forest, I make the solemn decision to abandon my parents. I will find my own place to hibernate. I enjoy the countryside yet there are so few folk around to donate blood. It might be better if I were in a city. I could walk the streets at night rather than the trails with their wagon tracks. I could meet ladies and dance until dawn, then hurry away to my apartment, throw the curtains closed against the sunrise, and take a three-day nap. Perhaps I could purchase a strong box full of nitrogen-rich soil to serve as my boudoir. That is what Saint Dracula did, I've read. It does help with one's complexion. I've tried that. However, I shall not be turning into a bat. No, that is quite impossible.

When my parents have finally broken down—literally crumbled away—I may return to claim the villa for myself.

Yet to whom would I leave it after I, too, break down into nothing?

3

"No," says Father as though I were six years old and asking to go alone to the corner store. "You would be recognized, perhaps attacked. You could not go among them openly. Surely you've determined that. No, it's best if you stay here with us."

"We are quite safe here, dear," Mother adds, looking up from her crocheting.

How can I tell them I no longer wish to live with them? It is not the same as turning eighteen and demanding my own life out in the world, free from theirs. I would get a job, then find a cheap place to spend my off hours, drive a modest second-hand car between them. I would shop for groceries on Saturdays, sleep late on Sundays, catch a movie once in a while. And I would meet people, perhaps a lady who might fancy an evening with me: fine dinner, a show, then moments of snatching affection from each other, followed by the inevitable midnight kiss.

Then back to the job Monday morning. There would be awkward smiles throughout the day, and plenty of lunch gossip with colleagues: the latest on sports, celebrities, politics, the next movie or album or game or election, whatever they bring to the table. And I would change clothes every day, except for weekends I find myself alone. I would hire a good tailor to customize my wardrobe. I'd even purchase an armoire. And bookcases. Oaken furniture that would last for generations. And there would be portraits on the walls, and small tokens scattered about on a desk, a side table, a nightstand, a shelf, things to remind me of my family, of their line, all the way back to the original sin, when God first decided to bless us with His greatest curse: eternal damnation.

That is the kind of life I would expect were I a normal fellow about to leave home and the protection of the parents.

"Allow me to deconstruct your bizarre proposal," says Father in the same snooty academic voice he has used most of these thirteen years whenever he needs to address me on a serious matter. As a physician, he had no bed-side manner. "You wish to go out into what we might call 'polite society' and live your life, such as it is, much as you did thirteen years ago. As though nothing significant has occurred since that time—since you joined us here. And yet you believe no one will notice you, will have no disparaging thought when gazing upon your completely normal countenance, will fear nothing at the sight of you. Everything will be perfectly perfect. Do I have it correct?"

"My dear boy," Mother speaks up, lowering her crocheting to her lap, "your father is correct. What are you thinking? We stay here for exactly the same reason for not staying *out there*."

"She means well," says Father with a knowing wink—minus the eyelid. "We have made arrangements to be able to stay in this villa for as long as it takes."

I squint. "Takes? For what? Your deaths?"

"If you wish to call it that."

I throw out my hands. "We are already dead!"

"That, too, is only in a manner of speaking."

"We sure aren't living!"

"And you have such knowledge of the difference," says Father.

"I do. I went to medical school. Just like you, and more recently, too, so my information must be a lot fresher. I know the disease we have. True, there is no cure. Yet living in isolation like this is no kind of life, either."

"It's the only life we can have," Mother interjects.

"You need to find a suitable pastime," says Father.

At that point, I have to turn away. My pale face, a sheet of flaky skin hanging down my cheeks, will not let me go on. My throat had become dry—*drier* than usual. I cough—somewhat painful without the usual phlegm most people would have pulled up.

"I do understand your concerns," Father starts up again. "We are fortunate to have simple pastimes. I read and your mother sews. What do you do? I know of others who must carry on as playboys, much as they did in life. It is embarrassing. They make a nuisance of themselves and frighten people. They give us an unsavory reputation. Most of us want nothing more than to be left alone, to be away from people."

"Except a rare sip of blood," adds Mother.

She gazes at me with her nearly toothless grin, no doubt hoping to see a warm smile on my face that reassures her I will stay.

"I only want to be away from you," I say, and even before the final phoneme falls I wish to take it back. Their faces flash something that's brighter, more aggrieved than I've ever seen. When I brought home a village lass for some private blood-letting they were aghast, told me I had broken the compact they had with the village. Now, though, they appear more in shock at my words. I try to smile. "I mean that in a nice way."

"What nice way could that be?" asks Father. He proceeds to remind me of all they have done for me, both before my transformation and since. He adds many details, *ad nauseam*, that serve to layer guilt upon me like a birthday cake. I stand humbly, taking it; I deserve his redress.

"But on the other side," I speak up when he falls silent, "is the other thing you have done for me: to bring me into this world with this affliction, with these genes, when you knew the odds were high that I would likewise suffer the same as you."

That shuts them up.

My heart quivers as I take a breath, a purely instinctual habit and not one I must do to keep living. After all, I do not live, and that is the crux of the conundrum.

"Listen, Father, Mother. I apologize for my remark. Yet the truth behind it remains. I'm unhappy here, even sharing all of your keen daily pronouncements, even watching you wile away the hours with your pastimes. I enjoy the sharing of blood and all the family history you offer whether I ask for it or not. Besides, for better or worse, you are my parents and for that reason I have accepted this arrangement. What choice did I have? You set up everything, a trail of blood drops, as it were, leading me from that chapel in Makarska to this run-down villa. There were detours, of course. We've discussed them at length many times. Even so, I went through hell three times seeking a cure—"

"All in vain," says Father, adding a chuckle.

"Then I died."

It was not a glorious end, no sirree. It hurt. It was rather like pins and needles had been injected into my veins, slushing prickily through my body. I screamed until I could endure no more and collapsed into something like a coma. When I opened my eyes, I had not expected to be in a dark room, a sheet over my face. I no longer hurt, so I swung my feet to the floor, stepped across the room to the closet, and dressed myself in the clothes hanging there. Then I walked out into the night.

I stare at them in turn, back and forth, my eyes dark and piercing. Theirs gray and dull.

"If I rejoin society," I tell them, "I'll need some kind of treatment to make myself presentable. So I don't cause alarm. I know that. Perhaps I can return to that clinic in Zagreb. They owe me. They could give me one of their treatments to improve my skin condition, which is actually what they specialize in, something to lessen the dry patches, the flaky skin, the red blotches. Perhaps I could regrow hair, too."

Father frowns. "Do you mean the same clinic that killed you?"

I shake my head. "They did not kill me. They tried to help me. Besides, I pressured the director to try something that wasn't ready. Stem cell research suggested it would be effective—"

"Which is how they killed you."

"No, Father! They did not kill me. God killed me!"

"God?" He laughs like only an aged vampire can laugh: dry heaves with a raspy whistle. "There is no God. It is all myth and superstition. Something to keep the masses in line. You know how much horror has been done in the name of this God thing, don't you? Far too much."

I wave my hand at him. "He has been taunting me all my life. At the end I made a deal with Him. I told Him I would accept my fate and stop fighting it if He would let someone live who I had harmed. He kept his part of the bargain, and so here I am."

Father tries to laugh more, deliberately cranking up his guffaw to impress upon me the degree of ridiculousness I have attained.

"You gave your life so another may live . . . ."

"Yes—in short." I purse my lips, thinking of Alma Jónás.

My eyes close and I'm back there in Sárvár—after Budapest, before Zagreb—as she comes out of the bathroom, a pixie wrapped in a big white towel—white, the symbol of purity. I sit cross-legged on the floor, my back against the side of the bed. Dropping the towel, she climbs over me and sits on my lap, facing me. Her body is covered in tattoos. Jewelry adorns her nipples and navel. She rises, takes me in her hand, and settles upon me. A brief ecstasy returns to me—the moment of emptying my soul into the universe—

"You told us everything about that poor girl previously," says my mother. "Seems a waste of a life, if you ask. Better if she had turned vampirish and stayed with you. Then you would not be so lonely. Oh, I feel the regrets you must have, not having a partner to bring into this life, to share your misery with. That is not what we wanted for you."

I tilt my head. How sad Mother is, how cold she can be when she doesn't intend to be.

"You need for me to find a female vampire to comfort me in my misery? Are you truly saying that?" It is such a joke that Mother makes, yet she doesn't take it as humor. "Are there matching-making services for our kind? What would I put in my profile? Loves midnight strolls, passionate kisses, drinking Bloody Marys? I'm sure I could use a photo from twenty years ago. I'd lie about my age, too. It just might work."

Father roars with laughter and I frown at him.

"Don't be so cruel," I say to Mother. "I am alone and do not wish to be. And yet I would choose this fate over cursing another person to be wounded in our way just to be a partner to me. I'm not that kind of vampire. I'm a good vampire."

Father steps from the shadows in the corner, a book in his hands, holding it up like a silver cross, as if to signify how I've interrupted his reading.

"There is but one kind of vampire," he says. "We do, however, come to this situation in multiple manner. We do each have our grievances, our trepidations, our loathings. Some do believe God has deliberately thrown them down while others, like your mother and I, accept the biological explanation for our lot in life."

He means our genes, our disease, our affliction—as certain a curse as anything garnered from living in a biologically diverse world. None of us chose this, yet all of us must exist with it. We have tried for centuries to end our line, to cut off the curse, yet that old demon *Love* visits and thus a child is made to carry it onward.

All I can do is nod pensively, like I do every time this discussion has come up during the past thirteen years.

"So I will leave here." My voice is calm yet full of boastful bravado: I am finally abandoning my parents, ha! "I will leave here and make my way to Zagreb. I will see what treatments are available to make myself look respectable. Now that I am . . . *whatever* I am, I need no longer fear dying. I only need a make-over. I got myself here without shocking too many, so I can make my way out from Villa Székely with little more effort."

"What if you're found out?" asks Father.

"Given the present day and age, I expect I would gain sympathy. They wouldn't run me out of town. Rather they would assign me to an asylum, a sanitarium, a clinic and wish me well. We live in a better world now than our ancestors did. It's Romantic to be a vampire."

Mother is grim, her crochet forgotten. "Romantic!"

"Where will you go? How will you live?" asks Father, as though he had never given a similar thought to his own escape. Here they are, so comfortably ensconced in this rustic villa. And yet, with so many years and some money they have not put forth any effort to restore it. We dare not alert the neighbors, he explained when I first arrived.

I moved into a pair of adjoining rooms once used as bedrooms. One has an ancient bed still occupying it, the other does not. I use the desk in one room, scribbling my so-called memoir, and stare for days at the books on the shelves. In the other room, the bed beckons by old habit yet I never tire. We do not truly sleep. Instead, there is a kind of hibernation after we feed—or too long without feeding. And so I stand, staring at the bed, wondering the only thing I can think of for a bed: how it would feel joining some lover within its folds, pretending I am healthy in every way, and not, in truth, some monster that God has abandoned.

It is simple, really. What does it take to maintain a comfortable life here in this villa? Each day as I stroll its long halls, sweeping cobwebs aside and waving clouds of dust to the ragged carpet with every step,

I'm reminded we spend nothing on its upkeep. There is no electricity at this address. No heating oil. It is not a problem; we do not feel hot or cold. We feel nothing; we have no temperature. For water, there is a well and a pump to bring it up from the bottom of the hill to a tank in this villa, yet no administrative office below sends us an invoice, so we take as we like. The curiosity, naturally, is that we do not *like*. Water is its own curse; its touch can burn like acid.

Surely we have needs that must be somehow purchased, you might think. Food? Drink? Medicine? Not for us. We have no need of food, although we could throw together a lavish dinner if an occasion called for it. However, we are a simple family; we do not entertain. Only the occasional blood donor. Indeed, our invitations are unsent because we expect them to be unanswered. Such reputation! Perhaps if we offered more drink. Drink means wine, yet the dozens of bottles in the cellar remain lined up like soldiers. There might be need of medicine, yes, though it is not the sort of potion available in a local pharmacy. Believe me, I've tried everything. Nothing improves my situation. I've reached a state of equilibrium: I do not worsen yet I do not improve. My degree of inhumanity is constant, my appearance permanently set at a certain degree of *pathétique*. My parents have reached their own degree of stasis; it is difficult to tell their ages by looking upon them. That is the only kindness God allows.

"Perhaps a bit of plastic surgery would make me presentable to the royal courts of the land," I say, adding a laugh. "Then the world can be my oyster once more."

"What oyster?" Mother inquires.

"It's an expression of perversity," Father explains, unamused.

4

WHEN I STEP FROM MY ROOM, SMALL CANVAS SUITCASE IN HAND, DRESSED for travel, there is Father, leaning against the wall in the corridor, dressed for reading. We do not smile at each other and I lower my gaze.

"So that is your decision," he says.

I'm not sure by his tone whether it is a question or confirmation.

"I cannot stay here any longer," I respond. I cough, clear my throat and repeat my statement with more certainty. "I'm sorry. But thanks for all the blood."

His lips purse, hiding a grin, perhaps. I cannot hold back mine.

Then something weird happens. He reaches out and embraces me, actually pulls me close and holds me tightly. I drop my suitcase and wrap my arms around him. We never hugged even when I first found them in this villa. We never hugged during my childhood—not beyond my earliest years. Not even when I went to live with my aunt. Perhaps they feared contamination.

He releases me, steps back. Reaching into his trouser pocket, he retrieves a wad of bills, hands them to me.

"For your expenses. . . . To get you started in your new life. That is, your newest life. There are many, as you know. Let each be a unique experience you can cherish. Return any time you wish and tell us of your adventures. If we don't see you for, say, another thirteen years . . . well, then we shall assume you are happy. Somewhere. You can write. Or use the new thing . . . the E mail. Is that what it's called?"

"You need a computer for that. You don't have one."

"Ah, technology! Always rushing us into the future. Alas, we are too quickly left behind. There must be a good stationary shop wherever you might go. We are content with our old things. Words are still words. Give us some any way you can. All right? Would you do that? Your mother would appreciate a note from time to time." He wiped his eyes. "I would, as well."

I pick up my suitcase, ready to step around him.

"One thing more," my father says, his hand out to stop me.

"What is it?"

"Your mother . . . ."

"Yes?"

"She wishes you well, obviously." He looks down. "However, she is upset. Therefore she cannot see you off. Please understand. Take no offense. She is a delicate woman. Passionate, yet fragile. Her heart cannot bear this parting."

"I get it. Tell her I will write."

"We left you when you were a young man. For your own good, we believed." He tried to chuckle. "Now you leave us, also for your own good, it seems."

"That's ironic," I say with a fake laugh.

"It is. The world goes round on irony, it seems. Our cast seems also to be ironic. The human yet not human beings who walk the streets, who drink the blood, who are at once romanticized and cursed. Be careful out there, Stefan."

"Right. It's a forest out there." I smile at him until the silence grows too warm. "I will be careful."

We stare at each other another moment, checking each other for souls. Mine has been locked away for thirteen years.

"Where will you go first?" asks Father.

"I suppose I'll go to Budapest, check my account. A boy needs some cash if he is to be a playboy. Then to Zagreb for a spa treatment."

With a plaintive nod, he steps aside and I stroll down the corridor, take the wide staircase down to the main hall, dusty and cobwebbed. It seems a place meant for me to leave.

CR

Moonlight paints my path: a midnight journey to the village and points beyond.

As in years past, I have made myself up as pretty as I can be, all the better to not draw stares from those I pass. When I came to Europe from America, I had perfected my costume. I had a mask fashioned by a theater arts company. It matched my passport photo. The wide brim of the Homburg shades my face from undue gazes. The woolen scarf is an appropriate accessory in this season; it also covers my throat and its unsightly skin. Otherwise, I wear a formal suit as befits my status as some kind of a count. Father remarked on it once. I like to think big. My family has money, property, leisure time. I dress for the role I wish to play. My longcoat finalizes my ensemble. I walk in a stylish pair of brown boots straight from the early 1900s when coaches were drawn by horses. Always in fashion.

I know not the year as I stroll the gravel path, down this hillside to the road below. It could be any year and I am only mistaken because of my affliction. How many years have passed? Thirteen? Or a hundred and thirteen? Was I born a hundred years too soon? Or too late? How long will I live? Live! What is *living*, anyway? Mere animation? Or the beating of a heart? The cruel processes of aging? The collapse of the body's biological structures, bones becoming dust, flesh evaporating? I found no answers in my family's library.

This road is a strange place, fog drifting across my path, a moon which teases me, pulling me back to the past. Perfect for a vampire finally out on his own terms.

Thirteen years and I can still recall my adventure. I came here to find a cure and found it could not be found. I think of my desperate visit to that old chapel in Zagreb, seeking a blessing which I hoped would protect me from God's wrath. The holy water turned to acid and burned the priest. They kicked me out.

Before my trip to Europe, I sought a diagnosis from a colleague in Utica, New York. I flew all the way from my home in Oklahoma City just to see a doctor I trusted. No answer to my condition: not a skin disease, not a blood disorder, just . . . something else. I went to New

Orleans, seeking non-medical treatment, following what I found on a website. That, too, failed to arrest my affliction. I knew then my only recourse was to return to my ancestral home.

To get from Oklahoma to Hungary proved a laborious operation. With the strictness of air travel, the screenings, the questions, I knew I would not pass muster. So I drove to the port of Houston and bought a ticket on a freighter. As one of a dozen paying passengers, I eventually arrived in Rotterdam. I kept to myself while aboard.

From Rotterdam, I took three trains across Germany, heading for Budapest. I slept through a stop where I needed to change trains and arrived in Munich. My feet were numb, encased in sturdy shoes. Dogs on the street smelled my gangrenous feet and chased me, bit me. I awoke in a hospital with a few toes cut off. I limped, hobbled my way out of the hospital and tried to catch a flight to Budapest.

I sat next to a Goth girl—black everything except her pale skin, oversized boots, leather jacket, tattoos and piercings, earbuds helping her block out the world. That was Alma Jónás. I offered her a ride, asked if she would help guide me around the city on my errands.

Settling into the hotel room, I experienced distress and Alma got medical help. Later, she visited me in the hospital, brought me some plum pie. She couldn't go home, she told me. I saw the bruises her father had given her. So I became her new daddy. Being sick, I needed her help to get on the right bus to Sárvár—and off the bus at the spa.

They did not wish me as their customer, so we had to find other accommodations. In a small lodge at the edge of town, I came to the truth of my condition. I was transforming and could not stop it. Lost in her own world, Alma didn't mind that aspect of me.

I knew how it would end. So I tried to send her back to Budapest. She cried, made a scene, so I relented and welcomed her into the rental car I'd gotten. We drove to the Croatian border. I felt faint; a peek in the rearview mirror showed me I was loosing it again. Ahead were border guards stopping every vehicle. Alma did the only thing anyone could do: she cut her arm and fed me.

It keeps playing through my mind, nearly every day for thirteen years. Later she fell ill, blood poisoning, I'd thought—just as I was preparing for my treatment at the clinic. I was out of my mind, not making clear decisions. Perhaps I shouldn't have proceeded. Perhaps it wouldn't have mattered.

What did matter was that I made a deal with God before I went under the anesthesia. We had been sparring for some time. I begged Him to let Alma live: I would stop fighting my transformation and accept what I was meant to be. He agreed—and you know the rest of the story. I proceeded to my new home, found my old parents.

So now I leave that place. The gravel path ends at the edge of a paved road. To my right the road leads to the village; I usually take another path to the village, one that cuts through the forest. To my left the road goes on to the Plitvice Lakes, the national park with myriad waterfalls.

The fog has thickened, covering the road. A driver would have difficulty seeing someone like me walking along the road.

As I wait for the night bus to Korenica, I feel a weight pressing upon my left shoulder. I see my old friend has alighted, perhaps to express his farewell wishes.

"Good evening, Milo," I say to the little brown bat that has taken me as a friend for three years. We met in the forest below the villa when I thought to go out and have a picnic—a poor excuse for nostalgia, thinking of a past picnic with someone I once loved. Milo sought some fruit I had cut and placed into a bowl. Peaches, I recall. I let him have all he wanted. "So how are you? Come to see me off?"

No screeches tonight. He clings to my lapel, nuzzles my cheek as though he is my baby. Or my pet. It seems *de rigueur* for a vampire to have a pet bat. It's in the literature. Of course, the vampire *becomes* the bat more often than not. That's in the literature, too. I don't subscribe to those stories.

I gather Milo in my palm, brush his soft, furry back with my other hand. He seems to purr—more of a low-pitched chirping. He is sad, I sense. He is the only friend I can talk to.

"I must go away now," I tell him in a gentle voice. "I cannot live any longer with my parents. I tried, but I was only fooling myself." My sigh seems long in building, so much relief in its expression yet quick in its expulsion. Milo screeches. "Yes, yes, I know. And thank you for sticking with me through thick and thin." I shake my head. "So many clichés."

Gazing up and down the road, hoping to see the bus, I return my friend to my shoulder. I hear a low rumble through the fog. Yellow lights blink in the distance. The bus approaches.

I adjust my hat, lowering the brim over my face. I pull out some bills, ready to purchase a ticket. Most passengers will be sleeping. They will not notice me.

The bus pulls alongside me, doors opening. I wave my gloved hand in thanks and step aboard.

"Korenica," I mutter, as though the driver couldn't guess. I hand over the money. He gives me a ticket.

Making my way down the aisle, I count eight passengers: four are asleep, two reading, two focused on their music, plugs stuffed into their ears. I slump in the last seat, my back at the rear window.

I hear a faint squeak. I gaze downward and feel something moving in my coat pocket. It is Milo, climbing out.

"Hello, friend," I coo. "So you wish to see Budapest with me?"

His eyes flicker, he wriggles his nose, and gives me a warm squeak.

"That is much too far from home," I remind him. "I'm sure your family will miss you."

I lower the window beside me. A cool breeze rushes in. I know he understands. He crawls up to my face and licks my cheek, then flings himself out of the bus and into the night.

Now I am alone.

5

TIME, THEY SAY, IS A CRUEL MISTRESS. I'VE GOTTEN THAT IMPRESSION FROM the two-hundred-eighty-seven books I've read these thirteen years. In the family villa, surrounded by our rustic estate, nothing has changed. The seasons came and went, yet we could gaze from the windows and see much the same countryside. In the far distance I noted the cathedral steeple in Korenica.

As the bus approached, I suddenly realized that I should expect changes in the world I would be entering. What could thirteen years have done to this land? What has thirteen years done to me? I am the same, cruelly unchanged. Perhaps it is a blessing: to not have devolved further than how much I had when I first arrived here. God has a sense of humor, after all. Well played, Sir!

It seemed an old bus yet well-maintained. The seats were clean. The smell of cleaning fluid teased my nose, as though the vehicle had been freshly scrubbed for my visit. As I sat in the last row, I watched the world outside, dark in the night, the moon aglow, the road flat and smooth.

The passengers were dozing off, yet I cannot sleep. I might give it a try yet an hour or so is the best I can do. It is really more like going into a trance than true sleep. I tune out for a while but do not become fully unconscious. Therefore, I do not dream. That, too, is both curse and blessing. The theater is closed; a stern ticketmaster, arms crossed over his mighty chest, shakes his head and bids me go on to more practical matters. After I feed, however, I may slip into the abyss for a few days. That, too, is a dreamless void.

I recall the days when strangers appeared on our land. At first one or two, then whole family groups. They appeared to be from another country, looking nothing like the locals. They did not pause for long, so I was inclined to pay them no mind, merely watched them from our tower. Sometimes they picked fruit from the trees in our unmaintained orchard, yet because we do not cultivate them actively I hardly felt they were stealing. When they set themselves to defecate, however, I was compelled to shout from the tower for them to move on. Later, I began to go out in the evenings to confront them.

"This is no abandoned estate," I informed the trespassers. "My family lives here, so don't linger or vandalize. Keep moving."

They did not understand my English, nor my Hungarian—which had improved over these thirteen years, as well as passable Croatian. Once in a while there would be someone who understood English. We spoke minimally. They seemed afraid, journeying from far away to somewhere else that was far away.

"What happened?" I would inquire when my appearance did not put them off. Children stared at me like I was a circus freak.

They had faced war, a conflict between several parties. They were caught between all of them. Their cities were bombed, their citizens gassed, left to die. They elected to leave, packing what they could, and walking west. They had heard there was sanctuary in Europe. Right or wrong, they had few choices, so they marched west. Through Turkey, to the Aegean coast, paid for a ferry to Greece, then continued the march north. And they soon arrived in Bosnia and my family's estate near the border. Croatian or Bosnian, which is which, none can see for certain in that part of the mountains. They traipsed across our estate on their way north. They hoped to arrive in Germany.

It started about the time I arrived at my family's villa, apparently, though I did not occupy myself with news of the outside world. I was concerned with my inner world, with the changes I had undergone and fathoming how I would be able to go on, to *live*—using that odd word for this awkward kind of existence. I wondered how I could exist for another hundred years or so. How many books could I read? And what would I do with that knowledge?

Syria was a wasteland, Turkey in flames, Greece a hodgepodge of angry farmers and sailors against everyone else. And to the south were invasions from Africa, from Libya and Tunisia, heading to Sicily and Italy, hoping for an easier life. The nations of Europe were overrun. How could any city make room for a million more inhabitants? There is not space nor the funds to care for so many immigrants. And in these groups, from Syria and the Middle East as well as from Africa were soldiers of the radical religion determined to spread a caliphate across the world and wipe out their age-old enemies.

My father is the historian, reading stacks of books over the years. As a physician, he treated the physical maladies of patients who most hospitals would not accept. He treated the deformed and the insane, the unwanted, unwashed denizens of the lower edge of society, sent to the asylum in upstate New York. Mother treated the residents who were deemed insane, either truly without minds or merely labeled insane by the state and sent away to keep the state tidy. In his leisure, he educated himself on the geopolitics of the post-war decades. That would be post-World War II, as historians labeled it.

Conflicts happened, and with the introduction of so many foreign people into the heart of Europe, further conflict erupted. There were daily bombings, devices constructed in apartments and placed on the streets. Gangs of foreign men roamed the streets like packs of wolves, harassing and assaulting native-born citizens, especially the women who soon dared not go out alone. With danger spreading outdoors, women were forced to stay indoors, or had to be guarded by male relatives whenever they went outside. In this way the religious laws overcame the civil laws. The invaders wanted the religious laws to be supreme and through the daily behavior of the invaders, everyone's behavior came to fit the religious laws. Women were supposed to stay at home, they decreed, and when the streets became too dangerous, women did stay home. If they went out, they needed to be escorted by fathers, husbands, or brothers. That, too, followed religious laws. That change shifted everything: jobs, entertainment, government and civic duty, even whether or not you could have a pet.

This is what the visitors to our estate told me. Some were heading back to Syria, tired of the world they found in Europe, tired of the world that had changed. The Europe they wanted to go to was not the Europe they found. Escaping a strict and harsh life in the Middle East, they found the same strict and harsh life spreading across Europe. There was no longer freedom for the individual, the family, or the community, only the law of the land, which now came from religious dictates, not democratic propositions voted by the people.

I've talked with God—though many would doubt me—and He is as dismayed as me whenever we have discussed these recent matters.

The things mankind comes up with! (I'm paraphrasing.) So many of them purport to speak for me when, in fact, none of them actually understand the language of the heavens.

How about me? I asked. I think I understand you.

Well, Stefan, I allow you to understand me. It's part of our deal. An addendum to our compact. I let your friend return to her life before meeting you and you ceased fighting your transformation. That was our agreement. After all, I cannot work wonders all the time, or else I'd never be able to rest. Seventh day, you know. Celestial golf. Even a god needs a day off.

I had to nod at His frankness.

Perhaps you could use some kind of . . . now what are they called? A prophet? Someone to speak for you. Then everyone would accept your demands without question. No more mankind fouling the nest, as it were.

Yes, Stefan, that might be a good idea, and yet I've tried. Nobody listens any more. That *internet* thing you guys invented, it's ruining everything. Oh, for a muse of fire, they moan! Everyone now believes they are gods, one and another, all pontificating the way things should be. A few angry words tapped out on a small screen. I can't get a word in edgewise. But I'm too busy to complain, you know. Too many stars going nova, too many baby sea turtles lost in the sand. Let the people do as they please; they will anyway. Someday a flood may come, or an asteroid. Depends on what's available. I'm not vindictive, mind you, just practical—

The bus shook me from my trance, as I entered a different world. I remained in the Old Country, my mindset of another era. My habits had solidified during the past thirteen years.

Yet I retain the powers which my affliction has given me: first, the power to frighten. Dogs and children are easiest to disturb. Women are either seductively attracted or immediately flee in horror. Men stand their ground to fight me, especially if women and children are present. The weaker ones will likely flee. Second, within my thin, decrepit body I have strength no one would suspect. And surprising speed should I need to escape. And I cannot be killed. I do not feel pain—or much of any sensations, yet I can sense many things, like a clairvoyant.

There are loopholes. Separate my head from my body and I cannot control my body and thus fall limp and, for all intents and purposes, cease to live. My animation ceases. Drive a wooden stake through my heart and the impact will stay my hand. I would not actually die, however; I am already dead. You might, with the ripping of my heart via stake, cause some blood to spray out. Good theatrics. There is that: a sure sign that the stake has struck an artery. Nothing more. I would recommend the head severing to stop me once and for all.

Head severing seems to be a popular exercise in the new Europe, I've heard from recent visitors passing through the estate, returning to the Middle East. Things have calmed back home and the rebuilding is underway. I wished them well. They, in turn, wished me well but in a decidedly somber tone.

What will I find when I arrive in Budapest? Visitors have told me Hungary resisted the waves of refugees, built fences and walls to guard the borders. The grand council of European nations chose to ostracize Hungary and thus its economy suffered. Eventually, they were forced to unite with neighboring nations, working together. Isolated on my family estate, I knew none of this; only news from passers-by going in each direction educated me.

I hoped my bank still stood and was in operation. We get a letter once or twice a year that summarizes our holdings, taxes paid, fees charged. The letters had not ceased so I presumed our bank would be able to give me some funds by which I might conduct my affairs. By now, with investments in a trust, our family should be significantly wealthier. I expect to seek treatments with my share of it, superficial improvement, granted, and then search for a suitable estate of my own. There is not much for me to do to pass the time, but I would prefer to pass this time away from my parents.

The bus pulled into the station in Korenica. All was quiet in the town save the engine of the bus, a loud, irregular rumble which made me think of older times. It was easy to forget the world had changed so much. This sleeping town, lights off, had not changed.

Stepping off the bus, I realized I hadn't thought my grand journey through very well. The next bus would not be until morning. I had no room for the night. My fellow passengers were going home; I'd left my home. Only a half-hour gone and I was already making mistakes.

As the others dispersed, I studied the signboard, perusing the map of the area and the timetable of other buses. The Plitvice Lakes region was well-advertised. The weathered picture still showed the waterfalls and rivulets. A tourist destination, yet tourism had fallen off during the war. As with any natural wonder, however, it remained something to experience. Except for me. I do not do well with water.

Another picture caught my eye: a castle tower sprouting from the treetops of a forested hill. I recognized the villa I had called home. The picture's caption announced the place as the home of vampires. A caricature of Saint Dracula adorned the poster. Was someone selling tickets? Did someone offer a tour to the estate with tales of monstrous beings haunting its corridors? It had to be true.

I wondered how many wagons of the curious had rolled onto our property. How many tourists had trudged up the gravel drive? How many living humans had traipsed through our dusty, cobweb-filled corridors hoping to be frightened by a vampire lurching from a closet? Didn't they know we put ourselves away at sunrise? If they were inspecting our villa during daylight hours, they were missing a lot.

Rubbing my chin, I found two whiskers hanging on—and finally understood the odd noises I'd heard echoing through the villa while I tried to rest. I could not actually sleep, not even in the dirt-filled coffin made available to me, formerly used by my grandfather István. Father insisted I not concern myself with the arrangement. It made sense: once in a while, the lid would be opened and curious eyes would peer inside, see a sleeping vampire dressed in a dinner jacket, and gasp in awe. The tour guide would urge them to only take a quick glance, then carefully close the lid. They would not wish to awaken me.

Father has set us up as circus freaks, the props of a horrible legend, and in that way we pay for our sins. No doubt Mother played along, but it was I who got the curious eyes of strangers. While in my state of repose, hibernating, unable to move about, my body shut down for a short period while my mind remained alert. I am helpless during such a time, and vampire hunters throughout the ages have known that fact. Find the coffin in which the vampire sleeps and *voila*! instant fame with the hammering of the wooden stake. Preposterous!

6

I HAD SLIPPPED INTO A TRANCE, SLOUCHING ON THE BENCH AT THE BUS station, when a voice awoke me. It took a moment for me to decipher the old man's Croatian: *"Čekao dugo vremena?"* —Waiting long?

I pulled myself awake, straightened on the bench. With some effort I dug into my brain, replied: *"Samo jednu noć."* —Only one night.

He was standing, bent over, one hand curled over the knob on the top of a white cane. Wearing dark glasses, the man slowly turned and lowered himself beside me on the bench. He continued speaking, as though he believed I understood. In thirteen years living in Croatia, I had not bothered to learn more than a basic level of the language. After all, I hardly spoke to anyone outside the villa.

The man paused and rudely sniffed the air as though detecting an odd scent. Probably it was me, moldy as I was. I cannot bathe and I have no hygiene products. No Bath & Bodyworks store over here. My neighbor on the bench remarked on the odor.

I yawned, not used to explaining myself, then apologized, said I was sick.

He laughed, apologized back to me for his remark.

And so we became friends as we waited. Matej was eighty-six years old without being a vampire. He was also blind so my appearance did not alarm him. He said he'd been blinded during the 1993 war, when he was held in a camp by the Serbs. It was to torment his mother, who was also held captive. Her face was the last thing he saw and she had died soon after. I told him wars invent new ways to be cruel.

He shook his head.

My problem? I wasn't sure how to respond. I was trying to go to a clinic for treatment of my affliction. Affliction? Yes, it seems that my body is decaying. Infection. He thought that was sad, unfortunate, that I probably had difficulty associating with people because of the smell.

I chuckled—the raspy hack that counted as a chuckle now.

"It is not easy to be old," said the blind man beside me, his Croatian words soothing. "Everything hurts. You never know when something will break down, go haywire, and you can't fix it yourself. One moment fine, the next stopped, hard limits, not able to do anything for yourself. So you have to rely on strangers to get by. Your own family, they won't have anything to do with you. It's fine to be on your own when you're young, but not when you're old and can't take care of yourself. It is a miserable existence."

"Indeed." With a dip of my chin, I thought he'd described my own condition perfectly. "Worse perhaps is being a handicapped person, always needing help, even to do the simplest things. Like taking care of one's bathroom needs. How embarrassing! Or else a person who is disfigured, let us say, by disease or by accident. Hard to look at. So no one helps them. They don't want to get close."

"Yes, that would be horrible, too."

"The only reprieve is a quick death," I offered.

"Quick death? What answer is that to a problem?"

"It ends the suffering."

"Yes, I suppose. Yet there is so much more to life than to suffer pains and wants. Remember youth? That is worth every pain of old age. There is so much beauty—even for an old blind man. And love. You can't imagine the joy of making love when you're blind. Feeling your way. You appreciate how your hands can see for you."

I laughed.

Matej and I sat together on the next bus, a sleek new vehicle that ran smoothly on electricity. A plaque by the door announced that fact. It made little noise and I almost did not notice it arriving. I could have slept through it. Matej commented on the comfort of this new bus—a much better ride to Zadar than he had experienced before.

"Zadar?" I asked, panicking. "I want to go to Zagreb." I tried to say it again in Croatian.

The only way to take a bus to Zagreb from Korenica was to go first to Zadar, my friend explained. However, Zadar, on the Adriatic coast, seemed far out of the way, a drastic detour, going west to catch a bus going northeast. That is the only way, said Matej. Unless I wished to take a string of slow local buses, maybe four of them, to connect with the same bus coming from Zadar.

So I coughed, slumped in my seat, folded my arms over my chest, and pretended to listen to Matej as he continued his stories of the war. He did not hesitate offering up the most awful details. He seemed to delight in them, as though he sought to shock me.

"Yes, such horrors," I lamented in Croatian. He sounded much like God complaining about everything we've done to ruin the world. "I'm surprised you don't sound bitter now."

"That was long ago. A man cannot remain bitter for so many years or he ceases to live." He cleared his throat. "Besides, I don't blame the men. I blame the devils that took over their souls."

I noticed some other passengers watching us, listening to us.

"Yes, I see."

"A weak man is a good home for a devil," he continued, "and so many weak men fill a war, seeking after all manner of things, pride and duty, glory and reward, grasping after their own worth. All the things devils feed on. Then they become monsters."

It took a moment of careful review in my mind to put his Croatian words together. When I understood, I told him I understood.

"There are many kinds of monsters," I responded in a low voice. No doubt the other passengers could identify who the monster was on the bus. I kept my Homburg on and pulled the brim low over my face, as though I was trying to sleep despite the morning sun coming through the windows. "Some monsters are merely men who battled their fate and lost." I thought of myself, naturally. "They have no hatred in their hearts, yet they have the appearance of a monster. And thus ordinary people shun them."

"Yes," Matej agreed, pulling the collar of his coat tighter against his throat. "I have known those kinds of monsters. The pitiful ones. Like me." He laughed. "I am a reminder of what men can do to one another and it frightens people—ordinary people, as you say. The people who do not know, do not understand, and do not care."

"I know exactly what you mean."

He scoffed at my sympathy. "I get through life with a government pension, yet what do I do each day but defend against all manner of accusations: I was a coward, I lusted for blood, I was stupid to get caught, I did not protect my mother from rape, I collaborated with them, I did not try to escape, I gave away secrets, or even that I dared take up arms when war itself is such a vile thing, they say—as though lying down at the first sight of the enemy is the righteous thing to do. People are weak today. No one will take up arms against evil—and they claim that makes them holy." He took a breath. "You can take up arms! You can fight for justice! Many have fought for God and many have fought against someone else's god. The ideas that fill people's heads, they are like cancer—and I've had cancer, and beaten it; I'm on my way to get one more check-up to be sure it has not returned, like I care so much how I die." He took a longer breath. "Dying does not matter. It is the end of pain, and that is a good thing. Isn't it?"

I placed my hand on his arm. "I agree."

Then I took some time to replay and understand his words. I asked him if he knew Hungarian, a better language for me. He did not, yet he praised the Hungarians for standing strong against the "unholy hordes" of invaders. I assumed he meant the endless streams of refugees.

The sunlight was becoming unbearable. I felt it touching my face and it burned. Sitting on the shaded side of the bus to begin with, I shifted my position and got some relief. Yet it was only a matter of time before the boundary of light would come upon me again. I could only shift a little more.

It is not as legends have told. We do not burst into dust whenever sunlight hits our flesh. People wish it happened that way. Sunshine is caustic; that's all. It simply burns our skin, like anyone stretched out on a beach. However, the burning is more severe and quicker. Our skin flakes, peels—down to the epidermis, which is a painful experience. But we do not explode like they show in films. If that were possible, I know many of us would welcome that kind of speedy exit: suicide by sunshine.

But I digress . . .

It was noon when we arrived in Zadar, a city I had never visited, perched on a peninsula paralleling the coast. A series of long barrier islands separated the city from the Adriatic Sea. A charming old town, orange-tiled roofs over pale stone buildings. The bus delivered us to the central station in the newer district, where modern office buildings rose like monuments to success.

I helped Matej down the steps of the bus but he shook off my hand.

"I'm not an old woman!" he barked. I apologized.

Coming into the city, I noticed an airport. I momentarily wondered if I could fly to Budapest. But the old concerns filled me. How to pass through a security checkpoint looking as I did. I would be pulled aside for closer inspection. I would have to explain myself. If I had a hideous disease, I could not mingle with healthy folks aboard an aircraft. I was as good as a leper. My destination was Zagreb, anyway—

Matej tugged at my coat sleeve, bidding me farewell. He was off to his doctor appointment. I offered to guide him. He knew the way, had been there many times. He rattled his cane.

"Then how about you guide me?" I asked.

"You want to see my doctor? You got some problems?"

"Remember my bad smell."

"Yes, you stink!" He laughed. "I hardly notice now."

"It comes and goes. Fresh air helps."

"If you want to go to Zagreb, you'd best stay here." He meant at this bus station. "I'll be fine. No one bothers an old blind man."

"I wish you well, then, sir."

"And you!" He laughed. "Keep away from the monsters."

I nodded, then realized he could not see that.

"Thanks," I said.

I turned to enter the station, to get a ticket for the next bus, the one to Zagreb, as Matej started across the street.

Upon our arrival, I noticed the people loitering around the station. Some were waiting for buses. Others seemed like they had no plans, no particular tasks, happy to observe the bright autumn day. Or they were looking for a score, anything to entertain themselves or improve their financial lot. I wasn't comfortable seeing such people there. They were the sort who enjoy harassing people like me: the odd-looking ones.

Someone cried out and I turned to look, shielding my eyes beneath the brim of my hat.

Matej was on the ground, knees against the pavement. Two youths were trying to empty his pockets, right in the middle of the street in the middle of the day.

"Leave the man alone!" I shouted automatically—but in English. I put the words together in Croatian and shouted again as I hobbled toward him. "*Ostavite čovjeka sam!*"

As I approached, the two thugs looked up at me, grinning. They were not Croats. They could be from Turkey, I supposed, or elsewhere in the Middle East. They did not understand either my English or my Croatian, ignoring both my commands.

They removed Matej's wallet from his trouser pocket and a folder of papers from his coat pocket. They patted him down as they stood over him.

"Let him go! Return his belongings!" I demanded in unapologetic English. "Or I shall thrash you."

They did not comply, so I reached down and grabbed the collar of one man, lifted him away from Matej and tossed him hard on the pavement beside me. He seemed surprised that a weak, sickly man like me could do such a thing. His partner paused; I threw a hard backhand slap at his face, knocking him over.

They both got to their feet, sizing me up.

"Give me his wallet and whatever else you took from him."

"No," said one of them.

"You steal from an old blind man? How pathetic!"

I took Matej's white cane and swung it hard at the knees of the man who'd said "No". The cane cracked but so did the man's knee. He collapsed with a cry. The broken cane now had a sharp point. I wielded it like an epée, returning to my college fencing, and lunged forward, jabbing it into the belly of the second man. I held back; the jagged end only went an inch deep. When I withdrew the wooden stick, blood flowed out of his belly.

I froze—*What have I done?*

The sight both alarmed me and excited me. I did not feel heroic, yet I had acted for good. Was God watching?

I also realized my lack of nourishment on this long trip. I saw the blood seeping out and dropped to my knees. Bystanders no doubt saw me trying to help the wounded man. What I was actually doing was lapping up some of the blood before it could flow away. The brim of my Homburg hid my unnatural act.

I stopped when I heard sirens.

7

"UNHAND ME!" I CRIED. "I AM THE VICTIM HERE, NOT THE PERPETRATOR!"

Everything had happened so quickly yet it seemed to move in slow-mo animation. Certainly I could have fled. I could have broken through the crowd and run as fast as my feeble legs could take me. Some would see my direction and follow me or send the police after me. Moreover, Matej was my friend and I couldn't leave him wounded and alone. So I stayed, wiping my mouth on the attacker's shirt, then standing tall when officers arrived.

They asked what had happened. Who was at fault? What injuries were sustained? What role had I played in the mêlée? I announced that I used to be a doctor, of sorts, and tried to help the man who had taken the cane in the gut. I introduced Matej as a stranger who I'd spoken with only briefly. We had been on the same bus, the one arriving from Korenica. We had talked on the bus.

"I saw him being attacked by these two vagabonds," I explained in my best Croatian. *Skitnica* means 'vagabond' in Croatian, one of the more useful words I'd learned for those people who traipsed across our estate. "He was unable to fight them, and they broke his cane. He did not know it was sharp when he held it up in defense. The man ran straight into the point."

A few bystanders shouted a different account. The officers pushed me back, dropped down to examine the victim, the *skitnica*, wounded but alive. His accomplice had run away, however.

"It was amazing to see an old blind man fight off these youthful thieves," I said. "Yet it's a pity the cane broke and presented a sharp tip. He did not know that, being blind. When I saw the attack, I ran to him, but it was too late."

The lead officer glanced at me. Something caught his attention. He pointed at my face. I guessed his words asked how my face had gotten blood-stained. I wish I could have blushed.

"When I ran to him, I tripped on the cobblestones and fell against the victim—that man."

The officer insisted I be taken to a hospital and checked. My friend Matej, too. He was slow to get up. An officer insisted he remain flat on the pavement. An ambulance was coming.

◌

Once more within the folds of a hospital. I passed the mirrors without record; the security cameras ignored me. One firm hand grasped my boney arm, guiding me through corridors. Two more officers followed. A nurse led the way to an examination room. They were required to examine me. In the first instance, I would be checked for injuries. In the second instance, they would determine if I'd acted in the manner in which I had stated. A third reason was to determine if I were even allowed to be in the country at all. I had no papers.

I felt weak; I had successfully avoided hospitals for thirteen years. I have not had a comfortable relationship with them throughout my life. In fact, it was a hospital, *née* clinic, where I died.

Of course, *died* is a relative term. '*Umro sam u 2014,*' I might say, and it would be accurate. I died in the year 2014. There is a record of that fact somewhere. Unless the clinic tried to cover-up the flaws in their treatment protocol that sent me over the edge. I knew that was entirely possible. I had not helped matters, either, rising as I did in the pre-dawn hours and departing their facility without a word to anyone. Clinic staff would have discovered the bed empty, the sheet drawn over my face and body dropped on the floor, the clothing in the closet gone, and perhaps, if they were clever, they might have detected footprints as I stepped into the corridor and exited the building. There might be proof of that.

I needed to explain myself to the nurse sent to check my vitals in this small room. The walls bore posters instructing how to detect and care for sexually transmitted infections. The graphics were stark. One poster displayed the anatomy of the male apparatus, a cross-cut artist's rendition which displayed its inner workings. This was the room for the bad boys.

I had to smile at this choice of rooms. If this were the only one available, then I knew God was again enjoying some amusement at my expense. I had to appreciate the irony in that turn. I am not without a sense of humor, many have told me over the years. "You're a funny guy, Stefan," I recall Penny telling me, echoing the sentiment of others. I was never quite sure how to take that remark.

"You have a very low heartbeat," said the doctor in a soft, precisely articulated, textbook Croatian. She pulled a stylus from her white lab coat pocket and tapped several places on a flat computer screen she held in one hand. I had never seen such a device before. "Were you aware of that? It's dangerously low. I almost could not detect it." She shook her head. "Maybe this is malfunctioning," she muttered to herself, tugging on the stethoscope around her neck.

When she left the room, I saw two police officers standing by the door. How was I the target of investigation? I saved that old man. Now they were only interested in how I am still alive. And whether or not I belong here.

When the doctor returned, I put on my warmest smile.

"You should be careful," I spoke in a low voice, "for I am cursed with a disease."

"Disease?" She stepped back.

"It's not contagious, but it may be rather, umm, icky." Yes, I used the English word 'icky'. There is no Croatian word that carries the icky sensation. "You need not concern yourself with my fitness. The blood on my face and coat is not mine. It's from the man I was trying to save. I have medical training."

She could only stare at me with her dark, unsuspecting eyes. With a dismissive brush of her blond locks, she turned her attention to the computer tablet she held up, obviously avoiding looking at me. I could not blame her for that. I am hard on the eyes.

She tapped to another screen.

"We should run more tests," she said without looking up.

"I will not pass those tests," I muttered.

"Pardon?"

I realized I had spoken in English. She replied in English, as well.

The hour for secrecy had passed, as the day lurched into afternoon. Thankfully, I was protected from sunlight inside this hospital room. Still, I could not have a good appearance. It had been a couple hours since my lapping of blood from that vagabond.

"You speak English?" asked the doctor, name tag: Dr. Marija Juríc. "We thought you Croat."

"Apparently," I said, continuing in my native tongue, "I am many things, not all of them suitable for whoever I may happen to meet. If you want a Croat I may be a Serb. If you want a Serb, I may be one of those Hungarians. If you want a Magyar, well then, I just may be an American lost in Europe. Who can tell anymore? The world is mixed up and insane."

She pursed her lips, blinked. "It makes no difference to us. We treat everyone. It is our moral duty."

Then, for the first time in my examination, she gave me a warm, sincere smile. It struck an antenna in my heart and suddenly my whole being seemed to blossom, like a flower unfolding its petals to the sun. It was a glorious feeling I had not felt in thirteen years.

"You must be homeless . . . . Yes?"

"I left my home, yes." I waited a decent pause, gained the dramatic effect, and continued: "Seeking treatment for my malady. That would be in Zagreb. I did not intend to arrive in Zadar. My mistake."

"I understand." She glanced at the closed door. "And you met the older man on the bus, became friends, and then when he was attacked you helped him."

"That is all true."

"I wonder why they hold you . . . ."

My dry, cracked lips pinched on their own. "Perhaps they believe I want to be held by someone . . . anyone. It is another malady of which I suffer."

She looked up from the report. "Pardon? What did you say?"

I had mumbled. It was more to myself yet I suppose I hoped she might hear me, might understand my plight, and might give me a hug. I would settle for a one-arm around the shoulders squeeze. That would be enough. Vampires do not get many hugs.

She returned her attention to the screen on the accursèd computer thing, as though it was a living being—unlike me, who was not.

"What year is it?" I asked—right out of the blue, much like a vivid red streak of blood splashed on the pure white floor tiles of a sterile laboratory. I could do math and calculate that figure myself. However, the urge to have it confirmed overwhelmed me. That is the way the mind works after being isolated for so long.

She gazed at me, puzzled. "Have you been away so long?" She put a grin to her lips, saw I did not appreciate her humor, and restored her serious façade. "The year is twenty-twenty-seven. Why do you ask?"

"As you surmise, I've been away for a while."

"How long has it been?" She had a delightful accent, the mix of English and Croatian. "Were you in prison?"

"Prison?" I had to stop and think. "It was a kind of prison, though I committed no crime." I shook my head, feeling the years press upon me. "Look at me, Doctor Juríc. I could not bear the reactions of people I passed on the streets, so I put myself away. I hid from everyone. It was a terrible life." I laughed awkwardly. "Life! What a strange word. So cruel yet so useful to describe the constant animations of cells that choose to serve together for a common purpose: gathering fuel and seeking sex. Continuing the species. What is the point? All that effort put forth in staying alive long enough to make another of yourself and start it all over again. The long game. A hideous joke! God is a carnival master with a poor sense of humor. With too many trained beasts. And clowns. He has harassed and hounded me for many years, even after I surrendered and accepted my fate."

"You seem . . . agitated. Is that the word?" She tried to smile, failed.

"Yes, the right word."

Her pleasant countenance struggled to calm me.

"Please understand," she said. "I am required to take some tests, to make sure you are safe. There is an epidemic of diseases brought by refugees and migrants. The law requires us to check everyone who is not a resident." Another glance at the chart. "You do not have resident papers . . . ." She gave me a hard stare. "And you speak a lot of English. More than I can follow. I do not use it much . . . . How long have you been here? In the Hungarian Federation?"

I blinked, surprised that enough of my eyelids remained to perform that act. I thought of my father and his history books. He was not one to dwell on the daily affairs of states and statesmen. He preferred the past, the older the better. The end of the Second World War was his cut-off date. Everything happening since then was irrelevant to him. Everything happening since then was caused by that war. Too many discussions over the past thirteen years. The present did not exist in our isolated villa. Nor did the future. We no longer subscribed to the local newspaper. And the Internet was merely a myth.

"If you must follow the laws, then . . . ." A pause for effect. "Then, of course, you must. However, I don't think you will find anything in my chemistry that would preclude me from being on my way to Zagreb. I'm the picture of health," and my guffaw accentuated my sarcasm.

And sarcasm is only truth in a straightjacket . . . .

She accepted my offer to be her comedian of the day. It was all I had to offer. With a word to a nurse, the materials were brought in and the procedure commenced. It was difficult to find a good vein. I rather impressed the nurse as a dying drug addict, my veins too wasted to be of any use. Yet I existed!

Well played, God, well played!

I helped as best I could, making a fist, gathering what blood I had into one location in my arm, advising her to try there. She did, got enough to stain the vial, perhaps a bit more. It was the right color yet too thick. The passage through the needle was too narrow. She tried a larger gauge and stuck me again. No, I did not feel any pain. My nerves have ceased to function that way. Finally she was satisfied, applied a bandage, and exited.

The guards were still there as the door opened, swung shut.

What was beginning to seem like another thirteen years ended when Dr. Juríc returned, a frown on her face and an ominous wave of her computer tablet. Poor Juríc, I mused, watching her preparing her words, I knew her well—

"Your name is Székely?" she asked like it was a game show quiz.

"That's very clever. I told the police my name."

"You had no papers so we needed to confirm your identity."

"Confirm my identity? How?"

"We checked your DNA markers against the database in the federal residency archive. You attended a clinic . . . . Zagreb, correct? We have a match. It is a new requirement. So many people have no papers . . . the migrants, that is."

"I'm not a migrant. Well, here in Zadar, I suppose I am. Forgive me. I shall try henceforth to be less migratory."

"Stefan Székely . . . ."

She said my name as though it was a mantra that would call down God in a bolt of lightning. 'What?' God would demand. 'What has my little vagabond done this time?' He would ask. 'Just send him on his miserable way and never speak of this incident again.' That is how God is; we met once thirteen years ago.

"Yes, that is my name." I watched her contemplating the shocking revelation. "Yet living—existing—in such isolation, I never call myself, nor does anyone else. It is easy to forget who I am."

"Mister Székely, the tests are strange. The results are not normal." She tapped the screen, switching back and forth between two pages, apparently not believing her eyes. "You have none of the diseases we test for, so you are not a danger. That should make you free to go on your way." She regarded me with a little more positive façade. "You are not in any criminal database, either."

"You see? I'm just a nameless nobody on his way to nowhere."

"It is not so clear, Mister Székely."

"They said if my tests are clean I am free to go. Witnesses confirm I was helping my friend. I acted in self-defense—the defense of others, however the words go."

"There is no record of you since that clinic. And your name appears again when you crossed the border—the old border between Hungary and Croatia . . . thirteen years ago."

My head felt heavy. "Time flies."

"The only records of you."

"It's a small world after all."

"No tax records, no—"

"My bank handles those matters."

"And here you are . . . alive."

"They kept those details all this time? How sweet!"

A frown spread across her face. "And the other detail in the tests, a medical detail, is . . . . I'm afraid to say it, but your test results, Mister Székely, they show nothing. Not at all within the parameters. The data is off the chart. Highly abnormal. I have never seen anything like these numbers. They suggest you are literally dead."

A grin spread across my face, cracking the skin at the corners of my mouth. "Told you."

8

I AM LITERALLY DEAD, SAYS THIS DOCTOR, ONE WHO SHOULD KNOW. AND yet I go about my assigned tasks with a modicum of displeasure, for that is what God has decreed as my punishment for evolving from an egg and a sperm, for daring to develop into something approximating His great creations of the past. Imperfect. It is a curse, I understand. A thing of beauty, in its own twisted way, yet it lasts forever. No, I am not a bad person, just a dead one.

"You are a strange person," said Dr. Juríc, "yet we cannot hold you if you are clean, have none of the diseases."

The police officers would have questions for me, she expected. None beyond those relating to Matej. I was a Good Samaritan, who happened to be a Hungarian-American, just in the right place at the right time. Take notice, God. Keep score.

So what can be done with such a forlorn person? What is the right dispensation? What papers are needed so this *skitnica* can be on his way, being of no harm to anyone?

First, a doctor-ordered blood transfusion. Because I had so little in me, enough to be literally dead. Thank you, Dr. Juríc, for the resupply. In a few hours I felt like my old self—about five years younger than the day I arrived in Zadar. Spry, limber, ready to take on the world. It was a kind of miracle. I gazed at the clouds as I walked the streets of Zadar, expecting God's bemused face to show, or a lightning bolt to strike. One can never be sure which.

Second, a stop at an office of residency to get a card made for me. I would become an official resident of the Hungarian Federation. After all, there is documentation that I lived—there's that pejorative word again—that I *resided* within the bounds of the Federation prior to the formation of the union of Hungary, Croatia, Serbia, Slovenia, and parts of Romania, Austria, and the northeast corner of Italy—remaking the ancient Hapsburg empire despite themselves. The area of conflict for concern was in Bosnia—not a member of the Federation, having a Muslim population. That area was occupied by Turkish forces, much as in days of old. My father had long lectured on the Ottoman expansion and I had tuned out most of it. He reminded me of our friend Vlad Tepes and his sticky solution to unwanted guests. Indeed, the Turks now held fast to the land south of my family villa. It became apparent to me that what goes around comes around—except I am never to be born again. That would not follow the pattern.

"You've been too long away from the news reports," the minister of paperwork sneered at me in rough, country Croatian. He stamped my papers with the official seal. "You best return to your living place and be ready to defend against the horde."

I smiled like a two-year old child. "What horde?"

"All of them beasts from the Levant," he growled. He was a beefy man, bald with hanging jowls. "They come in waves, calling themselves refugees but it's mostly men of fighting age. No women, no children. Some people say it's all a plan to take over Europe. So we fight against it. We fight against their advancement."

"If they are fleeing a war zone, people should be more welcoming."

"I said they're mostly men coming. If they are fleeing, then they are cowards to leave their women and children behind. No, it's something else entirely."

"What could that be?"

"I blame the damn Germans!" He roared, then looked around like he wanted to hit something. "They feel the guilt of old wars, so now they accept anyone who has a sad tale. Many free things they give away if you can get there."

"They are coming for jobs?"

"I hear not many ever get a job, so they stay on the state benefits all their lives. It's been fifteen years and it only gets worse. More crime.

Ah, I hate thinking about it. Worse than here—you know, in Bosnia, back in ninety-two, -three. The way women were treated. Now these invaders want to turn their new home into the same kind of filthy, cruel place they left."

"I thought they were fleeing a bad situation."

"Maybe it started that way. It's worst in Germany—and Sweden— and France. You can't go in some places because the immigrants keep you out, even though it's your own country. Used to be."

"I remember reading about the refugees years ago. Before I stopped connecting with the world."

"That is a good plan. Yet now you better keep in connection if you want to live. Every day there is fighting and bombing." He cleared his throat. "You know last week they blew up the cathedral in Köln. The grand cathedral, standing for hundreds of years. Magnificent building! I studied it in school, when I wanted to be an architect. Another attack by the nameless horde, razed the cathedral to the ground! Horrible!"

"Yes, horrible."

I could not imagine such wanton destruction. Who tears down age-old monuments? He told me what happened to the Eiffel Tower being bombed a couple years before, how it fell over, killing dozens of people on the ground.

"They want to transform Europe into a wasteland of barbaric laws. It's the way of the places they left. Idiot governments!" He had to stop and catch his breath. "We do not want any transformation."

"I know something about transformation." I restrained a chuckle. "It's what God demands. Perhaps. Oh, well. Who really knows what God wants? I've tried to discuss it at length with Him but He cuts me off every time."

"You should just pray to God. Keep it simple. Ask for strength— physical and moral. Ask for a squad of guards to walk with you, too. Keep some pork in your pockets." He dared laugh, then thought better of it and went quiet. "We cannot joke like that. They'll cut out your tongue if they hear you."

I could only nod. My skin felt thicker, softer, with good color, as though I was only a hundred years old. I turned to the window in the office, saw a gleam of reflection there: the desk, the computer screen, the chair, but not, sadly, me sitting in that chair. Suddenly my heart seemed to collapse, like a rubber ball with a puncture, the air escaping rapidly.

I shrugged. "It matters not to me. I don't wish to encounter any of them. I don't care if they are fighters or refugees. I'll keep to myself."

"Yes, I see you're old. Probably die soon anyway. But the rest of us have families. We want to protect them from these invaders."

"That I understand. Yet I've been away for thirteen years, living on my own, far away."

"True? What made you leave?"

"My parents."

He grinned, his brow furrowing. "Parents? They died?"

"No, they refuse to die. So I needed to leave."

The bulldog laughed, slapped his fat hand on the desk.

"I hope to get my own place. You know, find a nice girl, have a family, build a wall, hire guards, the usual."

"You sound like a good planner."

He handed me my newly minted papers. "Don't wave that around. People who don't have them will kill you for them. You need this to go anywhere in the Federation, ride public transportation, get hotel room, do almost anything. Get a job, purchase a house. Be careful as you go about your travels."

"I will. Thanks."

◌੪

The express bus was a sleek monstrosity, a mostly white vehicle with red and blue stripes that would make the three-hour trip in two hours. All in splendid comfort. I could use some splendid comfort, being who I am and where I've been. A handful of days being wined and dined in lovely Zadar left me ready for a nap.

I stood in the line that snaked around the bus and ended at the vehicle's closed door. A couple dozen people waited, some with tickets in their hands, others without. I purchased mine at the ticket counter in the station an hour before, so excited to be leaving that I fumbled through my Croatian. I was confident in being on my way, having detailed discussions with the attentive clinicians in Zagreb.

Finally the driver arrived wearing an old blue uniform with red epaulets, very militaristic. He was a burly sort of man, the kind who could lift a bus with one hand and change the tire with the other hand. A thick moustache covered his mouth as he warned us to stand back. He opened the door and climbed inside the bus. People started to board but he shouted at them to wait, to get down from the steps. Perhaps it was not meant to be a pleasant ride after all.

Once we were allowed to board the bus, I moved down the aisle to the back row. I thought my presence would be less noticeable there. I had no inclination to have happy conversations about children, dogs, or grandmothers along the way. I sat in the last seat and found another man sitting opposite me, across the aisle. He seemed overly dressed for a fine autumn day, one where the golden sunshine sends people like me into the shadows lest we burn and flake. He looked me over, then stared out the window.

When the bus was full, the driver stalked down the aisle checking tickets. As he worked his way toward me, I began to have a strange feeling. My senses are more acute when I'm full of fresh blood. I can hear the beating of hearts several seats away. I can hear people's thoughts two vehicles over. I can detect irregular blood flow in the veins of the person next to me. I glanced at the fellow across the aisle from me.

He wore a scraggly black beard, had deep-set eyes, and a ball cap pulled down over his forehead. His coat was thick, like he was quite rotund beneath the garment. Yet his face did not indicate he was a fat person. His bewhiskered throat seemed to be that of a slimmer man. He caught me looking. I could not say who was more surprised. My appearance had improved and I could pass for a sickly person on a bus ride home to die among my relations. My neighbor stared a moment too long, passing the threshold of politeness.

I got up and bumped my way forward, crashing into the driver coming down the aisle. He had curses for me but I squeezed around him and took the front seat, right behind the driver. As far away from that *skitnica* in the back as possible.

When the driver returned to the front, since he had not checked my ticket, he demanded I show it to him. I handed the ticket over. He regarded it only an instant before demanding I get off the bus.

"Why?" I asked. "I just bought the ticket."

It seemed in my flustered state of affairs in Zadar, I had chosen the wrong date. I was not due to travel until the next day.

I tried to argue that it was all the same, tomorrow or today, but the driver would have none of it, no matter how clever my poor Croatian was. I smiled sincerely, even though my lips cracked. More curses and a feigned shove off the bus. I got the hint.

As I took a step down to exit the bus, I glanced back at the fellow in the rear of the bus. He was standing rather than sitting. He had opened his thick winter coat. He reached across his waist—

The world erupted in a spray of colors, the explosion beating me to the ground, falling into numbed silence. Around me the thick smoke convinced me I'd advanced to heaven at last. People stepped over me, others dropped against me and did not move. I saw blood droplets flying through the air like rain, some landing over me.

I picked myself up, found it difficult to walk and fell onto my hip. I crawled across the pavement as best I could until someone helped me up, lifted me and half-dragged me away from the scene of carnage.

9

MEDICAL PERSONNEL THOUGHT MY GHASTLY APPEARANCE WAS THE RESULT of being hit by shrapnel from the explosion. I concurred, unwilling to tell the whole story again of how I transformed into a vampire. It worked for a while. In time, I became a fixture of the hospital, like others who survived the blast. It was part and parcel of the new world, everyone agreed. It was a new normal. No one asked why it had to be that way. No one wondered why the world could not be the way it had been, say, thirteen years ago when last I looked out and saw only good. Instead, everyone had become weak, unwilling to fight, taking the easy road of submission.

The drugs they gave me to sleep did not work. My body absorbed them, encapsulated them in convenient little tumors, and I went on as I had always gone. None seemed the wiser. No one took delight in tales of vampires any longer. The real world was much more horrific than anything that could be portrayed in films. I doubted I could shock anyone were I to declare my true form.

I was the last survivor released from the hospital, perhaps because I appeared to have the worst effects. Almost everyone aboard the bus died, except the driver and myself, who were thrown clear, and the four or five sitting at the front who were severely hurt. Thirteen people outside the bus were injured; two of them later died. The Zadar bus bombing. We made the news worldwide, which I suppose was the goal. The bomber could not have known us, could not have had hatred for any of us as individuals. He simply wanted to make his mark on the world, to show he existed—well, for a brief moment—and perhaps hope others would praise him for his sacrifice.

"Where will you go?" asked my young doctor, named Markovic, when I was signing forms to be released. It was eight weeks later than I had originally expected to be on my way. They thought I should stay longer, being an old man, yet I insisted I continue on my business. My extended stay had given me plenty of time to practice Croatian.

"I have only one direction," I said in English, adding a wink. "To Zagreb. By bus. Again. What are the odds of two bombings?"

Markovic mugged. "Let us hope your trip is uneventful."

He liked practicing his English with me, though he sounded like a robot, checking for the right word before speaking it. We had talked at length about all manner of medical issues yet never happened upon the obvious one: my vampirism. He didn't give much attention to my genetic issues. The only serious injury I'd sustained was a broken leg. Compound fracture. When I had tried to get myself up and take a step, my tibia shattered. Bone fragments punctured my flesh and jagged slivers protruded. I was nothing but skin and bones that day anyway. They pinned my leg together, stitched it up, gave me lots of good transfusions.

Senior doctors insisted that someone in my poor health not be released but Dr. Markovic argued that as long as I was of no harm to others, having no communicable disease, they could not keep me against my will.

"Zagreb will look beautiful dressed in Christmas lights," said Dr. Markovic. "I'm sure you will enjoy them."

"Thank you. I've not seen Zagreb lit up for the holidays," I relied. "I was only there at the end of October my previous visit."

A short, stout nurse entered the room, presenting a fine wooden cane, carved with forestry motifs, a truly elegant accessory.

"We have gotten something for you," said Markovic. "You will need to lean on it as you go about your business."

The petite nurse grinned, her dimples flexing. Ana had always been kind to me during my stay, despite my horrid appearance. She had even flirted with me on occasion—I called it flirting, anyway. In our dreams we had planned a wonderful life together, five children and three dogs, in a villa on a mountaintop.

"Thank you," I spoke, barely above a whisper. I had lost my breath at the tender gesture. "I will remember your kindness every time I rely on its steadiness to keep from falling."

Ana touched my arm, yet I felt her parade of corpuscles through my shirt and jacket. She was in excellent health. I looked up and met her eyes and she shyly glanced away.

"You sure you don't want to come with me?" I asked Ana, knowing her reply already. Markovic translated my English and she shook her head, smiling all the while. "At least I asked," I said with a grin. "*Hvala za vašu ljubaznost.*"

"You welcome," Ana replied.

03

The second bus trip was successful. I got to Zagreb without incident. I disembarked at the central station. A man in bus company uniform assisted me getting off the bus and getting my bag. The bag mostly was for a spare set of clothing and my official medications. I had not been taking the pills, knowing they would do nothing for a dead body, but I wished to please the medical staff. They had done so much for me— right up to the edge of what God could do were He willing to bend the rules on my behalf. But rules are rules so I didn't expect any such benevolence.

There were signs, certainly. The rain storm that bombarded us at the half-way mark. The car crash we had to wait for, then carefully go around. The landslide that partially blocked the road. I knew God was trying to keep me from arriving in Zagreb, the site of my death. It was a sore spot for both of us. He dared not do something drastic to halt me; He was limited to things no one would suspect were His doing.

Stepping off the bus, I stared up at the gray sky, a cold and wintry ceiling, and I grinned like the madman I'd become.

Thirteen years since last I set foot on these streets . . . .

I took a taxi over to the clinic where once I had sought treatment. The office building which had housed the stem-cell research clinic on three of its six floors no longer occupied that block. Instead, a new,

67

larger building of glass and steel, sixteen floors high, stood there. No more the ornate concrete and carved stone of traditional architecture, styles that held heritage like a family photo album. The old town of Zadar had been preserved, like a living museum of the quaint manner everything used to be. Zagreb, however, had moved further forward and nothing was recognizable. What surrounded me was a city that could have been a city anywhere in the world.

The taxi driver said the new building had been there for ten years.

"Ten years?" I muttered in English. "What happened to the former building?" I asked in Croatian.

"It was torn down," he replied in Croatian, with an English sneer. It was obvious that the older building had been torn down, he meant me to understand. I was such an idiot.

"What happened to the clinic inside?" I asked, just to provoke his annoyance. "There was a medical research facility inside."

"Oh, that place," said the driver. "It was a big scandal. They went out of business. People died there. Lot of crazy things they did there."

"Went out of business, huh?"

"That's what I heard. And I don't read the news so it must be a big thing for me to hear about it." He laughed.

No more stem-cell research facility. That did not necessarily mean that a stem-cell research facility no longer existed, only that this one company had been forced to close. Perhaps they had moved, changed locations. Or another clinic had opened to continue their research, separate from the scandal of the previous clinic.

I wondered how many others had died. Perhaps only me, a foreign fool who thought he knew better than the scientists. Yes, let's try this, let's do it this way; I'll accept the risks, just give it a try and we'll see how it goes; I'm desperate anyway, desperate to try anything, anything at all, and even if it may not work, this is the last hope I have.

My lips struggled to grin in response to my thoughts.

The whole purpose of taking this trip was to return here. I expected them to treat my poor skin, so I might then present myself among mortals without alarming them. I knew they could do that. The doctor, Kovačević I recall his name was, talked up their skin treatments based on extensive stem-cell research. He was quite the salesman. That was all I wanted now. I wanted to look pretty, pretty enough I could go to the ball and no one would look askance. So I would be allowed into the ball, glass slippers or not. Poor me! I had lost the Prince Charming I used to see in the mirror each morning.

"Thank you," I said to the driver as I climbed inside the car.

I gave him another address.

As we drove, we came upon a group of police manhandling a group of civilians who apparently were protesting something in front of some government building. My driver paused, then changed directions. I continued to watch the battle through the rear window as we sped away. Police wielded batons over the heads and backs of the protesters. Protesters threw rocks. Then something exploded in the middle of the crowd. An armored vehicle rolled out from a side street. The police retreated into a tight line in front of the government building and the armored vehicle unleashed water cannon discipline on the protestors. Most fled. Some tried to stand their ground but they were bowled over by the powerful spray. In the winter cold, the water was particularly sharp.

"What are they protesting?" I asked my driver as we turned and I lost sight of the incident.

"They protest many things. Who can say what it is today?"

"They seemed to be young people."

"The youngsters protest the most. They get heads full of ideas from their schools and they demand what they want." He shook his head. "My own son was a protestor. Now he is in jail . . . one year already."

"What was he protesting?"

"I don't know. Something unimportant, I'm sure. They won't let me talk to him."

"Didn't they get a lawyer for him? Was there a trial?"

He turned and glared at me, even as the taxi barreled on down the narrow street. "You are not from here, are you?"

"No," I replied, lowering my chin to my chest. "I'm sorry."

"One thing is they want borders to be opened, let everybody in, no matter we have people already here with no jobs. They sing songs of union, everybody one big family, like it's religion. We are the world."

"I heard of that when I was in Zadar."

"Zadar! Oh, the bus bombing. You hear about that?"

"Yes, I know about it." I wanted to rattle my cane and tell my side of it but I thought better to let him talk.

"A guy from Middle East, that one, wanted to scare people into converting. So tell me how blowing up people makes anybody want to join you! How is that supposed to work?"

We shook our heads in unison as he turned the corner and slowed to match the circumstances of the old town streets. He had to be careful maneuvering the vehicle. Up the slope we went, then into a parking lot. I gazed out the window.

There it was, still standing: Svete Katarine, or *Crkva sv. Katarine* in Croatian: The Church of Sainte Catherine, first built in 1620 by the Dominican Order. Thirteen years ago I visited this church begging to be baptized, a way to keep God from killing me. It was just before my procedure at the clinic.

The church stood as colorful as before, perhaps repainted during my absence. No Christmas lights, like many other buildings in Zagreb. That was a rebellious act, I supposed. The lights that celebrated one holiday were offensive to people who did not celebrate that holiday. So everything had become muted, reduced to common secular gray. Like the wintry sky overhead.

Dusk covered us as a cold wind rolled down from the mountains north of the city. A scattering of snow flurries followed.

For some reason, I dropped awkwardly to my knees as I faced the church. I set down my cane and pressed my hands together.

Here I am, God. Back at the scene of the crime. Although you and I both know I did nothing wrong. If you are in charge of everything, you have the power to prevent this curse from falling on me. What did I ever do to deserve this? Even if an ancient ancestor of mine upset you, why bear your revenge upon me, who has never done anything to you but a few bad jokes and avoiding church services for most of my life?

I looked up, opened my eyes, let the church fill my vision. A spot of moisture emerged in the corner of my eye. Before I could touch it to see if it was real, it slid out of my eye and ran down my cheek, hung on my chin a moment, and dropped.

Thank you. Thank you for that reminder of who I am. Who I want to be. Someone who can shed a tear. I am filled with tears, you know. I need to let them out.

The taxi driver honked the horn, impatient even as he saw I was praying.

"Won't do you no good," he shouted in Croatian. "It's closed."

I fought to get up, straight and tall, leaning on my cane, staring at the church. The doors were shuttered. A concrete barrier stood before them with a warning sign for good measure. Thirteen years ago they had stood open, welcoming any and all. I had walked in, no official papers or answering a list of questions, no armed guards to pat me down or check my status.

I took an unsteady step forward and hit a wall. I looked closely but saw nothing. I felt a buzz when I put my hand up. It rippled through my arm. On the ground, at intervals in the pavement rose small bulbs. I guessed they emitted a kind of electric field around the church to protect an ancient building from the attacks of those who thrive on destruction and the futurists who insist everything old must go.

"You can't go in," my driver called. "Transparent wall. They got them around many places. So terrorists can't destroy them."

I turned, nodding my understanding, and got back into the taxi.

"Where to next?" asked my driver.

"There is no place else for me." I had spoken in English, thinking aloud. "How many people get to revisit the site of their death?"

"You need hotel?" he asked.

I broke out of my trance. "Yes, a hotel."

I told him to go back to the clinic. I did not know the name of the hotel where I had stayed before my procedure at the clinic but I knew it was only a few blocks from the clinic. I might as well complete the Zagreb tour by staying at that hotel.

Actually, I was wrong. In my mind I had walked to the hotel after I died. Now that I could see the streets again, even under the Christmas lights, I realized I had walked only a block over to the parking lot of the hospital and drove the rental car to the hotel. Yes, I arose from my death bed and still could drive a car! There is no law against driving while dead.

So we went up one street and down another, looking for that one particular hotel. I guessed it was this way, but the landmarks evaded me. It was a small place; they served breakfast like a B&B, but it was more than a family-run establishment. It was on a slope, I recalled. I had made sure to set the parking brake.

And there it was! The name had changed, a new sign set over the entrance, but I recognized its configuration. A facelift, yes, but it was definitely the same building, and it was still a hotel.

"Please wait until I make sure they have a room," I said.

Inside, the lobby seemed dirty, run-down, as though only youthful hostel clients were guests now. A plump old woman came out of the back room at the ringing of the bell. She seemed angry I interrupted her TV show.

"What do you want?" she growled in Croatian.

I asked for a room, examining the floorplan on the countertop. I traced the walking route with my finger, found the room where I had stayed. Where I had stayed with that Hungarian girl I'd met at God's choosing, some kind of test for me.

"Is this room available?" I asked, pointing to one particular square on the floorplan.

"Yes, all available," she intoned like it was a set phrase.

"One night." I thought a moment. "Maybe two."

We did the formalities and I returned to the taxi to get my bag and settle the fare. The driver told me to be careful in this neighborhood, now full of 'mussies'. He pointed to the mosque on the corner, which had not been there thirteen years ago.

"It's closed now. People want to tear it down," he said. "Payback for bombing the cathedrals."

I took my bag up to the room I had stayed in thirteen years before. I slowed, studied each portion of floor and wall, though they likely had been scrubbed a few times since then. If only one piece of lint were the same, I mused, then I would know I was home.

The last time I had gone up these stairs—the same steps, different carpet possibly—I was returning from the clinic. Alma was sick and I had taken her to the hospital. It was next to the clinic, but I had to go have my procedure, so I left the hotel address with the hospital staff. If Alma recovered before I was finished in the clinic they could send her back to this hotel. I had already paid for the room.

My hand went to the doorknob, remembering the last time I had touched it. It burned a little as I turned it. The door gave way. I pushed it open, let it swing wide, and I gazed into that room where I saw Alma stretched upon the bed that night, asleep. I kept the lights off so as not to awaken her, to not alarm her.

By then I had made my deal with God. I would accept my fate, to transform into this thing I've become, if He would let her live. A simple exchange. She was innocent; she did not deserve what was happening to her and I knew I was to blame for that. God agreed.

She awoke when I closed the door behind me. God kept his part of the bargain. She no longer recognized me. She was frightened of the stranger in her room. It was as if we had never met—just as I'd asked. I spoke only a few words, in Hungarian so she would understand me, then left money, thinking she could return to Budapest and start a new life with it.

That was the last I ever saw of Alma Jónás.

I stared at the bed. It could be the same bed, unless they replaced it during the years. Beds do wear out. Yet it looked the same, was in the same position in the room, had the same romantic red velvet drapery around the head of the bed like it was supposed to be a honeymoon suite. I smiled. So much lost—so much that could have been. So much . . . pain. It's always pain that stops a good dream.

I set down my bag and hobbled over to the bed.

Removing my coat, I lay upon the bed, imagining Alma once more beside me, so light she did not press down the mattress.

10

THE DREAMS THAT DESPERATE MEN HAVE, ESPECIALLY OLDER MEN SUCH AS me, and especially the dreams they have of younger women, have a special quality to them, both strikingly vivid and engulfed in sorrow for times past and chances missed. The knowledge that one has passed a marker and can never go back is a pain that never goes away. What once was is no more. The man becomes a husk of himself and he knows women look at him with disgust or amusement. There is the biology which fails. There is the mind which turns into a house of mirrors. There is the world of customs and laws and good deeds which cut and claw into men, turning them into hollow men or, at best, fills them with straw.

Although I am a vampiric vagabond, I have those dreams. At first I was surprised. It was difficult to confess my age, especially frozen for ever more at the precise age of my transformation. In the dream land I frolic with nameless, faceless women of young and less young ages, of beauty or simple prettiness, of playful affection or mere politeness. Seldom romantic passion. It is a curse, certainly, but also a blessing to see the scenes unfold like petals on a flower. To see the fruition of desire—enough to cheer for them, the happy dream couple, and wish joy for the person that is supposed to be me in that dream and the girl or woman who is whoever I want her to be but who is usually never anyone I can have or ever could have had. That is the trick of dreams. Then you awaken to reality, which is worse.

That is the way God has arranged my daylight hours: a theater of the absurd. I am stuck on stage, my boots glued to the platform, and the cast comes and goes, the curtain rises and falls, and sometimes there is applause. I often forget my lines—

I awaken in a casket of confusion, forgetting where I am, who I am, what I've become. My skin has produced a phenomena I used to call 'sweat': a cold, clammy layer of moisture which I have seldom known in thirteen years. During my stay in the hospital, I was given blood transfusions. They were trying to restore me to health.

Now I was a couple days from my last draught of red. I would soon need more. Sure, I rushed to leave, in a great hurry to be away from my parents. I didn't think through everything. All I knew was that I would take the bus to Zagreb, visit the same clinic, and they would feel guilty about killing me and give me free skin treatment. Yes, I believed that. My mind had become so dulled being in the same house for so long, always with the same company, forever reciting the same scripts, the same words and the same responses. I had to leave.

Certainly, I never expected to be on the wrong bus or go the wrong direction or be injured in a bombing or stay in a hospital for weeks and then, finally, to be on my way to my destination only to find that it no longer existed. I could appreciate the irony; in fact, irony is my middle name: Stefan I. Székely. I remember the dear young man in so many movies who, when he fails in his quest, returns home to his parents' joyful crowing: "We told you so!" Yes, sonny has failed; we were right: we knew he would fail; we told him so. He cannot succeed without our loving care, ever-present tutelage, and thoughtful guidance. He will never out-grow us! Oh, no—never!

I lay on my back, unclothed, as only a figure who is without beauty can recline while feeling secure in his skin. The door was locked, chained, bolted. The clothing had rubbed my poor skin raw. I needed to air the death stench, the cool mildewy scent that attracts maggots and flies. Most people do not care for it.

With my arms extended out from my body, I could reach the edge of the bed on each side. I grasped the bed cover in each set of fingers. It was déjà-vu: the feel of the fabric, the tightness of my fists. Although this was the same room and perhaps the same bed, I realized I had never actually slept here. We checked in and I went to get food. Alma felt ill. When I returned, she was worse so I took her to the hospital and told the doctor what to look for: blood poisoning. I had my own procedure to undergo. She recovered—

The events of that day swirl constantly around my head.

I wonder if she returned to Budapest as I suggested. Thirteen years ago . . . . If it had been me, saved from death and given a sizeable check and some cash, I would have gone. I would start small and build up a life of my choosing. I would remove the piercings, cover the tattoos, wear sensible clothes. I would try to fit into society, because it is bigger than me, and the penalties for not fitting in can be great. That's what I would do.

But I am not me. As much as I cannot fit in now, I mourn the days when I found it so easy. I never rebelled, never fought convention. I was the good boy. Adults liked me. Whenever I made my way through the echoing corridors of Old Main, the insane asylum where my family lived and where I was born, I interacted with only adults. I learned from them; I learned what a clever boy I was, a wunderkind! Outside of Old Main, I was not a clever boy; I was the misfit, the weirdo, the monster. No matter how much I tried to do as others did, nothing felt right, nothing helped me fit in. I should have embraced my outlaw status.

Now I had money and time. I could be an outlaw again. Hah! I am an outlaw despite myself. It is not enough to buy my own estate and live happily ever after. There is no princess to save. No dragons to slay. Only books to read. Yet how many pages a day can be read? I am not my father. I cannot work my way through a library like he does.

What book shall I leaf through today?

The question is absurd.

What window shall I look out today?

This is the curse. Time . . . .

Endless time . . . .

And always the pain of existence. The body's constant discomfort. The mind's noisy rattlings. The glacial breakdown of cells. The march toward dust. There is no end.

I sigh and the odor of decay fills the room.

'Tomorrow is a new day.' Mother has said that for the past thirteen years. Tomorrow will not be a new day, not this time, I vow. Tomorrow will be a regression! I shall reclaim the evil that I was meant to be, back when God first put His little plan into action. Let us see what horror I can foist upon the world. If all I am meant to be is walking death, let me gather a parade to march with me!

ↁ

I fed last night. When the stars filled the cold sky I stepped out from the hotel and strolled about the neighborhood, found a small, wooded park. A young couple sat on a bench there, smooching like young couples do. Probably they could not do so at either residence, so they met in the park. After dark.

When they saw me, the man spoke angrily, demanding I go away, furious that I had disturbed their moment of affection. I did not move so he stood. He repeated his words. I stepped forward and the winter moon lit my face, my true face.

The man cowered, blocked his eyes. My eyes burrowed into his mind, held him frozen there, kneeling in the withered grass. The girl got up from the bench as her lover weakened. She asked him what was wrong but he couldn't answer. She went to him, to check him, placed her hand on the back of his head.

I reached for her, grabbed her wrist and spun her into my embrace. Her breath spilled out, the scent sweet, as her eyes met mine. The trick is in the eyes: with practice we can hypnotize our victims. In a flash her body weakened, slumped in my arms. The scent of blood within her aroused my fangs. Adjusting her better within my grip, I held her gaze a moment then lunged at her throat.

I felt dirty, of course. I am not a bad vampire. That is what I have told everyone I meet in my dreams. However, that is not who I should be. Not if I am to survive. I have not learned much in thirteen years. I had it easy. My parents provided everything, even occasional blood donors from the village. I never learned to hunt.

Finished with the girl, I lowered her to the bench. She had fainted in my arms. Her lover lay on the cold grass, lost in a stupor he would struggle to rise from like a bad hangover. I spoke no words but thought a prayer for her. I wanted to beg for her forgiveness. I am a monster; I cannot help myself.

But that was not me. *Not now.* I would never apologize again. I would take whatever I wanted, what I needed. And I would never ask for forgiveness.

The night was long, the dawn coming soon, when I returned to my hotel room, stripped off my hunting clothes, and stretched out on the bed. The blood tasted so fine. It warmed me, killing the mildew. I felt the fresh red coursing through me. For a while I could feel alive again. Like old times. If I wished, I might venture out into polite society, rub elbows with the average and the ordinary, and I would be one of them.

Oh, this? they might ask, pointing at my bad skin. *Why, I was in a bus in Zadar when it was bombed.* They would be amazed yet believe me. That is the worst I would appear to them. I could pass for normal, for human, if I allowed myself to hunt as freely as I wished.

For that, I needed a decent hunting ground. An area full of people, enough of a population that I would never encounter the same host twice. A city would do nicely. A city I knew my way around. Such as Budapest. The city where Alma lives—perhaps; I should investigate. It is where my bank is located. It is where I could purchase an elegant loft in the trendy Terézváros district, fill my home with famous artwork, hire a comely maid, a stoic manservant, and sleep away the days while hunting at night. I could write poetry again.

And I would eventually write to my parents, just to let them know where I was—

No, I will not write. Not for a while, certainly. Let them wonder.

I am a bad vampire now.

෯

The Budapest I knew thirteen years before no longer existed. The first thing I saw as I arrived was a squad of police blocking the avenue. I was driving along in a red Opal XV, the latest model with the rocket fins, rented in Zagreb. I was nervous driving for the first time in thirteen years, but it's like riding a bicycle, they say: just keep your feet on the pedals and steer.

"Identification chip not detected," the husky female voice from the dashboard intoned, programed for English. The rental car guy showed me how to switch it to manual drive.

Even so, the voice command function was not helpful. And the constant alarms whenever I veered too far to the left or right, or got too close to the vehicle in front of me were distracting. The beeps that sounded when I lifted a hand off the steering wheel were annoying, too. By the time I had crossed the old border between Croatia and Hungary, I had the hang of driving again.

In Budapest, they seemed to be holding back traffic so a platoon of soldiers could finish clearing a rabble of protesters. A lot of billowing smoke ahead, as though a bombing had already occurred. Or it was smoke intended to deter them from remaining in this government sector.

I looked beyond the crowd for the spires of the Parliament House, the city's massive landmark set alongside the Duna—the Danube River to foreigners. A famous symbol of the city and its distinguished past as the capital of a great empire. Can't miss it.

As the people in the rental car office told me, years ago when the nations of central and western Europe were so quick to welcome wave after wave of refugees from Syria and other locations, Hungary alone resisted. The nations of Europe condemned Hungary's hard stance as anti-humanitarian, even though many of the refugees were terrorists in sheep's clothing. Hungary built a secure fence along its borders to prevent migrants from entering. Travelers swung south, crossing through Bosnia and Croatia. Bosnia was sympathetic to the refugees, yet they recognized the impossibility of accepting so many people into their small territory and sharing limited resources. So these nations banded together again and the Hungarian Federation was formed.

I felt proud, being of Hungarian ancestry, yet I would rather they have banded together out of a common pride or for their common benefit, for economic matters, rather than for defense—

I stared ahead out the windshield at the noisy crowd being roughly dispersed. That was the old me. The one who was kind and generous, who never wished harm upon anyone. That is the case with many, I realized as I watched people being manhandled, handcuffed, beaten with sticks, and hauled away meters in front of my car. A nice person will be nice up to the point when someone comes along who takes advantage of that niceness. Then the nice person will sprout talons and ravage the instigator. How dare you force me out of my niceness! Now that you've dragged me out of my nice person shell, you must fear me! That is the situation now.

I watched the Hungarian soldiers rounding up perhaps a hundred who had not fled the scene. I almost wanted to cheer for them, for the soldiers doing their duty, preserving the public peace, maintaining the laws. Because that is who I am now.

You are war-weary, tired and hungry, so a nice person takes you in, shares food with you, gives you a place to sleep, offers to help you find a job or teach you skills for a job, and you accept all of it. But then you complain the food is not like you had back home. The customs are too different, so you want to have the customs here which you had back home. You don't particularly want to work or to have to learn a new language or obey new laws. And all around you are the women, exotic to your eyes. Even the daughters of your nice host you take as fair game. Your holy book, and the man who tells you what the book means, gives you permission to do as you like. So you rape and steal and destroy everything in your new home. You dump trash on the streets because it is not really your home, it is your enemy's home. You set off bombs because you are bored, annoyed, or feel offended that your new home is not like your old home. Your host is a fool or else a nice person you have tricked. Either way, your host is beneath you, not worthy of respect. However you treat your host, no matter how badly, is permitted. What will your god say about your behavior? Is it for you, for your wounded heart? Or is it part of a plan to take over the new land, as though you are a soldier in civilian garb? Are you just a small pawn in a larger game that has been playing across centuries? You no longer care about what you left behind, no longer desire to return to your homeland, even after it is rebuilt. Your present location is your new home, and you do all you can to make it as much like the filthy wasteland you left behind. And you do not even thank your nice host. Because he is dead now, and you live in his house with his daughters as your sex slaves.

The man in the car rental shop in Zagreb had been very effusive. When he saw my old American passport among my papers, he spoke to me in English, happy to give it a try. Years ago he had been to a university in the United States. He studied aeronautical engineering in a city called Wichita in a state called Kansas. His chest puffed a bit. He got a Ph.D. there and returned to Zagreb just in time to have to fight against criminal bands trying to cross his country. He had to take up a rifle instead of a computer.

I thanked him for his vivid account of the weekly occurrences in Germany and France. Not a week went by there without three or four bombings, or attacks with knives or guns, or driving trucks through crowds. Hardly any outdoor festivals were scheduled anymore. Barriers were erected everywhere to limit traffic. Even so, a vest of homemade explosives worn by someone who did not care about killing himself, much less total strangers, was still an easy thing to do.

Like the fellow at the back of the bus in Zadar!

Yes, like that one—

I turned on the windshield wipers, clearing the snow flurries that melted on the glass, still watching the battle on the street ahead.

Now, the man in the car agency warned me, Turkey had joined the Crusade. He used the word 'crusade' deliberately, I suspect. Much of Greece was occupied and half of Bosnia was under Turkish control, like in the old days of the Ottoman Empire. I quickly estimated how close they might be to my family's villa. So what was I doing in Budapest? Affecting the nightlife playboy routine while my parents and our ancestral home were threatened? I felt guilty for leaving.

But that was the old me. The new me, the bad vampire, wanted only to have my own place, do my own thing, and enjoy what years I had left. Perhaps a hundred or more of those years. It depends on the blood supply.

I could see blood on the street ahead. Normally I wouldn't touch it. But it had been a long drive and I felt tired. I'd hoped to simply arrive and find a comfortable hotel for a couple nights, meet with my bank's account manager, and have a good Bloody Mary for dinner. That was what I'd hoped for. But times had changed.

11

I WAS STOPPED AT FIVE CHECKPOINTS WHILE MANEUVERING MY CAR through the narrow streets of old Pest, the flat east side of the Duna. Steel or concrete barriers were set up everywhere, reducing the traffic flow. I could have gotten to my destination quicker by walking, even with my hobble and the use of a cane. Each time the same standard questions and showing my papers. I had to think in Hungarian once more. In thirteen years my parents dabbled in set phrases, just for fun, but since I never expected to return here I did not use my time to study and practice. My Croatian was better at this point than my Hungarian, yet there is something about one's ancestral tongue which comes straight back full and strong when under stress. I had the right accent, at least. I was waved on each time I was stopped.

Around me were 20-story skyscrapers, dwarfing the old Parliament House. That great historic structure showed its age. Perhaps it had been attacked; some of its spires were missing. One wall was blackened as if from fire. It was no longer in use, I was told by the hotel clerk when I checked in. The new Hungarian Federation headquarters was a huge edifice east of the central business district. I could glimpse a giant cube of dark glass and steel through the gaps between the skyscrapers. Budapest now looked more like the New York I had visited as a child.

My lodging was tall, as well. I parked my lovely red Opal XV in the underground garage and met the rental agent there. I had paid for concierge service. I rode an elevator up to the lobby to check in. I felt good, looked good. My face appeared possibly five years younger than my true age. And thank goodness for proper papers!

Up to the thirtieth floor of the Grand Hotel Attila, sitting in a plush lounger in the express elevator, I went with two assistants. One young man, blonde and blue eyed, looked Swedish. Perhaps he had fled an overrun Sweden to live among other traditional Europeans. Or his parents brought him to Hungary as a youth for the same reason. He carried my suitcase, which had hardly any weight. The other assistant was a dark-haired young woman with a perky face, like she knew she was the best at her job. She carried my key—a plastic card with a chip embedded in it. We had that back in Oklahoma when I was last there. Thirteen years ago only the important people had cards with chips. I had feared being tracked by chips on the cards in my wallet. I feared a lot of things back then. Now things would fear me.

I glanced at Ms. Perky, trying to glimpse her throat but her dark locks blocked my view. Her short bob cut danced on her shoulders and I was intrigued, wondered how her blood would taste. I imagined she would sip cocktails after work. She did not seem like a beer drinker. Or perhaps, in the privacy of her home, she would toss down a vodka & tonic. I do not drink alcohol since my transformation, but I don't mind if the blood I consume has been tainted with interesting flavors.

The blonde boy set my suitcase on the rack, retreated to the door as the girl went systematically around my suite checking everything. The water ran true, both hot and cold. The windows were clean. The bed was the right softness, gave way just enough. The white towels were without frays. She explained how to program a security code into the system so I could lock and unlock the door without the key card. The code would also work on the private elevator which whisked me up to this penthouse suite. When she determined everything was to my satisfaction, she handed me the key card.

As she extended her hand, palm up, the key card resting there, she exposed her wrist—exposed the lovely blue veins of her wrist—so close to the surface, almost close enough to—

I bent my head to look closer, to sniff her blood.

"Sir?" she asked, taking half a step back while continuing to hold out her hand.

"You can speak Hungarian, if you please." I took the key card from her hand. "I need to practice. It has been years."

"Yes, sir." She grinned only slightly. "We have staff for that. Please call the front desk to arrange lessons or conversation partner."

"Conversation partner? Excellent. I shall do that."

The pair departed and I unpacked. Two sets of clothing, nothing for sleeping. No swimsuit needed. I stripped down and stood before the full-length mirror to the side of the main bedroom. I could just make out the outline of my form, a tracing of arms and legs and torso. No details within those lines but it was a start. I stared a long time at the two blurs that were my eyes in the mirror, deciding what color they must be now. The world had a rosy hue.

Because it was daylight, though gray and gloomy for the winter, I pulled the curtains shut, glad to be away from even the faint, filtered sunlight. My skin immediately relaxed, as though it no longer needed to fight photosynthesis. I took deep breaths. From behind the closed curtains I peered out through a small gap at the world: the cold world of the Hungarian Federation. I counted thirteen tall buildings which had not stood thirteen years before when I was here.

If the world could be rebuilt, so could I.

"I require a computer," I spoke into the wall panel after placing my open palm against it and watching it blaze with green fire. "A laptop will do. Whatever is popular."

"Which applications will you need?" came the female voice.

"I need to do some research, searches for businesses, and so forth."

"It will be brought to you immediately."

"Thank you."

ᘓ

Everything I wished for, I received. I enjoyed that kind of life. I strolled like a lord about my penthouse suite: a large bedroom and another idle room for sitting and staring at whatever might appear on a large screen set in the wall, an office alcove, a bathroom as large as the bedroom, and a corner dinette—were I to have the urge to cook for myself. At least the means existed, though I only used the refrigerator and a goblet or two. I filled the sink with dirty dishes—the goblets; someone washed them whenever I wasn't looking. Someone rearranged the bed coverings, too, with a lovely red rose set upon the white pillows even in the dead of winter, as though I were a lover who needed pampering.

From my thirtieth floor penthouse, I gazed out the windows at the city below. Snow fell one night, continued through the following day, covered everything, the streets and the rooftops. It was beautiful. The greatcoat-wearing guards standing watch, the green- and red-coated soldiers marching past, also beautiful. The red and gold lights of the holiday season blinking on and off. Traffic was plodding, as if waiting for spring before making the next intersection. I did not go out among them, only watched. From on high—like God. I wanted to be sure it was all real before I messed it up.

I ran my searches and found several clinics and spas in the city. A lot of places to make myself look pretty. Like a movie star. That would have to do. There is no cure for the illness yet plenty of treatments for the symptoms. Indeed, whenever hotel staff arrived bearing this or that thing which I had requested, they seemed pleased with my appearance. I was a man of mystery. As such, they seemed to fight over who might satisfy my desires, whose turn it was to mount the elevator and deliver to me whatever I had ordered.

When the snow had been cleared and all seemed calm, I carefully dressed for the world and made my way down to the grand lobby. There, a member of the front desk staff called politely to me. People looked. I didn't let on I was the target of the call but stepped in as dignified a manner as possible over to the front desk. I was then shown to another desk where a hotel manager in dark suit sat behind a magic screen. The front desk clerk introduced me to the manager. We were supposed to be best buddies, I surmised by the warm smile and firm handshake.

"Some of your form is incomplete," said the hotel manager, with a pinch of his narrow, waxed moustache. His manicured eyebrows also pinched above his eyes. "There was . . . uh, an inquiry this morning—standard operation, certainly, nothing to be concerned about really . . . an official of the Residence Committee, naturally—as expected, umm, because you have, umm, been with us here, as our guest, for more than two weeks, you see. We promised the official that we would see that the information was complete."

He produced a stiff paper form and slid it across the desk at me. I had written my answers on it when I checked in.

"If you would be so kind." He offered me a pen.

He pointed to a blank line: FOGLALKOZÁSA / OCCUPATION.

"I am retired," I said with some annoyance in my voice. Time was a-wasting. I could only be out in daylight a limited period, even a gray and gloomy daylight, before I would begin to flake. And they want to know my occupation! "That is the reason I left it blank."

"Yes—*persze*—sir, certainly. They probably wish to, umm, be able to check with your employer—former employer . . . if any issue might come up—matters of State and the like." He again pointed to the blank line. "If you would be so kind as to put the occupation you had prior to your retirement . . . and your employer information, that would be . . . umm, such a delight."

I pursed my lips. "A delight? Really?" I hated his smugness, the way he said *persze*, like saying 'but of course' in a snooty tone.

The hotel manager blushed, pointed again to the line.

"I used to be a doctor of some kind," I decided, pushing the pen to the line. Last employer? I wrote *Oklahoma Blood Institute*. They had fired me over some missing units of blood. "No need to call them."

He watched intently, eager to snatch back the form once I lifted the pen. "Excellent, sir, excellent. We hope not to bother you for trifle things ever again. Pardons."

"Is that all?" I asked, standing.

He also rose, daring to shake my hand. I refused and he bowed his head. "Yes. Thank you, sir. So sorry to take this time out of your day."

I turned for the exit, the slowly rotating doors that shoveled people in and out of this building. As I stepped into my portion of the rotating doors, a well-dressed couple outside halted, watching me. They waited until I had passed through before they took their turn. I glanced over my shoulder at them as I continued down the sidewalk. Everyone was treating me like some kind of celebrity.

Catching sight of myself in a wide storefront window, I knew that I existed. My figure in the glass was a firm outline. Considering my lack of proper nutrition the past week, I was pleased how I was represented in the reflection. My deep brown longcoat with the sable collar, the Homburg I always wear, and my boots, Hungarian brand in top-grade leather, gave me a striking appearance. Or perhaps it's the elegant new walking stick I now wielded.

I saw that expression of awe once more as I entered my bank and the account executive in charge of my family's holdings immediately recognized me. He stood, came out from behind his desk to greet me, a head bow then a hand for shaking, calling my name and adding 'sir'.

I had to pinch my bald eyebrows. My eyes burned. My nostrils dry, ready to bleed. Yet I stood tall because I am who I am.

"The portfolio is prepared," said Gustav, whose life and career is dedicated to my family's fortune. He takes a fee each month. A week earlier he had promised to have everything compiled and calculated, ready for this very important meeting. He has indeed accomplished the task. "We trust your stay is comfortable?" He seemed to enjoy speaking English, raising his voice so fellow employees could hear.

"Everything is fine," I said in a soft voice. The rich and famous are not entitled to be loud and disgusting. "Thank you."

He led me into a boardroom where four gentlemen sat around the long, polished wood table, black suits like undertakers. Each stood and greeted me. I did not shake their hands; too much trouble reaching around the chairs. The doors were closed. Communication devices were placed in the center of the table, into a tray my host explained blocked any signal going in or out of the room. Privacy was assured.

Then, over the next four and a half hours, we delved extensively into the numbers that comprised my family's fortune.

℣

In Budapest, the great capital city and burgeoning metropolis of the Hungarian Federation, home also for thousands of Germans, French, and Swedes who fled their overrun homelands, you can get anything. In 2028—the New Year celebrations had ended—there are miracles to be had. Anything for a price. Apparently, say my bankers, I can handle any price.

When I tap the tablet on my nightstand a young woman comes to my suite. I hear a buzz at the door and I pick up that tablet. The screen changes from black to blue with eight round symbols. I press my finger to the one that says OPEN DOOR and the door to my suite opens. I need not get up from the bed. In steps my assistant. I call her my 'assistant' because she assists in returning my body to a state of comfort.

Later a staff person showed me how to set up the system so I did not even need to tap the OPEN DOOR button. Instead, the designated assistant would be identified automatically and the door would open for her. My assistant could come and go as I directed without me ever having to get off the bed.

As for my assistant—I actually have seven, one for each day of the week, as appropriate for someone of my means—I must be careful. Hence the need to make use of several. My body is delicate, fragile, prone to injury if there is too much stress placed on bones, muscles, and internal organs. Pleasuring me requires a special touch. It took a few weeks to locate who had that touch.

My treatment begins rather like a standard massage. Every inch of my figure is worked. I need the blood to circulate. I need muscles to tense and relax. I need bones to hold weight. My organs need to be coaxed into service from time to time. I cannot simply lie upon a bed every day. I've done that previously—for too much of the past thirteen years. So my assistant engages my body to keep it in proper operation.

There is an extensive collection of cosmetic products, having all the proper nutrients and other chemicals I know nothing about, which are generously applied to the dry patches on my skin. What matters is that I am restored. My appearance improves. I do not accept the tanning agent, however. I wish for my skin's natural pale to remain. How else am I to know who I am when standing before a mirror? It is a luxury few may afford. In fact, fully half of each day is me preparing for the other half of the day.

Which brings us to the next stage. During the course of stimulating my body, something strange usually happens, a wonderful phenomena I recall from my youth. I have experienced this before. Now it is a poor reflection of the past. The erection. In my present condition, the effect is painful. There is only one way to get rid of it and my assistant knows the procedure. It is rather embarrassing.

Finally, the most important step of my assistant's protocol. We rest side by side. We lie in what I call the 'lovers position': arms wrapped around each other, legs entwined. Our cheeks touch and perhaps our lips, as well. There is a profound silence save for a few heartbeats—from my assistant. It is the most magnificent sensation I have ever felt. I gladly pay for the four-hour sessions. If only someone could invent a pill which would make you feel this way whether or not you have someone with you. I would buy it.

The problem, however, was that my assistants were new—before I came to understand that we now live in the future. The lovely female assistant, regardless of her name (although I preferred the brunette named Dorína), followed the protocol perfectly, as we discussed, as we agreed. Then, during the final stage, when we lay together in peace and calm, I sensed the right moment and snuggled against her neck, my lips at her throat. A fire arose in me; I could not withstand it. I lurched, biting her throat, going for the hot red I smelled there.

Instead of warm, supple flesh, my teeth pierced the outer layer only and crashed against something decidedly firmer. Something metallic. Not what I expected. I pulled back, gazed upon my assistant's ragged throat. What I saw was utterly shocking! I had to call the front desk to complain, to get an explanation for this odd situation. I was not so much angry, but I was caught in a painfully ravenous moment, dying for fresh red.

"It is the new standard," the concierge told me. "Most guests have no complaint as the personal assistant performs the duties all the same as a living girl."

"But she's—she's a robot!"

I should have suspected the first two or three times she visited me. She was much too perfect; no mere human could be so perfect. Her movements, her speech, her fingers' motions—without flaw. Whatever I said, she responded with the ideal reply. She spoke Hungarian, but also Serbo-Croatian, German, French, Italian, even English. I was able to tease out of her some American street slang, just for fun. And she was so attentive, as though the entire purpose of her existence was to focus on me, and give me everything I ever wanted.

Except her blood, apparently.

What I'd smelled was not her warm blood but the pneumatic fluid that coursed through her mechanical tubes. Well, pneumatic fluid is not the same, obviously. Blood has the particular properties which are essential in maintaining life—or death, in some unique cases. I used to work quite intimately with blood. I mean microscope intimacy. I ran tests to determine what was in each sample drawn. That was my old life: careful, measured.

Now I sought a fuller, wilder lifestyle—

Sleeping with robots left me weak from a lack of blood. I had come to realize over the previous thirteen years what amount I needed and how often I needed it to maintain animation. I was more a machine than a person. I needed lubrication, as it were. The need I had couldn't be adequately expressed to hotel management. Therefore, I retained a private physician, Dr. Szabó, who was good at keeping secrets, as he convinced me, then explained the complicated procedures for getting what I wanted.

So I began dressing in outdoor clothing, the full get-up since it was winter, and going out to satisfy my needs.

It was a minor thing at first, as the news bulletins reported. After several weeks, the reports moved to the front pages of the electronic screens set up throughout the city. No more paper newspapers, only in museums. What was shown on the public bulletin screens was always government-approved. The screens were set up near bus stops, moving walkways, and monorail stations, as well as in public buildings and shopping areas. One could also get news reports on a personal tablet, such as what I had in my room. Yet I still preferred the tactile pleasures of shaved wood, much like my father. I knew he would never be able to live in the future. It was good that he was stuck in the past there in the family villa with Mother—

Sure, I thought of doing it a couple times, but I never did. There is no store now where one can purchase stationary. So I did not write any letters to them. Perhaps they wonder, so many months later, what became of me, their son Stefan Székely, agent provocateur.

Besides, I could never tell Mother and Father what I've been doing. It would disgust them, the wild nature by which I 'live'—the word continues to sting. I didn't care; I was not a good vampire. Those days were long gone. I was too desperate a couple times, left my victims too weak. One died when I took too much while another made it to a hospital in time. Authorities thought it was the work of some terrorist cell and a manhunt ensued. A handful of ne'er-do-wells were arrested. Security was heightened throughout my district. The snowy winter, thwarting the endless rants of the hot-earthers, managed to dampen the violence, but everyone knew spring was coming and the war against the last orderly society would resume. I could observe it from my penthouse suite.

12

I AM A BAD VAMPIRE. I CONFESS THE FACT TO STONE WALLS, POLISHED mirrors, and in daylight hours to the inner chambers of my heart, empty as they are. To maintain my health (laugh, snicker), I indulge in what might be called public intoxication.

I prefer young females, not because of any fetish, but for the fact that they are generally smaller and weaker than me and so are more easily subdued. I have no fear or hesitancy attacking males. A weaker one or two have given me their red when a female was not available. Blood is blood, they say, though thicker than water. To me there is little difference in taste or potency between male and female. To my tongue, female blood tastes a bit sweeter, but that distinction is only detectable to a trained palate. I'm convinced it may be all in my head. It matters not which I prefer when I'm out on a cold February night with so few denizens also out and about in this fine city.

It is easy enough to follow a well-heeled lady from a bar or a cheap hotel—until a patch of shadow provides a moment's opportunity. A soft lull, the frozen instant, a quick bite, the supping, the closing of the wound. It takes only a minute—more if the location allows for longer feeding. An old habit, I am careful of the amount I draw; I do not wish to permanently harm my host(ess). In my new 'bad vampire' persona, I shouldn't care. But the old Stefan hangs around, talking into my ear, begging me to be less cruel than others might be.

The bodies they find add up, granted. They make headlines on the news screens of the city, perhaps also farther afield. Surely I cannot be the only vampire in Budapest. I cannot be the only undead fellow in the Hungarian Federation—discounting my parents. Or in the world, for that matter. How many might there actually be? Popular literature suggests tens of thousands, minimum. If we exist, we must be related perhaps back thousands of years. We carry the gene. We should meet, form a club. Family reunion. We could call it a 'supper club' and dine on specially selected blood in various vintages. Private, *persze*. Stiff initiation fee. Our suppliers would be compensated according to our financial prowess. For we, the undead of centuries past and present, have had so much time to acquire our wealth. It is embarrassing, I must admit.

Remember that spa in Sárvár, west of Lake Balaton? The spa where I was refused entrance because of my horrid appearance? Thirteen years ago? Yes, that one. I could buy that place now. I would own it and kick out everyone who treated me badly, especially that snooty front manager. Oh, yes, he may well have passed on into death or at least retirement. It matters not.

I could own that spa; it could be my private venue, a place for mineral bath treatments and relaxation for my vampire friends from around the world. They would raise a toast to me! Cheer me! Thank me for opening the world to them—as though none before had ever done similarly . . . as I have read or heard about in the grand history of Blood Type AB, so common in this part of the world and nowhere else. We are the 5 percenters of the world. It is our gene pool; a spa where our gene pool is celebrated? It seems too ironic to be real.

Yet I shall make it real.

So I ventured out on a snowy morning, the air full of flurries, before the sun could burn through the oppressive wintry overcast. I headed to my bank. We had not scheduled a meeting via the 'magic tablet'. I thought to go out for a stroll and arrive there at their opening. My timing was impeccable: the staff unlocked the doors as my footfall pressed upon the steps. The man grinned as if he knew me.

"Good morning," he said in an odd, British accent, standing aside and sweeping his arm wide to invite me into the bank's majestic lobby with its eight thick marble columns.

Those members with which I had transacted knew me and spoke to me in English despite giving them permission to use Hungarian. I'm becoming fluent again. But they humor me.

My personal banker, Mr. Német, was not there yet, not waiting for me. I acknowledged to an embarrassed secretary that we had not made an appointment. So another officer, Mr. Szöllösi, one of his lieutenants, took over the task to help me arrange the purchase of the infamous SÁRVÁR FÜRDÖ.

Thirteen years before, the hotel complex had been surrounded by a variety of pools for swimming and baths for soaking. Inside awaited a full range of services for both families with bored children and adults in need of something therapeutic. Arriving in my desperate condition, I had little confidence that I could find an ancient cure for an ancient malady. As it was, the resort seemed too much recreational water park and not enough treatment facilities. It didn't matter now. I would transform it as I liked.

"You are lucky," said Mr. Szöllösi, his Hungarian accent less thick than Mr. Német's. "The facility is in poor condition over the years. Not popular at all. Another owner tried to restore it and it succeeded for a few years. Then return to slow seasons. You can get it for a low price."

"Excellent," I intoned. "Name the price."

He did and I nodded my approval, even with his warning that the purchase would consume what he considered a serious portion of my holdings. That, plus a few more *Forints* thrown at it for refurbishing. I would not open it to the general public, anyway. It would be for only myself and those whom I approve. As he said, it is no longer popular. Besides, vampires need a special mineral content in the waters which would not agree with warm bodies.

Papers were pushed to me, with a pen. I signed and pushed the papers back to Szöllösi. He notated several pages from the papers on his electronic tablet, then invited me to enter my code numbers to prove I was who I wanted to be. Lastly, I pressed my fingerprints to the electronic pad. Done.

It was still early morning as I stepped from the bank's impressive vaulted doors into the simple world of the ordinary and average. I felt icky already. Modesty, Stefan; humility. It was difficult to remember. The past was so far away now.

I turned down the avenue, thinking to enjoy a leisurely stroll past the high-end stores—with so much at prices I could easily afford. Yet I didn't need anything they had. *Tsk-tsk.*

At the intersection ahead of me was a commotion. A lot of noise. A crowd gathered. To my right was the corner of the government district. The old parliament house stood further along the riverfront, and the newer Federation headquarters rose several blocks behind it. Smoke already columned a block away.

Suddenly an explosion. Everyone immediately ducked, then stuck their heads up to sneak peeks in the direction of the blast. More smoke billowed across the plaza. Screams. People were running from right to left across the street in front of me, escaping. Sirens wailed.

I scrambled up, as well as a vampire with a humbled leg could, and used my cane to guide myself down the slope, a minor grade, to that next intersection. The crowd which had gathered there before the blast scattered. Newer people stopped at the same spot. A man lay on the pavement, squirming against the concrete. His gloved hand clenched his throat; blood ran down his arm. A small shank of metal protruded from his neck. Shrapnel had struck him, torn into his neck, severed his carotid artery. His face was white, eyes desperate for an angel. Other bodies on the street were torn apart.

I pushed people aside and dropped to my knees, practically on top of the man's chest. As sirens filled my ears and people screamed, I pushed my face to his neck. I clawed his hand away and the gusher of blood increased, spurt after spurt. I set my mouth over the wound, gathering the expulsion like a kid drinking water from a hose.

A woman jostled me, demanding to know what I was doing to the poor man. Another said he'd called an ambulance. I had not the voice to inform them this man would never make it to a hospital, even if I left him alone. There was no way to stop the bleeding for such a severe wound, not in the time it would take to get him to a hospital. He was a goner as soon as the shrapnel sliced open his neck. There was no reason to let such a fountain go to waste.

When his gusher subsided and he was deathly white, I sat back. My mouth was red. My face, too (hiccough). I tried my best to stop the bleeding, I told the medics who arrived—yes, too late to save him under the best circumstances. As I predicted. A pity.

Pulling a handkerchief from my coat pocket, I noticed a strange figure standing a few meters away. I dabbed the cloth to my lips. The dark figure watched me and the body on the street. The figure wore a cloak with a hood—like Little Red Riding Hood always wore, except this one was black. The hood was drawn up so I couldn't see who the figure might be. I could not even be certain if the figure was male or female. I wondered if the mystery person might be in league with the bombers, checking the damage.

I turned to address the questions from the medics and when free of their inquiry the mysterious figure was gone.

No matter. I had feasted like a New Year's banquet prepared for the entire staff. I was full. Satiated. Drunk in our special way. I tried to walk but leaned this way and that, grabbing at the storefronts to steady myself. Finally, I waved down a taxi and climbed in—fell in, with my hotel's address card in my extended hand. I do not know how I ever got to my room or stretched out on the bed.

I slept for days.

ଓ

More snow was falling outside as I gazed out from the bed, too numb to move, barely able to remember what had happened to me. I lay in that waking stupor for another day and a half, watching the snowflakes dance in the sky. Pretty little things. Falling, drifting, coming to their end in a pile of their cousins. Like me.

I received communications via the tablet informing me the owner of the Sárvár Fürdö had accepted the terms of the sale and my bank had completed the transfer of funds. I now owned a spa resort on the west side of Hungary, near the mountain range which once separated Hungary from Austria. Now both were part of the Federation. I could handle the business from the bed, tapping on the tablet as my heart desired. The date of sale was not convenient but the facility could sit unused until I was available to tend to it personally. Whenever it suited me, I would initiate its renovation.

I was not yet hungry after my feast, but I grew restless and decided to go out and enjoy the cold evening. I was not searching for blood. I did, however, stroll along some of my usual routes.

As I got to the corner of one street in the bar district, I paused to check for cross-traffic. When I proceeded to cross the street, I looked up and there was the same dark, cloaked figure I'd seen before.

I halted.

An approaching truck honked at me and I hurried on across the street. The figure had disappeared.

I looked in each direction. Strange. But this was a bar district. Lots of people popping in for a drink, leaving, disappearing into the next doorway. A cold night. No sane person just stands outside staring at strangers. (I said no *sane* person; that excludes me—yes, I might stiffen with the cold but I do not *feel* the cold.) It was no concern of mine if someone wished to stand out in the cold. Coincidence.

When daylight came and I was safely behind closed curtains in my penthouse suite, I pondered while weak and weary whether the figure might be an envoy sent to invite me to join a secret club. It was like so many movies of my youth: the mysterious stranger follows an acolyte and eventually they meet. The older, wiser entity sees potential in the younger one, and there's the enticement: to learn more, to hone one's skills, to gain new knowledge, to get the best seats at concerts. The acolyte is impressed, intrigued, considers the opportunity. The wiser figure adds the final treat: the chance to gain even more power, and proposes joining a group where only the select few may enjoy its benefits—and the benefits are extraordinary, but always for a price. Usually the loss of one's soul is required, or a certain ability must be surrendered, as the cost of membership, to ensure sincerity.

Well, I was never one to join clubs, so a mentor's efforts would be wasted on me. This mysterious figure had to be something different. Perhaps a detective who was doggedly on to me, immediately figuring out my *modus operandi*. Nor was this likely the private eye I'd put on the Alma Jónás case, to learn what had become of her.

I thought I was doing rather well. Keeping to myself. No threats, no pressure, making my own rules. I decided when I hunted, who I fed upon, and how far I would suck the red before allowing calm to return to me and I departed. I was careful. I had read all the literature on the art of seduction and applied those arts with great effect.

That all changed rather quickly.

Making connections through my bank and my hotel residence, I began being invited to parties. Not the teenage, rock music, marijuana type of party of my youth but elegant ones requiring a tuxedo and top hat, a silk ascot, and the best behavior one could muster at a moment's notice. Indeed, social gatherings of society's elite. Within a few weeks, as Budapest's newest man-about-town, I was becoming known in high society. It was both exhilarating and disconcerting—

Oh, the ladies most certainly did swoon there in those parlors! Too many instances of indiscretions: a lovely lady draws me into a back room and there she inevitably faints.

"I don't know," I would say to the hostess of the house. "We were simply smooching, then suddenly she went limp in my arms."

"Oh, my! You do have a way with women, it seems, Mister Székely," Mrs. Someone or Lady Someother would say in charming Hungarian, excusing my sordid behavior. For such behavior is deemed Romantic and thus forgiven.

"Oh, and look: she seems to have cut herself on something," one of them might also note. "The jewelry these days! So avant-garde! Stick with traditional styles!"

I would agree: no point wearing cutting-edge jewelry if the edge cuts your throat so easily. The wounds would always heal.

Most gatherings were at the lavish home of one of the Federation's leading families. I met members of the parliament, and the leaders of commerce and industry, leading fashion designers, a few trendy artists, and too many dregs of the entertainment community—though they impressed me the least. I was welcomed like a lord, fought over and fawned over, coaxed into a clever speech on, say, contemporary politics here or a longer lecture on the vagaries of imported diseases there. A few guests referred to me as *Doctor* Székely, which I enjoyed.

None, it seemed, knew my humble beginnings, so great an actor was I. My high school theater experience was finally paying off. It was primarily because of my acting that I was invited to become a member of the board of a major Hungarian corporation (which I dare not name), although I declined. I needed only to attend a few meetings throughout the year and for that be handsomely compensated. Perhaps I would also give a vote or two.

I could see how summer would unfold: more parties. And business meetings. Investment opportunities. Handshakes and backroom deals. Lavish balls and cocktail gatherings. Introductions to more of the rich and famous, pithy diatribes to law and order, perhaps a sitting for a portrait (cameras would not capture my countenance). And always the sipping of blood. I would require a secretary to keep my schedule organized. It would be a busy life, full of promises, sordid delights, and perhaps some unexpected joy.

However, I welcomed my new-found indolence more. A harried lifestyle did not suit my naturally introverted disposition. As a man-about-town (note to self: reorder business cards), I was a full-fledged member of Budapest society and quite happy to receive invitations to every event whether or not I actually attended. At long last, I was a person of great esteem and interest. My parents would be proud of me. Perhaps it was time to write them a letter.

13

ONE FRIDAY NIGHT—ACTUALLY IT WAS PAST MIDNIGHT SO A SATURDAY—I had finished my latest feeding and was on my way home. On the way to my penthouse suite, I spied two dark-cloaked figures coming towards me, similar to the one following me the past few weeks. It had to be deliberate. At that hour only the drunk and destitute, and some wayward migrants, terrorists, and the like, were out.

Now that spring had arrived, it had been raining yet had ceased about the same time I'd caught my hostess. I had taken her from behind in a lonely monorail station. She likely did not know I was there until my hand grasped her throat. Then the bite: *hold . . . hold . . . and release*. She sank heavily in my arms and I dragged her to a bench. She moaned like she was drunk; her red tasted of alcohol. I placed some *Forint* bills in her raincoat pocket and disappeared into the night. The old, wrinkled bills were hardly used any more; the government let the cash wear out and didn't replace it. Everything now was electronic. Yet how else to give some money to someone without an electronic device being involved? An electronic device would make every transaction traceable.

I am a bad vampire, I have been saying, yet the past haunts me, will not leave me to my evil. So I pay for the blood I take. I have my own moral table, a simple system based on my own calculations. None have complained that I gave too little cash or took too much blood. Indeed, I remain quite anonymous.

But I digress . . . .

So two cloaked figures approached; we saw each other, knew we would pass each other. I hoped there would not be a stopping, not an encounter. After I have fed, I abhor meeting anyone. I prefer to return to my penthouse suite and enjoy the flood of fresh red filling my senses.

I guessed after a few heartbeats (metaphor, chuckle) they expected to stop me. As we approached each other's personal space, the two of them reached out and grabbed my arms. They threw me back against the stone wall of the building there, slamming me hard as though wishing to teach me a lesson—much like those filthy bullies in high school had done. Were these two also princes of the night? Did they expect to dine off of me?

"Unhand me, you louts!" I growled. The elevated language usually served to alarm them. Not this time.

A third figure appeared, not wearing a cloak but a longcoat like me, made of material for a rainy night, and a fedora pulled down to hide the face. This figure stood directly in front of me. It could have been the perfect robbery, though I had already given away the cash I bore and had no electronic devices on my person from which to extract a fee for my release.

"You have been careless," the figure before me, a man, spoke. No one else was around at that hour on that street. "You will get us into trouble." His words were English, his accent British. Not what I would expect in Budapest. "We see you. We watch you. And we are not at all pleased with your behavior."

"I . . . ."

I didn't know what to say.

"I'm sorry," was all I could muster. I shook my head to clear the cobs. "How do you know me?—know what I do?" Before any response, I grew bolder: "I have been careful. Never been caught. The reports blame migrants and terrorists."

"For a while."

The man stared at me; I saw he wore a mask, like the one I'd worn to get across Europe fourteen years ago, no questions asked. It had a fine authenticity and moved, shimmered like real skin. But I could tell it was a mask. In the Federation, all face coverings were banned in public areas. Security cameras could not identify people who wore masks or the foreign fashions of migrants and refugees.

"You don't know everything," said my accuser. "The authorities are starting to suspect us. We had an understanding, yet now—"

"Us?" I knew what he meant yet I asked anyway. "You mean people such as you and me?"

"People like you."

"But not like you?" I nodded at the two fellows who held my arms. "Not like them, either?"

"No."

"Then who exactly are we discussing tonight?"

The mask grinned; my interpretation was of a grin. He could have intended something entirely different.

"Budapest has five million people. That figure doesn't include the non-citizens, tourists, migrants—those who are not expected to stay, about a hundred-thousand of them." He glared from eyes that glowed red in the dark. "There are more than a thousand of us here."

"So that's five million blood donors for a thousand of the needy," I pondered aloud. "Seems a good ratio. I thought there would be more of us. Or just you, and these two fellows, I mean."

"We do not satisfy our needs in the manner in which wilders do."

"Oh."

I got it. Finally. I was acting like an uncouth lout, grabbing blood bags off the shelf, as it were. Stealing. Like I did back in Oklahoma long ago. Old habits. I shouldn't be so reckless. I needed to mature, to up my game.

"So what should I do, if you don't mind me asking?"

The man before me shook his head like he thought I was too stupid to understand. A wayward child who did not deserve to be in school, wasting a seat for a better child.

"Join a club, fool."

His mask was a full sneer, lips twisting into a commentary on my existence. Perhaps the mask was specially designed to reflect his true face beneath the mask. I wanted to compliment him for the device, ask where he had it fashioned. I would get one for myself.

"A secret society. There are five. Try the Kodaly Club. You can get what you need there and no one will bother you."

"You three gents are members?"

"Not that club." He sneered again. "That is why I recommended it to you."

I got the insult. They wouldn't want to be members of a club that would have me as a member. It wasn't worth pursuing. Or using the blade inside my cane on these smug louts. I was a champion fencer once upon a time.

"So . . . we are all . . . vampires?"

All three *shhh*ed me. "Geez, say it louder, why don't you!"

I lowered my voice: "I thought I was the only one. In Budape*sht*, that is. A large enough city, to be sure, but how rare is our condition? How rare is our blood type? There should be more in this region of the world. Legend demands it."

"We are many," groaned the fellow on my right, lightening his grip on my arm.

"How many? Do you also feed at night?"

The fellow on my left spit. A red glob hit the pavement.

"You are an amateur, *Stefan*," said my interrogator. He gave my name a particular snarky intonation. "Not all of us are wealthy like you, but we do all right. Our longevity allows us to accumulate wealth, but we did not have your advantages."

"Advantages? What? My parents left me money. I'm a trust fund baby—"

"Yet you hunt like a kid out of reform school. None of us can afford to be caught. State Security watches us. Make a mistake and it would ruin it for all of us." He gave my chest a shove. "So. Be. Careful."

The man stepped back, the others released my arms. They stared a moment more then exited in three directions, leaving me stunned on the wet sidewalk, the faint glow of a distant streetlamp distracting me.

 CR

I lay supine on the bed in my penthouse suite as Dorína worked her deft mechanical fingers up and down my body. I pondered the night's encounter. So many aspects of it frightened me. I had been watched.

They knew my name. They spoke English. They knew I had money. Suddenly, I realized I could have been kidnapped and held for ransom. Yet there would be no one to pay ransom. I am alone. Surely those who know everything about me would know that. So far, they only wished me to stop embarrassing them, to stop giving them a bad reputation.

I am a bad vampire.

Indeed! A bad vampire, yet not in my degree of evil but in how amateurish is my presentation. I am bad at *being* a vampire.

My mind raced. I felt my heart give a thump. I contemplated my options.

I'd suggested they were like me but they denied the comparison. Was it a matter of degree or were there other types of vampires? My family's genetic line forced me into one kind: the doomed. Could others suffer the same symptoms from different causes? During my research years ago, I learned of the psychic vampires, those deranged warm-bodied people who drew energy from healthy people simply by their evil presence; they had no disease. There were some people who fancied themselves vampires so much they even filed down their teeth into fangs, dressed in tuxedos and spoke with . . . a Hungarian accent. Like Béla Lugosi, the original film vampire. I'd modeled my high school Halloween party character after him. Yes, blasphemy!

My midnight accuser mentioned a club or a secret society. If it was secret how was I supposed to find it? And even so, how did they get their blood drafts? Hire willing donors? Weekly dinners? It seemed preposterous, something from a B-movie. Shaking my head, I knew I was living in a B-movie. There would be no end to it, however, no final credits, no walk-off music.

I waited as long as I could, holding off feeding, allowing my body to suffer, to begin withering. My pale cheeks became sallow, my dull eyes withdrawn. Hair fell out again. My joints ached and my organs ceased to gurgle. I was dying; that is, I was returning to the poor state I had possessed while running away from home—before my wealth bought me the care I needed to maintain a public façade.

Then it was time to feed again.

They knew my haunts, my patterns, my behavior. And they were watching, they said. I reached for my tablet, tapped to call my personal physician, Dr. Szabó. He understood my condition—we agreed I had a strange variant of *acute porphyria*, not vampirism. He would treat me according to symptoms without delving into my true state of affairs. I requested a transfusion of Type AB. That was a special case, lots of authorizations. It had been easier to go out and hunt. Now I was too weak to hunt.

Yes, sorry, I've let myself go . . . . It is not a pretty sight, I admit. Yet a bad vampire can, must endure all manner of hardships, put up with all manner of insults and incriminations to survive. He will get even, you can bet. The bad vampire always gets even. It's a literary trope, so it must be true!

CR

Perhaps it is time to travel. Now that spring is in bloom, renovation can begin on my spa resort at Sárvár. The first thing to do is rename it SZÉKELY FÜRDÖ to distance it from the reputation it had garnered as the biased monstrosity that rejected me previously. A fresh start. That would remove me from the strictness of Budapest nightlife.

I cannot be watched as I go about my business.

Everywhere I went in Budapest I seemed to draw a member of the vampire clan. They always made their presence known, made sure I knew they spied upon me. I met one at a social gathering; he stood in as a server but gave me the evil eye when dipping the tray for me to take up a wine glass.

Budapest was convenient, with old trolleys and the new monorail system, as well as standard bus lines. Everything I truly needed was near my hotel home, anyway. I started to use the monorails to go to the edge of the city to hunt. But there were always cameras on the trains. Otherwise, it was good to occupy the penthouse suite and let the bank pay the hotel each month. I went about my business.

However, as I planned my move to Sárvár, the quaint little town in the west, I had to make preparations.

I purchased an automobile; only the poor say 'car'. Mine was the latest model of Mercedes, the V-class, with more subdued fins. It was large enough for me to be driven in comfort wherever I might need to go, relaxing in the rear seat with a hired driver operating the vehicle, yet not too large for me to handle the driving myself should I wish to, that is, in better weather and road conditions. My choice of color was black. Like my heart. I ordered the windows tinted. A refrigeration unit added in the rear seat area. It would be convenient to store a unit of blood there for long trips.

"No, no, I don't mind a stroll," I told the dealership's manager in perfect Hungarian. "My last time walking the streets of this fine city. I'll return when my automobile is ready."

Spring was rolling over the somber city like a warm blanket over a child's bed. Tepid breezes, flowers daring to bloom, and the sunshine less meek, now so bright and golden—a terrible turn of events for me. I would need to spend more time indoors. The advent of spring made my past haunt me more: the coming summer days full of bike rides, rolling in the grass, a picnic.

I was ready to continue to my next location. And when I arrived, I would finally write that letter I had promised to write to Mother. To Mother, yet knowing Father would be reading it, as well. *You've done well for yourself*, I imagined them thinking.

The concierge located an old shop that printed stationary. I went to purchase some one evening. So used to the night's hourless obsidian, I paid no mind to the time. Once outside and several blocks away from the hotel, I realized such a shop, run by a mom and a pop, would likely be closed at that hour. At least I could have a look, I decided, see what kind of shop it was, perhaps see some stationary samples through the window. A night stroll was good for my skin—whether I chose to get some red or not.

I had no plan to hunt. I had promised the local vamps I wouldn't. Not much, anyway. They made it clear that I might ruin their little arrangement with the city's powers-that-be. A few members of their cult sat in high places, they implied. I'd been upsetting the status quo and they would have none of it. So they followed me, just to intimidate me. And—

There was one now!

For the love of Saint Dracula! I cursed, seeing the cloaked figure on the corner ahead. I slowed my pace, hoping the figure would move on.

Does everyone have to wear the same dark cloak with a cowl? That was what made them stand out.

"You fellows keep keeping on my trail," I spoke in full voice. "I've kept to our agreement. Fewer red kisses. More care, less news. Surely you must be impressed by now."

I stared at the dark-cloaked figure. No movement.

"Can't you just leave me alone now? There are plenty of throats in the city, enough for everyone."

There was no response, the figure unmoving on the street corner, so I stepped forward until I arrived at the curb on my side of the street.

The figure did not retreat.

"I said I'm being careful."

These damn cultists! Always playing the mystery tropes to the full. That was the chief reason I disliked them. I had enough of that kind of drama back in my high school days.

"Besides, I'm moving away soon. You can report that to your chief, Lord Baltimore or whatever his name is. Then you won't have Stefan Székely to fuck with anymore."

Suddenly the dark figure came to life. (It is only an expression; for the undead, the lexicon sticks like a second skin.) The figure moved: shuffled, one foot to the other, as though the first had grown numb standing there. Anyway, it served as proof of life (another unfortunate term we use). I wanted to laugh aloud at my clever thought. The *life* of the undead. I should be on a talk show. Even these dire cultists should appreciate my humor.

The figure stepped toward me, advancing into the street. Naturally, there was no traffic at that late/early hour, not in this commercial district where the sane people had long departed, safe at home and fast asleep.

"Don't you know me?" asked the figure from the shadows of the cowl. It was a woman's voice.

"No! Why are you following me?"

I was tired of their attempts to threaten me. I refused to join their circle. So they kept following me, spying on me. Watching me!

"I've been searching for you," said the woman. Her tone was flat, less alive than my personal care robot's voice.

I paused after stepping into the street, studying the figure: shorter than me, shoulders hunched, the cowl slipping back, off her forehead. The nearest streetlamp blessed us with a bare sliver of light, marking the space between us.

"Why?" I asked, feeling this might be different than those cultists bothering me. A sigh escaped. Suddenly I felt weary. "I just wish to be left alone. I have nothing left to give."

The shadows shifted within her cowl while still shielding her face. Something was different. This was no cult goon, I understood in that instant. However, I was still ready to defend myself if an attack came. Perhaps she was just their decoy.

"You gave everything . . . to me."

That was a response I did not expect.

I shifted my stance. "What do you mean?"

Gloved hands rose from out of the slits in her cloak, but thankfully they held no knives. They took hold of the front edge of her cowl and turned it back, folding it upon her shoulders. The lamplight graced her face at long last and I recoiled at the sight.

The woman was older than I expected. Her skin, like mine used to be, was in a horrid condition. The classic signs of acute porphyria, a vampire in the making. It was sad; I felt sad for her, I realized—and I wondered next why she had come to me. I was no scientist. I had no cure, only expensive treatments that barely kept me suitable for public display. A dose of red worked best. What could I possibly do to help her? I wanted to be charitable, but—

"Now do you know me?" Her eyes tried to blink, eyelids worn away, withered lips drawn tight, exposing a bad set of teeth, a few missing. "I'm Penny."

Part Two

14

HER GLOVED HAND WENT TO HER FACE, RUBBED AT HER EYE A MOMENT, then the other eye, as though she believed there might be a tear ready to fall after all this time.

"You used to call me your Beloved."

The words hung in the night air like poisonous fog.

"I doubt I'm that now. Or anything to you."

Staring at her, I was overwhelmed by the sensation of my mouth hanging open so far I could've swallowed a bat. My heart cranked up, roared to life, pounding like a jackhammer in my chest, as though I was fully human again and did not realize it. My legs weakened and I leaned harder on my cane. My eyes could not, would not, accept what they saw. I blinked, shut my eyes a moment, opened them and stared again.

"Penny . . . ."

A feeble sigh escaped through my lips.

Her chin, with a dry patch of skin hanging forlornly from its lower edge, dipped to acknowledge my understanding.

My first thought was how absolutely horrible she appeared, a train wreck of disease. I didn't dare touch her. My second thought, which rumbled through my head a half-second later, was how she could have found me. Barreling a close third behind that question was: Why do you look as awful as I did when my transformation was at its worst?

I couldn't speak any trite expressions; no 'long time, no see' would do. She thought I was dead. At least, I'd left her with that impression.

In the minutes before I began my procedure at the clinic in Zagreb, I'd panicked and called her long-distance to tell her I was sorry and that I loved her. It had been weeks since I had last seen her. Then I died.

Literally died.

And she never heard from me again. She had to believe I had died. That is what she would have thought. Or else, knowing what I'd told her about my affliction and the accursèd transformation, she would have assumed I had completed the transformation and deemed myself unfit for her. She would understand that I would hide myself away from the world, just as I'd suggested many times while suffering through the process.

Yet here she stood: knowing who I am, who I had become, and coming to me nevertheless.

"I cannot even begin to fathom answers to the obvious questions," I spoke. I sought more words, measuring them for kindness. "You have found me. I never expected you would ever go looking for me. I never thought—"

"I hated you, Stefan." Her words, soft spoken yet sharp, pierced me like a wooden stake.

I pursed my lips, a child being scolded.

"Hated? . . . Hate-*ed*? What does that mean?"

She *pfft* at me. "What does anything mean now?"

"Indeed."

"We are the same now."

"You mean . . . you have transformed? Like I did?"

Her nod was glacial, a whole winter of ice.

"But how?" I asked with a shrug. "You don't have my family's genes. How could . . . ?"

She tilted her head, looked straight at me like she believed her eyes could stab through me. I felt the razor tips of something cutting me. I wanted to step back.

"When you raped me."

"When I . . . *what?*"

"That night. We made love. Then you went further. I told you to stop but you continued."

"That? I was hot for blood. I told you! I needed—needed the blood that flowed from you—"

"It wasn't yours to take."

The love making had been desperate. I wore a knit ski mask to hide my horrid face. She wanted to make me feel better, meaning more human. Then I thought to please her by going down there, like lovers do in the movies. And there was a spot of blood. She cursed at the blood, believing her period had already ended. The taste of her blood sent me into a fever rage. I never hit her but I treated her roughly, held her down while I dined. Finally satiated, I relented and she curled into a fetal ball, weeping.

Then she had sprung up, gotten dressed, and tried to leave my apartment. I ran after her, apologizing, but she said I had raped her. I reached for her, to stop her and make her listen. She grabbed my wrist to take my hand off her—and her grasp tore the skin from my wrist. She dropped the sheet of dried skin right there on the sidewalk and went to her SUV, drove away.

And that was the last I ever saw of Penny Park.

"I hated you," she repeated. "But now I know—I understand—what you were feeling, what motivated you. Trying to survive, to hang onto your humanity. I know because I am suffering that now. I don't blame you for what you did. I hate that it happened, but . . . I know you were not in control of yourself. So . . . I don't hate you. Not now."

My chest felt lighter. "Thank you. I am forever sorry for all of that. I have felt that regret every day since it happened."

"For fourteen years? Every day?"

"Fourteen years is a long time. That's plenty of hours to think about everything. And I do mean everything. All the regrets. The what-ifs. The if-onlys. So many days I wished for something a lot different than what happened. I wished I had lived. I would have returned to you, Penny. Believe me. You can believe that."

She rubbed her eyes again; the old habits die hard.

"I believe you."

I stepped forward, arms extended. "If you ever thought to give me something to comfort me in my death, those words were perfect."

We entered an embrace, spontaneous and mutual. In my arms she felt bone-thin beneath her clothing. I could feel the shallow beat of her heart, the slow sludge of her organs, the dying within her body cell by cell. I wanted to cry. She wanted to cry, as well. Yet we were cursed.

"So you are dead . . . ." Not a question falling from her parched lips but a steely confirmation.

I nodded but she could not see that while in our embrace.

"Yes, dead. Trying to keep going, however." We parted yet stood close. "And you?"

"Not dead." She seemed to chuckle at our perverse phrases. "I am dying, yes, but unlike you I will never recover."

"You have the disease," I said, again the master of the obvious.

"Your disease. The one you gave me that night."

"I recall it was afternoon. The shades were drawn."

"True. An afternoon tryst. They used to be good for us."

"I remember."

"Now we are old," she said, her voice trembling. "One of us dead, the other dying."

I reached for her again, another embrace.

"It cannot be any sadder."

She gazed up at me. "When I am dead, will I be like you? Kind of living? Or will I be like any other human, put in the ground forever?"

"I think it is the latter. A cemetery, a coffin, words of calm, and the R.I.P. on a headstone. You're right: it can be sadder."

"Oklahoma seems so long ago and far away. Now I'm the same age you were when we parted. An old woman. In a useless, pointless life. While I can still call it a life. I feel like one of those lepers in a Bible movie, shunned and falling apart day by day. Until there isn't anything left of me. Nothing. Only an ex-lover who remains . . . who remains alive, or whatever you call your present state of existence."

"We call ourselves the undead."

A pensive nod. "Like in the movies."

"Exactly."

⋘

In my penthouse suite, I helped Penny remove her cloak, the hotel staff none the wiser. Then I washed her. For me, water was acidic. So I used several packets of sanitary wipes, mostly alcohol; they sting but kill the bacteria which caused the odor of death. A few inches at a time, arms and legs, showing her what to do. Then I turned away and allowed her to complete the process for her personal areas. I closed the door of the bathroom behind me and waited.

After a long time, she appeared, wearing one of the soft, white robes the hotel provided. And the cushy hotel slippers. Her bare legs were bone thin, skin scaly with the brown, dry patches that were the first sign—and the second, third, and so on . . . to the end. Yet there was a faint glimmer of something a little more positive that flickered across her face. Her fingers went to her head, once more attempting to rake the thick hair that used to lie there. She flashed embarrassment, forgetting once more there was no hair. Part of the process: learning to accept what we no longer have.

I called my personal care assistant to work on her. The cosmetics made a big difference, dulling the itching and burning. I caught a weak smile flashing upon her face. When she was soothed, I ordered food, what I thought would be easy on her stomach. I had no appetite as the transformation plowed through me. Broth and bread would do to start. Served on a white tray, with a flower in a small vase.

In this large suite, everything in the damning shade of white, I sat across the wide room, beside the curtained windows, giving her plenty of space as I watched her eat: hesitant at first, finding her speed, letting her stomach awaken, then with more enthusiasm. It seemed she had not eaten for a long time. I cautioned her to take it slow. My stomach twisted, knotted as I watched her.

After a while I rose and strolled across the room, over the white carpet to the white tile floor of the dinette. I opened the refrigerator. I retrieved some of my special stock, expensive because it was hard to get, dangerous even. I found a straw in a drawer. As I returned to her, I pressed the straw through the opening I made.

"Here," I said. Irony spilled over my hand, dripped on the carpet. "Drink this."

I handed her the unit of Type A which I'd been saving for a special occasion. This was the occasion.

She didn't blink. Accepting the bag into her two hands without reservation, she clamped her lips around the end of the straw.

"Slowly . . . . Very slowly. Like a fine wine."

She sipped like an elegant lady at a garden party, all the socialites in their fine fashions.

"Be careful not to drip. White carpet."

With the straw between her lips, she gave me that sideways glare that immediately took me back to our days together when I would say something stupid but she had the kindness not to call me on it. She would just give me that look. It was Penny, I knew for sure.

Without her cloak and cowl, I saw her once glorious black hair had mostly fallen out, her scalp bare and scaly, discolored, a couple of red lines curving over her crown, one of them sutured, the stitches recent. It took all the tenderness I could dig up to gaze at her with the same love I could never believe she had for me when she'd gazed upon my horrid face long ago. She was right when she said people stick with the ones they love: the burn victims, the cancer survivors, the amputees, the quadriplegics; we don't give up on those we love. It may be hard, but we don't give up—

However, I had died. I could not expect anyone to stick with me in that circumstance. It was different. I was letting her go—to save her, not forcing her to be with me even though she had promised. I was doing her a favor. We'd planned to get married, after all. Then this affliction came upon me, like a time bomb going off, and I could not stop it. I had to let her go.

Finally, she sat back, the blood gone. I took the bag from her.

Her hands went to her face, brushed her scalp. She remembered I was in the room and chuckled to herself, turned to a painting on the wall: a graceful horse and rider trotting down a dirt path through a colorful arbor on an autumn day.

"I drove away," she said, a grating sadness coloring her voice, then stopped to ponder. She bit her ragged lips. "I wanted to shower but I had to get to the station. My report was scheduled and I needed to do a live intro in the studio." Her head shook, then her chin touched her chest. "But no time. So I went straight there. No changing clothes. I threw on a blazer borrowed from Jen, my producer. I did the story. I smiled like I was happy. Then I hit the door, left."

She turned in her chair and regarded me. Then, perhaps seeing my expression, she averted her eyes.

"I was a mess when I got home. I drew a bath and soaked for hours. You know? I wanted to wash it all away. I wanted to wash you off me. I let out the water and watched you go down the drain. Bye-bye, Stefan."

"I deserved that," I mumbled.

"I told them I was sick. I took some days off."

"That's why I didn't see you on TV. I wanted to be able to see you again, even looking at your news reports."

"Yes, well, about the news reports . . . . You know our so wonderful meteorologist, the one who won the awards? He needed a raise. So the station bigshots fired all the experienced reporters. Like me. And they hired newbies at half the salary. So I was out of a job."

"That was unfair."

"It wasn't overnight. They dragged it out." She squared herself in the chair. Her dull eyes seemed to brighten, to burn bright in an evil way. "My turn came several months later."

"So what did you do?"

"I came looking for you. Of course."

"Really? For fourteen years?"

"Sure. I thought you might've found a cure." Her dry, cracked lips pinched into a grin. "No, not at first."

"What happened?" I asked far too innocently.

That seemed the next reasonable question, not an interrogation. It seemed to be asking about a cure. Or it concerned her next step. In the cool darkness of this hotel room, a sanctuary for the dead and undead, the question was an invitation to spill it all.

"A lot happened." She seemed to want to cry then yet there came no tears. She rubbed her eyes anyway. It was only the tightness of her voice that gave away her distress. "I don't want to think about it."

"Here you are," I said as gently as I could. "You found me. How did you find me? In all the world? In this large city?"

She pursed her meager lips, somehow proud that I had noticed her investigative skills.

"You said you needed to go to a bank in Budapest. Then you would go to some spa. So I went to every big bank in the city, asking about

119

you. Of course, none of them would divulge the name of a client. I left notes for them to give to you."

She glared at me. I shook my head; no notes received.

"Then one day you walked into the bank I was in. Well, I thought it was you. So I followed you. Creepy, yeah? Stalker. And it was you. Then I had to decide what I would do, what I would say, or if I hadn't gone too far into this to see it through."

"See it through?"

"The confrontation." She cleared her throat, a dry, raspy growl. "It's always the confrontation that sells the movie. You know, he meets her or she meets him, and one of them is in shock. The other one smiles smugly, quite satisfied in the revelation. Cut to commercial."

"You've seen it through . . . ." I waited for her to finish my sentence, like we used to do for each other, then went ahead. "Or is there more? More you plan to do?"

I could have feared a knife or something else intended to strike me down at that moment. After all this time, any jilted lover would enjoy the dramatic confrontation, she had said. Yet I was too tired to get up and stand in a defensive stance. I only had my sword-cane as a weapon. Over there, leaning against the chaise-longue. Or one of the four steak knives in a drawer in the dinette. If she wanted to kill me, I would yield.

"My plan is . . . since this thing came over me . . . is to get through the day. Just get to the next freakin' day. Just see the sunrise again. The damn sunrise." She choked, coughed. "Why?"

She shook her head for a long time.

"I really don't know. Each day is worse. Right? You know what it's like. I don't know why I push myself, why I go on . . . . But I guess the bottom line is I just wanted to face you, give you the big confrontation scene, you know, see your sad, pitiful face—see you seeing that my horrible face matches yours. Both of us hideous."

She picked at a loose flake of skin on her cheek.

"Now I've done that. Now we are fit only for each other. Two ugly corpses. Are you satisfied? Happy to see me? Glad I'm now like you, infected and dying, a life wasted? Is that what you expected? I see you. It's you. What do you think? How do you feel? Are you sorry? Yeah, of course you are. I see that in your face. So I guess I can die now."

Her voice broke. There should have been streams of tears, not just the dry sobbing and a raspy, painful grating noise. I felt her utterances scratching me, like sandpaper across my soul, drawing beads of blood. Except I no longer had a soul. God had snatched that away from me the instant I died.

"You can't die," I said, "not until you've told me everything."

She looked up, held up her hand to block my view of her face.

"If I do, will you stand with me and face the sunrise?"

I glanced at the closed curtains, the sunlight already strong outside though our room was dark.

"Sunrise?"

"Isn't that what vampires fear most?"

"Well, it's . . . ." I swallowed hard, understanding. "Yes, I will face the sunrise. I will do that for you."

"Thank you, Stefan. That's the kindest thing anyone's ever said to me."

15

WHEN THE TV STATION MANAGER TOLD ME I WAS BEING LET GO, I HAD A few months to find another position. Not a good time of the year for hiring, though. I started packing the day I got the rejection from the last of the stations in the Oklahoma City market. I returned to Denver, moved in with Mom, as painful as that was. She didn't give me any of that "I told you so" crap, thankfully. She understood. Dad immediately tried to fix me up with good Korean men again but, obviously, that was not of any interest to me. You know his thinking: Better for me to be a good little housewife than a single career woman.

A few months before I left the station, you called me, Stefan. You knocked my cell clean off the desk it vibrated so hard. You were saying something about having surgery. I don't remember it all now. But you said you loved me, and if you didn't make it to forget about you. I tried to tell you something important but you were too frantic sharing your worries with me. You barely heard me say I was pregnant.

When you finally got what I was saying, you told me flat out to get an abortion. You said I shouldn't let your cursed genes continue in the world. Your exact words. Remember? I never wanted children, Stefan. But we did it. It was the day you raped me. Before the rape part. The love making part, when we loved each other, before what happened next. If you want to downgrade it to sexual assault, go right ahead. But sexual assault with unwanted penetration is rape. Doesn't matter if we already made love with consent. I withdrew consent when you decided to use your tongue and I said to stop. But you didn't stop. You needed blood. You were a monster. It was the worst day of my life.

Until a few years later.

I got some spot reporting gigs around Denver, just free-lance stuff, but that hardly paid the bills, you know. Mom let me stay rent-free, of course. Dad let me work in his office, secretary stuff, but no nepotism for him. I got paid the standard wage as the other 'girls' in the office. You can imagine how much I loved doing that. I did that for a year. I never got hired on full-time at any station. I even went to interviews at stations outside of Colorado: Kansas City, Tulsa, Fort Worth, and even Fresno out in California, of all places. I felt good about getting the weekend anchor slot there. But no.

Then I heard about a special program in Korea. You know I spent some summers there when I was young. I even lived there a year while I was in college. If I had to, I could still speak Korean. So I applied and went over there to be an elementary school teacher at a private school in Seoul. All the rich kids. If you can imagine me teaching little kids. I was the so-called English teacher, but because I looked as Korean as everybody else, they kept speaking to me in Korean. It's easy to forget a language if you don't use it. Well, it came back to me. I must say, the kids loved me. And I loved them. I really hated to leave. It was not my calling—broadcast journalism was supposed to be—but it did lift my spirits. It made me feel good after the TV reporting disappointments.

After I returned to Denver, still living with Mom, I got an adjunct gig teaching journalism at Santa Fe Community College. I'm sure not a teacher, Stefan. I know it, but it was a job. I needed a job. Maybe they learned something from a real broadcast journalist, maybe not. A few were paying attention, took notes. Most just checked their phones all through the class. Made me feel like *What's the point?* I couldn't see myself doing that the rest of my life. So I sent out more applications and samples of my work. I got a few more interviews, but no hires. I felt really close in Columbus, Ohio: got second and third interviews. Meanwhile, I taught more classes. I thought life was finally becoming real—the reality check they tell you about, right?

Then I got the reality check for real: the mirror.

Remember the mirror, Stefan? We used to stand naked in front of that wide mirror in my bathroom, side by side, staring at ourselves.

One woman, one man. You were slender, a geek. Me with no boobs. We were a couple. Those were good days. But you know mirrors can lie. You told me that more than a few times. Especially when you started poking at those dry patches on your face. You cursed the mirror. Then you turned them down or covered them, you said. You refused to look at yourself. But I saw you. I looked at you, Stefan. I was your mirror, and I saw you falling apart. Every single day. I still went ahead and put my eyes on you, no matter how bad you looked.

March 15, 2020. The next worst day of my life. I stared at myself in the mirror. I saw the patch on my cheek. Brown. Scaly. Itchy. Mottled edges, sort of diamond-shaped. If I had never met you I wouldn't have a clue what it was or how I might have gotten it. I would try what you did, what I first suggested: apply some lotion. Dry skin needs lotion. And hydration. I can't laugh anymore at how many times I told you to hydrate. Your skin was too dry, so hydrate. Remember?

You know me: I hydrate like a fish. So that was not my problem. I tried lotions, which softened the patch—patches, eventually, on my face, shoulders, back, also my chest. There didn't seem enough lotion in all the stores of the mall to cover my needs.

But I did know you, so I had a clue. A creeping feeling started to run up my spine.

I know what you're thinking: Why does she have this problem? She is not Hungarian. She doesn't have those genes. And she eats a ton of garlic in that Korean food. I wondered that, too. It made no sense. But there I was, naked in front of the mirror in the bathroom, examining myself, staring at my brown-patchy skin, wondering what to do.

And my mother walked in!

"What are you doing?" she asked, half in shock to see me naked.

"I was about to take a shower," I told her. "I was checking these . . . a few spots of bad skin."

She stepped closer and took a look at them. She doesn't have any medical training, but she is a mother. That must count for something, right? But she had no idea. Then it was déjà-vu all over again: "You better see dermatologist."

Just like I told you, Stefan.

That was the day I about died. Long before the day I almost really died. And the other times I almost died. And now, again . . . almost dying. I love that you had a unit of blood saved for me—

Burp. Excuse me.

I continued spot reporting, wearing a lot of make-up. I didn't feel good standing in front of a class so I quit the college. Meanwhile, I did research. I found the clinic in Utica you went to. Made an appointment like you did, expecting to meet your old flame, that Leslie woman. Remember her? You never told me very much but I guessed you guys had a nasty affair and that's why you came to Oklahoma. Am I close? Go ahead and nod. Yes, like that.

Let me tell you this, Stefan. I went to that clinic, got checked, got tests done, got a negative result for anything they had heard of or had seen before. I asked about Dr. Leslie.

She was no longer at the clinic.

"Moved to another?" I asked the doctor who checked me, a tall guy named Dukas. Was he there when you were?

He hesitated saying anything, just mumbled that she had left the profession. That phrase: 'left the profession'. What does that mean? Being a doctor is a good paying occupation, so why would she leave it? I did some research. You know me. Called in a favor from a reporter friend in Buffalo, got her address.

Leslie lived in a trailer, out in the country, in the forest outside of Batavia. I mean, not in a trailer park. Alone out there. It was the whole redneck set-up, pardon my Korean.

So I go up the steps and knock on the door, thinking she must have a brood of kids and that's why she quit medicine, something like that. But no. No kids. Just a lonely old woman.

I ask if Leslie is at home.

"You a bill collector?" is what the woman said right off.

I assured her I wasn't. Just looking up an old friend from college.

"I don't have any friends from college," the woman said. It was her: Leslie, your old lover. "Not anymore."

She looked horrible. Her hair was falling out in patches, the rest of it dirty and crisp as straw, prematurely gray, almost white. She wore a ragged bathrobe, also filthy. What I could see of her face and hands, she had some disease. A skin disease. I know you like irony, Stefan. A dermatologist with a skin disease. Okay, a cardiologist having a heart attack, same thing. Agreed.

So we talked. I have a caring face, you know. People talk to me. We stayed on the steps, though. I'm not sure I wanted to go in that trailer. It seemed quite dirty and a bad odor drifted out. But she confirmed what I suspected. She had caught something, couldn't get it treated—or it resisted treatment—so she wasn't allowed or didn't want to continue working with patients. I understood.

We talked about you eventually. I just said I knew you. We worked together on a news story. Blood bank something, right? She didn't have very much affection for you. She blamed you for whatever her disease was. The *affliction*, as you like to call it. You did have an affair, right? I get it. She was married and you two worked together, had a fling. Her husband divorced her over it. Daytime drama stuff. And you ran away to Oklahoma.

And about a year later you developed a dry patch of skin.

It's been a long time. What I've been through since then—yeah, I can't begin to think now the way I was thinking then. Everything is different. I'm very different. I want to cry at every sunrise—because it means I have to make it through yet another day—but my eyes won't make any tears. You complained about that, too. It made sense to me after I met Leslie. She's probably dead by now. Or else transformed. What I saw on her skin was a phase I have already passed through, Stefan. Two years ago. I recognized it when it covered my entire body. I thought back to how that Leslie had looked, and I think she had the same thing, the same affliction.

I'm fucking Korean, Stefan! Asian. A garlic eater. Why me? Leslie is whatever kind of European, probably Scottish or Irish, I guess. And we both got the same problem. She had it first. And it is the same problem you got. The same problem that caused you to transform. You said it was genetic. But how about for us? Put it together! Add it up!

You gave it to Leslie. Think about that, Stefan. You gave her the disease—the vampire disease.

Then you gave it to me.

⚬

"Mom, I have something to tell you. Please sit down. Give me your full attention. This is important."

Of course she remembered meeting you when she visited me. She was very happy I met you. She talked about you all the time, Stefan, like you were the perfect boyfriend for me. So it hurt so much to tell her that I thought you had given me a disease. She thought I meant one of the typical venereal diseases. One of the easy to treat diseases. A few shots and done. I suppose it is a venereal disease if it can be passed through sex. That was beside the point, though, when I had the talk with my mother. She lost her love of you pretty quick.

"Neither of us knew it could be passed on," I tried to explain. "He was suffering from it but I insisted on making love with him anyway. He even wore a mask, his face looked so bad. He thought how he looked would scare me away." I choked up. Mom patted my back. "I wanted to show him I still loved him, that I would keep on loving him no matter what."

"Love is strange thing to people," said Mom.

I cried against her shoulder.

"So it's partly my fault. Both of us . . . we weren't thinking clearly, logically. Not being careful."

"You hooked on love, nothing you can do."

"But now I have something. It's like what Stefan had. Already I see it becoming worse. My skin has more patches."

"We find good doctor for you. We not gonna let it hurt you."

"I already checked with a doctor. And so did Stefan. I know he tried everything to find a cure. Or at least some kind of treatment. And he— he went to a clinic in . . . Croatia, I think. They were trying some kind of experimental treatment. That was the last thing he said. He called me, said he was going into surgery."

I cried more, hugging my mother.

"Did he . . . die?" she asked.

Sobbing, I said, "I never heard from him after that."

16

SOMEHOW I AWAKENED EACH DAY. AND IN THOSE FIRST FEW BREATHS I realized I wasn't dead.

The sunrise burning through the window began to hurt my eyes. I would turn over, face the wall. I was back in my childhood bed, you know, in my childhood house with my mother doing her daily tasks outside my room. I was supposed to be a career woman. I would make her proud. And show my father I could be successful without one of those upwardly-mobile corporate husbands. He sent me to college to learn some trade. I learned broadcast journalism. I was making my way up the ladder just fine before the fate thing stepped in and pulled the ladder out from under me. Or, maybe it was this god you kept cursing. You always said he had it in for you. By hurting the ones you love he hurts you more. Is that it? That's kinda sick, actually.

Our first date . . . remember it? I took you to church. The Korean church. We sat together, we sang the songs, and listened to the sermon spoken in Korean, and you never once even tried to hold my hand. You were a gentleman. I learned a lot about you from that first date, Stefan. I knew then I could love you from that day on.

So I returned to church, my mom's. I spoke to the preacher about God and fate, all the things that sin can cause in our lives. I tried to understand why this was happening to me. I had lived a good life, no obvious sins. Unless you count sex before marriage. But we were not promiscuous, you and I. No, we were hardly porn stars in bed. The preacher suggested I was thinking too hard, that diseases sometimes come without committing sin first. I'm not sure that was comforting.

I thought of that idea each morning as I went through the routine. Get up from bed, make sure I was alive, then step out to the bathroom for a morning pee, checking the color and volume. Then I would pull off my nightgown and stand before the mirror. I would study myself, top to bottom, focusing on every part from my head and face to my shoulders and chest, belly, and legs. I turned one way then the other to check my hips, my butt, the back of my legs. I pulled one foot up onto the countertop to examine my toes, arch, heel. I checked my calves as best I could, twisting around as far as I could. The back of my knees, back of my thighs. I would lift my hair to see the back of my neck. I ran my fingers through my hair and always some would come out, clinging to my fingers.

Facing the mirror, I would take stock, compile my assessment each morning. What was new? What patches changed, which disappeared, what new ones appeared? Any changes in color? Texture? Shape? What itched, what didn't? I leaned in close, putting my face almost against the glass, examining my eyes, pulling down the lids and rolling each eye from one side to the other, up and down. I looked inside my mouth. My tongue pressed on each tooth to determine if it was loose or not. I studied the color of my tongue. I became as obsessed as you did, Stefan.

And so I could see my body change every day. I saw the shifting of my body from healthy to unhealthy to disease-riddled to what I am now: a dying husk of a human.

This is what you did to me.

For about two years I stayed at home. I helped my mother the best I could but I seldom went out. If I did, I bundled up, slathered on tons of make-up, wore dark glasses. Nobody could recognize me or see the ugly patches on my skin. I certainly could not work in any real job, not where others would see me, stare at me, wondering what I had and be afraid to get too close. It was hard enough picking fruit in the grocery, seeing how other shoppers avoided the fruit I had touched. Not even the exact piece of fruit; I mean, all the Granny Smith apples. They went over to the Gala apple bin. Or they skipped apples altogether because I stood beside them.

I saw some doctors and they gave me papers certifying that I had a debilitating disease. I got some money, disability checks each month. I gave them to my mother for her trouble, taking care of me. Otherwise, I tried to stay out of her way, to make life as easy for her as possible. After all, she now had a poor daughter who was dying from a venereal disease. Such a scandal in the Korean community of Denver. I felt sorry for her. She became less active in the community, too.

All the blood tests in the world showed I was perfectly healthy. Or the tests could not identify our special affliction, whatever markers it had. See? I learned medical jargon in my research. In my doctor visits. Everybody was getting tired of seeing me. First, I was ugly. Next, they knew there was nothing they could do for me. I was wasting their time, even if they might feel bad for me.

You went far and wide searching for a cure, for treatment, and finally you tried something dangerous. You called it experimental, so I assume it was dangerous. And it was, wasn't it? You died, right? You sped up the transformation. You got it over with quicker. You saved, what? Five or ten years of suffering? How long does the transformation usually take if you don't try strange treatments? About ten years, I'm guessing, if you don't have the genes for it. Like me.

I didn't try any experimental procedure like you, Stefan. No, I let it come at me at its own pace. Two years from the first symptom—a dry patch of skin on my cheek—to being too gross to be seen in public. Wasn't it about one year between your first dry patch of skin and your death? You hastened it. I didn't—couldn't just kill myself quickly. No matter how much I hated what I saw in the mirror each morning. No matter how people shunned me. No matter how much Mother cried every day, how my father refused to talk to me. Yeah, even over the phone. Even then, I could not kill myself.

I did fantasize about it. Nothing violent. That's not me. I checked medicines that would let me sleep deeply and never awaken. I bought some. One night I put a handful of pills in my mouth. Then I spit them out when I began to feel dizzy. I did not swallow any of them but they burned my mouth. It was like a warning from God. I was not allowed to take the easy way out. I had to own my suffering.

I went on to sleep—what we call sleep, right? You close your eyes for a few minutes, then awaken. Try it again a few minutes later. And again. Maybe you can be unconscious for an hour. With a pill—if you can keep it down—a few hours. So not only are we falling apart but we get no rest, no reprieve, no break to enter a dream and be tormented by the comparison between the joys of our dream land and the hard acceptance of reality when our eyes open again. It's a triple curse.

My mother came into my room, that room where my dolls still sat on the shelf like I was seven years old. She told me it might be best if I moved into a nursing facility. They could take better care of me in that kind of place than she could at home. I knew she was right, but it felt like a knife had been stabbed in me. All I did every day, every night, was lie on the bed or sit by the window, staring out at some strange fantasy world that was forbidden to me. That was no kind of life.

Of course, it was supposed to be a kind of death.

"If you can walk maybe you go someplace and enjoy yourself?" my mother suggested.

"I can walk just fine. Sometimes there's pain in my joints but don't need a cane yet."

"Then you can go to . . . like see a wood or a lake. Just be alone and you can enjoy nature . . . . Then you talk to God."

Her heart was in the right place. Perhaps if I did go out, away from other people, I might feel better. I didn't know how dying out in the beauty of nature made it any easier, but it was worth a try.

I could drive a car but I needed to renew my license, which had expired while I lay in bed. But I didn't care. What are they going to do? Fine me? Lock me up in a jail? So I drove—slowly, carefully; it had been a while—out of Denver and up into the mountains.

I'm sure you know the feeling, Stefan. When you stand among the tall pines, the cool breeze caressing your skin, blowing through your hair, and the sky is as much below you as above you, there is a special sensation. I never had that sensation quite like the day I arrived on the top of that mountain. It was so far up there from the world I left. I threw off my clothes, let the wind scour my body, tug at the skin tags and the flakes, rip off the ones that were loose. I let the sun cover me, burning the dead skin away, melting all the brown patches into pretty designs. You don't believe me, but I did. I stood bare naked under the sky. It felt so good to not have fabric rubbing my skin raw. I was so hideous-looking—yet no one was there to see me. I no longer cared what happened to me. Arrest me, let me die, whatever. Who would touch me, the way I looked? I was a wild animal. Maybe a werewolf? I could be a werewolf, Stefan, you know, just staying out in the woods, hunting like a wild animal. Except I was losing hair, not growing it.

As I stared at the sun, hoping to go blind, I heard a voice. Maybe it was God, who knows? Maybe it was a park ranger, or some camper shocked at the sight of me. The voice said: "He lives." That was all. I heard it repeated. When the wind blew harder I heard it louder. Maybe it was only the wind. But I heard it clearly.

I stayed overnight, no tent and no food, just me and my affliction. My SUV was parked below, about an hour's hike down the mountain. A pile of clothing was my bed under the stars. I stared up at them, counting them, and for a few pleasant moments I could forget what was happening to me. I could remember better days.

"He lives." I thought about it. It sounded like so many sermons I'd heard, referring to Jesus rising from death inside a cave, something like that. I know the story, the resurrection after three days. If you, Stefan, had died, then maybe—just maybe—you rose after three days, too. Maybe you were alive again somewhere. It sure seemed as good of an option as anything I could think of.

"He lives."

God was sending me a message. *That fucker still lives.* Yeah, that's exactly what He said, straight into my ear. *So why not go find him? That's something to live for, isn't it? The chance to confront him, the guy who gave you this disease, this affliction. Now you have a purpose. Go.*

17

First, I had to renew my passport. It expired after I returned from that year of teaching in Korea. You can imagine how difficult it was to get good pictures. I tried eight times with different make-up and a wig. I tried with glasses, nothing too dark, but that was not allowed. It had to look like me when we were side by side, the real me and my photo. No, I wasn't as clever as you. I didn't have somebody make a theater mask for me. The rules are different now. I just sucked it up and showed my true face to whoever needed to see it.

You haven't been out in the world for a while, Stefan. Am I right? It's twenty-twenty-eight. The world has changed a lot, especially how difficult it is to move from country to country, especially on airlines. Unless you really want to go through all the checks you might as well stay home. It is no longer a fun experience. And it's worse if you don't exactly look healthy. Or if you're going to a conflict area like Europe. I was both.

I did all the research I could while I waited for my passport. I paid extra for express service but it was still a month's wait under the best circumstances. Where was I going? Don't you see me, Stefan? I was going here. I remembered you talking about a clinic, about Budapest, and about some spa, a mineral bath kind of place. I remembered all of that, so I searched for them online. I found the clinic in Zagreb. They had a website. But the information was old. It had not been updated in five years. When I tried to call the phone number on the website, there was only a message—I guess it was Croatian. It had been a while, so maybe they had gone out of business. If they did something dangerous, too experimental, and someone died, then . . . well, that could shut a clinic down very fast. I've done stories before on medical malpractice, shady doctors, and the like.

So I turned to the banks in Budapest. Lots of them. No way to get useful information that might relate to you. And that was assuming the GlobalTalk app put all that Hungarian into correct English. Not much else I could do from my house in Denver. I had no journalism friends over there, either—

Wait a minute. Back up.

I dug around in the attic of my mind, opened boxes and checked everything related to Stefan Székely. In one box I found a statement about the funeral of your parents. That was in Croatia, some town on the coast. In the same box, I found a statement that you made about having property near that town. The family estate or something. So I got on the internet again and searched for all the Székely-related stuff I could find. On the MyWorld app, I saw that coastal town: Makarska. Then I went in different directions, using the satellite view, zooming in and looking for any castles or other structures that were big enough to be the estate of any historical family. I only found one that was near that coastal town. It was marked as 'abandoned ruins'.

That part of the world was known as the Hungarian Federation. Both that town on the coast and that castle further inland were within its boundaries. Maybe you don't know, living inside it, but outside, the Hungarian Federation is frowned upon by most of the other nations of Europe and the United States. You can't go rogue in this day and age. Especially not a country. Everybody has to go along with the general consensus, which is, of course, as everyone knows, not a consensus but an admonition, a direction, a protocol for exactly how someone or a group—I won't name names—wants the world to be.

So for me to get into that Hungarian Federation, where I guessed you would be if you were anywhere, I had to apply for a visa. It's not a standard form. It's six pages long. Some of the pages have boxes for me to write out my answer to the question. Not just check a box or write one word but write out a multi-sentence response to questions like why I want to enter the country, exactly what my business would be there, and the names of anyone I expected to be in contact with, plus their contact information. It had to be handwritten. And more photos. They wanted face, of course, but also full body pictures, front and reverse, top of head down to shoes. The instructions required women to dress modestly in photos, wearing 'suitable garments'—so wear a nice dress like you're going to church. There was a long list of what was not suitable for the photo. A set of fingerprints was required, all ten fingers. And notarized medical certificate of 'reasonable health' which they provided in the application packet, for two doctors, not in the same office, to fill-out. There should be documented test results showing no evidence of any of a dozen communicable diseases. They had a list. It took me two months to get that packet together and send it to the Hungarian Federation embassy all the way over to . . . to, well, down the street from this hotel. There is no embassy in the U.S.

Six months later I received my visa from the Hungarian Federation processing office here in Budapest. I was almost dead by then. A big flare-up of symptoms had me in the hospital for a couple weeks, but there was nothing to be done but treat the symptoms. It seemed to go away on its own and I returned home. My mother thought I shouldn't go traveling.

But I had to go.

I booked my flight. The closest major airport I could get to was Munich. There were no direct flights to Budapest except from Poland and Russia. Air routes from European countries had been suspended. Did you know that? For two years now. They're trying to punish the Hungarian Federation for deciding their own fate rather than going along with the demands of the boys in Brussels. The powers that be. Yes, the jackboots are getting thicker there! At the same time, those countries aren't any safer, allowing in more immigrants, migrants, refugees from everywhere. I know, I know, that's none of my business. Things are peachy-keen and hunky-dory in the U.S. of A., right? Not really. Every day it seems somebody has to protest something and the police are putting them down. No, we have the same level of fascism as other Western nations. I had to wonder how different, how worse the Hungarian Federation might be. How worse could it get?

But you want to know how I found you . . . .

CR

"Explain this mark," said the airport security officer, a stout woman with her hair in a bun. "And these, umm, patches of darker skin."

"It's related to my period, ma'am. It clears up in a few days."

She shook her head, like she felt sorry for me. Then she poked her wooden baton at my ribs, remarked how they showed too clearly, like I was undernourished. Not grounds for barring from flights, fortunately.

"You pregnant?" she asked, waiting to check off something on her clipboard.

"No, ma'am. I was once before."

She looked up from under her eyebrows. "Give birth?"

I frowned, shook my head.

"That looks like stretch marks right there," she said.

"That's just my bad skin. It comes and goes."

Check. Her pen scratched the paper.

"You're free to board your flight."

I stepped down off the stool and grabbed my clothes. As I began to get dressed, she watched me intently. The procedure required her to make sure I didn't sneak something from my clothes into one of the body cavities she had already inspected.

After all, there was that passenger who packed his colon with some explosive, a new kind they said was transparent on scanner machines. Looked like an impacted bowel. When the flight arrived at Boston, he detonated his ass. You didn't hear about that? Three hundred dead. And there was a woman who put explosives in her vagina. They caught her before she boarded but she and a gate attendant were killed when it went off prematurely. Now everyone is checked thoroughly.

I wasn't pulled aside for closer inspection because of how I looked. No, it wasn't because my face looked sickly compared to my passport photo. Everyone is pulled aside now. It's the new normal. You haven't traveled for fourteen years, Stefan.

Flying is not for me.

Now there are five security lines at the airport. One for women, one for men, and one for anyone who thinks they are something other than woman or man. The fourth line is for families with small children; they can be inspected together. The fifth line is for those special people who have the premium Safety-Seal status. For a price almost as much as the air ticket you can undergo the series of inspections outside of the airport at a nicer facility as late as five days before flying, rather than do it at the airport on the day you fly. I suppose the rich and famous get a lighter touch than the rest of us get.

The rest of us pass through two different machines that scan us for explosives or hidden snacks. We go one at a time into a closet-sized room where we can toss out anything that may not be allowed on the plane, which is everything nowadays. Not even a ballpoint pen. It has a point, you know. And you might have to write something. You know words are dangerous. No chewing gum or mints, either. Choking hazard. Yes, one would-be terrorist actually tried to choke a flight attendant by shoving a whole box of mints down her throat. Other passengers restrained the guy.

Only one small bag is allowed now anyway, small like a purse, and you better have medicine in it or something else you must have with you at all times. No exceptions. And no electronics of any kind, either: no phones, computers, tablets, nothing with an 'on' switch. Not even the thumb-sized MP3 player I used for some Reiki music to help me stay calm. Had to put it in my checked suitcase. The only thing worse about flying today are the standing positions at the rear of the plane, the new cheap seats. Fortunately, not on international flights of more than four hours. Also we are not allowed to bring our own food or drinks onto the plane, but we can buy snack boxes and bottled water for around thirty dollars. No carbonated drinks or alcohol on board, either. Soda can explode and alcohol offends some passengers, makes them want to blow up the plane, you know.

But first, we must go through Personal Inspection. All the women go into the next room—like the men go into their room—and when there are about five of us, the inspector gives the command to strip. We are watched closely to see that we don't try to hide something as we disrobe. There are cameras watching us, too. They say the videos are deleted after 72 hours, long after we pass the inspection, but who really knows if the more attractive women are somehow shown off by employees to their friends. There have been cases where some PI video got on the internet. The faces are blurred, which they say preserves privacy, but you could see everything else plain as day.

The woman inspector goes around to each of us. After disrobing, we must stand with our feet apart, arms away from our chest, until the inspector gets to us. Leaving Denver, I was in a group with two teenage girls and their mother, a twenty-something woman in business attire, and two grandmothers. There were shoulder-high screens to provide some side-to-side privacy, like so the young girls wouldn't see their grandmother. The inspectors check everything, treat everyone equally bad. I was in the security inspection line with a bunch of men when I got to Chicago, so I was alone in my inspection room. I got the full treatment, just big Officer Stanley and little me. And the cameras. Thankfully, I passed. A new group entered as I dressed.

I took my purse, which had its contents dumped out on a table, put everything into it again, and exited. Outside the door was a long path to the boarding gates, marked off by electrified security ropes and a stern guard every hundred feet or so. If anyone tried to climb over or duck under the ropes, the current would be broken and a siren would sound. You would not catch your flight after that.

At the boarding gate, I sat down to wait. My skin started to itch under my long-sleeve shirt and slacks. I wanted to scratch but I feared drawing attention to myself. An airport guard came by with a sniffing dog, working their way around us, then departed. The dog paused at me, maybe smelling the ointment I used to make my skin less dry and flaky. Not enough distraction to warrant further checking, I guessed, as the guard gave me a nasty look, then pulled the dog away. Maybe he didn't like my sexy vampire face.

Finally, we were called to board. I stood a little too quickly, much too pleased to rush ahead to the next step, and felt a wave of dizziness. I recovered before anyone noticed. If someone had and reported me, I could have had more inspection to make sure I was healthy enough to fly. They don't want anyone getting sick on the plane.

As we lined up to go down the gangway to the aircraft door, we paused once more at tables for agents to dig around in any bag going on the aircraft. I only had my purse. In it was a magazine, just news and commentary, no big deal, I thought. But it was. The agent tossed it into a trash bin. He gave me a look like he wondered what my political views were and whether or not reading that kind of magazine might set me off, might make me want to do something dangerous aboard the aircraft. He never suspected that what would likely set me off had already been happening ever since I arrived at the airport.

Now I would have nothing to read on the flight, nothing except the ladies magazines they provided, so I would know how to fix my hair for the man in my life or bake perfect chocolate chip cookies for my 1.5 darling children. Honestly, as long as I could breathe easily, I planned to just sleep for as much of the flight as possible.

If you want to have the privilege of flying, you must go through the process. So the only people who fly any more are those who can't get there any other way, like crossing an ocean. Heck, I drove all the way to Utica, New York from Denver rather than fly there.

18

THE FIRST TIME I VISITED EUROPE WAS ON A SPRING BREAK TRIP WITH MY sorority sisters. We did the London, Paris, Rome tour over ten days. That was a very different situation from what we have going on now.

Arriving in Munich was not a whole lot better than in Chicago. As we filed off the airplane, we were searched again. You never know who might grow bombs in their bosoms during a long flight. More scanners. And health inspectors giving us the once over as we filed past. Some were stopped and questioned. Some of those who were questioned were pulled out of line and taken to a screening room. More questions. Then a blood sample and a tissue sample and a 6-hour quarantine. At least I had a cot to lay on. I even fell asleep.

Despite how I appeared, nothing was wrong in my tests, so they let me into the country. My suitcase had long been stolen from baggage claim, though. I went over to the airline office and complained. I got some compensation, but for a woman in my delicate condition, not having my lotions and ointments was pure evil. With the dry air on the plane, my skin had worsened by weeks. I needed a long, soaking bath in a vat of lotion. I couldn't wait to get to a hotel and do just that. First I had to purchase my body care products again.

With only my purse to comfort me, I went from store to store in an arcade just outside the airport, buying what I needed. Not knowing German, it was difficult to choose. And the staff women kept walling me off, hoping I would go to another store. They sneered at me, at my appearance. I wanted to shout: "I'm a human, too!" But I didn't feel human. I tried to remember what it was like to brush my hair back out of my face and let the sun warm my skin. What it was like to not wear make-up. You used to call me a natural beauty. Now I needed to cover myself, first with cosmetics, then with clothing that hid my delicate condition. I was lucky they even allowed me to enter Germany.

And then came the zombie horde.

Perhaps it wasn't that dramatic, not like on a TV show, or like the drugged-out protesters you find at every public event now. They seem to just show up and attack anything, whoever happens to be speaking, licensed or unlicensed. It seemed to be a new kind of drug-craze. I don't mean real zombies—if zombies can be considered real. Political zombies.

I was exiting my fourth store, had a large bag of products in my hand, and I heard shouting. Then a small poof of an explosion. I saw a line of police, armored up, marching against a ragged mob of these protestors. The poof was tear gas I guessed as soon as I smelled it. I ducked into the store, but the store clerk forced me out—literally pushed me outside and shut the door, locked it. She knew I wasn't one of the protesters. I had bought expensive products from that store.

The mob was backed up by the police line, forced down the street in my direction. There was no place to hide. I tried to run but my feet were numb and I tripped on the pavement and fell. The mob caught up to me, going backwards, and I was swept along with them. I tried to move to the side to escape. I got into an alley, hid behind a trash bin as the police line passed me. Then the violence began. Rocks by the mob, rubber bullets by the police. Then one of those homemade bombs was tossed at the police. The police switched to real bullets. A new line of police came to the front and started shooting. The mob grew bold and rushed forward with anything they could use as clubs. I saw the first line of police officers struck by the mob and fall. I saw the mob people drop with gunshot wounds.

As I tried to escape, something was thrown at me, hit my head. I felt dizzy but I kept going, crawling on my hands and knees along the pavement, trying to not lose consciousness. My whole body hurt. My hands and knees couldn't take the roughness of the pavement. My skin was tearing, bleeding. More explosions, screaming, shots—

ᴒ

"You will be all right," said a female voice in a German accent.

I opened my eyes and saw I was in a hospital bed. The lights were bright. I raised my hand to shield my eyes and saw that my hand was bandaged. My other hand was likewise bandaged. I tried to sit up but my body ached too much. I winced and sank back on the bed.

The doctor leaned over me, checking my eyes with an instrument.

"*Fraulein* Park," said the doctor, "you came here by police carrier."

She seemed to think I would know what that meant.

"There was attack in Neue-Geigerstrasse. Very bad. You were hit on the head. The police cleaners found you. Lucky they decided you were not protester. They go another place. So you are here for to be treated."

I looked at her name tag: DR. FRANCK.

"I just arrived at the airport . . . ," I started, then lost the strength to speak.

"Visitor. *Ja*, they showed your flight credentials."

"I didn't . . . . I wasn't in the protesters." I got the words out, took a deep breath. "I came out of a store."

"We understand." Dr. Franck pointed behind her to the sack on the side table. The store bag of my lotions! "You were shopper. So you were not in a good place at bad time."

"No, I wasn't."

"Now you need to rest."

I certainly felt like resting. "How long . . . ?"

"How long here?" She glanced at the tablet in her hand. "Almost two days. You were unconscious when they brought you." She pointed to my head. "We closed the cut on your head. Very bad." She explained that a piece of broken glass, probably from one of those bottle bombs, had cut my scalp down to the bone. Lots of blood from the wound.

I reached up to feel my head, but my bandaged hands could feel nothing. My hands were bandaged because I had scraped the palms crawling away from the attack. I had scraped the skin off my knees, as well, and they were bandaged.

"You have a long scar but when your hair grows out nobody can see it. So no worries, *ja*?"

"Yeah—*ja*."

She didn't understand that I was already loosing my hair. I doubted it would ever grow back again, certainly not thick enough to cover a scar on my scalp. But I was still alive, at least.

All this way, through all these hassles, just to die in a protest I had nothing to do with. That's the kind of irony you love, right, Stefan? I came to find you, maybe just to die trying. But then came the kicker, as they say. The doctor told me more.

She noticed my skin problem. Three days without any self-care and I was looking quite ragged: dry patches all over me, boils and flakes. The usual rash. I looked worse being under-hydrated and underfed during the flight. So, being a doctor, she naturally wanted to treat my problem before releasing me.

During my three days there, she had examined me and talked with a colleague in dermatology. The colleague had seen something similar years before. So this Dr. Gottlieb, the director of the women's wing of the hospital, examined me, too. In fact, a whole team took a look at me—like lifting the sheet and seeing my whole body in all its hideous glory. It was a classic case of the visiting-American-with-bad-skin syndrome. When I asked Dr. Gottlieb if that earlier case was named Stefan Székely, she grinned. The name was familiar. Yes, he had the same problem, but worse than me. She said they'd had to amputate your toes. They had gone gangrene. After a dog bite. I had to smile; that sure sounded like Stefan's kind of luck.

But he left one night and they never found him. She wrote up her notes and published an article about the case. It was just a short note, a curiosity. None of her colleagues across the medical world in Germany responded. So it was forgotten. For fourteen years. Then I walk into her examination room—well, not literally; I was being treated for injuries sustained during a protest—and happen to also have the bad skin syndrome.

"I'm on the way to Hungary," I replied when Dr. Franck asked if I knew anyone in Munich.

The real question was why I came here. Tourism? Nothing much to see these days, nothing but protests. Lots of crime in the streets. A single woman was not safe day or night in most of the city, the doctor warned me. I should hire a pair of female bodyguards. A group of three women is safe. As for her, now female doctors were only allowed to treat other females. And male doctors only treated men. New laws. The constant arrivals of migrants—they no longer called them refugees— had turned her beautiful country into a third-world slum. But the politicians could feel saintly, at least—her words. The EU—now turned into UE ("United Europe"), a model of what they thought the United States had tried to be—seemed content to give away their heritage to the mobs from the south and the east.

She fretted, remarking in sad words on her family line going back to Charlemagne. She was proud of that, yet she never would mention it now. King of the Franks, she answered when I didn't seem to know who that was. Nothing old, nothing sacred, nothing European could be allowed to remain, she told me in a hushed voice. So the trend was new or 'Modern' and third-world everything. That would explain the strange architecture I saw at the airport and along the streets. That also explained the noise that awoke me every morning: the calls from the minaret loudspeaker of the mosque outside. The next mosque over, several blocks away, was slightly out of sync, making for a horrendous cacophony battering the windows.

"Hungary? You mean the Hungarian Federation?" she asked. "You don't want to go there."

"But he went there."

"You knew him, the man fourteen years ago?"

"Yes. Unfortunately. I'm looking for him. I want to kill him."

She looked sternly at me, perhaps wondering if she should call the police. I grinned, shook my head.

"He hurt you, this man fourteen years ago?"

"Oh, did he hurt me! Look at me. This disease I have. My horrible appearance. He caused all of this. I hate him."

"*Ja*, I see. He gave you this disease."

I wanted to cry then, but my eyes would not make tears.

"He took my heart and left this disease in its place."

Dr. Franck nodded, crossed her arms over her chest. "*Ja* . . . ."

She went to retrieve the chart on the side table, tapped through its pages as all doctors seem to do while thinking what they might enjoy for dinner.

"It seems," she spoke with her back to me, "a new disease we only see very rarely." She faced me. "Many new diseases coming from the migrant community but this is not one of those. We will need a few more tests."

She smiled to encourage me, then left the room.

I was not encouraged, though. My mind burned with hate. I knew I was not fit to leave the hospital. I had no idea how to continue. Yet I'd come too far to stop or to go back.

Listen to me, Stefan: the only thing driving me on was my hatred for you. Honestly, I wanted to kill you. I wanted to find you and face you and show you what you did to me, what I'd become because of you, and then I would hammer a wooden stake into your damn heart.

19

STOP! JUST STOP IT! THERE IS NOTHING YOU CAN DO, STEFAN, SO STOP trying to say comforting words. Are you a scientist? Have you done research? Do you want me to hate you again? Just listen!

They kept me in that hospital for two weeks, running all kinds of tests. I felt fine, ready to leave but they insisted I stay until they could determined what it was I had and try to treat it. There was some talk of me spreading it around, like with any STD. I wondered, too. But I knew your experience was unlike anything anyone had studied in medical literature. Except for the varieties of porphyria, from mild to acute. I remembered that word: *porphyria*. You called it the 'vampire disease'. That is what you said you had.

I wanted to tell them that, but I feared they would want to keep me longer just to study me. Isolation, the whole works. A lab rat. I didn't want that. I wasn't going to be having sex with anyone so no chance of passing it on. But I wasn't concerned about doing something bad to someone else. I was the victim. I *am* the victim here!

Talking with Dr. Gottlieb, I learned you escaped in the middle of the night. I told her you do that kind of shit, just run away without any note or phone call or text message. Like a bat. Don't laugh. She didn't. She told me you asked about flights to Budapest. By the time they figured it out, you were in Hungary, so no chance to stop you at the airport. You were carrying a rare but serious contagion, she said. She wanted to alert authorities in Hungary but her boss said it was out of their jurisdiction and since she never had medical proof of whatever you had, it would just be a goose chase. So you got off scot-free, Stefan. In case you wanted to know.

But I knew the truth: you had to go to Budapest to access your big fortune that your parents left for you. Isn't that right?

And what would you do with that money? Pay for research into a cure for us? How long would that take?

"Mother, I get it," I said, calling long-distance. "Now I know how he felt. Not only the physical pain but everyone shunning him, fearing him, surrounded by hate. He always said God was after him, out to get him, trying to do him in. Like there was some game of revenge going on and God was winning. Yeah, he started thinking like that. Yeah, probably because of the disease. It was getting into his head. I mean physically, eating brain cells. I don't know. I'm not a doctor. But he changed. He was so twisted when he left."

"Maybe he got worm in brain," said Mom, helpful as ever. "So he maybe think he's vampire but not really turn to vampire."

"Mother, stop reading those books. It's just fiction."

"But you said he was turning."

"Transforming. That's what he called it."

"But what he transform from? And to what?"

"From a normal human into . . . into some abnormal human."

"Then the vampire is abnormal human?"

"Mother, it's not the same. He isn't a vampire!"

"Then somebody got to be the vampire or nobody write the stories about it."

"He—he is not . . . a vampire. . . . I think."

"You said you going to find him in his old country. Because that's where the vampires live. You said so."

"Mother, no!"

"Then why you go so much trouble finding his old country and him in it?"

"Because I want him to see what he did to me!"

I was shouting by then. Nurses ran into my room to see what was wrong. I waved them off, smiled politely.

"I have to go now, Mother. Nap time, okay?"

"You call me if you find him."

"When, not if."

The unpleasantness of the symptoms was real enough. You had them; I saw how they affected you. Now I had the symptoms. I knew from direct experience how it felt. I simultaneously understood your insanity and hated you for sharing it with me. It does drive you crazy. The internal burning along your nerves, the constant ache in your stomach, bloating in your intestines. And the damn dryness. The weakness and pain in the joints. Yes, that could be a lot of diseases, a lot of better known and more easily treated diseases. But there's one thing that's different: no test to detect it. No signs pointing to useful treatments, much less a cure.

It is a transformation. I get it. It is not a sickness you get over. It is a process that ends only when the transformation is complete. And what that transformation results in is something I fear. I feared what I would see when I found you, Stefan.

But now that I see you, you look pretty decent. Your skin is white and smooth. Healthy-looking. But you do look older than your true age—although you can move around well, like someone younger. You have some hair on your head. Your eyes are clear—a bit bloodshot, red in the night. I think I see lipstick on your lips. That's cheating. And you walk with a limp and use a cane. Pain in the joints? And missing toes. It seems you've recovered somewhat. What are you now, about sixty? But frozen at forty-five. Looking seventy but spry as a thirty-year old.

Did you find a cure? Is that why you look better? Is there some of that for me? Or am I a different case and what worked for you won't work for me?

How do I look? Like walking death, I know. Even I can smell my grave rot. My ghoulish breath. I'm dying inside and anyone can smell it on my breath. My body has shut down its immune system. Germs are partying on me and in me, and all their shit is making the stink that's ruining your beautiful hotel suite. I'm sorry. No, not sorry at all. I want you to remember this odor. I want this room to reek of death. Then you'll remember me and what you did to me, Stefan. Then you will remember everything I did to get here just to see you looking at me and hearing your heart burst—that's the only joy I can have.

Do you feel guilty? Wait, there's more.

The border crossing is not a carnival ride. Remember the airport in Chicago? That was a delightful escorted tour full of champagne and giggles compared to crossing the border. No unhealthy people can be admitted into your precious Hungarian Federation. No, I totally get it. I wouldn't let in sick people, either. Anybody who looked even a little sick, just a cold or a cough, got pulled out of line and checked closer. So you can imagine how I was treated. I definitely looked sick. But they didn't simply turn me around and put me on a train back to Germany.

I was released from that hospital with a better outlook. The fresh blood helped. I got skin treatments, too. It was like being in a spa. I bought another set of clothing and more lotions and creams. There were a lot of questions, the same questions, throughout the journey.

I arrived at the border on a slow train from Munich, stuffed with migrants heading back. Recent raids had filled the deportation trains—Germany through the Hungarian Federation to the border of Bulgaria. It was the only transportation to Budapest.

The train stopped at a processing facility. Everybody off and into holding pens. It was raining then. Eventually I got under the roof. The wait was a couple hours just to get up to the inspectors. I looked around: both the well-dressed and the ragged were treated bad. The people who showed their Hung Fed passports, though, went straight through the gate and boarded the next train to continue the journey with only a couple questions, a nod and a smile. If you're not a Hung Fed citizen, you wait. If you look sick, you go to yet another crowded holding pen . . . where you'll probably catch another disease.

A stout woman in a white lab coat examined me in front of all the other women in that pen. Most were not concerned but some watched me to see what to expect. I did not have to strip down. It was a quick check. I did not pass. Another woman led me away and took me into another room where it was warm, unlike the holding pen which was outdoors but under a roof. In fact, I think it used to be a holding pen for cattle. So many people being sent south now.

I waited, standing for a couple hours, then I got a seat for another hour's wait.

When my turn came I was escorted into the next room and told to disrobe. Three women checked me—checked absolutely everything.

Cavity search. I had a health certificate from the hospital in Germany, offered to show them. They found it in my purse, digging in it without permission. Oh, well. You found it, good. The certificate states I am healthy, have nothing contagious, even though I have skin problems. I'm undergoing treatment but nothing serious that would cause any problems for the public. Signed by two German doctors. Official.

When they allowed me to put my clothes on again, I realized that I had missed the continuing train. That was the least of my worries. I would catch the next one, or the one after that, or some other damn train to Budapest, once or twice a week. Whenever they decided I was of no threat to the Hung Fed. I kept telling them but my Hungarian is so non-existent I knew I was wasting my voice.

There is no long-story-short, Stefan. They put me in a large room with about fifty women and long metal benches. That was not enough seating so most women occupied the floor. A water cooler on one wall, toilets against the opposite wall. By toilet, I mean commodes, three of them fixed to the wall. No walls, no privacy. Like a jail cell. The room smelled awful.

"What happens next?" I asked a woman who dared smile at me.

Of course she didn't understand English.

Another woman came over, a blanket wrapped around herself. Under the blanket she seemed to be naked. Seeing my curious eyes, she opened the blanket a bit to show me her pregnant belly.

"Where are your clothes?" I asked, not caring if she understood me.

"Take," she answered in a thick accent.

"They took your clothes?"

"Take." She gestured with one hand: a tearing away motion. "Take."

Someone had literally ripped her clothes off her. Who could be so cruel? And she was pregnant. Officials had given her a blanket, at least. I looked around. Several women had blankets wrapped around them. It wasn't for warmth; it was clothing. But other women I saw, the tough-looking bitches, seemed to have plenty of extra clothes piled up like they had stolen whatever they could just to hoard them, saving them for a rainy day. Later, I saw them selling clothing to the food service women who came into the room.

"How long have you been here?" I asked the woman. I gestured to

153

my wrist like I wore a watch. She seemed old enough to know what a wristwatch was. People look at their phones for the time now, Stefan. But I lost my phone when my suitcase was stolen.

She shook her head. Holding up her hand, she wrote on her palm with the tip of her finger: **3**.

Three days? I wondered.

No, three weeks, she indicated by counting on her fingers.

My heart sank. I literally lost my strength and had to sit. I dropped on the floor, butt first, and a pain shot up through my body. A physical pain. My spirit evaporated.

Three weeks to get approved to enter a country? At the border, too! Ridiculous. And I had the visa already. But I looked sick. It's only the vampire disease; no exclusion for that, right?

No wonder nobody wants to come to your fucking Hungarian Fed. Tourism is kaput. Stay home everybody. You are not wanted here. But I wasn't a refugee from some war-ravaged land. I was not an economic migrant looking for work. I was not fleeing justice. Or injustice. I was only looking for my ex-boyfriend. I used the word *fiancé* so it sounded more serious. I wanted to call you 'bastard' but there was no reason to insult your parents. I said it was for love, I had to find you, but that was the biggest lie I ever told. Well, second biggest.

It didn't matter to them, the inspectors, or whoever made decisions about who gets in and who does not. And if you do not get in, you wait to go back. You do not just walk back through the gate into Germany. If you were even a step inside the Hung Fed, like where the holding pen is, then Germany doesn't want you. So you wait. You wait until someone who doesn't know you decides to let you on a train—if you have money or position. Or else, if you have nothing, maybe lets you walk through the gate, and you stand on the other side of the fence, where you're free but entirely on your own.

One day I had that chance. An official came into the holding room and announced amnesty for anyone wanting to go back to Germany. They had collected too many guests. I could have walked through the gate and been back in Germany but with only a fucking blanket around me. At least I would be free again. That wasn't what I wanted, though. Not me. I'm stubborn like a bad rash. No, I had my goal, my destiny, my purpose-driven hate. I had to finish it. All the way to your face, Stefan, wooden stake and hammer in my hands. So I refused the offer.

And so I waited with my blanket around me and my dying body for six more days. Then my number was called. Earlier that day, my friend, the pregnant woman with the blanket? She miscarried.

20

IT FELT LIKE GRADUATION DAY WHEN MY NUMBER WAS CALLED. I GOT UP off the concrete floor, stretched my aching back, brushed off the ants that were eating my skin, and walked awkwardly through the sitting crowd to the open door, blanket wrapped around me. I feared the door would close before I could reach it.

I smiled at the guard but she did not return a smile.

"You speak only English?" asked the officer in the inspection room, a woman with a reddish face, blonde hair in a tight bun. Her golden uniform had seen better days, needed dry cleaning. Her blue epaulets suggested some middle rank. Her English was hard to understand but I did my best because my life depended on how well our relationship proceeded.

"I'm American." I was neither proud nor ashamed, just hopeful of finally being let out of this detention facility. "I speak English. And some Korean."

She looked up from my papers. "Kor-ee-ah?"

"Yes. *Annyeonghaseyo.*" I grinned with effort. "It means 'hello'. My mother is Korean."

Then I thought she might think I was really Korean, not American. The Hung Fed hated people from other Western nations, I'd heard. From Asia and Africa even more.

"She taught me." Better to say only one of my parents was Korean. I wanted to be sure she believed I was an American. But I need not have worried.

"No very many Kor-ee-antz come dis vay."

"I believe it."

"No many Amer-ee-kantz."

"Really?"

She ignored my remark. I was trying to be friendly, to show I didn't blame them for the treatment I got in the holding room. I just wanted to get on with my trip.

"Age?"

"I am forty-five."

She stared at me, not believing. I'm sure I looked older in my poor condition. I hadn't seen myself in a mirror for a few weeks. I could pass for fifty on a good day.

"It's true. Forty-five."

"Family?"

"Only me on this trip. My parents and brother are in America."

"Child?"

My first thought was the woman who miscarried in that holding room. Two other women had kicked her during the night, trying to steal her blanket, which was all she had. Then I realized this official was asking about my children. I thought a sympathetic answer would be a good sob story, a poor mother separated from her child, so I said: "He is in America."

She nodded as she wrote on the forms, checking boxes. She applied a stamp here and there, turning the pages. The stamp left a bold, red square framing the shield-and-crossed-spears logo of the immigration department. The seal of approval.

She asked more questions and finally turned to a new page.

"Reason come in Hungarian Federation?"

Nodding and forcing a smile, I gathered my thoughts. I had been practicing my speech for several days until I had the perfect statement. I had memorized all 240 words. I was a broadcast journalist in another life; I could speak clearly and persuasively. No matter how I had been *abused* I was going to get through this interview and be on my way to Budapest.

"I wish to enter the Hungarian Federation," I began, pausing for a breath, "to find someone very important to me: my fiancé. He was—"

Before I could say one more word, the door flung open and another woman officer called to dear comrade at the desk, alerting her about a disturbance. There was fighting in the holding room. I had learned the word for 'fighting': *küzdelem.*

She jumped up and rushed out the door.

I sat there, listening to shouting and the noises of violence. I stared at the desk. I saw my papers laying there. I noticed the stamp. And the ink pad. Suddenly I was filled with terrifying energy. My hand moved. I pulled it back. My hand leaped again. My hand landed on the desk, then on top of my papers. There it was: my hand grabbing the stamp, hitting the ink pad, pressing the stamp to the big blank square on the last page. And back again.

It was just a formality, right? She was stamping the other pages with no hesitation. I was done, ready to go.

Then the papers were in my hands. One hand grasping the blanket, holding it closed around me, the other hand taking my papers.

And then I was standing, walking out of the room, holding out my papers like a movie ticket. I stepped lightly down the corridor, barefoot against the cold concrete. Then I realized I couldn't simply run out, not with only a blanket. Where would I go?

Another woman in uniform appeared out of nowhere. She halted me, took the papers from my hand, looked them over. She gave me a stern nod and led me down the corridor. A door opened and she waved me into the room.

It was a kind of cataloguing room. The woman dutifully checked the papers again, then searched for the right numbered bin that held my belongings. She handed the small bin to me and I gathered up my shoes and my purse and everything that had been in it, including the folded Euro bills and credit cards. I was really surprised: my wallet looked intact. The photo of you and me in the Barnes & Noble bookstore at Quail Springs Mall was still there. You know, back in the days when we both were so good-looking.

I was quickly shown to another room, like it was close to her lunch break. The room was filled with discarded clothing, collected into large boxes. I helped myself to the pants and shirts, one each. I reached for socks—she nodded they were okay—and almost accepted a pair of panties that appeared clean. I'd been wearing my one and only pair for what seemed ages. Of course, I had stopped having my period years ago when the transformation started. Can't afford to lose blood when you're becoming a vampire, right?

She waved me off, indicating I had gotten my quota. It was cold outside, so I gestured like I was shivering to beg for an outer garment. She pointed to a box in the corner. I didn't see any coats there. But I went over and pulled out a long, black cloak. A cape with a hood. Little Miss Riding Hood. That was me. Perfect for hiding my ugly face from the world. It was similar to wearing that blanket but with a cowl to shield my face.

Then she led me outside. I waited only a minute before a man from the train parked on the tracks there waved me aboard. He climbed on after me. The train began to move immediately. I stepped inside the car, squeezing between people to sit on one of the hard benches. They begrudgingly allowed me space. I felt like I had lost 10 pounds. I had not eaten a good meal for weeks. All around me I saw sad faces full of hardship. I wondered how long they had waited before being allowed into the Hungarian Federation.

I was the last person to board. They would never wait for just one person, especially not some quarantined sickly individual. Somehow your god liked me. So I was lucky. I was damn lucky, Stefan. And you didn't even know I was coming for you.

෨

Abused. Did I mention that? I was wearing only a fucking blanket when they let me into your fucking country. Is that the way you guys treat women? Women with a proper visa? Okay, I'll allow for some mix-up, some pure bad luck, a case of overreach, bias, prejudice, ethnic hatred, whatever. Things can happen in a foreign country. I suppose it could have been a lot worse. Who knows? I could have been raped or killed. Who would ever know? Who would report what happened? I'm lucky. Probably my horrible appearance kept potential attackers away from me. Nobody wanted to touch me.

When I entered that holding room I wore my only set of clothes:

shirt, pants, socks. I stopped wearing bras when the transformation made my skin irritable. I needed clothes, though, dirty as they were, wearing them for several days. I needed to cover my dry patches of skin. I needed to cover the red blotches, the brown crusty spots, the flaking, the boils, so they wouldn't think I was a walking bag of disease and send me to an even worse place.

One night I was huddled in my corner with my friend, Wilda, the one who was pregnant. She was beside me, her body pressed against mine, half for protection and half for warmth. To pass the time, I had been teaching her English and she was teaching me German, although I think she was actually from Prague. We should have been learning Hungarian, I know, but neither of us knew it.

Suddenly, hands grabbed my feet, pulling me out straight. Hands yanked at my cuffs as other hands pulled the snap loose and ripped the zipper down. In three seconds my slacks were jerked off me, down my legs, over my feet.

I sat up and grabbed at my pants, but a woman pushed me down with her foot as the pants went into the air. The two women assaulting me laughed. One reached out and ripped my shirt open, the buttons flying. She grabbed at my shirt collar. Then she threw me down on my belly and ripped the shirt off my arms, tearing one sleeve away. In a flash, I was on the concrete floor with only a shirt sleeve, plus my dirty panty.

Wilda fought with them, trying to grab back my clothes from the stronger women. They kicked at her but missed her pregnant belly.

Seeing me shivering on the floor, Wilda shook her head and shared her blanket with me. In the half-dark of the room, she could not see how ugly my skin was. She wrapped her arm around me and held me tight, her big belly against my back, her blanket pulled over us.

We complained to the guards but all they did was give me my own blanket. It was ragged and had holes in it, probably some fleas, too, but it was either that or nothing. My clothes were somewhere in the room, in someone's pile. I couldn't see clearly who attacked me, but I could guess. The gang of women in the center of the room.

CR

Someone was talking angrily about the Hungarian Federation one day. That woman and a couple others sitting with her got into a heated discussion about the government leaders, how they were all *vampires*. My ears perked up. One woman got too loud. She said she heard there were attacks by vampires in Budapest and better to wear garlic around your neck. Another said government leaders were vampires. Suddenly the doors opened and guards rushed in and grabbed them. We never saw them again.

So I eventually got out—or in. Into your country, the glorious land of free Hungarians, plus Croats, Serbs, Slovenians, Slovaks, Czechs, Romanians, some Austrians, and anyone else who decided to flee the decline of the West for a sanctuary where vampires could run free. Is that it? Your home, Stefan? Do vampires really run the city? Are you in charge of this now?

I arrived by train wearing the one set of clothes they gave me, and a cloak that made me look dark and mysterious. I had my boots back that they took when I was put in the holding room. With my bad skin worsening during my stay at the Border Hotel, I needed lotion quick. I had the money I'd brought, thank goodness, so I shopped and I found a youth hostel to bed down in.

It was no longer a hostel, just a run-down B&B. We used hostels when I toured Europe with my college friends. Not enough business now to keep them open for young travelers. There were no more young travelers. It was too dangerous, too much hassle. For a cheap price I could share a room with three other people. Shower and toilet down the hallway. The woman at the front desk almost did not let me in at first glance, but I assured her I was healthy enough. I showed my health certificate.

"No foreign people can enter Hungarian Federation if they got any disease," she intoned in English like I had never heard it before. Maybe it was something everyone was required to memorize. Everyone was telling me that. I saw it on signs in restaurant windows.

My papers were stamped. I showed them to the woman. She read them carefully, probably more for her amusement than checking my status. Then she gave me a key card and waved me off.

I had the room to myself the first two nights. Like I said, not so much business. Especially in winter. Then the snow came. A few older travelers, looking for a cheap overnight space, came and went.

Each day in Budapest I went from bank to bank, just taking a look, hoping I could get information about you. I dared ask for you by name: Stefan Székely. As a reporter I learned to read people; I can guess from their facial expressions and body language if they are hiding the truth. Many of the people I talked with—in English, of course—seemed to recognize the name but wouldn't say anything more. If so many knew your name, I felt confident you were here. So I kept looking, no matter the pain my body was blessed with.

Finally one day I was standing in the lobby of one bank, the mighty MAGYAR FEJLESZTÉSI, of course, but in their new location east of the Hungarian Federation headquarters building. Next to that children's amusement park with all the miniature rides. I stood in line, staring out the windows, watching the children play.

I was next in line to conduct my business, looking dreadful but not caring a damn—and in you walked, all prim and proper, an aristocratic gentleman, with your dark hat and your cane, dressed all in black with that red silk tie. Of course I couldn't be sure it was you. I expected a decrepit creature, a gutter snake, a predator of women, a bloody mess. But you, this debonair figure, were the closest I had seen in Budapest.

So I followed you—that figure, whoever he was. I followed you for weeks, learning your patterns, catching glimpses, studying. I observed your comings and goings, your midnight strolls, your victims. I could have turned you in to the police, yet I wanted to deal with you myself. So I stalked you. Until I was sure it was you.

At the bombing in the government plaza, where you sucked that wounded man dry, I was certain that vampire was you. Then I knew who you were, who you had become. I was ready to confront you— even before I could buy a wooden stake and a hammer. In fact, I still don't have them.

Now it's your turn to be lucky, Stefan.

I may die before I can kill you.

21

PENNY LAY IN A DEEP SLEEP, THE KIND THAT COVERS US WHEN WE ARE empty—or when we have feasted. I watched her petite figure stretched out on the bed, a child's body ravaged by disease, a broken doll. The absence of clothing is more comfortable; the friction of fabric irritates the skin, causing chafing. A covering of nitrogen-rich soil helps the skin's tone best yet I couldn't order such a thing to be brought up to a penthouse suite without certain questions having to be dismissed. The benefit would only be temporary anyway.

The unit of Type A helped to bring back her color. Yet, in the end, her story, told over three days, was exhausting for her. She gave me leave to do my business and return for her. She gave me a shopping list. Besides items such as cosmetics and lotions, the list included a wooden stake and a suitable hammer. For her, my smile was sincere: that method of death is only legend. Animation needs the head, the brain. If you wish to halt animation, the head must be separated from the body. The stake is merely symbolic. Many have carried on, even weakly, with splinters in the chest. But I didn't have the *heart* to tell her the truth—

(My heart does not actually beat; it clicks rather like a clock—a clock that needs rewinding.)

I cannot fathom my existence now, not with this woman dying on my bed. The sight of her is horrible, like she has pulled herself out of a grave and wiped away the dirt. Yet the death mask—indeed, the death body cast—remains. She is dying; that is plain to see. Yet I cannot look away from her, this woman I loved. I called her my Beloved. I wanted to marry her, just to see her every day, to touch her when we were close, to lay with her in the night and know I was not alone.

Now she is here, yet I feel even more alone. Responsible for her, for the disease that runs through her like machines harvesting her life one cell at a time. My gut is a knot. My heart is compressed like a deflated ball. My head is so twisted around I cannot think straight. I must do something, however.

I stare at her naked form, covered in dry patches, red blotches, scars, and boils. And smelly blue-green fungus.

What have I done?

There must be something medical that could save her, restore her, even reduce the disease in her. Must be some way to halt the affliction, my family curse, in her. She is not of my family. I gave her this disease, some variant of it. Just as I did to Leslie years ago. I never knew that would happen.

When the affliction came to me, I knew it was genetic; my parents suffered from it. My whole family line seemed to get it. So why did they keep passing it on to another generation? Youthful love wins out over common sense.

What is the evolutionary benefit of this kind of creature? Was the human form only a kind of chrysalis, an interim stage before our final flowering as monsters?

Staring at Penny, unconscious on the bed, I cannot help but think of Alma, who also had been sick and dying on a bed in Zagreb. I had thought it was a kind of blood poisoning. I took her to the hospital. I told the doctors what it was, what to look for, what tests to run. And I was correct. Yet she did not improve.

I turned to my friend God, though we had a 'frenemy' relationship back then, pretending to be on the same side while forever plotting pranks.

I was serious when I demanded that God fix her, make her whole again, back like she was before she met me. I made a deal with God for that. I heard His words clearly. When I died, He said: "Done." The deal was done. I was done.

Had I used up all my favors from God?

I wondered.

What could He possibly want in exchange for healing this person named Penny Park? She does not deserve this fate, or anything that has happened to her to bring her to my door. Let her go. Let her rise whole again. Happy and whole, like she never met me.

Like you did for Alma Jónás. Anything. I will do anything, whatever you demand. Just save Penny . . . my Beloved.

∞

"You are the strongest person I know," I whispered into Penny's ear. I straightened the few strands of black hair on her head. "And I'm so sorry for all that you've gone through. I really had no way of knowing another person could face the affliction from me. For all I knew, it was a hundred percent genetic." She seemed to be asleep. "Then again, I did try to hide away. I avoided you. I told you how hideous I was, yet you came to me. We came together for love. I did not want to share this disease, this transformation, with you—with the world."

Because her eyelids had withered away, along with her eyebrows, I had lain a soft cloth over her eyes to block even the faint line of light leaking in between the curtains. For those who have transformed like me, we can be awake for days. We grow weak gradually and need to feed. Then we may sleep for days, more a coma than sleep. We have no dreams. For Penny's type of suffering, she remained weak but taking in some blood helped her regain strength. She was in the sleep phase now, unconscious for almost two days, her skin cold, dry, blotchy and pungent. Like death.

We are a decrepit bunch of aberrants. I wanted to die, to be away from everything, but I could not die. So I followed my parents' clever-by-half plan and stayed away from everything real as best I could for fourteen years, hiding in the villa—which is a kind of death. The only fate worse than death is spending eternity with your dead parents. Yet I overcame even that. I struck out on my own, made it to some kind of a success, at least a narcissistic, self-indulgent kind of success where I focus only on my own needs, my own pleasures. Some would say that is success: never having to go daily to a job, to labor for many hours each day, to always get whatever you want. Yet at what cost? I had sat in several drawing rooms during the past few months, pondering such questions as I observed the high society rituals with amusement—

I made a deal with God to save Alma, who was just an Hungarian Goth girl I happened to meet. She helped me when she didn't have to, and I thanked her with some money. She thanked me with a moment of sex—and she began to die.

Dramatic pause.

And Penny before her.

And Leslie before her, the same.

So this affliction is contagious. Sex with a vampire makes you also a vampire. Or, at least, you *look* like a vampire while on your descending path to the abyss. It is not enough to simply cease having sex. It does not give me a milligram of pleasure, anyway. It's purely mechanical. Everything works as it should, certainly, except the nerves which bring euphoria, which is the drug that makes us want it so often, especially in our youth. In the village, the women I would meet to exchange blood for sex never suspected I gained no enjoyment from it. Their blood was what I needed.

Sex is no longer the problem. It is the affliction that rages through my Beloved—

She *is* my Beloved, as much now as ever before!

I loved her so much, yet I wounded her. I condemned her to a horrible death. For nothing. There never was malice in my thoughts or deeds, yet she is more the victim of this curse than me. I had no choice in my parents, the family line, or the cursed chromosomes we pass on. Yet I did have a choice—

If I had known what would happen . . . .

Now it is my ultimate responsibility to help her. Dammit, to undo this curse! I must do something to save her! And I do not even care if she fulfills her promise to drive a wooden stake through my heart. She could do it today, if that would undo what I've done. It will not stop my animation, yet if it brings any joy to her, I freely tear open my shirt and hold forth my chest for her weapons.

଺

Perhaps God is only in my head, like a petite muse, or the notorious humoculous. A voice which I myself create. People talk to themselves all the time. They speak as though they are actually two persons—dual personæ. I do not mean a kind of schizophrenia. Normal people ask and answer themselves and none think lesser of them. It does help to sort out the important ideas from the chaff swirling in the background. However, back through the ages, is this dual-personæ the origin of God? The prophet, the one guy in the tribe who has the dual-personæ: he thinks it is the deity who speaks to him. He convinces everyone that this deity makes public service announcements only through his voice. Is that possible? Today, with trillions of dollars' worth of very complex communication technology, people still can find someone claiming to be a channel for a deity's messages. Or is that just the dual-personæ talking, one side to the other side, believing each is a separate entity instead of two sides of the same microphone?

So if I hear the voice of God, is it God or is it just me? I heard His voice quite clearly in the middle of the night when He finally agreed to our deal: my life for Alma's life. Me off to the dead, she back to life. I accepted. It could not have been a dual-personæ situation because I saw immediate results. I did not do that; I was not there to do anything for Alma. Only God could have lifted his gnarly finger and waved her healed. Not me, not my inner voice or any trickster phantom in my third eye. I could blame only one.

As for me, I was already dying. Nothing I had tried to stave off the progression worked for long. And it returned ever quicker and more virulent each time. I simply gave up in the end. The final experiment failed. I suppose I knew it would fail, yet I went ahead anyway. Just to get the death over with. Was that it? That doesn't seem like me. I'm a practical person—used to be.

If there is no God, then who did I give myself up to?

If there is a god named God or any other pseudonym, rocking the book covers in different bookstores, then it all could work. All I should have to do is beg for Penny's life. I beseech the deity to alleviate her suffering. I offer something of value in exchange for that service. But I have nothing left to give; I have given my life already. One and done. I cannot go to the well too often. Or ever again. Mathematics suck. And so do vampires (laugh, snicker). What else can I do? Tell jokes, go on a comedy tour? Raise money for research? The reality is too serious.

I have a spa resort needing renovation. I could offer that. Perhaps that would be enough. It is worth something. I could turn it into a summer camp for religious kids.

Who am I kidding? God is not kid-able.

I close my eyes and fall softly beside my Beloved on the wide bed. Like her, I am free of the irritation of clothing upon my skin. We make such an ugly couple now. Indeed, the mirror on the ceiling over the bed, intended for voyeurism, is now a testament to our abuse, though we barely make any mark upon its glassy surface. We do not stand before mirrors and gaze upon the totality of our lives as we used to do, planning our lives, dreaming. The dreams of a vampire are red: vast sheets of red, endless red, oceans of red, spilling into red, washing over red and flooding us with ever more red. Until we awaken days later.

Nights later.

It is time, I can feel in my gut, in my heart. I must feed.

I will feed for her, for my Beloved.

If I cannot maintain myself, how can I care for her? How will I find a solution to saving her?

I call my private physician, Dr. Szabó, and order another supply. Two days, he tells me. I agree; it is the best he can do accommodating me. I can only hope my Beloved sleeps until then. Without stepping off the edge into the abyss.

I dress and go out as the dastardly sunset finally fades to black. Now I have until sunrise to meet my needs.

Follow me, God. Watch me. See how low I stoop for the love of my life. Is this what you want to see? Is this your entertainment? Save her, please. Save her from me.

22

THE STORES HAVE NOT YET CLOSED AT THIS EVENING HOUR. I RIDE THE monorail east to the edge of the city, through District XVII, almost to Pécel, where the large box stores are. It is the newest development. There is little need for an automobile in the city now; I purchased mine chiefly so I could drive to Sárvár. However, I must wait for additions I ordered to be installed. Another week, they said.

I get out of the monorail station and, behold, there is the shopping experience I've always dreamed of: the wholesale hardware complex. It spreads along the highway like a cancer growth.

Entering, I blink at the bright lights, pulling lower the brim of my Homburg.

"Where might I find the wooden stakes?" I ask the first store clerk I encounter, speaking in standard Hungarian.

"You want to make a fence?"

I'm not sure I understand him. I explain further.

"It is garden department. People use them for gardens."

"Of course they do," I respond. What else could I be thinking?

He points to a back corner, tells me the aisle number.

I give a wry grin, tipping the edge of my brim in thanks. Gardening department. That would make sense.

Curious eyes follow me as I pass through the store: this dark, mysterious figure still wearing his wide-brimmed hat indoors. You do not want to see my head, folks. Nor my face. Believe me. The veins are dark, like a spider's web, and some of them redden when I think evil thoughts. It is part of the curse.

And there they are, at the end of the aisle. Four bins hold different sizes. Pine. Very nice. The 20 cm stakes seem the right size. I hold one up to my chest. Yes, enough length to grab hold with one hand while using the hammer with the other hand. When the act is done, half its length should be enough to break through the sternum and pierce the heart with enough of a handhold remaining. As the designers likely considered. I take one, then return it to the bin. Too many splinters. I do not wish my Beloved to hurt her delicate hand while holding it. I choose another. Then another.

"Can you smooth the edges?" I ask a handyman wearing a store apron. He nods without a smile. His shift is almost done, I sense. His heart beats quicker, but irregularly. There's a skip I hear when I stand close. I stare at him as he works: he is my age, yet alive. Perhaps not for long. See a doctor soon. I send my thought to him. And lay off the fatty meats.

He runs the piece of wood through a sanding machine, gives the smooth, shiny wood to me. He asks if I am satisfied. I nod, accepting the stake. It seems perfect.

"You need only one?" he asks, pointing back to the bin.

"Yes, if it is the right one."

He gives me a queer look, like my answer is not clear. Yet I spoke correctly: '*Ha ez az egyik legjobb.*' I suppose it isn't, but that kind of understanding is really between a vampire and his deity.

I stalk away, exit the aisle, head for another aisle to find the right kind of hammer.

In too many films the hammer is a rubber mallet. That seems the most practical. You do not want the hammer to split the wooden stake. A metal headed hammer would do that. The ball-peen hammer also is unsuitable. So I select the rubber mallet as my hammer of choice, one that is not too heavy for my Beloved to wield.

I head to the cashier stations, choosing the live person over the scanning machines. The woman there wears a scarf around her neck but I can still see the rough ends of two scars uncovered by the scarf. Eyeing my purchases, a wooden stake and a rubber mallet, she gives a smirk like she knows what they are used for.

"Lot of talk about vampires in the city," she says to me, her voice low. "I don't blame people for keeping ready."

I pull the brim of my hat down a bit to shade my face.

"Only pathetic rumors," I say.

ଓ

They stand as one to block my route. Again. We know each other well, it seems. The night is too familiar, the blood too red. Yet they harry me all the same. Can we not keep the streets free for passage?

"Back for more?" the pudgy one in the middle calls out. He is the one who held my right arm the first time we met in the empty streets of this commercial district. A chubby vampire is rare. I think his name is György—not that it matters.

"More of what?" I reply quietly, eager to continue to my destination with a minimum of annoyance. I have important duties to perform.

"More midnight fun," the oaf laughs.

"You don't speak Hungarian any longer?" I ask, first in Hungarian, which draws a blank face, then in English.

"More Englishmen comin' every day to the Hungarian homeland."

"Is that so?" I study them. What trouble will they instigate tonight? I have better plans. "I hadn't noticed. It's not my area of expertise."

"Smart ass, ain'tcha?" It is the one on the left addressing me. He pretends to know me well. Has a scar across his forehead, and no ears.

"Hungary is the white homeland now!"

"I presumed it was the homeland of the Magyar."

"The what?"

"Magyar. Also known as the Huns. Hence the name Hungary. You did attend some school, didn't you?"

"Yeah, 'course—"

"This is our country now! All the ragtags can keep out!"

"I doubt the Huns are exactly your kind of people. We came from central Asia originally. But then so did a lot of people in Europe."

"You got white skin, is all."

"Granted, though that may be some of my vampirism showing."

"Yeah, no more. Europe for the Europeans!"

"Who exactly is that these days? How many generations must you prove born on this continent to stake your claim? Pardon the pun. And how far east do you maintain is *your* land? All the way to the Urals?"

"The what?"

"Hah! He said 'urinal'."

"The Ural mountains. They run north and south, dividing Russia from Siberia. It has been the traditional boundary between Europe and Asia for a long time. At least for cartographers."

"Car-who?"

"Mapmakers."

"We don't need no maps here! We run this city."

A cynical laugh would have been appropriate but I yielded. "Then we all must surely be lost."

I appear to be joking. The four of them share their amusement.

"Where is your esteemed leader?" I ask to break up their noise. Everything echoes through these streets at night. I refer to the tall man who did all the talking that night when I first met these 'others'. "Lord Baltimore . . . ?"

"His name is Balthazar, mind you."

"Baltimore sounds better. More Marylandish."

"Youz best not say that!"

It is easy to imagine the rest; no need to bore. An escalation of jibes and insults, threats and suggestions about my mother's bed partners. It will end the same. We scuffle.

Such a pity they see no other option for a discussion of our mutual differences. There is shoving, an eager hand upon a resistant shoulder, as usual, and the awkward backwards motion. It is actually beautiful the ways a pre-maturely stiff body can move. Our vampire eyes catch the action in wonderfully translucent panoramas of rainbow hues. If only cameras could record it: the way a cane hiding a sword can come to life. The way a silver-lacquered blade can slash, the sharp edge not only cutting a fair mark but adding insult to injury with the burning touch of the silver upon the skin of these young vagabonds who fancy themselves true keepers of the blood.

A hand drops onto the pavement and everyone stops. Yes, young hooligans, it's all fun and games until someone loses a hand.

"He took off me hand!" growls the uglier one. There is no blood but the appendage lays in the filthy gutter like a rubber duckie. He stoops to retrieve it. "You bloody cunt!"

He starts at me and I lift the blade, high parry *deux*.

"I suggested earlier that you lads unhand me. Do you recall? Now I have unhanded you."

The lout is boiling with rage but his friends hold him back.

"Find a stitcher and reattach it. Good as new."

I switch my blade back and forth, the sign of a master fencer—well, perhaps thirty years ago. It is enough of a show for them. I do appear dashing!

During the scuffle, they knocked from my hand the crinkled sack I was carrying. The wooden stake tore through the paper. The hammer fell out with a thud on the pavement.

"What is that?" they all seem to demand at once.

"Some tools," I reply, returning the blade to its sheath, their lesson learned.

They hold their wounds, watching the cuts sizzle, seeing the smoke drift into the spring air. The cuts do not draw blood. The silver hurts, however. Now they are too surprised by my odd purchase to focus on anything else.

"I have need of these items," I speak firmly.

"You can't go round carrying a stake and hammer. It's against the rules."

"It is a private matter," I say, though I owe them no explanation.

"Private? You got no rights to private matters. Balthazar wants to see you." The British accent is delightful.

"Ain't gone be for nottin good," the second vagabond explains like an agèd college professor.

"For what matter?" I dare ask, assuming they can dig out an answer from idled brains.

"Balthazar will tell you when you get there."

"Be there tomorrow night."

"Yeah, at midnight."

I hold up my cane, sword sheathed, resting it against my shoulder.

"And where exactly should 'there' be?"

"We gonna take youz there," says stumpy.

"So you better be here, right here, right this place—"

"Tomorrow night, don't forget."

"Don't forget or miss or you gonna be sorry."

"I pass through this intersection on most nights. If Lord Baltimore wishes to have a conversation, I am ready to exchange words."

"Balthazar!" the ugliest one demands.

"Whatever his name might be, I have more pressing matters with which to deal now. Be off and tend to that hand."

My feint unsettles the oaf and he lunges at me with his attached hand, knocking me to a knee. He curses at me as his friends try to quiet him. He won't have any of it. He breaks from their grasp as I rise to my feet, unsheathing the blade.

"Watch out!" cries one as another shouts "He got the blade again!"

The oaf lurches, grabs my coat lapel, tears it downward. Buttons pop. He grabs my red silk tie, chokes me. I kick upward with my knee and he backs away. When I have some space, I pull the blade free and swing it as hard as I can.

I hear the cursing before I see the cause of their foul words. I stand back, loosening the necktie that had been pulled too tight. Then I gaze down at the ugly, pudgy face, eyes still open, rolling back and forth on the pavement at the feet of these hooligans. Poor György.

"Sorry about that."

And I am genuinely sorry. Cutting off a head is a sure way of killing a vampire. Works every time. However, it breaks a code. It sets things in motion that cannot be stopped.

They state the obvious: I cut off his head. What follows are curses, complaints, threats to tell on me. I've heard it all before—in my school days. They swear Baltimore will hear of this. And this incident will come to the attention of their so-called supreme leader, someone they call Azov—*Lord* Azov, if I heard them clearly.

"I trust you three can clean this up before sunrise?"

They are too stunned to respond. Blank faces, gaping mouths.

I reach up and tip my hat, bidding them a goodnight.

"You can't just kill people on the street, you know!" one calls after me as I walk away.

"He is not people," I shout, not looking back, "he is vampire."
"You still can't go around killing!"
I laugh; it echoes through the streets.
"He was dead already."

23

"I THOUGHT YOU LEFT ME," SAYS PENNY, LITTLE MORE THAN A WHISPER, when I enter the bedroom of my penthouse suite, cane in one hand and the sack from the hardware store in the other.

"No, I'll never leave you again."

I can barely hear her: "Yes, you will."

Her eyes burn through the darkness, a faint red glow that leads me straight to the bed.

I slip off my coat and set down my hat. I drop the sack on the foot of the bed, near her shriveled feet. I sit beside her, lean over her. The sensations of another life flood me. Her dark eyes meet mine, the red of hers matching the red of mine. I can finally see her soul. And she can see where my soul used to be.

"I brought you a gift," I say with a twisted grin.

I reach for the sack, pull out the wooden stake.

"You did it," she mumbles. "You really did it."

I show her the hammer. "It's a set."

She opens her mouth to speak, half her teeth gone, tongue coated in something gray. Her throat is deep red, streaked with white strings of mucus. It is not a kissable mouth, nor a kissable moment. And yet, it is the only thing to do. She reaches for me, pulls my head down and our lips meet. Mine are full, close to normal; hers have almost withered away, leaving her gums and teeth exposed even when her mouth is what we would call closed. It still counts.

"You do love me," she moans when our kiss ends.

I nod, a silent confirmation of our present state of affairs.

"I will have my private physician see what he can do. He is coming soon, bringing more blood."

She thanks me, wants to close her eyes but cannot. Gesturing at the cloth that has fallen to the carpet, I retrieve it, place it over her eyes. Her hand takes mine, tries to squeeze it, yet her grip is so weak. Her hands and fingers are just bones, papery skin, veins red beneath. Soon there will be no pulse.

"I had a dream," she says, "a dream about you and me. We were in a meadow, like they do in a movie. Just running though the grass, hand in hand, smiling at each other. And the sky was so blue, cloudless and blue, so bright. It was a perfect day."

"It sounds wonderful."

"I want another day like that. Just one. Then I could remember that in my final moment."

"We had a day like that, didn't we? Long ago . . . ."

"Long ago doesn't count."

It was difficult to watch her mouth move to speak. Her words are jostled by the lack of lips. Collected spittle disturbs her words.

"There will be an end to this." I do not know what I mean by those words, both as I say them and after as they chime in my head. I think I mean that her pain will end. Yet I hope I mean that I will find a way to save her, too. There is not much time remaining—

The sunrise hits the curtains and we both look away.

"When you regain your strength . . . ." I must pause. My voice is too dry and scratchy. "Then I will give you what you have wished for, my Beloved. When you are strong enough to wield that hammer and the stake . . . ."

"Thank you." Her voice is an echo, fading in a canyon far away.

I nod several times, counting the slow pulses in her hand. One . . . two . . . three . . . . Snails crawl faster.

"He will be here soon."

I give her hand a squeeze.

CR

The burly man with the massive black moustache bulls through the doors as I rise from the bed to greet him. He carries a black medical bag and a small plastic cooler. The darkness of the room momentarily halts him.

"I come quick as I could," Dr. Szabó says in his gravelly bass.

"Thank you."

"Zere is protests again in government plaza," he says with a shake of his head. "Police block many streets."

"I'm glad you got through." I wave toward the bed. "Please . . . ."

He knows what to do. There is nothing he hasn't seen in his career, which is the reason I enlisted his aid. He knows my unique problems. He doesn't ask awkward questions, only does what is necessary and accepts payment for his services. He also knows English.

"How long?" he asks, staring down at my Beloved.

"Since what?" I ask, uncertain what he means.

"Since death." He gives me a hard glare.

"She's not dead. Not yet—I hope. That's the reason I called you."

He checks for a pulse, wrist then throat, waits for a breath from her nose. He straightens up.

"I thought zis is one of your . . . dinner guests."

"No . . . hah, not that. I never would bring such a person here."

"I see many such persons in my work."

"I'm not like those other . . . vampires."

He starts to laugh, realizes the seriousness of this house call and refocuses. He wrinkles his nose at the death stench.

I stand aside as he gathers his instruments and sets up an IV, the bag of fluid taken from the cooler. The other bag is a unit of Type A blood. He begins checking her from top to bottom.

"She will die within the hour," he grumbles after a few minutes.

My head is shaking before I can understand his words.

"No," I blurt. "Save her. Please."

He shakes his head, scratches his chin. "Zere is not much can be done now. We are too late."

"There must be something! You have to do something. How about a transfusion? Doctors keep people alive all the time, don't they?"

"Yes, sometimes. I must take her to hospital for zose procedures."

He stares at me, perhaps awaiting my permission.

"She is here legally," I say to answer the first question in his eyes, then the second: "She has the affliction."

"Yes, I see. All ze classic marks of ze disease." He looks back over his shoulder as though seeing what might be left in his medical bag. "I did not bring enough blood for transfusion. She needs to go hospital. You want me call ambulance?"

"An ambulance?"

"Yes." He waits. "Zere will be publicity."

"I know, I know . . . . But if it saves her life . . . ."

"Decide, Mister Székely."

The next heartbeat feels a year away. Then I nod and Szabó's thick fingers are tapping on the tablet. He speaks loudly into the tablet's graphical microphone, its blue colors flickering to match his voice, as he requests an ambulance.

"You should clean zis place," he tells me when he ends the call with a loud tap of his finger on the tablet. "Police will want to look. Can you be sure nothing is out of order?"

"Yes, everything is fine. I don't do anything illegal."

"Not here, perhaps." He narrows his eyes. "In ze city? Ze streets at night? Zere is talk." He glances at the bed where my Beloved rests. "You pay for my services. Now I give you ze advice for free: you are too outstanding. A mysterious person, yes—easy to spot in crowd or alone. And always a body with some marks nearby."

I step back. "It's a coincidence."

"Zere was a body last night. Without a head."

"I told them to clean it up," I mutter, but Szabó hears me.

"So, was you?"

I grimace. My hands wave of their own accord, as though they are re-enacting the scene. "I was attacked. I had to defend myself."

Dr. Szabó goes to the bed, prepares the body for removal, wrapping the sheet around her.

"Zis," he says, lifting the body in his arms, "will end you. Scandals are not my property. After zis incident, let you and I be done. I will see to her care at hospital but I won't be further involved."

"I understand. But I continue to rely on your discretion."

"*Persze*. Must maintain reputation."

We descend in the private elevator and meet the medics pulling the gurney through the lobby. The entire hotel staff seems to be there to see the event. I realize I am not fully dressed for public display. The stares burn like the sunrise. I raise my hand to block their view as I follow Szabó to the ambulance, down in the underground garage in keeping with privacy concerns. I climb inside to ride with my Beloved and we are whisked away to the hospital.

I follow the emergency staff that meets us—as far as I can, until they close the doors and tell me to wait.

Dr. Szabó followed in his Audi coupe. He finds me in the waiting room. I see his hand in front of my face before I notice he is there. In his hand is a mask similar to what I used fourteen years ago to get across Europe without drawing attention.

I gaze up at him, then accept it.

"You don't look so good, so . . . ."

"Thanks."

I get up and he hands me the sports bag he carries just for me, in case he must meet me somewhere to save me. In the bag along with medical and cosmetic supplies, is the spirit gum that will affix my mask to my face, saving me from embarrassment. I am without my longcoat and Homburg, however, left in my suite, but there is a black ski cap in my emergency bag. I pull it over my nearly hairless scalp.

"So you have everything now, Mister Székely."

I nod like I have just heard my sentence.

"So I leave you now." He takes a step and halts, like he wishes he could stay but has other appointments. "Good luck."

His footsteps slap the tiles as he departs.

Hours later a nurse gets me, takes me to a room where I have more privacy. A doctor visits me briefly just to confirm a few medical details. Then an administrator arrives to confirm the financial details. Papers to be completed. I ask if they can wait until I know the results.

"You still must pay, no matter the result," he intones in Hungarian.

"I have always paid," I retort in Hungarian. It sounds rougher than saying it in English. "I pay and I pay and I pay . . . ."

He leaves the papers on the seat next to me.

More hours.

God, it's me. Again. You know what I'm going to ask so can we cut to the chase and just get it over with? Save her. Just save this woman for her own sake. She has never done anything wrong, evil, or sinful. Her only weakness was letting me into her life. People make mistakes. Let her off the hook. Let her return to life. And I will do whatever you will have me do. You hear me, God? I thought we were friends. We did a deal fourteen years ago. Can't we do one more?

∽

There will come a time when you will do me a great favor, but until that time, you must do one small thing. You will think it insignificant among the explosions of stars and the incessant churling of crickets, yet it is necessary in order to close a door that must be closed. Will you do this act for me, Stefan? If you will, I will see what can be done for your Beloved.

I awake with a start, realizing I had fallen asleep on the floor, my cheek against the carpet, some lint tickling my nose. I had slipped off the chair in the waiting room. No one thought to touch me, awaken me, to get me up onto the chair again.

In my head were a string of words. I had to remember them. They were Hungarian, strangely enough, yet as soon as I heard them my mind automatically translated them into English. And that voice . . . it was unique: a vivid combination of a famous actor's bass rumble, an elephant's trumpet, and hummingbird's song. I cannot forget the tone of that voice, nor the words.

"Am I in a movie?" I mutter, picking myself off the floor. The room spins and I drop into the chair, grabbing the edges of the seat to steady myself. I am low on blood, I know. Too long without, waiting for Penny to come back to life. My mask has come off my face, lays on the carpet, sticking to it by the spirit gum. I snatch it up, knowing my face must look horrible.

I regain my bearings: hospital, waiting room, Penny somewhere. She's in good hands, I presume, but they will never guess her disease.

They won't know what to do about the affliction. Neither do I. So I dared pray to my nemesis; it was all I could think of. It had worked last time. *Dear God, it's me again . . . .*

Medical personnel pass by the waiting room. They seem in a hurry. So I worry they rush on behalf of Penny, which makes me even more anxious. She will not transform into a vampire, she will simply die. A real death. And not be able to continue among the undead, like they do in too many films. Ironically, I cannot also go into that real death.

How many hours has it been?

There is no window in this room, so I cannot guess which is closer, the sunset or the sunrise. For the undead, the sunset is welcoming; the sunrise is a threshold we do not pass. For the living, the sunrise brings a new day, full of new hopes, a chance to try again, while the sunset is a mark of satisfaction, a day that has been well-lived, and rest is their reward. Sleep . . . ah, reward for a job done well, a full day lived fully. As it should be. Yet the undead do not sleep, only hibernate in dark vaults of unconsciousness devoid of dreams—

"Mister Székely?"

I look up from my hunched pose, realizing I had closed my eyes. A man in medical garb addresses me. His tone is somber, as though he is not happy to see me. I suppose he wonders if I could be just another patient by my ghastly appearance.

"Yes," I barely can speak.

"We did the best we could," the man says in English. "She is stable, but she is far from—"

"She lives!" I cry out, jumping to my feet.

The man—Dr. Kovács on his name tag—falls back, avoiding my hug.

"She is still critical. I want to tell you the progress. Since it has been so long you are waiting."

"Yes, yes, progress!"

"She is still in very serious condition. It is too soon yet to—"

"Can I see her?"

"Soon. When we move her to a room—"

"Thank you, thank you!"

Dr. Kovács grimaces as I crush his hand between my two hands, shaking it. He pulls away, turning toward the door. He points outside.

"Some men are here to ask questions."

"I know, I know. Who's going to pay the bill. Papers. I have to fill out papers. I told him to wait until—"

"No, these men are from the security office."

"Security office?"

"State police."

Dr. Kovács shrugs, then exits with such dramatic flair, I'm sure he was in all the theatre productions during his school days. Or maybe that was me. Difficult to tell the difference any more. Am I the criminal or am I the victim? Or is it nothing more than reflections in a house of mirrors I stumble through and I am actually everything?

Less than a minute later four men enter, two in black suits and two in the dark green uniforms with red trim, members of the Hungarian Federation security police.

24

"*LÁTHATOM ŐT MOST?*" I ASK, DEMANDING TO SEE HER. "JUST LET ME SEE her, then I will answer your questions." Dr. Kovács knows English, the men from State Security not so much. "I need to see her! *Meg kell látni. I need to know that she is alive. Meg kell tudni, hogy ő még életben van.* Please." I stare straight into the doctor's eyes. "*Kérlek.*"

Dr. Kovács gives a quick explanation to the security men. In most cases, they are not so kind, not very willing to bend or give anyone any breaks. After all, their responsibility is to assure the safety of everyone within the borders of the Hungarian Federation, especially the citizens. They take the job very seriously. Hence, the hours of questioning about my business in the Federation. I was fortunate to have had my official papers updated or renewed or whatever that status might be while I was recuperating in Zadar from the bus bombing. They know about the bus bombing and my recuperation, much to my chagrin.

Chief Inspector Rusza nods. He is a big man, built like a side of beef, face hard as a granite mountain, black eyebrows as bushy as eagle wings, lips a line cut by a rusty knife. He is not going to be my friend.

"Yes, you may go," says Dr. Kovács finally. "They agree, but for only a few minutes."

I thank everyone there and follow the doctor out of the room. The security men have been assured there is only this one short corridor between the room where we are talking and the ICU ward.

Nurses are gathered outside the clear plastic curtains, everyone in medical hoods. I am given one to wear also. A nurse helps me seal it around my shoulders. I pull a gown over my clothing. They help me with the gloves. Then I am allowed into the cubicle where my Beloved rests. She is not contagious, the team leader says. Rather, the medical team does not want to pass any germs *to* her while in her weakened condition. Her immune system is dead.

As expected, all manner of tubes and monitors cover her like three octopi. A cloth covers her eyes. The machines beep and lines cross in blue and green. A respirator hums and hisses. She is alive.

"May I hold her hand?" I ask through the plastic mask.

The attending doctor nods.

So I reach for her hand, bandaged to hold in place the tubes and sensors, and I gently feel her fingertips. I stroke her bare fingers with my gloved fingers. I call her name, muffled through the mask. If she opens her eyes, the cloth will prevent her from seeing me. If she can look at me, she will only see a mask, perhaps be frightened, so I do not insist on removing the cloth.

I feel their eyes on me; a nurse or two, maybe the doctor himself, are watching me. Dr. Kovács waits outside the cubicle. Perhaps they worry I will do something to her. Or they are simply touched by my devotion to her, notable because of the deplorable condition she was in. As though she had suffered months of the most degrading abuse.

"You must return," says Dr. Kovács. It has been three minutes.

I continue to stroke her fingers.

"They will come for you if you do not return," he reminds me.

I hold her fingers tighter, plastic against flesh.

"I must insist you leave now."

I pinch her fingers harder, hold them.

"What are you doing?" he demands.

Her fingers move against mine. She clenches my fingers. Not tight, but it is enough that I know she is alive. My chin drops to my chest; I breathe deeply. Releasing her fingers, I turn to go.

ઉ

The questions are uncomfortably direct. I respond with a clear *"igen"* or *"nem"*—yes or no. Chief Inspector Rusza, standing like a statue in his overcoat, square jaw jutting, Neanderthal brow shielding his beady eyes, has a delightful way of shouting even the simplest of expressions too close to my ear. They confirm everything about my status, my movements, my business interests. They seem unimpressed that I have some wealth, own a spa resort, and live in a penthouse suite of the Hotel Attila. That actually makes me more likely guilty, I think. A man with unusual tastes is a man who might hold a woman hostage and abuse her for several weeks. Until she appeared to be near death, a grotesque distortion of human dignity. I cannot deny her appearance but I insist to them that I found her that way, in that condition. In fact, she came to me, looking for me during the preceding weeks.

"*És ha ő nem vissza?*" asks the chief inspector, wiping his spectacles with a white cloth. The handkerchief has the Federation crest on it. "*Képviselőkről, akik neki? Az orvosok? A halottkém?*"

"I don't know what will happen if she doesn't recover!" I shake my head. "That is not what I worry about. She will recover, she must! Then she will speak for herself. You won't need to be asking the doctor what happened. Or the coroner, as you suggest—geez, how morbid!"

There is a moment to translate my outburst, then the questioning continues. Rusza's face grows more red.

If they already know everything I have done since arriving in Budapest, then what is the reason for asking if I did all those things and went to all those places?

Rusza asks me about my Beloved and I tell them the whole story without mentioning my medical problems. No need to explain the affliction to the pre-dead. They seem tired after an hour of listening to me moan about my love life in Oklahoma. They understand that I ran away from her—nothing said about wanting to save her from the horrid appearance I had gained. It was only a lovers' quarrel. She was livid, vowed revenge on me. They understand that motive. She went to a lot of trouble to find me—and she did find me. With those health problems already presenting. No, I had no idea she was in poor health until I saw her. They doubt me.

"Listen to me. I'll even say it in Hungarian so there is no chance of misunderstanding: *Ártatlan vagyok. Én soha nem bánt vele rosszul.* I've never hurt her, never treated her badly. She is my Beloved. You got it?

189

Ő az én szeretett."

Finally, I think I've gotten them to understand our relationship and the reason she looks the way she does. She has a disease, obviously. That is the cause of her horrible appearance. But I did not cause that medical problem—officially, in their reports. In my gut I know it is all true: I literally did cause her medical condition, and there is nothing I can do to stop it, or reverse it, or make it less extreme. She is still dying on the other side of this hospital wing.

Yes, I should've taken her to a hospital sooner; I agree with them. That could be considered medical negligence under Federation law. I must be ready for charges to be filed, Chief Inspector Rusza says. Either a medical negligence charge or maybe something more serious: direct abuse of a human or, if she does not recover, aiding in a human death. Then a court will be involved, and the courts of the Hungarian Federation are not so flexible.

I can say nothing.

Then Rusza is barking at the others. He pauses to address me, asks for the key card for my penthouse. It's actually just a code to type in for the private elevator, I explain. Can I refuse? I really don't want people rifling through my stuff without me being there to supervise. I don't have any embarrassing possessions up there, but still—

No, I can't refuse, apparently, so it's a moot point.

"*Négy. Kilenc. Két. Hét. Három. Tíz. Négy. Hat,*" I speak, robotically.

Rusza scribbles down the numbers.

And they storm out.

င8

With the protectors of the faith gone, I can focus on Penny. Since the moment my eyes gazed upon her, my guts have been steaming, seeing the downward spiral of an angel, seeing the inevitable crash. Yet seeing her in that hospital bed, even after a team of doctors have done their best to pull her back from the edge of the abyss, I cannot stand up under the weight of guilt. It overwhelms me. Fourteen years of keeping to myself, hiding, fearing contact with the outside world, thinking I was saving her from me.

You're a sly bastard, I mumble to my friend above. You have to take everything so literally. I asked you before to do me a favor. Then I would stop fighting you, just be who I'm supposed to be: a monster. Not only do I appear as a monster but I'm also a monster in what I've done. Does that gratify you? Seeing me in pain? You let the one I love suffer this damning affliction. Why? To amuse yourself? Are there no famines? Wars? Storms to keep you entertained? What will it take to satisfy your desire for constant amusement? Newborn babies skewered on stakes? Will that do it for you? Newlyweds slipping into random woodchippers? Ascetics hanging from crosses? Is that the bar we must reach?

Dr. Kovács visits me. He sees that my guardians have left, but he says they will return and I am not allowed to leave the room.

"You may see her again, if you wish," he says, almost afraid to say it, glancing over his shoulder. "For a few minutes only."

Outside her cubicle, I don the garments that protect her from me, then I enter. A nurse watches me, to be sure I first do no harm.

I take Penny's hand, hold it gently between my hands, careful not to disturb the tape and tubes there. My glove is cold. I can't feel her, can't sense anything. I peel off the glove, holding my hand out of sight, blocking the view of my hand from the nurse, who is distracted by her colleagues, anyway.

My hand again touches hers. As our skin merges, I am suddenly thrust years into the past, to a vault of memories, seeing the days when we loved long and bright. Yet the heavy iron door begins to creak, swings shut a few inches. I panic, grab a photo album from the nearest shelf, and dash out just as the door swings completely shut. I escape, album in hand, as the iron door clangs, a bolt lock dropping into place, sealing the sacred vault forever.

My eyes are open yet I do not see the room around me, only the play inside my head.

I examine the dusty album in my hand, lift the hard leather cover, stare at the first page of photos. There is that picture of my parents in their last photograph, looking much as they did a year ago when I left them. There is a picture of a scene which I know nobody could have photographed. The angle suggests a bird took the photo while winging its way over Penny and me. We are sitting in green grass, in a meadow, and the sky is so blue, not a single cloud to distract us.

The last picture looks like a religious icon: a stylized portrait of an angel—an extremely stern angel bearing the marks of a queenly rank, poised in a seductive manner, breasts half-covered, eyes half-shut, her elongated teeth sharp and dripping blood. It is not a picture I have ever laid my eyes on before, and I do not know why it is included in this flash of memory. Or is it a vision?

I turn the page, anxious to be rid of the evil angel, and there I see my Beloved smiling, her warm face and body as whole and healthy as any team of physicians could ever arrange. Yet I am not in that picture. She smiles but not at me. I can only gaze at her, satisfied with what I see. From a distance.

This is what you want? I mutter to myself, addressing my frenemy, God. Clues to a mystery. Are You inside my head? Or am I talking to myself? What am I supposed to do? Will You grant me another favor?

I'm not sure if I'm still standing beside my Beloved's bed or I'm somewhere else, floating in storm clouds, but I hear that same voice as before. I think it is an answer to my questions:

"You must do one small thing for me. You will think it insignificant yet it is necessary in order to close a door that must be closed. Will you do this act for me, Stefan? If you will, I will see what can be done for this person you crave."

Not crave exactly. I desire, yes. God sounds as though he is fighting a cold. It must be chilly in space. You must dress appropriately.

Feeling dizzy, I pull myself together, even as I sense a jumbling of my cells, clumping together, the strange effect of gravity. At the same instant, I realize a deal is being proffered.

Yes! I accept. Tell me what to do to save my Beloved.

I hope that was enough. I'm falling so I cannot try again to take what is offered. The floor is hard when my head hits. The ceiling opens and I see an elegant Renaissance painting surrounded by clouds in a dozen hues. With chubby cherubs. It can only mean that a deal finally has been made. My Beloved will live.

25

ALARMS BLARE. PEOPLE ARE PICKING ME UP FROM THE FLOOR, CARRYING ME to a bed, laying me down. They start checking my vitals. Ladies, I'm all right, just a spot of light-headedness, nothing to worry about. Yet I know the real reason: it has been too long without feeding. I need blood.

It is daylight outside and the windows of the hospital do not have blackout curtains like my penthouse suite does. I feel my skin burning from the sunlight coming through the glass. I used to enjoy sunny days, I recall. Then I began to burn. I began to flake, my tender skin becoming like paper, flaking, sheering off, and blowing away like dust, the underlayer raw and beading with blood.

The sunshine arrives in this room through an azure sky half-filled with fluffy white clouds. Idyllic—or horrifying. Depends on your genes. The filtered light irritates me a little less. My eyes tend to burn, like from chlorine in a swimming pool. My skin does not burst into flames like in the movies. My skin dries and flakes to a dreadful degree; that is what is painful.

Still, I do not paint a pretty picture for medical personnel. They cannot get a pulse. My temperature is too low. They find I am lacking blood, the obvious problem. They perform emergency procedures as I watch in amusement. They do not know what I am, nor would they believe me if I told them. A needle enters my arm. And then so does blood, fresh blood, a fine woody yet delicate Type AB, tart bouquet with a mellow finish, perfect for an evening dining along the Duna riverfront.

My mind returns, as though it is a balloon inflating. Words fill my head, rows of them, pages. I wonder whether a voice really spoke to me or if I only imagined the words because I was fainting. I often talk to God though He seldom replies. I begged for another deal. Finally, He relented and granted me His favor one more time.

Or did I imagine all of it as I crashed to the floor?

Nurses tend to me, look into my eyes and see no soul. I'm coming back to life, one says. *Élet*—life! I want to laugh but I am too relaxed to move. I would prefer to be alive, with all of the beautiful attendant annoyances and delicious ironies, than to continue in my present circumstance. The best I can hope for now, however, is that my Beloved will recover enough to wield that hammer upon that stake and end this farce, God or no God.

Then they leave me, taking their frantic talking out of the room. As a group they abandon me. I hear another alarm. My powerful senses pick up the noise of the machines in the next cubicle going off, letting everyone know the patient is in trouble. I try to sit up, to have a look. Is it my Beloved who is in trouble?

No. It is an old man with one leg missing. He is crashing. Twenty people, it seems, crowd into his cubicle, all dedicated to saving his life. I heard he was in an automobile accident. God playing pranks again.

"A crowd of vampire cultists blocking the street," one of the staff says, repeating the police report. "He tried to veer, flipped over."

Euphoria permeates me as the fresh, warm blood courses through my veins, the only sensations of pleasure I can feel. My temperature rises. A strange tingle ripples through me, the opposite of the pins and needles that killed me. With that warming, I find my energy.

So I, too, arise, and go to my Beloved in her cubicle.

It is amazing how strong one can feel with just the right mix of antigens kissing the thirsty cells of one's body: welcome home, they sing! A fresh unit of blood does wonders for one's complexion, one's mood, one's will to live. One's sense of humor, too. However, once it enters my body, as I have learned, the fresh blood, no matter the type, likewise transforms. The corpuscles mutate to match what my body requires. The blood becomes a new, different kind of blood: Type X.

A vampire can accept any type of blood, thankfully. Type AB is my brand; it is the blood I had before my transformation. The affliction changed that, my needs and what satisfies my needs. The blood that comes out of me is . . . well, 'tainted' is a polite word.

"My Beloved," I whisper into Penny's ear. She moves as though my breath is a mosquito. The little bug injects an enzyme that keeps the wound open, lets the blood flow while it laps. And that seems quite normal to most people; never an accusation of monsterhood.

I take her hand in mine; I feel normal again, I realize, straight up off the table. I could walk out while they are busy with the old man. Yet I must tend to my Beloved.

"You must get strong again," I tell her. She winces. "You have to finish your mission. The stake is waiting, Penny. You want to end me, right? Come on, fight for your right to stake your claim." I chuckle. "You have a stake in this relationship. Use it." I cannot stop myself. "The stakes are high . . . . You must raise the stakes . . . . After all, you have a stake in my life."

A nurse calls to me and I bite my tongue. She asks what I am doing up from my bed. Before I can answer, she is called back to the emergency. They know me, know my devotion to this woman. I am staying with my Beloved, who is dying. Nothing of concern—although I have no mask or plastic covering on. Nor gloves.

"Can you hear me?" I repeat my words directly into her ear.

She looks so horrid, much worse than I ever did before I died. My gut twists, remembering how she used to be, knowing I caused this to happen. Suddenly I want to drive the stake into myself. Grief floods me. I almost feel tears in my eyes yet I know it's impossible.

"Penny, I—I'm so sorry." I watch her face for signs my words are heard, that my words touch her mind. "I wish I could go back in time and never meet you. Then you would be happy and healthy. Then you wouldn't be here . . . dying."

She stirs, followed by a sharp inhale, the first breath after crawling out of the grave. I lift the corner of the cloth over her eyes. They are open, without much eyelids—but is she awake? Is she blind? Have her organs failed? If not, they will soon enough. I grasp her hand; it is limp, boney, cold. I remove the cloth off her face and stare at her eyes. They used to be so beautiful, so dark yet radiating such love. I could always see her soul through them.

"St—"

The sound seems just a breeze, or a squeak of the bed. I listen.

"Ste . . . fan."

I hear her clearly. A word. Her parched lips move, form my name. I lean down over her face, put my ear to her mouth.

"If . . . ," she exhales.

I move to speak into her ear. "Yes, Penny, go on."

"If I'm . . . gonna . . . die . . . ."

"Please, Penny. You won't die. Recovery takes time—"

"I need . . . to tell you . . . ."

"You are not going to die, Penny. They will save you. Hang on."

"Listen . . . Stefan . . . ."

"I am listening, Penny. I hear you, my Beloved."

"I . . . ."

She slips under and I tap her cheek, trying to bring her back. I give her shoulder a shake.

"Penny!"

I kiss her. Our breaths do not match or mix. I speak encouraging words yet I know the truth. Finally, I accept the truth. The inevitability of the end. I never wanted to believe it but if this team of doctors cannot save her then . . . . They pulled her back from the abyss, but can they bring her any further away from its edge?

"Penny . . . how can I go on without you?"

I nearly asked how I could live without her, caught myself in a pang of semantic weakness. I cannot *live* without her because I simply am not living. I cannot live with or without anyone.

And neither can she—

The idea fills my head so quickly I think my brain will burst, blood flinging through the air, splattering the walls. I want to clasp my head to hold it in. With a glance at the ICU lobby, I see that everyone is still working on the old man. I gaze down at my Beloved's face. If only I could do something, anything, to save her. I cannot wait for God to work His miracle, no matter what our deal is.

"Penny," I call once more, "there is only one way to save you."

"Stefan . . . ." Her lips continue moving but I only hear my name.

"Tell me again, Penny."

"I . . . ."

She is not able to speak loud enough for me to hear so I go ahead: "Penny, I have an idea."

Right then her fingers firm and dig into my hand which holds hers. I give her my full attention. Her eyes widen. This is the death spasm, I recognize. The last gasp of a dying person, the final attempt to hold on to life before succumbing to death.

"I didn't abort," she blurts out.

"What?"

A nurse looks in on us, sees we are doing no harm, disappears.

"You have . . . a son. *We* . . . have a son."

"I told you to cut off these genes—"

"He lives . . . with my mom . . . in Denver."

"A son?" I cannot believe what I'm hearing. "You didn't—"

"After I die . . . ." Her grip on my hand lessens, then goes slack, her body falls limp. "Go to . . . him . . . ."

A long exhale.

I grab her hand, hold it up by the wrist.

"There isn't any time left. There is only one way, Penny. Only one way to save you."

Looking around the cubicle for something dangerous, I see a stylus on a tablet. It will have to do. I take it and stab it into my wrist, digging for a good vein, ripping it open. Thanks to these hospital personnel, I am flush with Type AB, already turning into vampire poison. I squeeze the wound as I press my wrist to her lips. I keep the blood flowing, running between her dry lips, into her open mouth, down into her throat, into her body. I give her all I can squeeze out with no regard for myself. Let me empty myself, if only she will live. Let my poison bring her back to life—even if it is a dark life.

Part Three

26

SURROUNDING ME WAS A STRANGE MIST, A FOG OF POISONOUS GAS THAT filled my lungs and covered my face. I knew my eyes were open but I could not see anything through the whiteness of the fog. It surrounded me, blinding me.

Don't worry, Stefan Székely, I've got your six.

I heard the voice again. The strange words repeated in my mind. Got my six? What does that mean? I knew it was some kind of slang from video games or police movies. Six, like on a clock, I suppose. The six is down on analog chronometers. On digital devices, no special meaning. You have my *down*? I'm going down?

Don't worry, Stefan Székely, I've got your six.

There it is again: the same voice, the same words. Coming through this fog, like a silver blade slicing through—clear, and sharp as a knife. Or a sword.

Don't worry, Stefan Székely, I've got your six.

I've got your six. Which means I'm protecting your rear. Or, the nameless voice is protecting me. Covering my back. Watching out. A general expression of support when used outside of military or police situations. I've got your six. All right. Thanks, I guess. The voice said it three times. Or else it was mere echo.

And then I awoke.

Instead of a fog-choked wood, I am in a hospital bed. Again. I have an IV dripping into my arm, and a dozen monitors stuck to my skin. The lights have been dimmed, thankfully. It must be the night shift. A low, unhurried buzz from a nearby nurse station assures me all is well. At least for everyone else; never can tell about me. Nothing on the monitors alarms anyone.

Thus, I must have been in this hospital already and had one of my spells. They picked me up off the floor, I imagine, began addressing my medical needs. I don't have many medical needs these days. And what problems I do have are addressed by Dr. Szabó.

Grinning, I recall one time he criticized me for my strange habits: "I don't understand zis obsession with blood you vam people have. It's ridic'lous. Is no such ting as vam people."

(He never used the word 'vampire'; that would've been too gauche for him.)

"If you die, you die. It's done. No more be acting in ze life. You get accident, you lose blood, so zen you need blood. If no accident, no need for blood. So why vam people always playing with blood? I know some Satan people in Budape*sht*. Zey too like blood. Zey pour it and drink it for ze ritual. Rub it over zeir bodies. It's crazy. Much crazy ze days are now. Like ze 'Blood of Christ'. Ze Christians, and ze Catholics. Old ways. Everybody loves playing with blood. And nobody gives ze blood. Low supply. Is more difficult to get blood now. More expensive. I got to pay lot more to zose people to get blood for you. People want, how you say, a *bribe*, to give me ze bags of blood. Special for AB blood. So you better find anozer way to play ze games. Ze end of vam people coming soon."

I could hear him now like he was standing in this room—

"Szabó!" my mouth exclaims when my eyes open. He is there, right at my bedside, staring down at me, big hulking monster that he is. Even in the dark, I can see a distressed look on his face.

He reaches his blood-stained hand up to his open collar, pulls it down, away from his throat. There is blood on his throat, mostly dried. He scratches at it.

"What does zis mean?" he asks in a deep, hoarse voice.

I stare hard in the dim light to see what he is referring to. He leans down to show me better. I see the puncture marks.

"It means, doctor, that you are one of the vam people. I'm sorry."

He shakes his head, paces, thinking of his next move.

"I was attacked," he says, crossing the room. "A group of youths. Zey were ugly, dirty, smell bad. Zey grabbed me and I fight zem. I used to be wrestler so I body slam one of zem, hit next man. Zey push me down to ze street. I tink zey are ze gay men, want get sex with me. He climb on me, kiss my neck. I try push him off. Zen he bites my throat. It burns, burns, burns like acid." He rubs his throat, remembering. "I kick off ze man and zey all run away."

"There are vampires in Budapest," I say.

"No, vam people are only legend."

"Legend?" I clear my throat, ready for a long speech. "All legends begin in reality, you know. Whatever happened way back when, in the mists of time, nobody knows. But somewhere, at some time, the gene dealers decided it would be good for survival if some of these people got this gene. My family got it. I have it. That is why I am a vampire. It was my time. It's nothing magical, it's science. Bad science, perhaps, but a medical disorder, nevertheless. I should've had you treating me for my dry skin long before I died."

"So now I'm going to die? Is it what you say?"

"No, not going to die."

"What? What is it? What's happening to me?"

I shake my head. "It will take some time, depending how much got into you, but—"

"What got in me? I thought zey suck out my blood."

"That's part of it. But the enzyme that keeps the blood flowing, it will contain the . . . let's call it the poison. That will change you. It will make your blood change . . . which will make you die. Which will keep you from actually dying. It's complicated. I tried to explain to you how it works. You didn't listen. So you die but you are not dead. And then you are, as you like to call them, a vam person."

He is aghast—not surprisingly. White as a Hungarian can be. His beard suddenly gray. The hair on his head receding more than I recall from the other day. His girth remains but he will lose that as his energy stays high and his appetite fades. He will only need blood, after all. No need to count calories.

Cursing, he rushes out of the room, nearly toppling a nurse coming to check on me. I act surprised to see her.

"What happened?" I ask the nurse in grumpy Hungarian, meaning my reason for being in a hospital bed.

She looks down at her tablet, pulls up my chart, dabs a stylus here and there, reads, gives two *hmms*. This must be a new shift. They don't know me.

As she attempts to explain in Hungarian, I recall just how frantic the cries of "Oh my God! What are you doing?" sounded in Hungarian. I was found out. Caught. Hunched over my Beloved, all they focused on was the blood. I was careful, didn't make a mess. But blood is blood; it's always alarming to see the red. It means something is wrong. And something wrong must be corrected. So they sprang into action.

They thought I was committing suicide, slitting my wrist that way —clearly distraught over the death of my lover. That I let the blood drip into her mouth was only a disturbing side feature. I wanted her to share in my death. Sick, perhaps, but not suspicious. I collapsed on the floor the same moment they reached for me to pull me off her. I had drained myself and fainted.

I notice the bandage around my wrist. Such a neat job, too. Tidy. I expect the sutures beneath the bandage are tight. And then, because they are supposed to shower me with kindness, they refill my tank with good ol' Type AB premium until I am no longer in danger.

"How is my Beloved?" I ask in English.

The nurse pauses as if translating, then smiles awkwardly and exits with measured steps.

෨

The sunrise is muted, clouds hiding the sun. I expect a doctor to enter but it is my old friend Chief Inspector Rusza, as bullish-in-the-china-shop as ever, accompanied by his band of ne'er-do-wells in crisp olive drab uniforms with crimson trim. His words precede him as he bursts into my room. I am hard-pressed to translate his gravelly Hungarian. It's something about my penthouse.

They went up there to see what evidence could be found linking me to whatever crimes had not been solved. Other than some medical equipment and empty bags of blood, they found nothing that would suggest I abused my Beloved. Just as I told them. No torture devices. No harsh chemicals. No ropes or duct tape, nothing but a wooden stake and rubber mallet. They found the receipt; perfectly legitimate.

Then they found my cane—

"Gentlemen, please," says one of the doctors, hurrying into my room, waving his hands to usher out the security patrol. "The patient needs rest. There was an emergency." This doctor's clear Hungarian I can understand. "You can post a guard, if you wish, but I must insist he not be disturbed for a few hours more. It is better if you come back tomorrow."

"We must make the arrest," says Rusza in my translation.

"As I said. Post a guard. He isn't going anywhere."

Rusza snaps his fingers and one of his stern henchmen moves to stand watch outside my door as the rest of them depart.

"Thanks," I say to the doctor.

So I have a little time to think what I should do. An arrest. Really? If not for anything related to the condition of my Beloved, then what? I've been a model citizen—

Ah! That stupid thug György. One of Lord Baltimore's lackeys.

Rusza mentioned my cane. Did they notice it contains a sword?

The doctor returns with two nurses.

"How do you feel?" he asks in English. "I understand you're related to another patient in our hospital?"

I'm in a regular room. Penny is in the ICU. As I get my bearings, I give this new doctor a solemn nod—Dr. Almássy, tall and slim, high forehead, balding, a tiny pair of glasses perched on his long nose.

He informs me he has spoken with Dr. Kovács about Penny's poor condition. News about her has been passed back and forth through the night. Now it is morning. The dark, rainy day outside and the closed curtains confused me. I thought I was in a foggy forest, like the one around my parents' villa.

"If you are well enough to go to her room," says Dr. Almássy, "you should let us take you there." His voice is not so bright, not animated like when he kicked the security men out of my room. "I must warn you. She may not want to see you. The nurses think so."

I can only stare at him.

"What you did was so shocking," he adds by way of explanation.

"I'm . . . sorry."

"I understand you have strong feelings for her."

My lips cannot form a smile no matter how I command them. The reality of everything finally crashes over me. I am drowning in pain— my guilt, my regrets, my horror—

"You want to see her?" he asks.

I nod, trying to cry.

"If you will accept she may not want to see you . . . ."

"I'm ready." My voice sounds odd. Like I'm underwater.

He calls for a wheelchair. They help me from the bed, set me down on the chair, covering my legs with a blanket. Otherwise, I'm wearing only a thin gown. Then off we go, out of my room, out from the wing, sorrowful eyes at the nurses station following me down the corridor. Rusza's guard falls in behind us.

Dr. Almássy turns to the guard, tells him to get lost. I like the tone in the doctor's voice. We have serious business to tend to. The guard insists he follow, as per Rusza's orders.

The ICU approaches, the cubicle arrives, and I see the bed where my Beloved rests. A nurse stands beside the bed holding her hand. They wheel me up to the bed, ask if I can stand. They ask me if I want to stand to see her for the last time.

"What?" I shake my head to clear the words.

Then it hits me: *For. The. Last. Time.*

My head rings, the words burning in my ears.

I rise from the wheelchair like a corpse from a grave, clawing my way up through the packed dirt, tearing open the sod and shouting to the world that I still live, that they were mistaken when they buried me, lost in a drunken stupor for a few days, not really dead.

And I stare at my Beloved's placid face. There is the trace of a smile there, like her final thought was a happy one. I take her hand in mine but feel nothing. No pulse, no slippage of cells, no gurgle of fluids. The tubes and monitors have been removed. They have cleaned her, made her look as best they can. I still see her as I did the first moment she came up behind me in the order line at the café section of the Barnes & Noble bookstore by the Quail Springs Mall in Oklahoma City fourteen years earlier, after we had arranged to meet for the first time following our hours of messaging on social media. She recognized me by my profile picture and called my name. I turned and there she was. The love of my life. My Beloved.

And here she is again: the love of my life, as always.

"My Beloved."

I gaze down upon her face. If only we had never met . . . .

"She said we have a son."

Once they see I can stand on my own, the doctor and nurses step back, huddle at the entrance of the cubicle, by the curtains. They draw the curtains to give us privacy.

"I am sorry, Penny. I mean it. Forgive me."

Then I hear Rusza's guard complaining.

Rusza arrives, shouldering his way into the cubicle, curtains flying. Dr. Almássy tries to keep him back, hands up like a mime pressing glass. Rusza is angry at the lack of security. He's got a job to do! Not even hospital staff may delay him! State Security has priority.

"Let him have this time to see her off," Almássy tells him.

Rusza glances at the bed. "She's dead. No need to waste time on a dead person."

"Please," insists the doctor. "Two minutes."

Rusza nods. "One."

27

"I LOVE YOU." REPEATING THE PHRASE LIKE A PRAYER, I STROKE PENNY'S head as though she has lush black hair. I straighten a few strands that still hold fast. The crusty patches are less noticeable now. Her ears have wrinkled in a way that makes them almost elven. A veil of calm has spread over her pallid face, eyes blank, decayed nose flat. Her eyebrows have vanished yet at the end of her right one, stubborn hairs have grown long and coarse, refusing to fall away; now they touch her lips, the lips that have withered and pulled back. Her teeth had shifted to fill the gaps of those that had fallen out.

I caress her head nevertheless, unable to know if she has really died or if she has died in our special way; I wonder if I managed to save her. Or if I've failed—

A hand falls on my shoulder.

"My condolences," says Almássy. "The disease was far along." His hand retreats as though he is embarrassed to touch me. "We tried our best, but . . . . It was impossible. If only she had come here sooner. I'm sorry, Mister Székely."

A different, heavier hand grabs my wrist, pulls my hand from her head and twists my arm behind my back. It's one of the State Security boys trying my patience.

"So we go," growls Rusza, waving his men to take me.

"Let the man get into some clothes, at least," Almássy demands.

They agree. Two of Rusza's men grab me by my arms.

"Wait!" I shout in English to Almássy. "What will you do with her?

With her body?"

"She will be taken to the basement," he replies. "Where we have the morgue. It is the standard procedure."

"Then what?"

I am desperate. There is no way for me to know if my sacrifice had any effect on her. Otherwise, my Beloved really has died. I need to know which result has occurred. She cannot be buried or—or, worse, cremated.

But Rusza's men are taking me away.

"Please wait three days. Give her at least three days."

"Three days?" The doctor is puzzled.

"Please," I insist as Rusza's men jerk my arms back, eager to go. "It's—it's a Christian thing. You know, the three days? Jesus? It's in the Bible. She was . . . devout in that way."

"Ah, I see. You want the Christian ritual. The old style. I remember the story from school days. We do not follow those old customs now. Hungarian Federation shuns religious stories."

"She's a foreigner. She came to find me."

"I see. So give her three days for Christians."

"Yes, give her three days. Please."

"As you say, Mister Székely. It will take a few days for the autopsy."

"Autopsy?"

The breath goes out of me. I slump in the henchmen's grasp. They pull me up.

She cannot have an autopsy. They cannot cut her open. That would end her for certain. I try to speak but the words do not come out.

"It's time to go," growls Rusza.

"Please, no autopsy!" I manage to cry as they drag me from the ICU into the corridor.

Dr. Almássy takes a step after us. "Autopsy is required when there is an unknown disease . . . ."

I hear him calling after me but his words become faint.

They escort me back to my room and the Security Force personnel supervise the placement of my thin body into my thin clothes. I usually wear loose trousers and a size larger shirt to minimize chafing, which is not a pleasant effect on the delicate skin I wear. The spring is still cool in the mornings so I had a coat. Plus the usual scarf. And the Homburg. My boots. A man of mystery. In two minutes I'm dressed for an official visit to the State Security headquarters.

A nurse scrambles to retrieve the tablet, find the right electronic form to sign. Rusza snatches the tablet from her hand, scribbles his signature on the screen with his fingertip, thrusts the tablet back.

Rusza's henchmen have seized me by my arms, bent them behind my back. It seems as though I am not showing any sign of pain. They press my wrists tighter, up between my shoulder blades. My shoulder pops. I feel it; we all hear it. The henchmen smile.

"Was that necessary?" I curse.

I feel no pain, of course, me being dead. It was insulting, however. Little abnormalities such as this constitute the totality of our so-called superhuman powers. Actually, what we are is *sub*human—subhumans with superhuman abilities. Some would kill for such abilities. Some would kill us for having these abilities. A thin line.

The henchmen push me ahead of the others, down the corridor, as nurses and technicians stare in shock at the treatment I am receiving. No one says anything. No one will stop them. Jerked from my hospital room, escorted down the corridor like a criminal.

Out the double doors into the public area, more eyes on me: the hideous man in black, eyes red, face a mask of flaking skin, bullied by the quartet of State Security men. I note their sympathy, yet none of them assist me. None dare risk their own safety coming to my aid.

And then we are outside. The morning sun slices through the gray overcast in three spectacular shafts resembling silver knives. My eyes wretch, shuttering against the light. I am blinded. My face burns, even when shaded by the brim of my hat. Within the henchmen's grip, my body falls limp. I am hardly carrying myself. I'm moving at their whim, like a puppet.

As if on cue, a large black van with an official emblem on the side pulls up before us, its door already open, its interior dark, as inviting as a newly upholstered casket.

They push me forward and I stumble, tripping on the curb, and fall awkwardly. In that instant I fear hitting my head on the runner of the vehicle, slamming my forehead. Someone grabs my shoulder and pulls upward, hands catching me, keeping me from falling. Suspended a second into mid-fall, I twist around, turning to my right as I crash downward. But I don't hit anything. I hover, face down, inches from the pavement.

I see men in black, a flurry of long coats, each figure with long hair and a pale face—a dozen of them! One takes hold of my arm and, as I fall, my shoulder slips back into place with a satisfying snap. Yet my forehead still bangs against the edge of the vehicle.

Gunshots ring in my ears, retorts echoing between the walls of the hospital wings. I search for their source. I search myself, too, checking whether I am a target or an innocent bystander. I worry more about a wooden stake against my chest, or a slice of silver coming too quick for me to dodge.

More hands grab me.

Everything goes black, like night yet deeper, the blackest black I have ever experienced. I become aware of being apart from my body, seeing everything from a higher vantage, as though I had transformed into a bat and flown above the fray. I see Rusza and his goons in a tight circle surrounded by a dozen members of a gang, one of the vampire cults that curse the city. The flash of gunshots, blasts going outward from Rusza's circle in every direction, yet none of the cultists fall.

In the next moment I'm bent double, forced into a container much too small for comfort. Indeed, that seems to be the point: discomfort. Everything is black, cold as an arctic winter night. My skin literally freezes inside my clothing. Within seconds I cannot move. I sense my cells crystallizing. I do not shiver. My mouth cannot form words. Then sleep comes to me. I cannot resist. Cold arms wrap around me, calming the inner fire. This is what dying feels like.

◌◌

Never before had I felt such deep, penetrating cold. Lost in a profound hibernation, I can only dream of ice and snow, alone in arctic wastes. Then a few tingles cause my skin to flinch. More tingles run through my body, like the intense pins and needles I felt when I was dying in that clinic in Zagreb. The pain was too much and I passed out, entered a coma for three days. And arose in the middle of the night—

"He lives," a baritone voice announces, his words closer to my face than I would wish.

"I wait too long," a deeper male voice declares. The echo makes it difficult to understand but as I think it over a few times I am able to decipher the utterance. It is Hungarian; in my mind I translate it into English. I've been here too long.

The stinging increases until I want to scream but my tongue and lips are still frozen. My bronchial tubes are pipes of ice. I feel the thaw wetting my clothing, moistening my skin. My knees shift, break from their contortion, my elbows following. After a few more minutes, I can extend my body, pushing it straight out against the floor—a hard, cold surface. I shiver—a little at first, then in full-blown spasms I cannot control.

A girl's laughter interrupts my misery. With effort, I push my eyes open. Two hands hold a tall beaker above me. The girl is pouring some dark liquid over me, drawing the flow in a line down my body. It seems the liquid helps melt my frozen body quicker. It smells like wine. She giggles as she pours, amused by my wriggling.

"Enough, Maria," calls the male voice in rough Hungarian, deep and penetrating. "Do not waste it."

"Apologies, Master," says the girl in French-accented Hungarian.

I kick wildly and bat my hands against the floor, against my body. The shaking subsides as warmth floods through me. My bones crackle, muscles cramp then relax. My mouth feels hot and I swallow the spittle that forms from the thaw.

The girl stands. She wears a red gown, a dress with rips and tears, the ragged hem almost brushing my face. Like she has worn the same garment for decades. She holds the beaker up next to her face, like a spokesmodel in a television commercial, gazing down at me with a crazy smile.

"Leave him. Come here. Sit beside me, Maria," says the deep voice. "You have done well, my pet."

She steps lightly across the floor; bare feet slapping against a moist surface. Thawing has left a puddle around me. My fuzzy eyes follow her form over to a raised platform. In fact, it is a stage and seven steps lead up to the top level. A large chair with a high back fills the stage. It is occupied by a massive figure, twice as tall as a normal human, it seems. Perhaps it is the devil himself. Or God—and I must answer for what I've done.

The girl goes to his side and bows her head, then kneels beside the throne. It cannot be called anything but a throne. The figure sitting on the throne reaches down with a long, muscular arm and pats the girl's head. He gives her dark hair a few gentle strokes.

"This is Stefan Székely," says the baritone without fanfare, affecting a cultured, upper-class Hungarian.

I hear the baritone step away, the slip of shoes echoing against the concrete floor, the swish of moisture from the puddle swept across the surface. My eyes still cannot focus.

"Stefan Székely," the figure on the throne thunders, helped by the echo in the room. Perhaps he uses a microphone for dramatic effect. It has to be a large room by the degree of echo, though it is too dark for me to see into the corners or see if there are others present. I sense there is an audience, shuffling in the periphery of my vision.

My eyes burn as they thaw; I try not to look too hard.

"You asked that he be brought to you," says the baritone. "On the matter of my assistant's cruel and unnecessary murder. And, as you have complained, other behaviors which are not congruous with our commune."

The voice begins reciting a list of behaviors, actions, and problems attributed to me. He takes great pains to make it all sound ominous. I rest on the floor, wet and miserable. I just want to hold Penny's hand and wait three days.

"Is that all?" asks the deep voice from the stage when the baritone finishes the list.

"Yes, Lord Azov."

"Is he awake?" asks the man with the bass voice.

The figure with the baritone voice turns to regard me on the floor.

"He can hear us, yet he is not yet at a point where he can speak."

"Go on," the bass voice intones.

"This Stefan Székely, being newly arrived in our city, set about on a wilding scheme which has threatened exposure of our commune to

State Security. Our man in State Security headquarters has done his best to deflect concern about this behavior, yet it becomes difficult day by day, week by week. Székely is well-known among the social circles of Budapest. It has been difficult to act against him. You complained about his wilding, so we gave him warnings. Yet he continued this behavior. Eventually his behavior resulted in the heinous murder of my assistant, a good vampire named György Samsa. Therefore, we have brought him here to answer to you."

"Well done, Balthazar."

The name stabs me. It is my old nemesis, Lord Baltimore, who is prosecuting the case against me. If only I had been granted my own attorney. It seems a decidedly unfair situation. I have never been in a vampire court. I'm a happy-go-lucky vampire. At least being here— wherever here might be—I've escaped the clutches of Rusza's State Security gang. But I wonder: where am I? The frying pan or the fire?

Neither, I demand. I would rather be presiding over a solemn vigil for my Beloved, waiting for her to arise.

"In the matter of my assistant," says Balthazar, "Székely lopped off his head with a blade hidden in his walking stick. My other assistants witnessed the act."

I want to shout that they attacked me first, that I was defending myself. The thick-necked thug leaned down at the wrong moment. But I cannot yet speak—

"While György Samsa was of little value in our commune, he was my assistant and he was one of us. His murder is an insult to you, Lord Azov, an offense to us all, and is clearly against the accepted laws of the commune. For this act alone, aside all others, he deserves severe punishment. Add to this affront his consistent and deplorable record of careless, provocative, and on-going misbehavior and the verdict is obvious. Guilty as charged. Székely must be sent forever out from our commune. I recommend punishment before his dismissal. He should receive the basest form of punishment. What now is your decision, Lord Azov?"

A gravelly roar fills the room, emanating from the throne on the stage. It seems to be the judge and jury's throat-clearing ritual.

As my eyes clear, I see a more defined figure sitting on the throne.

The man is huge, shirtless, leather trousers and boots black. On his head rests a helmet with fur and horns, something a Mongol warrior might wear to strike fear into a Great Khan. Crossing his muscled chest are tattoos of wolves, bears, and hawks. Running down his bare arms are snakes, fangs drawn, tongues flickering. His hair is long, braided at the ends, hanging over his shoulders, probably down to his waist were he to stand.

I see a petite female with long, black hair sitting next to him upon the wide arm of the throne. Another pet. The one he called Maria still kneels at his feet, one hand pawing his boot as if polishing it.

"The basest form of punishment?" asks the deep bull voice.

"I speak of exposure."

The occupant of the throne laughs. "Not beheading?"

Balthazar scoffs. "Exposure will provide the accused an enduring punishment. Beheading is mercy."

The giant on the throne chuckles. "True."

"I said György was a poor assistant," Balthazar continues. "In truth, he had little value. One moment a bumbling fool, the next a vicious thug. Yet there are extenuating circumstances we should consider."

"What are they?"

"His parentage. Though we remember him for his brutish behavior and his crude humor, his willingness to start or join a fight—and he was an ever-faithful servant, usually giving minimal effort or thought. Perhaps he was not a very commendable participant in the midnight commune, yet he did have a good start in darkness. As one of the royal footmen, he was made by Princess Marija late in the previous century, and since then residing thirty-two years in Budapest. Before his rebirth he was one of four sons of Kristóf and Dorka Samsa. He had in flesh one son with a maid of the royal household. And seven children-in-blood followed."

"So he is worthy of retaliation."

"We remember his wit, his joviality, providing a constant source of amusement for myself and my associates. And he always paid ample homage to you, Lord Azov. For that grace we ask for your favor."

The bull clears his throat. "It is your choice."

"Exposure is appropriate," says Balthazar in an uncomfortably flat voice, as though he is used to speaking the courtly phrases. "We would be satisfied. It is enough to honor György."

All I can think at that moment is the popular myth that exposing a vampire to sunlight will instantly cause its body to burst into flames or explode into dust. It makes for a dramatic effect in films but it is hardly accurate. Biology simply does not work that way. I want to explain it to them; I have medical training, after all.

"Though Székely is new to the dark world, he must know what is proper and what is abhorred by us."

"How long?" asks the devil in his bull voice.

Balthazar regards me again. "Can you speak?"

I grunt, trying to push out a word. I fail.

The devil on the stage grumbles.

I try again: "Y—Yes."

"When did you enter the dark world?" asks Balthazar of me.

I cough a while, then: "Thirteen years—no, fourteen now."

The devil slaps the armrest. "This one is young."

"But there is no excuse for—"

"Like a babe," says the devil.

"I lived alone," I suddenly cry out, like a thick dam has burst. The Hungarian words spill out. "I've only been among others like you for one year."

Balthazar scoffs. "Nevertheless!"

"What do you know of our laws?" the bull voice demands.

"What laws?"

I had not studied anything. I was too busy learning to function as a vampire. I only tried to understand what I had to do just to survive.

"From the day I became this," I say, forcing my vocal apparatus to produce the Hungarian words, "I have been alone. Indeed, I lived with my parents, also vampires. Yet they taught me nothing. When I came here—to Budapest—I did not know there were others."

"We are everywhere," Balthazar says.

"I didn't know. Only myths—legends—and my family."

"You lived a lavish life, nevertheless!"

"My parents left me funds—"

"You do not know our laws?" the devil questions.

"Actually, no." I suck air like I have been running all day. My lungs are still thawing, the ice crystals stinging. "There is no book to read, no notes to peruse. But I'm willing to study." More breaths. "I know more of the Hungarian Federation's laws than those of your community. I always thought I was keeping out of your way. I never wished—"

"He does not warrant exposure," someone calls out from the side of the room.

"No! Expose him!" others call.

"No one's been impaled for a while."

"No mercy for a vampire killer!"

"Expose him!"

"Trial by sunrise!"

"Let him burn!"

The outcry from their fetid breaths fills the room with the odor of ferrous oxide, like we are all made of rust, the agent of iron that runs through our blood-obsessed community.

The giant on the stage waves his mighty hand and the shadowy crowd around the perimeter of the room falls silent.

"He is newly dark."

"Laws are laws, Lord Azov," says Balthazar.

The bull grumbles. "Exile, I shall consider."

I cough, not to get anyone's attention but to clear the spittle. "I can leave town. No problem. I have property in the west."

"Property?" Balthazar seems suspicious.

"Not much. A poorly-run resort. With mineral baths. It needs a lot of renovation."

"We don't care about a spa." Balthazar turns to the devil. "He needs to be exposed, Lord Azov!"

"This matter is wasting my time," grunts the devil. He regards his dark-haired pet perched on the arm of the throne. They grin lovingly at each other. "Better pleasures await the unholy."

The girl—or woman, small as she is—stretches, raising her arms over her head. Her black dress pulls tight, circumscribing her lithe figure. She yawns. "Let him be exposed."

"See? Your own lady agrees," Balthazar laughs.

"I want to see a vampire burn," she says. "Is that what happens? I never got to see that. Balthazar, what happens?"

The prosecutor steps forward, bows. "The sun will burn his skin, turn it to paper. The skin will dry to dust. Some may tear off and blow away. Often the internal viscera becomes visible. Sometimes the bones appear. It is quite painful."

"Will he die?" asks the lady.

The devil chuckles.

"No." Balthazar ponders a moment. "It is appropriate punishment because it does not kill a vampire. It does not give the vampire relief from this existence."

"What does it do then?"

"It—frankly, my lady, it ages the vampire. Exposure to sunlight decays the body fifty years for each hour of the sun. It varies with the individual and the directness of the sunlight."

"So he grows old instantly?"

"Yes, my lady."

She grins. "That is what I want to see."

The devil scoots forward on the throne, his huge hands grasping the armrests and his horned helmet slipping to one side of his head. A pair of pouty lips press outward.

"Then we shall see this one exposed," he says with a decisive grunt. One finger rises off the throne's wide armrest. "For the entertainment of my lady, let him burn. She has been without amusement lately."

28

"BUT YOU SAID I WAS TOO INNOCENT FOR PUNISHMENT. DIDN'T KNOW THE laws. Not responsible for my actions. Like that. I'm new here. And— and my Beloved just died. I need a break today."

My desperate words wouldn't have much effect on this Azov guy's decision. He seemed a cruel sort of creature, given over to diplomacy only by the whim of his pet. Balthazar was smiling, looking back and forth between Azov and me, awaiting affirmation. I hated seeing him pleased. That hurt most of all—until I would be stood under the hot sun. As for the girl—the woman perched at the devil's knee—she was twice as scary as her master.

She hopped down from the stage, step by dramatic step, her black leather boots with extra-thick soles and jangling silver buckles making up half her weight. Like everyone in the room, it seemed, she sported the same unruly black hair and deathly pale face of a Goth.

As she approached, she squinted, eyeing this crippled prey. I knew she would not bite me; there would be no point to it. Yet she was the one to decide my fate.

I squirmed on the floor.

"Besides, I was arrested by State Security," I cried out, switching to English.

"We took you from them," Balthazar snarled, also in English.

"I was taken from a hospital." I had to catch my breath. "Where my Beloved died. I'm in mourning!"

"Your affairs are of no concern to us," said Balthazar.

"But—you should just let me go. My mourning will be punishment enough for whatever I did. I have lost my Beloved!"

"Be-lov-ed! Be-lov-ed!" the crowd laughed.

The din increased, everyone calling for my punishment. Only that Lord Azov held back their fury. As the master of ceremonies, Balthazar raised his hands to encourage them. Then, with one wave, the giant on the stage silenced the crowd. Balthazar was caught with his mouth agape in mid-cheer.

I gazed up from the floor, my eyes more clear. I was in some kind of warehouse. Boxes and crates stacked up along the walls. Shelving full of tools and construction supplies. Palettes of lumber rising to the ceiling, and the ceiling was high with fluorescent lamps lighting the room. In fact, the so-called stage I first saw as my eyes adjusted to the thawing, was just sheets of lumber stacked up—made into a stage. The throne, also, was not a piece of furniture but put together haphazardly to look like a throne. There was no Devil's Ball here, just a throng of ne'er-do-wells playing night court.

Were they even real vampires?

Balthazar I could see as a true vampire, and probably his cohorts, but I didn't know any of the others taking pleasure in my discomfort.

This woman, however, petite yet with an aura of power protecting her from harm, seemed most like a vampire of anyone in the room.

She stood over me like a conquering heroine—so close I expected she was about to do something cruel to me. Her boots had spikes and studs; they could cut me. I anticipated a swift kick somewhere—face, ribs, groin. As the hem of her black dress danced around her knees, she straddled me, one boot on each side. I could have stared up under her dress; it seemed she expected that. I stared up the outside of her dress, instead, straight up to her chin, where three silvery studs reflected the overhead lamps and stringy black hair framed her ghostly face.

As I stared at her, I realized she had the appearance of someone I once knew. Or so I imagined. You never forget your first Goth girl. Considering just how long a vampire might exist, it's possible to cross paths with many people, dead and undead. In the literature, they may cross centuries. I am just a little short of fourteen years in the dark world. Yet here we were.

"*Ön Alma vagy? Az Ön neve Alma?*" I dared ask.

I prepared for a hard physical rebuke, a strike against my challenge. But I had to speak: I thought this woman looked like Alma Jónás.

She stopped her fidgeting, settling on the best angle, hovering over me, and regarded me like a cat that had cornered its mouse.

"*Honnan tudod a nevem?*" she demanded, asking how I knew her name. She lifted one oversized boot, let it hang in the air above me. With its spikes dangerous, she brought the boot down upon my chest. A grin flickered across her lips as she asked a vampire's most important question: "*Mi iszunk egymástól?*"

—Have we drunk from each other?

A kind of vampire greeting, I supposed. The idea of one drawing blood from the other. The making of a vampire. It was cute, but wrong.

Yet what did I know? I had never met another vampire, save for my parents, not until I arrived in Budapest and started walking the streets in search of a hot drink. I had no idea of vampire customs. All I knew came from some bad films.

"*Nem,*" I replied, with a shake of my head.

She removed her boot from my chest. Suddenly, she squatted, her rear almost touching my face, the gap between her knees showing everything.

"Are you Alma?" I asked, then switched back to Hungarian: "Did you meet a man on a plane from Munich to Budapest about fourteen years ago? Did you help him around Budapest?" My Hungarian was clear enough. Textbook perfect. With each question, she seemed to search for an answer within herself.

"What you doing there?" called the devil, Lord Azov, from up on his make-shift stage.

She turned in her squatting position to address him and a raw string of words cut through the air, struck the huge man like a volley of arrows. He waved her off as he seemed to shrink upon the throne. Rather than face embarrassment before his audience, he flung his hand at her dismissively, like she was a silly creature not worth his rebuke.

"I was Alma Jónás," she said in a cool, harmless voice, turning back to me. Her Hungarian was also clear, not the slang-strewn dialect she had used with Azov. "I am not that person now."

I tried to sit up but found myself still weak. It had been too long without a feeding. I might fall into hibernation. And then I was frozen to immobilize me—and left to thaw out. I lay vulnerable to anything. The way things were going I did not expect to see the sunrise.

"So you are the Alma who accompanied me to Sárvár?"

Her face reflected puzzlement. "To Sárvár? For what reason?"

"The spa resort. West of Lake Balaton."

Balthazar stepped forward. "What is this scene?" He threw his arm violently toward the woman. "The sunrise is approaching. She wants to witness the criminal's exposure. Let us get it done."

Alma stood. With hunched shoulders, she turned to Balthazar, coiled like a wild animal ready to pounce. Her face showed no delight. Suddenly her face darkened, flashed purple like fresh blood, and a rage of horror spewed from her mouth. He cowered under the force of her exhalation, her bestial roar, the noise of her war cry. Then, like the flick of a light switch, she reverted to her plain white Goth façade.

"Why do you interrupt me?" she cursed at Balthazar.

The devil on the throne roared with excitement. "Our queen has spoken!"

She returned her gaze at me. Something familiar played around her eyes. The Alma I knew had never been an expressive girl, always quiet, cold and aloof. Yet I had always sensed something kinder under her tough mask. She helped me in a dire situation back then. She could have walked away from me, forgotten me.

I recalled her bringing me plum pie while I was in the hospital.

"Have you enjoyed any plum pie recently?" I asked in English.

"*Szilvas pite?*" She seemed surprised again, yet something familiar, like a childhood memory, seemed to fill her consciousness.

Then I realized the problem. She was not supposed to remember me. That was the deal with God.

I glared up at her, standing over me, petite yet strong. The aura surrounding her crackled with energy. I worried how far I could push her to remember. She might turn her fury at me.

With a hard swallow, I prepared my words, back to Hungarian:

"Alma, how is it you are here?"

Her eyes narrowed, bushy eyebrows pinching over her pallid face.

It seemed as though she was searching through her memories. Her red lips pursed, caught between protruding white fangs. One hand rose and fingers clawed back her black hair—like opening the curtains to a new day, or to a new act in this theater.

"*Vámpír vagyok*," she said at last in her old voice, almost too quiet for me to hear—exactly like a painfully shy girl I knew almost fourteen years before. Her tone revealed neither shame nor suggested any boast. It was a merely confirmation of the inevitable. I'm a vampire, she had said. "Like you."

Like me? I sacrificed myself to save you from this.

My chest heaved, terrified as I sucked air. My body flooded with emotion, the burning sensation like my veins flowed with fresh, warm blood—my withered heart pulsing as my head ignited like a rack of fireworks—exploding.

She knelt down to dab the hem of her black dress to my eyes, to collect my tears—my wasted tears.

"What is it she does?" asked Balthazar angrily. He turned to Azov. "What is she doing with the criminal?" Back to me: "What spell have you cast on her?"

I wriggled on the floor, a full spasm of frustration, unable to get myself up. "My affairs do not concern you!"

"Affairs?" Balthazar snickered, waving at Azov. "You see? He calls them affairs. What will you do about this betrayal? Your lady deserves better."

"Betrayal?" boomed Lord Azov.

Balthazar waved his henchmen over. The thugs, grinning, rushed over to me, fists raised to strike.

The giant rose from the throne like a monument sprouting from hard-packed earth. His chin jutted as his rubbery lips rolled over some words, deciding.

"Stand away," he ordered.

She did not acknowledge him, remained in her stance over me.

"You know this vampire?"

Again she ignored him. No doubt everyone else in that room feared what would happen next.

He bounded off the stage, passing over the seven steps in one leap, boots crashing on the floor. The vibration shook the concrete under my body.

"Answer me!" he demanded. "What is this thing?"

Balthazar, twirling his curled moustache, had gained amusement. "Rule number one: vampire does not kill vampire. It is the foundation of our laws. He is the criminal here. He deserves the punishment. Our queen has agreed."

Azov waved him silent with a sharp clap. He stepped up to the small woman, towering over her and me, his body forming shadows in every direction from the ceiling lamps. His chin dropped to his chest as he glared at her.

"Who is this criminal?" he grunted and the walls rattled.

She kept her eyes on me. "I don't know."

"Is this thing a criminal or not?" The giant turned to Balthazar for an answer.

"It most definitely is," replied Balthazar. "Time is wasting. Dawn is coming. The sunrise approaches."

Other voices agreed, chanting for an appropriate punishment.

"For the life of my assistant," called Balthazar, "and for the honor of our kin—all of us, the Pesht clan! Even for all the tribes of our area. The Buda, and the Óbuda, too, though I loathe them greatly. For all vampire-kin!"

Cheers filled the room.

The giant spun around to her. "What do you want with him?"

A smile cut across her face as she continued to stare down at me. Clouds of doubt thinned, a ray of realization shone through. She tilted her head a bit, considering her options.

The devil stood jealous, Balthazar complaining, the shuffling crowd of miscreants energized by the drama.

"I know this vampire," the small woman announced to Azov. She paused, staring at the giant. "Let me speak with him."

"What has she to say to a criminal like him?" Balthazar demanded.

"She can say what she wishes," Azov grunted to him.

"Privately," she said.

The giant stepped back, waved at two of his burly goons.

"What do they have to discuss?" Balthazar cried, like he was about to lose his bet. "Let them speak here."

"Use the office," he growled at her.

"Will she be safe? Alone with that criminal?"

Azov glared at Balthazar, a stern reply to his question.

"Tie him down anyway."

The goons carried me out of the warehouse, through a set of doors, down a corridor and into a small room. The lights were too bright in the room. I squinted, tried to hold my eyes open. It was an office used during daylight hours. Several desks, office machines, and whiteboards covered with handwritten numbers. People worked here. A company by day, a vampire court by night.

On the wall were five framed portraits—company executives. The last one looked like the giant in the warehouse, but with a neatly trimmed beard and half-hearted smile. Lord Azov was a department manager—not actually a devil or king of the local vampires. Not surprisingly, Gergely Azov was named Employee of the Month. He probably worked insane hours.

The henchmen plopped me down on an office chair in front of the big desk, like I was there to interview for a job. The duct tape wrapped around my arms, fixing them to the armrests, was not part of the interview.

My hostess stepped to the front of the desk. She hopped up, sitting upon the edge. Her boots swung repeatedly against the front wall of the desk, making the metal panel rattle.

She studied me a while, as I tried to feel the tips of my fingers and toes. The minutes ticked by like hours.

"Stefan Székely," she spoke at last.

Looking at her, I had to remember her present age: fourteen years older than she actually appeared: so much like she did when last I saw her. And I was fourteen years older, too; Penny had arrived in Budapest at the age I was when I left Oklahoma. Now Alma was the age Penny had been back then. It all seemed too neat, like another trick God was trying to slip under me. Fourteen years gone in a blink.

"Yes," I responded.

29

"I DO THINK I KNOW YOU," SHE SAID IN THAT SAME SOFT VOICE SHE HAD used a long time ago, "yet I'm not sure how or where or when or why we were together." Her Hungarian was sweet, a lilting poetry. "So then . . . me and you were lovers?"

I tried not to smile. "It is a long story."

She was serious, her face hard. "Tell me."

So I recounted everything from the hour I snuck out of the hospital in Munich and flew to Budapest. I sat next to her on the plane. After arrival, I invited her to share my limo into the city. I asked her if she could guide me around for half a day as I conducted my business. I'd pay her for her time.

"Then everything went crazy," I told her. "You got help for me and I ended up in a hospital. You visited me, brought me plum pie, too, and later helped me escape."

She continued studying me, perhaps watching for a clue I might be inventing this story.

"We got on a bus to Sárvár, where I hoped I could make use of the spa to treat my affliction." She seemed to doubt me. "I was trying to resist transformation. I thought it was only a skin disease." A slight nod from her. "You didn't need to go with me. But you insisted."

Maybe she expected more money for helping me, I don't know. I'd already given her cash for her time and trouble. Her interest in going with me certainly was not because I was a strikingly handsome fellow. Not in my condition, which had worsened.

Yet that seemed to be her thing: the Goth façade, the obsession with death and all things macabre. When the spa refused us, we went to a small inn at the edge of town.

"At that inn, you took a shower." I paused to find the right words. "When you came out of the bathroom, you had a big towel wrapped around you." No reaction from her. "I was sitting on the floor with my back against the side of the bed. And you . . . you sat down upon me, on my lap. And tossed away the towel."

The jewelry of her piercings had tickled my skin as she straddled me, working us into a climax. I described that to her as judiciously as possible—as much as my Hungarian vocabulary allowed.

"That I remember," she said with a plaintive nod.

I let out a long sigh, feeling my body warming, as though I had just confessed to a crime.

She stared at me. "That was you?"

I batted my eyes, tried to nod.

She blinked; her eyelids were not withered away. Perhaps that did not happen with the way she became a vampire. I had to return to the legends I'd studied. She was not dying because of poisoning, like Leslie and Penny. I'd asked God to save her. She must have transformed in a different way—

"Yes," I sputtered. "Fourteen years ago."

She repressed a laugh, like she couldn't believe she'd had sex with this poor, weak vampire tied in a chair before her.

I told her what happened next: her illness, the blood poisoning, me taking her to the hospital. And I went on to my treatment appointment and died there. She recalled a hospital and a hotel. That was in Zagreb, I reminded her. We had driven there in a rented car.

"Hotel?" she asked, suspicious.

"Yes, I returned to the hotel after—" I leveled my eyes at her. "After I died."

She snickered like she didn't believe me.

"You may think it is funny," I said, adding a pathetic chuckle, "but I asked God to cure you. I tried to make a deal with God. To save you. I know it sounds crazy. But I was crazy back then. I promised I would stop fighting my transformation if He would make you healthy."

"Did it work?" she asked, a sly grin playing hide-and-seek just like fourteen years ago, perhaps knowing the answer already.

"It did."

I had to look away. Too disturbing to see her appear now as she did that night when I returned to the hotel. She had to have transformed soon after that, however, to be frozen at that age. A pang of sorrow shot through me.

"At that moment, it did. You were back in the hotel room, as fit as a fiddle. But you no longer recognized me."

"No? Why not?"

"That was part of the deal." I took a breath. Probably she would not believe what I would say. "God was supposed to make you as if you had never met me. So when I saw you again in that hotel room, you didn't know me. I was scary-looking. You were afraid of me."

She just stared at me. I could not read her face, could not guess at her feelings about this story I was telling.

"I don't remember," she said at last.

"That's what was meant to happen: you forgetting everything about what happened."

She nodded thoughtfully, her heavy boots coming to rest against the front panel of the desk. I sensed a strong vibration in her aura, but her teenage façade kept me on guard.

"I left you some money. And a bank check." I paused to see if that information registered. "I wanted you to start a new life."

"What new life?" She seemed confused.

"When we first met, you told me about your boyfriend. The one at the university in Munich? He beat you, so you were running away from him. That's what you said."

She shook her head like she didn't believe me.

"Back in Budapest your father wouldn't accept you, either. He hated the boyfriend, you said. So he beat you, too. When you visited me in the hospital, you had bruises on your face."

Her hand moved like she wanted to touch her face to check for bruises, but didn't want me to notice.

"It was long ago," I said, trying to be comforting.

A long, deep breath seemed to pull in the air of the room and her shoulders broadened, back straightened. Her face whiter.

"It's past," she said. "Before I became who I am now." Her face changed. "You try to confuse me! What tricks! If true, then you used me and I cannot forgive. Now you are only small vampire in a big city. Not important. You are criminal, they say. You must be punished!"

I waved my hands, my arms taped against the armrests. "I gave you money to start a new life, not for—not paying for sex or whatever. I thought if you had money you could have your own life, make your own way. You could start fresh. That's what I was thinking."

She looked angry.

"After all, I didn't need money where I was going."

Her expression softened, returned to the pale ghost.

"Where did you go?"

I wanted to laugh, but I didn't; my body rattled, however: one final shiver. My clothes were wet from thaw. My tears likely were moisture from the thaw, not true tears.

"I went to my parents' house. More of a villa. Two hundred years old, they said. Near the Plitvice Lakes." I shook my head. "On a hilltop. Surrounded by a forest. And a roost of bats."

She seemed shocked. "They let you live there?"

I smiled against my will. "They insisted on it. In fact, they set it up that way. Everything was directed by them for most of my life. I really had no choice. Until now."

Her stare was sharp, disbelieving. I tried to meet her eyes but they would not accept mine. I regarded Azov's portrait on the wall.

"I'm free now. Free of them both, that crappy villa, and all of their silly rituals. And the tourists wanting the vampire experience!" I ranted on about my miserable life under my parents' protection.

When I stopped, out of breath, she glared at me as if I had insulted her. What did I say? The sad story of my fourteen years as a vampire. Thirteen years for her. I shook my head.

"I gave up everything to make sure you would be healthy. I thought it was the right thing to do." My voice had gotten an edge. My chest tightened. "My life was my only bargaining chip with God."

"God tricked you!" She grinned, evil dancing in her eyes.

"Perhaps." I could not hold back my words: "If ever I felt cheated, it is here—right now—learning that, despite everything I did to save you from a horrible death or existence as unpleasant as mine, you became a vampire nevertheless. I used my one chance. I wasted my only wish! On you! But for nothing. Nothing! Now I don't have anything to offer God to save my Beloved's life."

God was certainly laughing at my foolishness, how easily deceived I had been. This is why we are no longer on speaking terms. He refused to help Penny. I was out of wishes. I was lost—

"Fuck you!" My whole being sizzled with hate and I shook against my bonds. "Just fuck you."

Our eyes met awkwardly.

"Fuck me?" she said in English like I had.

She slapped my face—not too hard, but hard enough to get my attention. She reached for my hand. I lifted it from the armrest. She clasped my hand, held it as though she could sense truth in my veins, reading my thoughts in pulses of blood. Her nails dug into my flesh.

"It was not nothing," she spoke, returning to Hungarian.

"No?" I wasn't sure what she meant. "What happened to you after I left?" I tried to see her face; she had lowered her chin, still holding my hand. "How did you end up here? With that monster on the throne?"

"Shhhh! Don't let him hear those words."

"Tell me what happened after I left you."

"Nothing happened."

"You were healthy." I caught my raised voice, dialed it back. "What happened to the healthy girl?"

"I changed. Like you. Stop making a big deal of it."

"It is a big deal! I gave up everything I had to save you, but you became vampire anyway. That is a big deal." I swallowed hard. "Was it your choice? Did you want to become this? Or was it forced on you?"

"Stop! You have no right to question me."

"I must know the truth! I have nothing left. My Beloved has died. I have died. Everything has died. Except you. And you go on living like that same Goth girl from fourteen years ago. What is this madness? What has happened in these fourteen years? It is madness! An unholy madness that covers the landscape like a hurricane, pounding us and drenching us until we are nothing but creatures of the night hunting for a sip of red before sunrise—"

"It is truth!" She drew her hand away, her nails cutting me. "You think it is carnival trick, like circus, but it is truth! Nothing you can do. We are night people, not your kind of sickly beings feeling sorrow in yourself. We rule here—"

"It is the same." My eyes felt full of tears but without the moisture. "You and me, we are vampires, like it or not."

Her face darkened, purple with rage. "We are not the same."

"We both died but did not really die—"

"We never die!" She was ready to explode. I cringed, remembering how she had handled Balthazar's demands.

"If I had left you as you were, back in that hotel room, you would have gotten worse and died after years of agony. Like my Beloved has. But I asked God to cure you, and He did. So you could go on with life, be happy and healthy. But you threw it all away!"

"No," she growled, slapping the desktop. "You not tell truth to me. Now I know you are fake vampire."

"No, I really am a vampire," I responded with pathos on my breath. "I'm the real kind of vampire. My transformation was genetic. It was inevitable, unstoppable. My parents transformed, too. They never told me about it, what would happen. I didn't learn until it started. I couldn't stop it. You saw that. As we traveled from Budapest to Sárvár, to Zagreb, you saw me change. Now I'm exactly what I was supposed to be: a vampire—the undead."

She stroked her cheek with a taloned finger, eyes half-closed.

"I saw a strange man in my room," she chanted, "dressed in black with a big hat. I was afraid. I cringed on the bed until he left. I can't remember what he said. I rushed to the door, to lock it."

With a push of her hands, she slipped off the desk, landing loudly on her thick-soled boots, practically banging against my knees.

"I tried to sleep. I thought it a dream. When I awoke it was late and manager checked on me. So I packed my bag and took the money. I returned to Budapest. On train I remembered the man in the room. He told me to start again."

"Yes, that was what I wanted for you—"

"Silence!"

I blinked.

"When train arrived, whole city was different. Not my Budapest. I didn't know where to go. People stared at me so I cursed them. I used the money for cheap inn and I thought and thought what I should do."

"And what did you do?"

She quickly pressed a finger against my lips, her nail scratching my cheek, drawing blood. Seeing that droplet, she leaned forward and her tongue unfurled, swept up the bead. She lingered—her lips moved over mine, pressing hard.

"Certainly I remember you," she said on parting, rolling her tongue over her lips. "It was you tasting my blood, true?"

I dipped my chin. She offered herself more than once to keep me going. She was a cutter, taking a razor to her arm to distract herself from the stresses of the world, so a snip to feed a vampire did not seem so traumatic.

"Tell me, my lovely little pet, how we did it?"

Her smile was wide now, her teeth bright.

"Did what?" I asked with a frown.

"The sex."

"You sat on my lap."

"Is it true? And you were like this?" She stood before me, her hips against my knees. "Like now?"

"Wait a minute," I said.

"Don't you want it?" The fangs framed within her smile seemed a bit longer. "Is it the reason you want me?"

"I don't want—"

Her hands swept up to my head, palms cupping my ears. Her eyes met mine. I tried to hold no expression but her eyes pulled apart the curtains that hid my soul—what now occupied that cavern where my soul once resided. What was there could only be a pit of despair, the abyss, the end of everything.

She settled over my lap. Her fingers opened my trousers. The tape fixing my arms to the chair was tearing apart as my body heated.

"I can't do this—"

"Let us see!"

She pressed against my lap. "Yes, you are a vampire! I can feel your spear ready to strike!"

She gave a laugh then shook against me, probably faking it at first but after a minute her moaning sounded genuine. Pieces of tape fell to the floor in crumbles, as though my body heat had burned them, changed them to dust.

"We can't be doing this," I muttered, teeth clenched, genuinely fearing pain. I fought the storm of sensations. Something swept through me. I felt like a young man again. Energy filled me, like she had plugged me into an electric generator. I was burning, a fever like I had never had before.

"You remember this? Hmm! Vampire sex is best." She ground against me. "I went to Munich. To boyfriend. He called, worry about me. No other place to go. He was different, talking sweet words. He introduced his professor, an old man named Arkady Azov. They study electrical engineering together, say it's important for making life—"

"Life?" I grunted, sensations beating me. Blinded as if by a bright light, I could see God hulking in silhouette, shaking his head at me from his cloudy throne. Everything was done, finished.

"And death," she spat. "Ah, you did well, my pet! Do you feel it? The energy? You look recharged."

My heart pounded like a train engine. I thought it might burst. I remembered what death felt like.

"He shared me with that professor, the old man." Her breath was harsh as she rocked against me. "I did it to make him happy. He got promotion. It was not only for sex. That professor, strange man, many strange ways. Looked like death, worse than you. Very difficult to have sex with him. Yet he could put me into spell, put me under his control, with a few words or a stare and I would obey anything."

I was gasping even as my body slackened, my fever drawing down, trying to listen to her, the noise of my reawakened heart so loud.

"He took me—used me. Abused me. Yet I learned much. I learned how much pain I can take, how much pain I can give. He always bite my throat, take my blood. I knew it was right for him. Like for you. It is life. Blood is life."

"Also death," I blurted between breaths.

"Yes, it is like death." She leaned down, kissed my forehead. "So I learned how to get what I want. First Munich. Then here in Budapest. Maybe Paris next. Or Vienna. Many fell under my tooth and claw. Like wolf! Taking sheep of the world. Arkady taught me everything, gave me his power, made me queen. Until I killed him."

"You killed him?" I huffed. "Then who is Gergely Azov?"

She slapped my face. "Lord Azov!"

"Okay, Lord Azov." I shook off the sting. "That's a Russian name, isn't it?"

She laughed. "You are so interested in everything."

Lifting herself off my lap, she dropped her boots to the floor and stepped backward against the desk. The hem of her mussed black dress fell, covering her sin. My arms were free of the tape, only a few strings remaining. I shook out my hands, stretched my arms upward.

"I just want to know what—"

"Be calm, my lovely pet." She patted my head, her nails scratching my ragged scalp. "Lord Azov is son of that old professor of electrical engineering. He learned the trade from best people, right from the beginning, one-hundred-sixty-two years ago."

"He's how old?"

"One-hundred-twenty-seven years in darkness."

"In darkness. He doesn't look a day over forty. So Lord Azov runs the Budapest operation."

She cocked her head. "Operation?"

"Like a gang. Isn't this your gang territory?"

"Is bigger. We rule the east. All the way to Timisoara. Others have the west. We will rule both sides soon."

"You mean the Pest side and the Buda side of the Duna."

"Then we rule all of Hungarian Federation!"

"But how can vampires ever be in charge when we can't even be out during daylight?"

"We make everyone go out at night. We make new laws."

"Oh, like in the movies. Listen, Alma, I need to—"

She slapped my face. I dared not retaliate, not with her goons just outside the door.

"You obey," she growled. "You listen, not me!"

"I apologize—"

"Is better to rule in Hungarian Federation than in Germany. Lots of Germans come now, escaping the devastation by the invaders. Yet here, vampires are hunted. Bad blood, they think. State Security always hunts us. Three executed last month. They want only pure society here. We are considered diseased, so they try to capture us and burn us in ovens."

"And what about that boyfriend?" I asked, expecting another slap to my face. My skin was already flaking away.

"Dead." She said it so innocently and without hesitation that I had to wonder if foul play was involved. She noticed my consternation. "It was the true death. Not vampire."

My heart slowed, fell into its usual stillness. "I see."

"He deserved death."

"Okay. An abuser. I get it."

"Lord Azov took all his blood, his soul—left empty sack."

"And you are . . . ? His pet?"

"Not pet!" Instead of another slap to my face, I felt a punch to my shoulder. "We rule together. Yet I will win. Soon." She grinned, pleased by what she had done. "You will help me. So I give you power."

Shaking my head, I said: "Seems more like you were taking power."

"No, I charge you up. Like Prius turbo. Now you can fight."

I tried to chuckle. "I believe you."

"So you will do something for me." She pointed to my crotch, then to my heart. "Use your power. It is time."

"What?"

"To kill Gergely Azov."

"What? Me? Why? How?"

Before she could answer, the door burst open. Balthazar pushed in, arms on his hips, accusingly. Two goons followed. I could not hide. My trousers were still open, our act clear to everyone.

"Look! See?" he shouted back to those in the corridor who followed him. "Another betrayal! Lord Azov will tear him apart limb from limb! This is worthy of impaling! What a sight it will be! Finally a spectacle! What a grand day to be a vampire in Budapest!"

30

IN A FRENZY, ALMA BEGAN ACCUSING ME OF ASSAULTING HER.

"*Már majdnem túl késő!*" she cried out, flinging her hands at me. She ranted until I could no longer follow her words. By then she had her fingers hooked around my throat, nails rending my flesh.

"No!" I shouted, struggling to break her grasp. I didn't know who was tricking who. She was accusing me of trying to rape her. "I am not that! She is! I was tied to the chair," I insisted in Hungarian. The tape had disintegrated from my body heat.

"Stop him!" shouted Balthazar.

Two ugly goons grabbed my arms, held them at my sides. Alma leaned away, feigning calm. She ordered them to take me back to the warehouse. She would inform Lord Azov what deeds I had done. And that would be the end of me. She laughed.

My first thought as they dragged me from the chair was what kind of power she said she'd given me and how I might make use of it to extract myself from this situation.

It did not take long for my body to react.

I lashed out with two fists, knocking the goons backwards. I leaped up, trying to pounce over their hunched bodies. Other goons reached for me but my legs spread at an unusual angle to kick at them. It was something only a martial arts star could do in an action movie. I had never done that before. It did not even hurt.

Then I was landing on the floor, boots catching, my hands ready for more. Energy boiled through me.

"Take him to Lord Azov!" Balthazar commanded.

Four thugs grabbed me, forced me into the corridor. The curious huddled along the walls, hissing and growling as my escorts pushed me through. I felt the energy of six men coursing through me but I was held fast by the foursome. They took me to the center of the room, directly under the spotlight, stood me before the make-shift throne of Lord Azov.

The giant still sat on his chair, unconcerned, petting the girl who had poured the beaker of liquid over me. She batted her eyes at him and he grinned.

"This criminal was seducing your lady," Balthazar announced.

Azov looked up, frowning.

"As you thought, our lady was taking too long. When we entered, this criminal was seducing your lady! We saved her."

Azov grunted, dropping his pet girl like a rag doll. He stood, hands on hips, glaring down at me.

"You!" he bellowed, arm raised, finger pointing.

The thugs let go of me, backing away as Azov descended the steps to the concrete floor. His heavy boots pounded the wooden planks and shook the walls. They knew I could not get away, but they wanted to be out of range when their master dealt with me.

It was Alma who started it, pulled me into her spell. I thought she was on my side. Then she asked me to do her a favor. She asked me to kill her master—this giant towering over me. He was probably seven feet tall. Broad-shouldered, barrel-chested, with arms like tree trunks, legs like bigger tree trunks. His scowl was unnerving. I could only guess who the true ruler in this territory was: Alma or this Lord Azov?

I took a hesitant step back, gave a quick glance over my shoulder: nobody there. Taking another couple steps, I glanced to each side: the crowd filling the perimeters of the room, pushing among the shelving that lined the walls. Metal shelving. Full of construction equipment. Tools. Sharp objects. My eyes shot over the items on the nearest shelf, perhaps a twenty-foot lunge. Hammers, saws, trowels, basic gardening supplies. I needed garden shears.

My focus stayed on the shelving as Azov inched toward me. He was grumbling something about how wrong it was for me to touch his lady.

I hated to keep silent on the matter but I knew nothing I said would be believed.

"What you doing with my mistress?" Azov growled, making two huge fists.

"Wait," called Alma from behind him. She had ripped her dress up to her hip, showing her leg, probably to make the situation look more serious. "Have pity on him. Just a stupid boy, a fool. It was nothing." She laughed: a steely, hollow sound.

Azov turned to her. "Never play these games."

"It is not a game, Gergely. It is—"

"Never call me that name!" he roared, raising a fist.

She bowed her head. "Forgive me, Lord Azov." She looked up. "He was so clumsy that nothing actually happened. It was amusement for me. That is all. He is so pathetic."

I didn't know what she was doing. Seduction? Lies? Betrayal? Then betraying the other side. Covering her own bad actions? Kill Azov, she had told me. But did she mean it? How was I supposed to do that?

"Alma, what's going on?" I shouted.

"I don't actually remember you," she said with a loud guffaw. "I was playing with you. Just kicking your mind like football."

"But it's true," I said, "what happened fourteen years ago."

"I don't believe. You are just kicking my mind."

Was this all part of her game? She had played games before, I could guess by the way Azov reacted. Now me. Her target.

"Wait—"

"Do as you like with the fool," Alma chuckled, "just let me taste his hot blood first."

"Take all you want!" Balthazar called.

"Perhaps I'll drain him," she sang in a cheerful voice.

She strolled toward me, Azov behind her. Sidling against me, her hands went to my hips, slid up to my armpits. Her fangs were drawn, her eyes bright red. She truly sought blood—my blood! She stretched up, swung her hand over my throat, clawed at my skin, then pulled me toward her.

"Take the blade from my boot," she whispered into my ear before she bit my neck. Not to my artery but to a harmless area. My hands went to her hips, like we were dancing. Azov growled, questioning what I was doing.

My hand went down to the top of her boot, felt hardness there, a wooden handle and a blade. In an instant, I retrieved it and pushed her away, exposing the sixteen-inch carving knife I wielded like a sword.

"What you doing with him?" Azov shouted.

Alma skipped away. "I want to see a fair fight, Lover."

"A fight?" His nostrils flared, eyebrows thrashing. "It is no fight. It is execution." He glared at Balthazar.

"Seize him!" Balthazar commanded. Three of his big goons started forward then hesitated. They had no weapons. "Go! Take him!"

None moved at me.

So Lord Azov lumbered forward—

I swung the knife and slashed his forearm. He held his arm back and swung at me with his other hand, a tight fist. I ducked and thrust the blade up at him as his arm passed, striking near his armpit. He howled more from embarrassment than pain. He fumed—then rushed me again. I went into full fencing mode, the energy that Alma's spell had bestowed upon me fueling me.

From *en garde*, I lunged, struck Azov's wrist, snipped a fountain of blood. The narrow stream arched into the air. He pinched it with his other hand as I retreated a step. Letting go of his wound, he reached for me with his other arm but I parried his hand and laid a deep cut across his palm. A line of red dripped on the floor.

"Maria!" he cried out, keeping his eyes on me, holding his wounded hand behind him.

"Yes, Master?" She bounded down the steps to the floor, went to his outstretched hand. Evidently she knew what to do. She held his wounded hand in her two, licking the blood that oozed in his palm. The wound would soon close.

"Seize him!" Balthazar cried again but his goons hesitated.

I turned in a circle, challenging them with the knife, ready to cut them. The tip and the edge were stained red.

"Silver!" cried Azov, feeling his skin burning where I'd cut him. He jerked his arm away from Maria. "It's a silver blade!"

The crowd around the sides of the room hissed and pressed back toward the walls, giving me space.

Maria was distraught, her master jerking his hand away. She leaped at him, grabbing his arm and pulling his hand toward her mouth. He fought her but she sank her teeth into his palm. He thrashed his arm back and forth, trying to shake her off but the girl held on with her fangs sunk into his hand. He was distracted—

I bolted through the shelving, toward the doorway, flung the doors open and the night unfolded like a snapped blanket. Vehicles lined the curb. I clapped my hands and three cars lit up, alarms going off. The one directly in front of me was a shiny black Audi Q9 sedan.

The door handle sparked when I touched it, my new-found energy rendering the security system inert. The driver's side door popped, slid along the side of the car. I climbed inside, grabbed the steering wheel, the door sliding closed. The engine ignited at the touch of my finger to the power button.

In my haste, I backed into the next car with a crunch, then lurched into the street like a bat taking flight—as the vampire court spilled out of the warehouse, filling the street, milling there like neighbors had called in a noise complaint.

"After him!" I heard Balthazar shouting, his whiny voice echoing down the street. His orders were cut off as motorcycle engines roared to life. Three bikes charged past him in hot pursuit.

I was away in a flash, the knife dropped on the floor of the car, my hands engaging the subtle intricacies of steering like a professional racer. I knew the streets, the turns, the alleys, the exact width of this vehicle to bull my way through central Budapest.

Only when I hit the Szabadság bridge and saw the wide expanse of the Duna below did it strike me that I was escaping for my life—such as it is, metaphor and all. As I crossed the bridge, I caught my breath. To my right, on the opposite riverbank, was the citadel of Szabadság.

As I exited the bridge, heading west, searching for a highway out of the city, I saw the motorcycles following, their headlights marking me. Further behind them charged several cars. Overhead two monorail lines crossed.

Somehow I pulled a donut in the middle of a wide intersection and headed north, tires squealing. My hands sizzled as the car skirted the hilltop fortress, trying to lose my pursuers. I urged the car over the curb, onto the park's sidewalks, and roared up the hill, circling the slope, through the trees, hitting Szertis Street and descending. Still they followed!

The residential neighborhood I entered forced me to slow, but I hugged every turn, cut through a couple backyards, laid rubber across the playground of a primary school just to make the next avenue, Villányi. I crossed between two moving cars and a fuel truck without breaking stride or causing them to brake. The lights changed after me. The motorcycles almost made it. One struck the fuel truck, sliding between the wheels, and the inevitable explosion lit up the night sky.

Two of the bikes stayed with me as another monorail line flickered, a train passing overhead. Another black sedan made it across the avenue, avoiding the wreck, rumbling over the old trolley tracks. I made for the highway, taking Alsóhegi Street. Opposite the train line was Budaőrsi Street, which would take me out of the city.

I kept spying that stretch of pavement, hearing the rough chug of heavy machinery. A light struck my rearview mirror.

Parallel to my street came a train, a freighter—like a miracle from God. I had one chance: the only crossing was Bocskai Street—a few meters ahead of the nose of that train engine. I took it—shrieking enough to wake the dead as the car made a wild 275-degree turn and rocketed over the double tracks maybe a meter and a half ahead of the train. My pursuers were not so lucky. One bike slid under the train. The other had to slam the brakes to halt in time. The train continued down the line, dragging the bike with it.

It was not a street crossing at Bocskai but a bike path, I realized. I spun the car around to continue on Budaőrsi Street—which became the M1, taking me out of the city, out past the shopping center and clothing factories, which made the world much darker. As dark as my heart. I passed the abandoned Volvo plant, the Swedes divesting from the Hungarian Federation.

The numbers blurred on the speedometer as I flew into the night.

31

LOST IN THE DARKNESS, I RACED DOWN THE COUNTRY ROAD—LIKE A BAT out of hell—doing 200 km/hr with headlights off. My vampire eyes could see quite well.

Then a figure swung up from the backseat.

My foot hit the brake, my hands gripping the steering wheel as the car fishtailed. My eyes were fixed on the road ahead, curve coming.

"Don't stop," said the silhouette.

"Alma?" I tried to spin my head around to check.

"Keep going," she said in Hungarian. "They are not stopping."

"I thought I lost them."

"No." She was a shadow in the rearview mirror.

"How did you get into the car?"

"I unlocked it for you."

I pursed my lips, shaking my head. I thought my new electric touch had opened the door.

"You really double-crossed me back there. What the hell were you thinking? You let them believe I—that I assaulted you. But it was you who climbed onto me. I was tied to the chair. You know the truth. Why did you lie? I'm confused. And angry."

She snorted. "You got away, didn't you?"

"That's not the issue." I slowed more. My mind no longer focused on driving. The energy she had apparently given me had dissipated. My tension evaporated, my body slackening, getting comfortable in the car seat. "What was that talk about killing Azov?"

"Lord Azov!" A kick to the back of my seat.

"Sorry, Lord A-hole, whatever. I thought he was your boss. Or your master, or whatever you vampires call your overseers. Your lover? All of the above?"

"Do not mock us. There are powerful forces you will offend. We are all subject to them."

"Like you?" Again I tried to see her in the mirror.

"You have no idea what dark forces can do." Her words sounded noble in Hungarian. "Not to be taken lightly."

"I've read those thick books about the dark forces. And the forces of light, too. Good stories. Makes for some dazzling special effects in films. But we are real—as real as the undead can be, I suppose. Not the products of either dark or light forces. The pathetic result of damaged DNA. Or put down by a fucking disease. Microbes. Bacteria. Viruses, whatever. No dark forces in those little creatures."

"You are young in the dark. Like me," she said, calm yet confident. "The difference is my maker was a master and gave all his power to me when I was reborn."

I sighed. "So many new terms: 'maker', 'master', 'rebirth'—a whole new set to learn. Me? I just waited for my family curse to kick in, a dry patch of skin the first symptom. And I tried to treat it with lotion." My laughter was genuine, filling the car with the amusement I'd pent up for years. "Now I'm being chased by a crazy gang of vampires of the biting persuasion. Like in the movies. They seem an odd bunch, like they're just playing vampire. More curious than menacing."

"You and me so different," she grumbled like I had insulted her.

"Yes, different. Different ways of contracting the disease. Genetic for me. Infectious for you. A bite, sharing bad blood, it's like any STI. Like people spreading HIV. Or AIDS. Makes us look as awful as those sufferers. Sharing blood is the worst thing you can do."

"There is blood in everything."

"Especially for vampires. Blood is power, yes."

"I give you power. Make you strong. You kill Lord Azov. Then you escape. Go home. Leave Budapest forever. I will reign."

"Just like that, huh? Believe me, Alma, I want all of that. Every last syllable that you said. Especially the you reigning part. Good luck with that. I think you have the temperament for it."

The car had dropped to a respectable speed, nothing to catch the attention of a constable out on this country road west of the capital.

We approached the next junction. At the center of the traffic circle rose a tall monument, a stone figure of some Magyar warrior, helmet and armor, spear in hand, surveying the battlefield that was now fallow cropland.

"You abandoned me," she said after a moment. I could hear the pout. "That is what you said. You run away. Just give money like I'm no more than whore for you."

"Not exactly."

"It's true!" She slapped the headrest.

"But you decide to accompany me on this car chase?"

I carefully negotiated the curve around the statue and its small yard, slowing to a walking pace as I gazed at the statue. The figure was twelve feet tall, mounted on a stone base a meter and a half high. Impressive. I had the urge to stop and read the plaque.

As I directed the car away from the circle, the road straightened and sloped downward, continuing across the plain. Lake Balaton was to the south. On each side of the road, the fields had been planted. Too early to show much.

"Why do you want me to kill him? Does he mistreat you? Like the boyfriend in Munich? Like your father? Like any of a dozen men you've known. Like I did?"

"You didn't." She huffed. "You are stupid but you never hurt me."

The horizon behind us was no longer black; morning was coming. A watery orange seeped above the distant hills. Below, where it was still night, lights stabbed the darkness.

Headlights! Singles and doubles, bikes and cars.

"You're right, they did not stop." In the mirror I saw her turn and look. "They are still after us."

"You cut Lord Azov. He will not give up finding you."

"No kidding." I sped up. "So what's wrong with him?"

"Wrong?"

"Why kill him?"

"He is my master. I don't want any master. I cannot be free until someone kills him. I cannot kill him because he is my master. There is a wall that surrounds him."

"Oh, I get it. He cast a spell over you so it's somebody else who has to do the dirty work. No problem. Why didn't you say so?"

"It is not joke!" she barked. Looking back, "Go faster!"

My foot got heavy and the car lurched ahead.

"What happens when they catch us? When they ram us, make us stop? Or we crash?" This was feeling like my desperate drive from New Orleans, where I'd sought treatment long ago, back to Oklahoma City: north of Dallas, a monster truck full of country boys harassed me, ran me off the highway. "Will you take his side again? Or I'm on my own?"

"Faster!" she shouted, punching the headrest.

"I'm going faster."

"They cannot catch us!"

"Not with you playing dirty tricks!"

"No tricks!"

"How do I kill him if we keep running away?" I glanced down at the gauge on the dashboard. "Getting low on gas, by the way."

"You got to drive as fast as you can!"

The same moment I jammed my foot down on the accelerator, the sky behind us erupted in a huge fireball. The burst of orange burned the rearview mirror and blinded me for an instant. I thought the sun had suddenly breached the horizon.

I took my foot off the pedal, applied the brakes, hard at first. The car jerked. I pushed down more and we screeched to a halt. Checking the mirror, I stared at the blaze a kilometer up the road.

"What was that?" I muttered and there was no answer.

The door flung open and Alma jumped out, standing tall, gazing up the road. I also got out and regarded the fire.

"That's where the traffic circle was," I said.

Alma continued staring, like she could see that far. Maybe she now regretted wishing her master's death.

"I guess they couldn't maneuver around it, not at that speed," I said without irony. "You have to slow down for those."

Without a word or glance, Alma took off running down the road in the direction of the fire, quickly lost in the darkness of the plain. She was limber for a vampire in big boots.

I never heard the crash, just saw the fireball rip the night. Further in that direction, the sunrise was cracking the horizon, red like blood, fading to orange higher, and the deep blue of the dying night above. A star blinked white over the distant hills—Venus, the morning star.

But Venus was not a virgin lover, the thought suddenly popped into my head. No, the morning star was always the symbol of Lucifer, the light-bearer, and this was a sign. It had to be. How was it that I was here, at this moment, to see it? Out in the Hungarian countryside? With my life—so-called life; my *existence*—in complete disarray. It had to be a sign. But not a sign I was looking for.

The montage of bizarre images from before Penny died returned to me, tumbling through my head like flashcards as I climbed into the car. My parents once more frozen in their ghastly final portrait. Penny and I lazing in a grassy meadow. The religious icon of a sexy angel, streams of blood marking her bare body. I shook my head to dismiss them. Hallucinations, only, I decided. I was low on blood.

I started the engine with a tap of the button and turned the car around. I drove back the way we'd come, toward the fire, slow enough not to hit anyone.

When I saw Alma walking hurriedly down the center of the road, her black dress flapping in the breeze, I pulled to the side.

I lowered the window. "Shall I give you a ride?"

She ignored me, not even a glance, and began jogging. So I directed the car around her and continued toward the accident site.

I rolled to a stop a few meters before the traffic circle. Headlights lit the traffic circle. As I suspected, a vehicle had gone straight into that statue. The stone base remained, the giant statue had fallen onto the roof of the sedan, caving it in. The front of the car had been crushed up to the dashboard, the windshield shattered. The car had hit the monument straight on. It appeared driver and passenger had propelled through the windshield.

Grass in the circle hosted flames, torched by fuel leaking from the sedan. On my side of the circle lay two bodies, one still ablaze and one wriggling, slapping out flames on arms and legs.

Tending to them were members of the gang, the goons ordered

about by Balthazar, and some of Azov's guards in biker leather.

Standing up on the bumper of my car, I peered over the gathering. It was Balthazar who 'lived'—in a manner of speaking. His bloody body remained intact. The other, from the position on the ground, had been the passenger of the vehicle. Such a heavy body and a tall figure—easy to be thrown through the glass. Sometimes the airbag does not have time to deploy. Sometimes the glass breaks in such a way as to create a Guillotine-like device. Such a blade may be enough to separate a head from a body. Simple physics.

And so lay Lord Azov, prone like a starfish, splayed on the asphalt pavement. His head had rolled down the road, veering into a ditch.

"I found it!" cried one of the guard boys, waving his arm.

As Alma arrived, I jumped down from the bumper. She halted next to me to survey the situation, arms stiffly at her side. No one there noticed her presence. Or mine.

She spun around like she could look no longer, hands covering her face. I suspected she was an accomplished actress. I heard sobs, and she eventually wiped her cheeks with the backs of her hands. I was inclined to believe her. Except she had lied before. She had betrayed me before. What would she do this time? She wanted me to kill Azov so she would be free of him.

From that moment, I no longer believed in magic, in spells, or in the laws of physics. Or the forces of darkness.

"You are to blame." Her soft voice rattled with an invitation to a night in Hell, all expenses paid. She was right to blame me for this mess. It was all my fault. Everyone knew that. If I had only—

"There he is!" someone shouted in English, pointing.

Others called out, too. Some of the goons formed a rugby scrum before me, ready to pounce, yet I stood straight and tall, challenging them. They hesitated. I guessed they feared my hidden powers. So they growled their displeasure as I retreated, stepping backwards to the car, thinking to lock myself inside. They could smash the windows and haul me out of the car, certainly, then thrash me to their heart's content.

Locking myself in the car still seemed the right thing to do. The big carving knife was in the car, too.

They rushed the car, pounding their fists on the glass. One window cracked. The side panels and hood took beatings. It was not my car, thankfully. One fellow climbed onto the roof and jumped up and down until the roof bent. I cringed in my seat to escape the dent. My hand touched the knife on the passenger-side floor. I gripped the handle, sat up waving the knife at the vampires clawing at the windows.

The glint of the blade in the morning light stopped them. Half the goons looked up at the sky, toward the eastern horizon, the orange dawn. A few held up their hands or arms to shield themselves from the light. They drew back, an expanding semicircle around the car door.

The game was over—

Congratulations, spoke a voice I did not recognize. It was English. I glanced over my shoulder but no one sat in the backseat. It seemed to have come from inside the car, however. Or from inside my head.

I started the engine, listened to the machine purr a second, then let the car roll forward to urge the crowd of vampire henchmen to step aside. Angry faces hissed and growled as I moved through them. One fellow bristled, looking were-wolfish. Maybe it was the lighting.

As the car approached the traffic circle with its broken monument to ancient warriors, four men struggled to heft Azov's huge body from where it had been thrown, moving the headless form to an undamaged vehicle. I saw Alma, hands to her face, striding behind. The happy widow playing the part. I wondered if I had managed to do her task by getting Azov to chase me. Would I get credit for his demise? Or cursed by it? Blamed for it? How would Alma reward me?

"Just leave me alone," I muttered. Anger surged through me. "I'm sorry we ever met."

At the edge of the circle the small crowd gathered. Through them I saw Balthazar lying in the grass, up on one elbow, calling commands to his goons.

I lowered the window a bit.

"Yes, sir," someone grumbled in a bass voice. "Coming, sir."

Through the circle of Balthazar's goons I saw Dr. Szabó, his heft doubled over, hunched as he hurried to Balthazar. He dropped to his knees in the dewy grass and began seeing to his master's wounds.

What I could see in the dawn light was horrible enough: an arm missing below the elbow, likely severed on broken glass, and a flap of skin hanging from the side of his face, cut to the skull. His forehead rested against his collar and blood gurgled down neck and shoulder. Already Balthazar was pushing away goons who sought to lap up his leakage.

"Get away," he growled. "Be gone! Leave me!" The goons couldn't help themselves; the scent of red was too enticing and the fact it was their master's blood did not dissuade them.

But Szabó? The goons had bitten him, exchanged blood with him, made him into one of them—but the newest of them, hence a servant. Having medical training made him handy. He had been riding in one of the trailing vehicles, I guessed.

"Doctor Szabó!" I called. He did not look up, tending to his work.

Balthazar complained about everything the doctor was doing.

As my car rolled alongside them, I lowered the window all the way.

"Szabó, come with me."

He didn't even look up, so focused on his duties.

"Leave these vam people and come with me."

"He is not yours to command!" cried Balthazar in English.

"He shouldn't be yours, either."

"You don't know what you've done!" Balthazar fought the pain as Szabó tried to reattach the lower arm with metal pins and screws. "Do you?" His sharp teeth gleamed in the morning sun. "You have created a vacuum of power. We ruled the east. We held the city. Lord Azov had great plans. We were going to conquer the west, unite the city under vampire law! Rule over the daylight hordes. But you!—You destroyed our plans! Someone will rush to fill it, this hole you created. Someone we would rather not have in Budapesht. We are doomed, all of us, east and west, everyone of the dark!"

"Your affairs do not concern me," I mugged, regarding Szabó. He did not seem to notice me. Perhaps he was under a spell.

"My affairs? It is our affairs! The whole city! The entire Hungarian Federation! You have opened the door not only for the other vampire gangs of Budapesht but for the master of all."

"You're just being dramatic." I laughed. "And such a poor driver. First be sure your passengers fasten their seatbelts. Rule number one."

"That's my Audi you're driving. Look how you damaged it!"

"Very nice. Thanks for the loan."

His curses were not in a language I understood.

I swung my hand dismissively. "So who is this magical mystery monster that will take over?" I tried to see Alma in the rearview mirror. "Did they have a child, this Mister and Missus Azov? A son, perhaps? A son who would wreck vengeance upon us? Oh, but he could only be about thirteen years old now, at the most, right? I doubt he's already vampire kin."

Balthazar grimaced. "You killed Lord Azov! Now *He* will come. The accursèd grandfather. Not the father but the grandfather! You've let in the worst creature to ever haunt the world since Saint Dracula himself. I speak of Maxim the Cruel. The Russian. Because of you, we are all doomed! I pray to all that is dark and unholy that it will be you, Stefan Székely, who shall be doomed first in the line!" He ranted on.

I raised the window completely before he finished, the glass tinted with a push of a button. I stared outside, measuring the road.

"You will be cursed!" Balthazar called. "For all time!"

"Yeah, yeah, yeah," I muttered.

"We will hunt you down! We will find you! You can never rest! We will send Maxim to settle the score!"

"Relax, Lord Baltimore, this is not how the world ends."

Right then the edge of sunrise broke into the traffic circle. I knew the precise moment because of the uproar of warning and anguished cries around me. The tinted windows of Balthazar's sedan protected me. I could not watch them, however, writhing in pain, caught in the morning light, burning. They huddled, cringed, turned their cloaked backs to the sunshine.

A loud clank startled me; the glass in front of me cracked. My hand swung up to guard against splinters. The hood had a long groove now. Alma swung the tire iron once more against the windshield as I turned the car away. The hooked end of the tire iron caught the side mirror, ripped it off.

I steered carefully through the mayhem. She threw the tire iron at the car, the length of metal flying end over end, crashing against the rear window.

"Stefan Székely!" she shrieked loud and long, trailing me for miles.

I knew she was displeased. Yet I didn't care any longer what might happen to her.

A bright point of light in the orange sky caught my attention once more: the morning star. As I stared, it twinkled.

32

KILOMETERS DOWN THE ROAD, A WARNING LIGHT BLINKED INCESSANTLY on the control panel like a second sunrise: fuel low. I tried to drive more judiciously to maximize the fuel but I did not make it. The engine shuttered, groaned, and went silent.

Passing Tatabánya, I saw recharging stations, but this vehicle, like a lot of classic automobiles, still used expensive gasoline. I also had no money, no bank card on me. Being a vampire, I had not gotten a chip implanted in my wrist like most citizens. I still used ragged old *Forint* bills that were quickly being removed from circulation.

Now I was stuck on the side of the frontage road between the town of Bicske and the Budapest suburb of Herceghalom. I calculated it was about 35 kms to reach the city proper. A leisurely drive if I had even a half-liter of fuel. Longer, if on foot.

Walking along a main highway? With traffic? And security patrols? In broad daylight? And behind on my feeding schedule? A vampire's worst nightmare. If only I could fly home—

You are safe now.

It was the same voice that spoke before, but close to my ear.

Unnerved, I sat up in the car seat, expecting a security patrol to be pulling up behind me. I was far from the deadly traffic circle now, so I thought some emergency vehicles might be racing there. I thought the voice might be a distant siren screaming through the breeze. I listened for more. Only the songs of birds cut the silence of the fallow farmland around me—and the whizzing of vehicles traveling in both directions.

Outside the tinted windows of the car, the morning sunshine bathed everything in gold. The crack in the windshield had spread. I could feel air blowing in. The glass creaked, snapped.

That must have been what I thought was a voice.

Sure, I feel safe here—answering myself. So long as no one stopped to check on this stranded car. Everyone had a place in the Hungarian Federation and if you were out of place, someone of an official nature would check on you, make sure you were put back into your place. It was all very neat. Orderly. Parental.

Yet I had no place, no proper place in this new society. The world had turned crueler in the fourteen years I had kept myself isolated, protected by my parents, sheltered from reality. And just as soon as I struck out on my own, I quickly got myself into trouble. I could never admit it to them, certainly. My behavior would embarrass them and a scolding would ensue. Perhaps I would visit them someday—

Do you believe me now?

The voice. Again. Like the whistle through a crack between metal panels of the car. Faint yet distinct. I listened for more, just to confirm the source. Nothing.

"Believe what?" I dared speak to . . . myself.

The silence inside the car was deep. My ears rang. The sedan was well-insulated. The steady din of traffic along the highway continued.

I told you I would have your six.

My six? Protecting my rear. Gotcha. But how? In this car chase? I did nothing but keep my foot on the pedal and steer like crazy. That statue did the rest. Right time, right place. It was a miracle.

Yet you chose that road.

"That road?"

Or did you choose it?

"It was the first road out of the city—the M1."

The route was arranged for you and your vehicle.

"Well, thanks for that, I suppose. I'm done with car chases."

You escaped, yet your task is not ended.

If I weren't a vampire, I'd call myself crazy, check in somewhere. Talking to myself again. Hearing voices. Too long without red.

"My task?"

There is always one more.

"What are you talking about?"

I spoke just over a whisper—as though I was afraid to be heard even though I was alone. State Security had drones flying everywhere, watching and listening to citizens. Say the wrong thing and they would swoop down on you. Or the drone could just zap you: disabling your vehicle, stopping your heart, whatever was needed.

"I was trying to flee for my life—which is, ironically, impossible." Rage started to boil in me, remembering the past. "I already gave up my life. I gave it up for another—who betrayed me! Queen of the Vampires! Hah! I made a deal with God to save her years ago. Then she went and changed into a vampire anyway."

The next moment of silence made me afraid. State Security was about to pounce.

That is the reason you are a fool. The voice snickered. *You know this already. God makes no such deals. I, however, accepted your offer. Have you forgotten?*

I opened the door and jumped out. I stood frozen beside the road, in full sight of any drones scanning the area. The globe of the sun, still orange like a witch's bonfire, buoyed above the horizon, splattered rays across the landscape. The light stung my exposed skin. Better than being inside the vehicle with that spirit.

The words echoed in my head, like my skull was a huge cavern of nothingness. It was not just me talking to myself. It was—

The morning star. The sunrise. The fireball from the crash. And I was free. Or maybe not. The dream, its images, the promise to protect me if only I would do something in return . . . .

"I must do something?" I asked myself, but the voice overheard me and began laughing in earnest. Right next to my ear.

We made a pact, you and I.

"And who are you?" I had to shake my hands, still twitching with energy. My body could not be calmed. "Are you even real? Or just one side of a dual-personæ?"

Oh, I am real, Stefan. As real as the sunshine that is burning your delicate skin.

"Right." I turned to the car. Its tinted windows would protect me.

The sunshine had marched across the plain, acre by acre, rolling over the crash site, engulfing the vampires there.

And you will be free.

"Yes, that is what I am now: free."

I returned to the driver's seat, closing the door, wondering about my vehicle at the dealership, being outfitted for a vampire lifestyle. My fingers burned as the last of the fire left them.

"Gotta go," I muttered. "I must get to my Beloved."

The laughter that followed me into the car was like the howl of a storm, a whirlwind.

Everyone thinks they are free, but we know the truth. No one is free. All are slaves. You know this, too. Slaves to something, different things, and all must do whatever is required in order to continue.

"Continue?" It was awkward having a conversation in my head with a total stranger. This was what madness sounded like.

These fellows of yours, always concerned with continuing. They wish to go on without decay, without loss, without pain. That is why life is finite. No one really wants to live forever. It is much too long for your feeble containers. The hours are too great. There is not a library large enough to accommodate those hours.

"Wait—what?"

Library. You do have a library, don't you?

"Uh . . . yes. It's actually my parents' library. My father's books. I've read a few—"

How many books do you have? Enough to last to the end of your continuance?

"What do you mean, my continuance?"

You wish to continue, do you not?

"Yes, I guess so. But not exactly in this form." I scratched my head, staring out the side window. "How long do I . . . continue in this form? I never asked for this, never wanted it." I closed my eyes. "Continuing. Is that the best word?"

It is the only word. Continuing. Not ceasing. If not a full, happy life of ninety-three years in a fragile state of opportunism, then a longer existence of perhaps two-hundred-forty-seven years in a form which can accept that term.

"You're awfully precise. Studied biology much?"

The laughter again. Unnerving. Not inside my head, but close.

"Nobody can live—continue—for over two-hundred years."

Whales can. Tortoises can. Vampires can.

"You never told me who you are. But I think I can guess."

I stared into the rearview mirror, saw myself: red-tinted eyes set in a ghostly façade. Not a pretty sight, like death microwaved. I was ready to fall into a starvation coma.

"I transformed because of my family's genes. It's a pre-disposition. I couldn't stop it, couldn't reverse it, no matter how I tried. So I finally accepted it—in exchange for another's life. The deal with God. I know it was real because she did regain her health."

God does not make deals. God will, if you prefer, offer you quite a wide variety of choices. A semblance of choices. Yet it is all smoke and mirrors. A dog and pony show. Enough to get your vote.

"But it worked!" I punched the dashboard so hard that loud Goth music suddenly jolted me in my seat. I scrambled to silence it, slapping buttons. "I know it worked. I begged Him and then she was fine."

The illusions are impressive. I will give Him credit for that. I, on the other hand, am as plain as day. You can trust me. I never play games. I never make promises, and I abhor dogs and ponies. I do not engage in smoke and mirrors. In fact, I am smoke and you, Stefan, are the mirror.

"You know me . . . ."

I stared out the side window, my gaze touching a blackened church off the highway that had caught fire, probably from lightning, knowing exactly what he meant.

Glancing into the rearview mirror, I startled at the sight of Alma's Goth face there. I turned away.

Looking again with hesitation, I saw my own face but now colored as red as the devil's face. I jerked my eyes away.

"What are you doing to me?"

Reminding you of unfinished business.

"What unfinished business? I've ruined several lives. I've lost my Beloved, the love of my life. I'm a fucking vampire for who knows how many more fucking centuries! I am not a happy camper!"

Remember how you asked me about biology? Remember how you

259

complained about your genes?

I nodded, sensing how tomorrow was going to turn out.

You cursed God for your family's heredity. Yet you believed God could change it. You made deals based on that belief. It was only a belief. You ask about biology, so I will tell you, Stefan. God did not change your genes. Throughout the long existence of this world, many have wished to continue beyond their fruitful terms, so some were given highly advanced technology. They could continue despite a death of their souls. I argued against it but, alas, I was overruled.

"Well, that was good," I mumbled.

Now listen, Stefan—for when I stop, you will need to begin your task. It is I who gave you the genes which allow you to continue. It is I who directs what remains of your continuance. Now do what you are told.

"What I'm told?" I gritted my teeth. "I'm talking to myself."

Are you?

"Yes! No. I don't know."

You once stated you were a bad vampire. Prove it.

"I meant I'm bad at being a vampire."

I think otherwise. The words produced a snooty echo. *You want to be bad, so be bad. Do something bad. What would you do to win back the life of your so-called Beloved? How bad could you be? The life of a stranger for hers? Two lives for hers? Three or four? How about a dozen innocents slaughtered so your lover may once again be in your arms?*

"But is that necessary? I know you're just playing games with me."

Let us imagine for a moment that this Penny Park you so adore has fully died and shall never rise again.

"But she will rise!" I punched the dashboard. "I have to get to her."

Let us imagine not. Then what shall you do? How will you mourn? Will you go on a rampage, killing without hesitation, slashing innocent folk indiscriminately? Would your anger overwhelm you?

"Now you're just teasing. She has not died. And I will not need to play your game."

Oh?

There was a slap to the side window. A white-gloved hand. One officer of the traffic patrol. Another officer peered in from the opposite side. Tinted windows made the vehicle suspicious. I rolled down the driver's side window, wishing I did not look quite so monstrous.

"*Jó reggelt kívánok*," I spoke in a cheerful voice, hoping my alter ego would not speak up. Good morning!

The officer on my side of the car asked what the problem was, said I couldn't stay here along the side of the road. It was dangerous for me and not safe for other motorists. The vehicle being so badly damaged concerned him. Had I been in a wreck? Was it drivable? I agreed on the safety issue, however I had unfortunately run out of gasoline. The opposite officer laughed, remarked on the old folks who still drove petrol-powered vehicles.

They chuckled at how banged up the car was, pointed to the cracks across the windshield. I could not drive it safely. I would need to have it towed. They kept giving me side-glances like they were checking me out further: what an awful looking fellow, their expressions suggested. Led a life of excess and it's caught up with him. Poor man. Needs lots of the plastic surgery to look half-way decent, decent enough to walk into a grocery without frightening everyone.

The officers smirked at each other, one nodding toward me.

I can hear your thoughts, I said to myself.

So can I, said my light-bearing friend.

We waited until a truck arrived, then I got out, shielding my face from the sunshine. I didn't want to announce I had any skin disease. After all, the Hungarian Federation frowned upon diseased individuals. I rode in the cab of the truck, Balthazar's wreck of a sedan chained on the flatbed. We headed toward the city, the driver calling on his radio for a body shop that was open.

Within a few minutes we rolled to a halt, joining a line of vehicles. Another checkpoint. I guessed State Security was looking for someone. The driver glanced at me, sensed my nervousness.

Now? said my invisible friend. *Will you act now?*

"What do you mean?" I muttered.

The driver asked me what I said.

Take what you need.

I nodded, understanding.

Leaning over, I grabbed the driver by his throat, pinching my gaunt fingers around his Adam's apple. His hand went to my grip, tried to wrest it away, couldn't. He fell slack. Then I bit deep into the artery and supped until the car behind us honked to move forward.

Needing to change places with the driver, I let him slump in the passenger's seat, large sweaty forehead against the window. He would awaken after a while; I did not drain him.

You see now how bad you are? I knew I could count on you. Now for the task . . . .

I let the truck roll forward.

"No task," I grunted. "I need to get this truck off the highway or else the jig is up."

The truck lurched ahead as I kept the interval tight. We moved a few meters and stopped. Repeat. Repeat. Then I was next. There was no place to hide, no ditch to leap into without being seen. They would find the bloody driver next to me. The jig would be up.

"*Lépjen ki a járműből, uram,*" said the guard, a standard uniformed State Security minion. At least he added 'sir' when he requested that I exit the car.

My hand went to the handle. Another guard stared in through the opposite side. The driver looked suspicious so the door was opened. The sleeping man was checked. He fell over, almost out of the cab. The blood was not so messy. I explained he had gotten drunk, hit his head, so I was driving him home.

I was pulled from my seat, thrown down to the ground. A higher-ranking operative arrived, barking commands.

They must have recognized me. A grim façade on ungainly frame, the ugliness of the undead. I tried to smile. Just another Hungarian Federation citizen down on his luck. It didn't take more than a second for the higher-ranking officer to react. He greeted me with a rifle butt in the face. I felt my front teeth loosen.

33

"STEFAN SZÉKELY," A BRAND-NEW DEVIL ANNOUNCED, FOR THE GOOD OF my accusers who might not have been able to identify me. The sound of my name always irritates.

When I opened my arid, grainy eyes, the world was fuzzy. I had a plastic hood over my head, like I was in quarantine. A small, heavily scratched window in front allowed me to gaze out at the sterile world:

There was Chief Inspector Rusza, dressed in an immaculate black suit, red rose protruding from his breast pocket. His arm was in a black sling, white bandages around his wrist peeking from his cuff. He had taken a bullet, I surmised.

"Stefan Székely," Rusza rumbled in his patient Hungarian, "I know who you are—and what you are. We do not welcome your kind here. All of you and your diseased comrades will be dealt with in due time. For now, we will get information from you. How much we get depends on how deep is your tolerance for pain."

Grimacing, I knew I had a low tolerance for pain. But as a vampire, I am mostly immune from such nervous system notifications. I should already be in pain, I decided as my tongue explored my loose front teeth, dentistry by rifle butt. The world was turning so fast I was dizzy. Rusza, then Azov, back to Rusza. The only thing I wanted was to retrieve the body of my Beloved and hope against all hope that I could save her from a true death.

"Do you know what we do with your kind?" asked Rusza, enjoying the moment. He tried rubbing his hands together, as though he was wiping blood from them, but the sling limited his gesture.

"Dinner and a movie?" I had no sense of humor remaining in me. Not after that remark. My last joke. You live your life seeing the irony in everything and suddenly—

I shook my head, knocking the plastic hood askew. I tried to straighten it, jiggling in my seat. I wanted to look out the window but I found my hands fixed to the chair's arms with handcuffs. A few shakes of my shoulder did not return the hood properly.

Rusza frowned.

"No," he said. "We separate the head from the body. Then we burn both, the bodies placed on racks in a large oven, the heads on spikes covered with hot pitch."

He grinned, perhaps expecting me to display a mask of horror. But I was tired so I yawned.

"If you wish not to suffer this fate, you will tell us everything you know about Gergely Azov."

I coughed. Someone behind me slid the hood around so I could look out the window at Rusza's ugly mug. Bloody residue from my cough marred the window.

"I would be happy to tell everything I know." I raised my voice to be heard through the plastic. "But because I know so little about him, it won't take more than a couple minutes. Do you have time?"

That answer did not please the big fellow. He attempted to slap me with his slinged hand, got it caught in the cloth and grappled with his other hand. By then he had lost his motivation.

"Especially, tell us about the woman," he grunted.

I grinned inside my hood. "Which woman?"

"The woman he protects."

"Protects? But she is—"

I thought back over my brief encounter with the vampire couple, Gergely and Alma. Such a lovely pair, the Azovs. Co-rulers of Budapest, or so it seemed. So they declared. Even Balthazar had referenced them thus, lord and lady. I had never been interested in politics or who ruled whom. I wanted to be left alone in my own little world. An old villa in a dark wood up in the mountains, for example.

Just let me out of here.

I told Rusza what I knew, not to forego any torture but to help my enemy get my other enemy. Friends do that sort of thing. And spurned lovers, too. We call it revenge.

"You are unusually helpful," Rusza acknowledged, furrowing his jutting chin. He seemed puzzled. Torture was slipping off the table and he seemed disappointed.

"I don't care much for them," I responded. "Nor you."

He wrinkled his nose. "Take it as you wish. We help each other for the common good. The Federation must be strong. We cannot have it full of subversive hemophiliacs. Only a pure state can survive."

"You don't like vam people being out and about? We can still be good citizens of the Federation. We don't get in anyone's way. Just a few nips here and there. Most of us—or so I hear—pay for our drinks at private clubs."

He did not seem surprised. "We know of these establishments. One day they will be closed. Perhaps tomorrow. First these two, the prince and princess."

"They fancy themselves king and queen."

"No matter the names. You are all diseased and criminal. I welcome your demise from the Federation. All of you. It is a great shame your kind ever started in this region."

"Most of us do not choose to become vampires."

"Yes, it is a disease—"

"But you will take information from us willingly enough."

He smiled. "Information is neutral and nameless."

"So you accept it, no matter the source."

"Yes, true. Whatever aids our work."

"You said you would let me go if I give you information."

He glanced at his associates standing by the door. His face was stone. One of the State Security men turned and opened the door. The others exited. He closed the door behind them, regained his stance.

"I will let you go if your answers satisfy me," said Rusza. "Also, you must promise to leave the Federation and never return. Go as you like, over the border into the heathen lands. Become a mussie, I don't care. They kill your kind just the same as we do here."

I sat up straighter. "Do I have your word on this?"

"I give you a few words on this matter. If you please me, I will let you go. I will assign an escort for you to the border and they will watch you step across into the insane nations of United Europe. Good luck there, though I care not what happens to you. Your kind are not welcome there, either. They welcome all the rabble of the savage world without mark or question. Except your diseased kind."

"You have a kind heart, sir." He seemed not to detect my sarcasm. Leaving was exactly what I'd planned to do before these interruptions. If these people would only get out of my way. "Thank you for your thoughtful logic."

"It seems the best way."

"Naturally."

I negotiated the removal of the plastic hood, then told him about the meeting I had with Lord Azov. We both chuckled at the title he used. I glossed over my private talk with Alma; bygones. I described the car chase in profuse detail, me as the set-upon victim, but ignored the strange voice which directed me through much of it. An auditory hallucination from too long without feeding. The result, I made sure to emphasize, was that Gergely Azov was now indeed dead. As dead as the undead can be. He had been vanquished at long last. Separation: head from body, the Federation way.

Pure accident, I confessed, though seldom is an accident pure.

We shared another chuckle.

"Azov is dead?" Rusza wanted to confirm. He had been fighting the Budapest gangs for years. The largest one was as good as destroyed. It seemed anti-climactic. He stared at me.

"Yes," I confirmed. "I saw his severed head retrieved from a ditch while I stood near the headless body."

Rusza smiled—then frowned. I began to empathize with him, to see this beleaguered man for what he was: a state operative, forced or compelled to do whatever would save the state. Dedicated. I certainly could appreciate that. We seemed to bond over my interrogation.

He directed his guards to release my arms from their restraints. I rubbed my wrists as I rested my elbows on the table before me.

"Is that enough? I think I've covered everything." I dared relax. "May I go now? As you offered?"

Rusza nodded, obviously running details through his mind.

"Although . . . ." He pursed his lips for a while. "With Gergely Azov gone, gangs from Buda and Óbuda will take over Pest territory. More trouble for us. And we hate Vilmos Czakó the most—worst of all gang leaders. After Azov. Both powerful, yet Czakó delights in cruelty." He shook his head, thick black eyebrows waving in the breeze he made. "And then also there is . . . Maxim."

I perked up at the name.

"Maxim?"

"Yes." Rusza seemed to shudder. "They call him Maxim the Cruel. A Russian vampire. Also commander of the western army. In every war since Waterloo. He got the disease then, they say. Stories, perhaps. He served Czar Nicholas the Second. Comrade of Rasputin. The devil's stepson. And abused as a boy by that devil. Never forgets it, lives off revenge. He grows stronger with each revenge." He ranted on about this arch-enemy, and then politics, immigration, the failing economy, bad weather, and the Russians. The clock on the wall waited.

My body shivered at the vibration he established in the room.

"I see."

You see now? It was the voice again, even in this sealed room, with only Rusza and one guard. *Now is your chance to demonstrate how bad you are. You have been given a task to perform. Do it.*

"Do what?" I mumbled.

Rusza glared at me, like he thought I was giving away secrets into a hidden microphone.

There are six-hundred sixty-five people in this building at the present time. If you know the code, you will be able to program the heating system in the basement so it shuts down. The hot air will build up and eventually an explosion will occur. A design flaw. Or perhaps a way to destroy everything at once in the event of an emergency situation. Like a foreign invasion.

"Are you serious?" I muttered into my shoulder.

"What did you say?" asked Rusza, leaning in.

This building, said the voice, *the headquarters of State Security, will collapse and you will have killed six-hundred sixty-five people. It is a good start. Then you only need one more to claim your lovely corpse.*

"Why do I want to kill everyone in this building?" I mumbled once more, lowering my voice further.

Suddenly Rusza seemed struck by an invisible hand. He froze as though in a trance, his eyes glazed over.

Because you hate State Security. And because you have a task to complete. One thing more: do not harm Niklós Rusza as he is one of my agents.

"You have an agent? To do your dirty work?"

Doesn't everyone?

"I don't."

He has a weakness which makes him easy to manipulate. You may not think so, yet he likes boys. Especially his nephews.

I shook my head rather than speak, and Rusza pondered my action.

"You have problem?" he asked, standing up from the table.

"I've told you everything I know. May I leave now?" I stared humbly at the big man. "I promise to leave the Federation as soon as I have the body of my Beloved from the morgue. You don't even need to bother with an escort. I want to leave here. And I will never return."

Rusza hunched his shoulders, wrinkled his brow, narrowed his eyes. I thought he was about to transform into a werewolf—perhaps his usual after-work ritual.

And my talkative friend had declared Rusza off-limits! An agent of the light-bearer. A bad actor. It made sense. So then he needed to leave the building before I could perform my so-called task. Or else stay here yet survive an explosion . . . ?

"How do I get to the basement?" I muttered a bit too loud, thinking to myself.

"You go to elevator by east entrance," said Rusza in a low voice, like he was speaking to himself. "Insert key, turn right, then push button for basement."

I looked him straight in the eye across the table. He blinked but his face remained placid, possibly still in some kind of trance.

"Are you sure?" I asked in a normal voice.

"Yes," he responded. His fat hand had been in his front trousers pocket. As he pulled it out, to point at the door, a set of keys fell onto the floor. His foot kicked it over to my chair, under the table.

With a glance around, I bent to retrieve the keys.

"Will that be all for today?" I asked, holding a steady smile.

"Yes."

I stood and Rusza motioned for the guard to come over and unzip my plastic suit. I climbed out of it, draped it over my chair, then faced the door. My traveling clothes stunk, like I had escaped from a grave. The breeze from the ceiling vent helped dissipate the odor.

"One-three-three-zero-nine-five-two," he added.

Nodding, I stepped toward the door, feeling some weight pressing on my shoulders. The weight of a bat, perhaps, yet nothing was there.

As I passed through the doorway, two guards standing at attention on either side, the voice returned to me:

Now do you believe? Now will you obey?

"This is what you want?" I mumbled, walking with measured steps down the corridor to the stairwell. I felt certain that within a second or two Rusza would reconsider and guards would rush me.

A number three on the wall caught my eye, indicating the level I was on. I went down the stairs to the main floor, exited the stairwell and strode innocently across the wide lobby, across its polished floor and under its high ceiling, chandeliers, past lines of people conducting their business at various desks and along counters. I attracted no one's attention. They were like statues. My travel clothes were mussed but I appeared normal for public even without my Homburg. I credited the truck driver's contribution.

I found the east entrance, as directed, located the elevator, pressed the call button, and entered when it arrived.

After this task, you need only kill the Queen of Vampires to fill your quota. Then your lovely little corpse will be yours for all eternity.

34

THE ELEVATOR DOORS OPENED AND I WAS IN THE BASEMENT. GUARDS GAVE me a look, turned their noses away, yet dipped their heads as I passed, as though I was Rusza himself.

As I strolled down the corridor to the power control room, I felt the heft on my shoulder of a very ancient demon, directing my steps.

Turn here.

"I really don't want to do this," I spoke aloud—just to be sure I was truly speaking the words and not imagining them. "So many innocent people. I don't know them. They have never harmed me. For most of them, it is only coincidence they are here today. Others work here, trying to feed their families on meager wages—"

You are worried about innocent people? How quaint. I thought you wished to be a bad vampire.

"Well, not too bad. I'm just a poor phlebotomist from Oklahoma, who never hurt anyone."

Except the ladies you met. I have your record right here. Shameful. You were a bad human, that is for sure. You should be proud of that, how many lives you ruined. An example for many.

"I am ashamed of that. If only I had known . . ."

I approached the doors. Ahead of me, a fat, bald man in brown coveralls exited, saw me and dipped his head in greeting.

". . . which is why I cannot do this."

Yet you want this, to assert your own power, to make your mark, to let the world know you exist. It is the curse of the accursèd. I have seen it for countless millennia. It never ceases to amaze, the depths humans will go to prove they exist. Even knowing existence is so short. And no more than an illusion.

"Perhaps you don't exist," I snarled, pausing at the open doorway.

"You need something?" the big man in the coveralls asked me, half blocking the entrance. His Hungarian was rough enough I had to ask him to repeat what he said.

"I was sent down here to check the readings of some . . . gauges," I responded in polite, textbook Hungarian. I needed to pause to think of the Hungarian word for 'gauges'—*mérők*.

"Everything is working perfectly," said the beefy man, apparently taken aback by my insinuation.

"Even so . . . I was charged with checking them."

"Suit yourself."

He stepped back into the control room. I followed, glancing around at all the machinery and the flashing lights that monitored everything, appearing clearly as someone not familiar with the business.

Turn left, said my guide. *The bank of switches on the left. Stop. Top row. Red buttons. Not the big button, the little ones. It is number six you want to push. Hold it down for six seconds. No more. When you hear the alarm, release it and press the same button again. Hold it for six seconds more and release.*

"Then I run?" I mumbled to the voice.

"What?" questioned Mr. Coveralls standing beside me.

"Excuse me." I acted perturbed by his presence. "I must do this—check this, these settings—without any distraction."

"And who are you?" He watched me intently. "You don't wear the proper uniform to be working here."

A breath. "I was requested to come down here and get a reading off one of these monitors. It's . . . it's kind of a gag, I suppose. A dare by my sick friends upstairs. Well, you know, what kind of friends would send someone down here to . . . to see what a reading was on a silly monitor? I mean, I've never been down here in my life—literally—don't know what it's all about. Just following instructions."

"You're idiot," Mr. Coveralls growled. He waved me back. "Get out of here."

I was very ready to exit, but my guide pinched me, made me halt.

You are not a bad vampire at all. You are weak. And a fool. When push came to shove you fell down. What are we to do with you, Stefan? Moreover what should we do with your Beloved?

My throat was tight, like invisible hands were clenching it, cutting off my air. I threw myself down the corridor, grabbing the walls to steady myself. I was surprised I had let such an incident affect me: my heart rate, my breathing, so not vampire-like. Calm and steady is our mien. So close—

"I cannot kill innocent people."

There are no innocent people here. Everyone is guilty. Everyone has slipped. Everyone has fallen to one degree or another, some forgotten, some never to be forgotten. You will not be killing innocent people.

"I don't see it that way." I glanced up and down the corridor. The man in the coveralls watched me. "There might be disagreeable people in the world. I've met a lot of them. But death—true death—never to rise again—that's a cruel end. I would not wish that on anyone."

Even those people who harm you, who get in your way, who prevent you from saving your Beloved?

"It is fate, dammit!" I punched the wall and Mr. Coveralls shouted. I turned away from him. "She is dead. It's been two days—or more. Are they cutting into her now, seeing what caused her death? Am I too late?"

It is not yet time. You may yet save her body.

"But will I save her?"

The clock is ticking, Stefan. What will you do? If you care about your Beloved, you will do anything to save her.

"No," I whispered, pressing my forehead against the wall. "I cannot kill anyone. Not deliberately. I am not a bad vampire."

The *tsk*ing echoed down the corridor and back.

So you have chosen. The life of your Beloved for the lives of all these strangers. Plus the Queen of Vampires. You have failed. Your Beloved shall remain dead, the true death, and never be in your arms. Your actions demonstrate you do not care for her. She died because she once met you.

"No! I do care for her!" I cried out, alarming the guards. "She is the love of my life! My Beloved!"

Mr. Coveralls stomped down the corridor toward me. I hurried to the elevator, shutting the door before he could reach me.

Returning to the ground floor, I stumbled into the lobby with all the people coming and going around me, some bothering to give me a glance then shake their heads as comment on my bad appearance.

"Please," I whispered through clenched teeth, "let me go."

You may always go. No, Stefan, you are not a bad vampire. You will never do what is necessary to save your so-called Beloved. Do not worry, I will see that she enters my domain with no questions asked. Express lane. She will find someone more suitable for her here. And you will soon enough be dust.

"She is my Beloved!" I roared.

You treated her so poorly. It is difficult to see your affection for her. You have lived a life of regrets. Now you are dead. Excuse me, undead.

"I must go to her."

In that vast lobby of the State Security headquarters building, all eyes seemed to be on me. Suddenly I expected a rush of guards to apprehend me. Then all would be lost.

"Save her. Please."

Everyone deserves second chances. Come with me. You may yet earn freedom for your Beloved.

I followed the voice. Actually, I walked through rows of desks and halted in front of a set of elevators as though I was led on a leash. In the elevator I found my finger drawn to the twenty-fifth floor, the top of the building. I did not even know what was located there.

Out the elevators I went, straight down a dimly lit corridor, no guards present. It felt eerie, the same as when I was a kid hiding from my parents in that huge Old Main building in Utica. I could crawl into spaces nobody would see. I could spy on the insane and deformed who lived in the asylum. Now I was searching for a place to hide—or a secret doorway through which to escape.

Here is your destination. Open this door. Put your shoulder into it. It tends to stick.

I did as I was commanded and the door opened. A bright afternoon burst upon me. I was on the roof, or nearly so. Glass surrounded the room. Up a few steps, the solarium had doors which allowed access to the actual roof. I could see mounted guns there which I supposed were to protect the building from rebels and rioters.

"Here?"

Outside, I glanced around the roof, saw the roofs of other buildings in the government district. I could just make out the Duna.

"This is the place? What do I do here?"

The gun is already loaded. It is always ready to defend State Security headquarters from rebellious crowds. The attendants are having lunch. You only need aim and pull its trigger. The fifty-caliber rounds will do the rest. Then we will know whether or not your Beloved will live.

"No, I won't do it." I shook my head vehemently.

You do not want your Beloved to live?

"I just want to take her away from here and live in our dark world together. Let me go to her."

Hands on the sights, Stefan. The levers allow you to direct the barrel down onto the plaza. You see people crossing in different directions at this hour. With a fluid motion, you may be able to dispatch all of them. Then your Beloved will be yours.

"I said I won't do it." And yet I felt my hands pulled to the handles of the machine gun. The fingers of each hand wrapped around the grips, falling into firing position. The barrel tilted downward as though its weight could no longer resist gravity. I looked down the length of the barrel at the scene below.

What would you do to return her to a full and healthy life, disease-free and wholesome once more? As though she had never met you. What would you do for that? Would you dispatch so many people you do not know, so many who may be criminals or may be innocent? Or does it matter if your Beloved is returned to health—forever?

The thought cut through me like a polished sabre blade, smooth yet with deadly effect.

I gazed over the edge, the railing keeping me from falling. The plaza was as wide as two city blocks. Large planters full of flowers or bushes marked it into sections. People sat having lunch. A line of children in school uniforms marched on an official outing. A pair of grandmothers helped each other across the smooth pavement to renew subsistence certificates, most likely. And a dozen soldiers standing in formation, perhaps on their way somewhere. They posed, one of them operating a small drone holding a camera. All on the plaza, maybe a hundred. One hundred-fifty, tops.

"One hundred is too many," I muttered.

They are nothing to you.

Sure, I did not know them; none of them. Who would miss them? Their families, certainly, but only the family. They always miss their loved ones. No one would miss me—

Time is running out, Stefan. You must act.

I could not be saved, but I could finally do something good. Not only return my Beloved to life but let her be healthy and unmarked as she should have been. As she should have been if she had never met me—if I had never commented on her social media page. As if she had never responded. And we never agreed to meet in that Barnes & Noble bookstore, never shared coffee, never dated, never lived together, never ever lay in bed side by side and fell in love.

Suddenly I had that power, the powers only gods had, to turn back time and undo events, make things never happen.

There is much you can do. In fact, I would be remiss if I did not inform you the third girl in the first row, the blonde, is the daughter of the Governor-General. Her name is Szófia, by the way, named for her grandmother. She regularly cheats on exams. Behind her, the brown-haired boy, Tómas, is the son of the Prime Minister. He likes to grope the younger girls. Exiting the bus now is—

"Stop."

My voice was weak, yet I knew my tormentor would hear me. I stared down at the plaza, filling with people.

Feel the blood sludging through your veins. Who did this to you? Is it God? Who do you blame for your condition? Is this the God who made those beautiful people below on the plaza? None of them have your affliction. Show God how you feel. The way He makes beautiful, healthy people while you He condemns to this painful existence of dry patches and blood craving? Show Him how you feel about his curses and his blessings. Go on. Show Him.

A spring breeze touched my cheek as I marked the plaza.

Look out at the city, the lovely creation of Man. See its beauty. Cold, hard stone crafted to impress humans. What effort they put forth! They expect it to last, to continue, forever forgetting the impermanence of humanity. There is the House of Parliament, ruined now, yes, but, ah, what a work of art! It can be yours, Stefan. The river Duna, the city, the country, and everyone who lives here to do your bidding. I will make you Governor-General if you obey me today.

"Obey you?"

I give it all to you, everything you see. You will be my prophet to the unclean masses. You will speak for me. One pull of the trigger of this beautiful invention of humanity, designed perfectly to affect elimination of humans. One wonders why they work so hard to discontinue each other. But I digress . . . .

"You digress? What the f—"

Take your place at the head of my legions, our followers. Do it, Stefan, and the world will be your oyster. Your Beloved will rule beside you, as healthy as ever. It is your turn, your time!

The doors on the buses opened. About fifty students in uniform, age twelve or so, filed out.

Do it, Stefan.

My finger grew heavy. I would never have to think of this moment again. And my Beloved would be saved! One moment and everything would become glorious. My sins would be undone.

The trigger did not move.

Look, there's a puppy. See? By the potted bushes. Spaniel, I think. And that young mother sitting on the bench nursing her baby.

I tried again, using all the strength of my wrist and arm to try to move the trigger. I closed my eyes so I would not see my targets. Let the machinery do the evil. I am not even human, of no account, with no responsibility. I shook the trigger as hard as I could—

"Halt!" shouted Rusza, crashing through the door to the roof with a pair of uniformed men behind him.

Sorry, the spell must have worn off. You took too long.

Startled, I turned and the 50-calibre gun spun around with me. I saw Rusza and his men. I raised my hands, hoping they would not shoot me. He had a pistol in his hand, his arm extended.

"On your knees!" Rusza shouted. "Now!"

When I hesitated, he shot me. The first bullet hit my chest, near my armpit. The second hit just below the first. I slipped, dropping to my knees, my arm up, caught in the trigger assembly.

He aimed again and the third bullet broke a rib. My legs crumpled under me, my full body weight crashing to the concrete.

With my arm stretched up, my hand hooked in the trigger guard, my wrist caught, the weight of my body pulling down on the trigger finally released the spring and the round fired. Straight into Rusza's broad belly.

I tried to lift myself a bit, enough to unhook my wrist and hand, but that motion caused another round to fire which flew past Rusza and shattered the solarium glass where his two assistants cowered.

I asked you not to harm my agent. Yet you did. Now you owe me. You dare not fail me again or your Beloved will never rise.

"That wasn't my fault!"

Let us go directly to the main attraction.

"Enough killing," I grunted, feeling weak, spent. "I'm already dead. So is my Beloved. There's no need to make more corpses. Can't we be at peace?"

I feel your pain. You're a thinker, a feeler, not a doer. And you got yourself wounded. First things first.

My body retched, shook like a seizure, contorting in unholy ways. I could control nothing. For a minute everything snapped and stung.

When I tried to rise, my wounds seemed to have been mended. Three bloody slugs lay on the concrete at my knees.

There is still the Queen of Vampires. She must not continue. Then this long chess game with your friend God will continue. I am winning, if you care to know.

The two men who had followed Rusza crept up the steps a bit, their eyes wide at the sight of me taking three bullets and standing again. They rushed into the darkness of the stairwell.

"The shots. They will bring more guards."

Then you must trust me. Not as you did the Queen of Vampires. I trust her behavior towards you will not cause you to hesitate when the moment arrives.

I leaned against the gun mount, waiting for my head to clear. In the sunlight my skin tingled.

"Where?"

It seems she has returned to the place where you met her. I believe you call it a warehouse. There is no heating system to malfunction, no mounted guns, so you must deal with her the old-fashioned way. May I suggest something silver?

35

"Oh, poor baby, how does it feel?" the woman's voice cooed, but in a whiny manner, teasing. Must be Alma repeating the Hungarian to someone I could not see from where I stood behind the shelving. She admonished the other for being weak, for feeling pain.

I watched, stoking my courage, making a plan. In my hand was the sword cane, offered to me by the uniformed doorman as I exited the State Security headquarters. It had been taken from my penthouse at the Hotel Attila, part of the evidence collected. He called to me, held out the cane like I'd forgotten it. I froze, afraid that taking it would mark me as the criminal and a throng of guards would subdue me. But I dipped my head to him, accepting the cane.

Looking between boxes of nails and screws, I saw it was Balthazar who lay upon a bed of plywood boards. The throne of Lord Azov had been disassembled to make this resting place. Balthazar was in the same poor condition as at the traffic circle. Still no arm below the elbow. Szabó's screws had not sufficed to reattach it, I guessed. Balthazar cried out, whimpering. He seemed afraid to let go his full anger or full pain or both.

"You always complaining too much," groaned Lady Alma, Queen of Vampires. "I need a strong partner to rule this city. There is much to do. Many more to bring together in blood. I need you to be up to the challenge."

"Ah—ah—ah," he cried.

In stumbled Dr. Szabó, carrying an armful of supplies.

"You always take too long," Alma snapped at the doctor.

"I had to go to clinic to get some of these," Szabó responded.

He set down his wares, arranged them along the plywood beside Balthazar. He went to work—again. I saw the severed hand and lower arm lifted out of a plastic box and held in place. Alma pressed the cut end against the other end as Szabó worked with a large screwdriver. Balthazar screamed like I never heard any vampire scream.

Alma leaned over him, kissed his mouth. "Be still, my Love! This man will fix your flaws. We cannot have you half a vampire."

"I can't—I can't," he moaned, his body in a spasm.

"You must, you must," Alma insisted. She ran her fingers over his head, down his face, her nails scratching the fresh stitches in his ghost-white cheek, then his throat. "We are almost there. One day more. Perhaps two. We will take this city. I promise you—for all of us."

Balthazar continued moaning as Szabó inserted the long screws, adjusted the angle, gave the lower arm a sharp twist to align it. A wrist bone was not cooperating—the triquetrum, it seemed—so he dug it out and tossed it on the floor. Balthazar howled.

I turned the sword cane around in my hands, watching the scene. I could rush them, spear the queen straight away before she could react. Szabó might intercede, however. He was big enough to soundly thrash me. Was he loyal to them now?

The doors opened and in strutted a dozen members of their gang, dressed in tattered, singed clothes, faces painted for battle—looking ridiculous. The crew circled their masters.

Alma stood to greet them, her black Goth dress flittering like bat wings. I tried to hear her words but the gang talked over her. A fight was imminent was all I could catch. Another gang. Or several. The city was about to be a battleground—

My old-fashioned wristwatch beeped, warning about the sunrise.

The gang's attention turned in my direction.

"Someone's back there," snarled one female vampire, curly blonde hair streaked with blood. She added a long hiss. They were all jacked up, ready to rumble.

"Who is there?" called Alma.

Three members of the gang stalked toward me.

I stood tall, my cane held behind me, and stepped innocently into the light as though I had every right to be there. I marched out from between the shelves, exiting the aisle for the open area.

Alma gawked. "You! How dare you show yourself here!"

"Want us to kill him?" hissed the blonde lieutenant.

"No, he is mine." She said more but her Hungarian was slangy and hard to understand yet I caught her tone.

"I'm sorry," I said in a steady voice. "I never meant for that crash to happen. They were chasing me, after all. You know that. It was Fate, that's all. Poor driving." I pointed at Balthazar. "Blame him, if you must blame anyone. He was the driver. Lord Azov was—"

"I know Lord Azov was the passenger!" she sneered. "They never would be injured if not for chasing you. You are still to blame!"

I feigned a bow. "Then I apologize."

"Maybe he aim ze car for ze statue," Szabó muttered in English, his back to us, "try to send Lord Azov through ze window?"

"Shut up!" Alma growled, also in English.

The lieutenant waved her hand at me, long nails threatening. "He's got something behind him." She took a step forward.

I showed them my cane, leaned on it. "I need some assistance now and then. An old vampire."

"You're not old," said Alma.

"I was older when the transformation came upon me. You, on the other hand, were changed rather dramatically, with or without your consent. Who can say? You should have left here and gone somewhere else. Maybe America."

"America!" She gave a full-throated laugh and the others joined in. "Is that not your homeland?"

"Yes, in a way. Here is my homeland, too. My real homeland. My ancestors were born here long, long ago."

"Same as mine," Alma replied. "Maybe same as yours. Same village. Hah! Who can say? It is forgotten now. We have nothing now. Only a chance to grab our future in this moment." She shook her finger at the vampire on the plywood. "Except this one—wounded. We will miss our chance because of his wounds."

"What is it you hope for?"

She glared at me, as though I had asked a stupid question.

"With Lord Azov as our leader we sat on our side of the Duna and enjoyed simple life. That was enough for him, the lazy giant." She spit blood on the floor. "And his whore! Always his plaything, the games, the silly pastimes. Never the power!"

The doors opened again and two male vampires dragged in the girl Azov had kept as his pet.

"She is the one!" Alma shouted. Her clawed finger pointed at the girl's face. "This Maria turned him away from power, made him weak. Then you wound him, and goad him into chasing you. Brilliant! I could not plan any better."

I started to give an alternate version of the plan, but Szabó pushed himself up, blocking my view of Alma. I glanced at Maria, her face dirty. Her white dress was savagely torn, like she had been assaulted. Blood stained the front of her dress. Her neck was also bloody. Her escorts dropped her on the floor.

"Why you bring this corpse to me?" Alma growled. "I told you to ruin her. To destroy her."

"We did, my Lady," said one of the assailants, a muscled skinhead.

"She looks quite awful now if you ask me," said another.

"And she's ruined, that's for sure."

The second vampire laughed. The queen stared at them.

"Ruined is not enough! Destroy her," called Alma in a voice that struggled to sound regal.

I took a step toward the girl. "Wait. What has she really done? It was Azov's choice, not hers. She's a victim—"

"Speak not to me about Lord Azov," Alma sneered. Her head had lowered and she glared at me from under her bushy eyebrows, like a wildcat ready to pounce. "You did your part. Now you are dismissed. Go, Stefan Székely! Run away!"

I took another step, leaning on my cane. Maria was on the floor to my left, six steps away. Alma was in front of me, four steps. Behind her was the plywood bed with Balthazar flat on it, and Szabó standing there. The vampire gang was mostly behind me.

You have a clear run at her, said my invisible friend.

Something was wrong. I came here to do an evil deed, to be a bad vampire, when all I really wanted was my Beloved returned to me and a clear road to Sárvár. We would spend our forever days together there, contemplating each other's decay.

This is your chance. Do it now.

Wait a minute, I thought as loudly as possible, hoping my guardian could hear me. I have to be able to strike her without anyone getting at me. The moment is not right. Not yet.

I took a step forward, using the cane to balance myself.

"You be careful, Lady Alma, he uses that cane as a weapon."

My eyes widened. Szabó, my once trusted colleague, was betraying me to my enemy. I held the cane away from my leg like it was just an innocent piece of timber.

"I know he is swordsman," Alma growled. "He is proud of the skill. He can take care of Lord Azov's whore. Off with her head!"

"Lady Alma," Szabó began, head bowed, "I don't think—"

I held up the cane as though taking fifth position, ready to parry anything coming at my head and shoulders.

The arm of one of her gang members immediately appeared before my face, attempting to punch me. I swatted hard at the wrist with the wood of the cane and the hand retreated.

"Stop!" Alma shouted. She regarded me sternly. "You want to be loyal to me? To follow me? You can be useful. First, prove your loyalty. Destroy this whore. She has done too much harm."

The two escorts picked up the girl and threw her at me. She landed on her knees, blood staining the floor from her wounds. Looking up at me, her hands were clenched together, a praying nun.

"I beg you, sir," she cried.

I could not look away from her teary eyes.

"End her!" shouted Alma. "Make her wish she had never met Lord Azov! Or me!"

I raised the cane, grabbed its handle and with my other hand slid the blade free. It glimmered in the lamplight and the gang members instinctively withdrew.

"I'm not an executioner," I announced, standing too proudly. "This is not the way." I held up the blade, challenging.

Alma laughed. "There is no way but to end her existence."

There is another way, said my guardian. *Parry trois. Then lunge.*

I knew what my fencing master meant. I saw it. There was Szabó, a shadow forming around Alma.

I slipped the blade to my right, feigned the cut downward upon Maria's neck. Instead, I made the blade loop forward and strike at the Queen of Vampires. At the final instant Szabó pushed her aside with his elbow and the tip of the blade entered his wide chest.

He stared at me, accusing, then dropped on his thick knees.

I pulled the blade free and swung again at Alma. She crouched on the floor where she had fallen. Just as she pulled herself up, the blade slashed down, striking her arm. The blade cut deep, above the elbow, hit bone, but did not sever the arm.

I'd stretched too far and slipped off-balance, my free hand bracing my fall. Maria rushed to me.

"Get him!" shrieked Alma. Her gang rushed me.

Maria pushed me down, and the gang tumbled over her. Under the pile I had the blade in my hand. The weight of them pressed my hand to the floor. Someone grabbed my hand, snatching away the sword. I saw it was Szabó.

The next thing I heard was a great scream. The vampires untangled and got to their feet.

Balthazar was like a bonfire, smoke rising from his flesh. The silver coating of the blade was burning him. The sharpness of the blade had separated his head from his body.

Balthazar's head rolled off the plywood, leaving a bloody trail.

Maria climbed off me, stood and reached down for my hand.

"Now I am free," roared Szabó. The previous wound made a red circle on his chest. He held up the sword, admiring the blood running down the blade. With his arm raised, he was exposed.

Alma snatched the long screwdriver from the supplies spread out on the plywood and shoved it up at him. The Phillips head dug into his throat. She hit an artery and blood sprayed. She ducked under the crimson fountain, tongue out, lapping blood from the air.

The blade fell from Szabó's hand, clanging on the concrete floor. I dove for it, Maria clasping at my trousers. My fingers just reached the blade. My skin burned from the silver but I pulled it into my hand, the leather grip comfortable in my grasp.

The Queen of Vampires knelt entranced by the fresh blood raining over her.

I snapped the blade forward, catching her sideways, through her ribs, and into her heart. Her eyes opened, staring at me, her expression like she couldn't believe I would do such a thing. The silver caused her skin to smoke.

"That will not stop me," she said, voice quivering.

I knew at that moment I had taken the wrong move. Pulling back the blade, I set to swing it again. But I felt a weight on my arm, holding me back. Two hands clenched my hand, covering the hilt, and together we swung the blade strong and true: across the slender, pale throat of the Queen of Vampires. The angle allowed the blade to pass between vertebrae, splitting the cord, and out the other side.

A jumble of black hair blocked my view as blood splattered over me—and over Maria. We sank to the floor together.

Szabó was a beached whale on the floor, a pool of blood spreading out from his throat and body. Balthazar was a smoking fire pit in the stack of plywood, tongues of flame teasing rolls of wallpaper. Alma's body rested against the stack of boards, upright like a crucifix. Her head had rolled across the floor to the members of her gang who stood stunned.

Beside me lay Maria, gasping, hands to her face.

I prayed for sirens—then prayed for no sirens, or a roll-back of the clock. Vampire time was unmoving, always in the present.

Not what I expected, said my guardian, the light-bearer. *Not at all how I would have done it, certainly, but well-done, nevertheless, Stefan. Touché! What's yours is now yours. If you arrive in time. Unfortunately, time is not something I can change.*

The paper rolls caught fire, then the flammable fluids burst. In an instant the flames shot up to the ceiling and crawled across the wall to the shelves of paint cans.

"We must get out of here," I shouted to Maria as we scrabbled to our feet. "Fast!"

I waved her to the office but she tore her hand away and charged in a different direction through the billowing gray smoke. I doubted her way was safe so I exited through the corridor, past the office, out to the street. As I caught my breath, something inside exploded. Alarms went off. Windows above me shattered, glass raining down on the sidewalk, smoke billowing out.

I glanced up and down the street—

Sirens!

I ran as fast as I could despite a bad leg and being covered in blood. Other people's blood. A vehicle would be quicker. I crossed the blocks to the car dealership, trying to arrive by the time they opened for the morning. The sunrise struck me between the buildings, burning me.

The staff inside the dealership was shocked at my appearance.

"You look like Hell stomp on top of you," cried my young salesman, Mr. Vörös, in English. His long red hair flapped in the breeze of his arm-waving greeting.

"It's true," I relented. "Rough night at the office." I pointed to the door to the body shop. "Is it ready yet? I need it today."

Vörös seemed aghast. "Are you in need of medical assistance?"

"I'm fine. How soon?"

He shook his head. "You sure?"

"How soon?"

"I thought two more days. Had to wait on refrigeration unit. Back ordered all the way from Beograd. Two more days. Maybe three."

"I need my car today."

"Today?"

"Yes, like now. This minute." I glared at him. "Got the keys?"

He seemed disappointed, like his boss would not like that he didn't finish a customer's order properly. I patted his shoulder.

He cringed. "Damn! Your hand is so cold."

"Sorry about that. I've been playing with ice."

He led me to the cabinet where the keys were kept, retrieved mine. He showed me how to program the sensor so I need only tap the door lock rather than inserting the key or pressing the unlock button. I did not have a chip in my wrist like most citizens so the auto-lock feature was useless. He started to tell me more, but I reminded him I was in a hurry so I grabbed the keys out of his hand.

"Do you have a spare shirt?" I asked my salesman.

"*Persze*," he mugged, going to his desk. He pulled out a clean white shirt, still in its clear wrapper, and nervously handed it to me. "Maybe it fit you?"

Tearing off my bloody shirt, I grabbed the fresh one and clawed the wrapper open. My hands and face were caked with dried blood but I pulled the shirt on anyway, not feeling at all shy. My skin seemed better, not so dry and flaky. I felt a hundred percent more human.

"*Hé, láttad ezt? A tűz?*" someone called to Vörös.

On the far wall in the sales room, a wide video screen displayed the warehouse fire from a hovering drone. Four employees stood staring at the screen. Medics were filling ambulances with sheeted bodies.

I jogged out the door, my shoes leaving blood stains on the white tile floor. I circled around to the body shop and saw my beautiful black sedan up on the rack, two men in coveralls working under it.

"Bring it down," I called. "I need it today. Now!"

Vörös hurried in through the front door, waving at them, calling for them to follow my demands. They did.

I hopped into my new car as soon as it touched down, pushed the start button, and roared out of the garage and squealed off the lot like a man lucky to be escaping from Hell.

I found the next main avenue and charged into the city, zigzagging through the traffic, taking a sidewalk and knocking over a vendor cart, cutting a corner with people scattering, running a set of lights at a five-way intersection with cars screeching—rushing to the hospital to save my Beloved. I had to stop them from cutting her open.

It was morning. The third day. Shifts would begin.

The coroner would see to his first case, the diseased woman from America who had come all the way to the Hungarian Federation just to curse her lover once more before dying. The report showed someone had written down her final words. She blamed him for the disease that eventually killed her. What a tragedy! Moreover, she should never have been allowed into the Federation, rejected for having a serious disease. Her body would need to be burned. First, examining her organs would shed light on the progress of the affliction. Perhaps they could identify it and then begin research on it, finding a cure or at least a reasonable treatment. The disease left such horrible effects on the face and body.

It made sufferers appear much like the vampires of legend. Perhaps that was where the legends began long, long ago: among a close-knit clan isolated in the Carpathian mountains, interbreeding and passing on the genetic disposition to develop this fatal disease in mid-life. Or, possibly, the members of that clan had developed immunity to it while outsiders—and clearly this woman with oriental features had been an outsider to that ethnic group—anyone who was exposed to it would be forced to endure the painful transformation into this hideous final form: the rotting corpse: the final stage of humanity: flesh and blood. Then dust.

36

"No, Mom, I'm all right. I'm sorry not calling for such a long time. Long story, you know. But I want to let you know, first, that everything is okay. . . . No, really. It's a little hard to explain.

"Right now? Well . . . to tell the truth, I'm relaxing at a spa. I can't say where. Government agents listening. You know, like mineral baths? At a resort. Yes, one of those. . . . No, it's not harmful to my skin. That's why I'm calling. It's supposed to be healthy, make my skin better. It's the minerals in the water. From a mineral spring. From underground. That's what they say. In the pamphlet, at least.

"Yes, like that. So anyway, I'm floating on a rubber mat in this pool, under a full sun, and it's no problem. . . . No, my skin's fine. Wait, let me get my shades. Too bright here. . . . Not just minerals. I was in a hospital. Had some treatment. Don't remember much, but . . . what? I don't know. Doctor stuff. Medical jargon. . . . I suppose. If they did pray, I didn't know it. . . . No, Mom, it wasn't like that. No exorcism, just normal everyday medical treatment. . . . Magic? No, I don't think there was magic, no voodoo, no nothing. I just woke up one morning and everything was fine, everything normal and healthy. Like I was ten years younger. I mean, like before the disease showed up. . . . Okay, if you say so. . . . Yes, I have great-looking skin, and my hair is growing back and my gums don't bleed and I can close my mouth all the way, my lips are normal again and—

"Thanks, dear. . . .

"What? No, that was Stefan. He gave me a towel. We aren't wearing a stitch! Ha ha, Mom! . . . Yes, Stefan. Székely. . . . The same guy. . . . Yes, yes, I know, I know. It wasn't what I expected, but he . . . . No, he did. Everything is all right now, Mom. Like I said. He . . . no, he didn't. It was like . . . . Okay, it was a miracle. You can call it that if you want. Tell your preacher. Thank everyone for me.

"No, he was some kind of man-about-town. Inheritance. He knew some people, got the treatment for me. I guess I was in a coma. . . . Like he was back then, yes. I told you. And he . . . yes, like that. I just woke up one morning and everyone was shocked. The guy was about to cut into me to see how I died. He fainted, I guess. Yes, it was kinda comical, the way they looked at me. . . . I know! Wish I'd gotten it on livestream. . . . 'Dead girl sits up at autopsy.' There's the headline.

"Yeah, but I was kinda naked, just that sheet . . . like in TV dramas, sure, Mom. No, I just walked out. Stiffly. I couldn't really talk. I pointed at the door and the guy held the door open. . . . No, he was white as my sheet, what do you think? . . . And there was Stefan pulling up in a big black car, right in front of the doors, as though he was picking me up for a date. Yeah, the ER entrance! The car door swung open and I got in and we drove away—

"Of course. So anyway . . . no, we didn't. Listen, Mom, we're at this resort. We plan to go—no, Mom, he owns it. He bought it before I got here. But now it's . . . no, now we have to leave. Things are getting bad here. Russian army? You probably heard the news. The border is open, lots of tanks crossing. Riots in Budapest. The government's gonna fall, for sure. Any day now. That's why we're enjoying our spa while we can.

"Maybe . . . yes, another day or two. No, he says a week. . . . Stefan. You know, the guy from Oklahoma who I lived with . . . . My *boyfriend*. Yes, that Stefan. Mom, there hasn't ever been any other Stefans. Who would name a kid Stefan, anyway? Not in Oklahoma, at least. . . . So what if I did. I named him after his father. . . . Yes, Mom. You met him. You hated him just like I did . . . yes, but now . . . wait, now he's . . . no, Mom, he's . . . different now. I forgave him . . . . You should, too. Okay? Everything is undone now.

"Well, for one thing he's a lot better looking. Sexy, even. There will be a wedding. Count on it. . . . Yes, we do that. But it's okay. Problem solved. . . . Mom! Of course, damn condoms. Besides . . . besides, Mom

. . . he knows about our son. He wants to meet him. . . . Yes, Mom, we'll be home soon. I promise. . . . You won't recognize me. But . . . what's that? Phone charge? Mom, it's twenty-twenty-eight. Don't you know international calls are free? It was ruled a human right. We can talk all day and night if we want.

"Soon. Just need to visit his parents first. He always wanted me to meet them, but they kinda died. . . . No, it's not weird, it's . . . normal for us. . . . Yes, Mom, I will be polite. I will show them how I feel about him. . . . I will call him Stefan. What else would I call him? . . . Oh, you're right. That 'Beloved' stuff is too . . . umm, old-fashioned. . . . My 'gentleman friend', I suppose.

"Yes, Mom. . . . I'll call him my Beloved. See if he likes it. . . . Right. Okay. See you soon! Bye, Mom. Love ya."

CR

We left the village at sunrise, walking the old road as the morning light spread over the wooded hillsides, pale sunbeams slanting between the trees. We held hands, jostling each other like giddy teenagers. We even paused for kisses, for laughter, for memories we wished to live again.

Coming to the gravel drive for the first time in nearly two years, I knew something was wrong. The trees were bare in June, blackened as if by fire. Lightning, I considered. I could make out the stone walls and tower of the villa, normally blocked by the foliage.

Seeing it, my Beloved wrapped her arms around me and laid her head against my shoulder. "I'm sorry."

I placed my hand over hers. "I'd hoped it would be green and pretty for your visit."

"Should we go up?" She released me from her embrace but kept her arm around my waist. "What will we find? Are they still here? Maybe they left because of the fire."

"I'm sure nothing would make them leave."

Pulling her by her hand, we hiked up the gravel drive. Signs of a fire marked the route. Broken pieces of furniture, artwork, tapestries, as well as household items littered the way. Someone had been here, and not for a tour of a vampire castle.

Near the top we came to a wooden sign, crudely painted, nailed to a tree, with words that looked like Turkish. A closer look and I decided the writing was actually blood.

In the middle of the parking area were the remnants of a bonfire. A lot of things had been tossed onto it. Books, pieces of furniture, clothing—burned to charcoal. The doors to the lower level had been torn open. Inside was darkness and a faint stream of smoke drifted out, swept away with the breeze.

I glanced at Penny.

Taking her hand, I led her inside my family home. Many walls were painted with more Turkish words. Piles of debris filled the centers of the rooms, items gathered and burned or soiled with bodily products.

I let go of Penny's hand and rushed up the staircase, charging along the corridor to the large hall where my parents spent their years, father with his books and mother with her sewing and knitting.

The doors were ripped from the hinges, one on the floor, the other hanging loosely at an awkward angle. I pulled it on down to be safe.

Peering inside the deep room, my eyes fell on the tall stained glass windows at the far end, broken in places as though rocks had been thrown. The shadows in the far corners did not hide any movement. No father or mother. My heart clenched.

Perhaps they had escaped before this invasion.

"Stefan," called Penny from outside the hall.

She pointed down the corridor. I joined her and we stared out the windows at the end of the corridor, a view of the forest.

Two posts rose from the ground, crossbars at the top. From the cross bars two skeletons hung upside-down by their feet. The corpses had been set on fire. Skulls were missing. Below them the ground had been trampled, the garden stomped into mud, as though a crowd of people had gathered. Nearby two stakes rose to about shoulder height, as though they were intended as substitute bodies. Atop the spikes were two skulls, blackened by fire.

We hurried to the front of the villa then cut our way around the overgrowth to that garden area. I cut down the skeletons. We found a shovel in the garage and dug two graves to ease the bones into. We placed the skulls on the necks.

I had never intended to run away and leave them unprotected. But what protection could I have given them? They were attacked. The villa would have been attacked whether or not I was here. No defense against determined actors such as the ones who happened to find the villa occupied by an elderly couple who used to be human. No grace period. Instant hatred. Immediate violence. That is the way the world works now.

"I'm sorry," I cried over the dirt mounds.

Penny's hands went to my shoulders. After a moment, she pulled me into an embrace. It felt good to be hugged.

"As you always said . . . they were old, old enough to die. It's just so awful how they came to their end. Is there no justice in the world?"

I squeezed her tight. There is none, I thought. Only what we make for ourselves. That's what the light-bearer would say. I wanted to take up the sword, to ruthlessly slay the slayers, to bring justice to the land. Yet no voice addressed my demands.

"I should have been here. I should have protected them."

"Then you would be killed, too."

"A son has obligations . . . ."

"I'm sure they were happy to see you go out into the world . . . just like you said before. What more could they ask of you?"

"To comfort them in their dying years?"

"That could be another century, right?"

"That is why vampires should not have children."

"But you're not a vampire any more, Stefan. You're human again."

"Tell me the difference."

She stepped back. "Yes, Stefan. When are you going to tell me how that happened? How they finally found a cure . . . ?"

My lips pouted, uncertain how to answer.

"The right combination, I guess."

"Combination of what? Drugs?"

I remained nonplussed.

"Something experimental, wasn't it?" she quizzed.

"Very."

"Tell me. What did you do?"

I looked her in the eyes. "I made a deal."

"A deal?" She glared at me. "You mean with God?"

I dared not regard her, glanced down. "What do you think?"

She gave me another hug. "Then thank God for that."

I clasped her hand in mine, felt the warmth there. "I'm sure He is happy to take credit. Him and . . . science."

After a long look at the dirt mounds and caws from local ravens, we made our way down the hillside, back through the forest, an hour's stroll along the road to the village. War was coming to this part of the world. I thought about telling the villagers. Perhaps they knew already from the attack on the villa. There was too much to say and no words to say it. Time to flee again.

A bead of moisture grew in the corner of my eye. Such a strange sensation: a tear. Fourteen years without any tears and now . . . .

Suddenly I felt a weight on my shoulder. I saw my old friend, Milo, had alighted there, claws clutching the fabric of my shirt.

"Hello, my friend," I said to Milo as Penny gazed at me in disbelief. "I'm glad to see you. It's been too long, hasn't it? I'm surprised you found me."

Oh, but I've always been nearby, waiting for your call, waiting for you to need me. Yes, just as I needed you. My agent, the blind man you met, the one named Matej, spoke highly of you. In fact, after you left him, he lent me his soul in exchange for sight. Unfortunately, he died before seeing very much. It was a good day, he said.

Penny asked what I had muttered and I shook my head.

"Milo," I spoke to introduce my bat friend to my Beloved. "This is Penny."

She is truly lovely. Well worth your troubles. Take care of her. And thanks for everything.

Thanks?

For your assistance. I could not have done it without you. Now my plans may proceed. Turks encroach from the south, Russians roll in from the north like they did back in fifty-six, and United Europe accepts all the refugees. No more the Hungarian Federation. Resistance is ending. The chess game continues. Vilmos Czakó will do my bidding for now. Maxim Azov will replace him.

That is a terrible plan! It will mean more deaths, more chaos, more suffering—Ah, I see: That was your plan all along. Disrupt the peace. Restore misery and pain. That is your modus operandi.

You do not approve? It is necessary. We cannot have order for too long. People get tired, become restless, the churches lose membership. Order is bad for business. Besides, you like being part of history, don't you, Stefan?

Never did I want to be part of that. Leave me out of your plans.

I needed your help. And there you were. You see, I have no arms, no legs. That puts a crimp on what I can do. So I found you, always walking the path so close to me. We worked together to achieve our mutual aims. Didn't we?

But I asked God for help . . . .

Now you know. Only I keep promises.

Apparently so.

Be on your way with your lovely lady. You have your life, crooked genes corrected at last—although I can't imagine why you would choose the finite option when you could have chosen the endless continuing. However, if you really wish to grow old and die, that is your choice. Who wants to live forever anyway?

"Not me," I whispered, catching sight of my Beloved in the corner of my eye.

Then I wish you well. Remember, Stefan: I shall always light your path, wherever you go.

Milo gave a screech and launched himself into the sky, winging his way into the forest.

"You have a pet bat?" asked Penny, pink lips pushed into the corner of her mouth, her classic smirk.

"Not actually a pet." I grimaced, searching for the correct words. "More like guardian. But a devil, not an angel." I breathed deeply, then shrugged. "Long story, obviously."

"Obviously." She smiled and took my hand, caressing my smooth skin. "We'll have time for a long story on our flight home. First-class, you said. VIP all the way, right?"

CR

Once more I winced, anticipating pain. The hammer came too close to my fingers, glancing dangerously off the wooden stake. A shudder ran down my spine.

"Try again," I instructed. "Better aim, please."

The young man swung the hammer once more and struck the stake true, driving it into the ground. A few more strikes and the line held steady. The tent rose at last. We tested the other lines, made sure they held. A wind was blowing through the trees and we worried the tent might collapse during the night.

"That looks good," called Penny from the open hatch of the SUV. She gathered the cooler and pulled it to the edge of the tailgate.

"I'll get that," said Stefan, tall and lanky like his father, dark hair and eyes like his mother. He jogged over to the SUV, skipping around a couple of tree stumps, and grabbed the big cooler.

I stood admiring him. And his mother. The perfect family.

Suddenly, a sour smell stung my nose.

"Even up here? This high?" asked Penny. "More fields converted to cannabis. Less for food crops." She shook her head. "What's this world coming to?"

"Looks like that field's on fire," I said, gazing down into the valley.

A breeze shook the pines, clearing out the odor from below. The fresh scent wafted through the air, and I sucked it in, filling my lungs. The breath of life—so sweet. The view from our perch on the mountain included the valley below and the distant peaks across the valley, a few with snow already.

"I hope it's not a storm coming," said Penny, again beside me and giving my shoulder a pinch. "I told you it was getting too late in the season to start construction on our cabin. Better to start in the spring. We could have it done in three months. Just a foundation slab is all we've got so far. Not much to look at, Stefan. Why are we even up here this weekend?"

"We have to start getting used to being mountain folk. No time to lose. We'll soon have our cabin in the mountains. As you dreamed. All the better to be closer to heaven, right? I hope God doesn't mind His new neighbors."

Penny gave me the smirk she was famous for. "If you say so."

"You still talking about God?" asked our son. "My friends—and our Political Officer at school—they say it's just a myth. Like the old stories to explain how the world works. I guess it makes people comfortable, anyway. Like Grandma."

"Must you talk about that awful school," Penny grumbled. "So strict and—wrong. We're getting you out as soon as they approve the forms. It's homeschooling for you, young man. No more indoctrination."

"It's not that bad, Mom," said junior. "We can talk about anything, as long as it's hypothetical."

"And your friends are certainly free to believe whatever they like," I spoke up. "Who can say what is real and what is not?"

"We used to have free speech," said Penny. "When your father and I were young. You could say whatever you wanted."

"And Mother Park, too," I continued. "She can say anything, even pray in public. Religious beliefs are still tolerated. At least for the old."

"Be nice," said Penny. "She accepts you again."

My Beloved gave a love tap to my shoulder. I feigned injury and she swung her arms around me, pulled me down to her lips. We kissed. A lingering lip-lock.

"Hey, you guys," said the teenager. "Get a booth, why don'tcha!"

Penny broke from our embrace. "We have a tent." She pointed with her chin.

"Good enough," I said with a grin. "Now, where will you sleep?"

The kid frowned. "The SUV?"

"Your father's kidding," said Penny. She turned to me: "Don't kid your kid."

A dark shape caught my eyes: a bat taking flight out of the forest, circling over the meadow and back again. I did not move.

"Watch out, Dad!"

I didn't cringe as the bat alighted on my arm, searching for a secure hold in my elbow, then clawing its way up my arm to my shoulder, posing like a pirate's parrot.

"Wow, it likes you," said my son.

"Is that . . . ?" Penny started.

"Just a bat," I said, studying the creature. "They live in Colorado, too. They're harmless. Probably eats fruit." I glanced at my son, acting wary at my affinity for flying mammals. "I once had a bat friend back in the old country."

"He did," Penny confirmed.

"Here," I said, stepping over to the cooler resting on the tailgate of the SUV. I moved slowly so as not to scare the bat away and retrieved a jar of plum jam, my favorite. I held it up.

"Could you open this?" I asked my son.

He took the jar and unscrewed the lid, held it out for me. Sharing a look of amusement, I dipped my finger inside, gathering a dab.

"Relax. There aren't any vampire bats around here," I said coyly, offering the jam on my fingertip, "so nothing to worry about."

It is good to see you again, Stefan.

The same voice that had haunted me in the Hungarian Federation.

I need your assistance.

"What?"

I told you I would call on you again someday. Remember? That was our arrangement. I have another task. Are you ready?

"Of course I'm not ready." I turned away from Penny and lowered my voice. "It's only been two years."

This is our arrangement. You and your Beloved are restored to full health. And your son, as well. So long as he acts with good intentions and causes no trouble.

"What do you mean by that?" I wrung my hands. "It's a medical affliction. That's all."

"Huh, Dad? What'd you say?"

Everyone knows medical afflictions are caused by moral flaws. It was proven millennia ago. However, do not worry. So long as he behaves well, he will not develop the affliction you so despise. As for you, there is something I need you to do.

"But I—"

It is time, Stefan. Put down the bat and follow me.

"Mom, what's wrong with Dad?"

Or perhaps I could make use of your son. Either way. The choice is yours.

SUNSET

The conclusion of the Stefan Székely Trilogy is coming soon.

Acknowledgements

Although actual places are mentioned in the novel, no disrespect is intended; nor is suggestion made of any actual impropriety by these entities. They are used fictitiously.

I always use music to assist my imagination. For this novel, I began with the playlist from the first novel's writing sessions: the music of Adrian von Ziegler, BrunuhVille, and selected songs of Coldplay, Evanescence, Tokio Hotel, and In Fear and Faith.

Eventually, I added new music: the original and various renditions of Queen's "Who Wants to Live Forever?" as well as the music of Eurielle, cellist Tina Guo (solo and with pianist Peter Kater), and especially the works of Shaun Taylor McManus.

During the period of revision, I also discovered music by Lucas King, especially the album *Dark Piano for Dark Thoughts* which helped to reshape several scenes.

Thank you for your inspiration and the amazing aural support.

About the Author

Stephen Swartz grew up in Kansas City, Missouri, USA, where he was an avid reader of science-fiction and quickly began emulating his favorite authors. Even after veering from science-fiction, his stories usually feature exotic lands and foreign languages, strangers lost in familiar places, and the occasional breakfast menu.

Along the way, Stephen studied music in college and worked at a wide range of jobs: from French fry guy to soldier, tax agency clerk, and TV station writer, before heading to Japan for several years of teaching English.

Stephen is now a Professor of English and has taught writing in New York, Pennsylvania, Kansas, Oklahoma, as well as China. He lives in Oklahoma, where he can be found working on his next novel most evenings and weekends.

Other books by Stephen Swartz

*Epic Fantasy *With Dragons*

A Girl Called Wolf

A Dry Patch of Skin
(soon to be a trilogy)

A Beautiful Chill

After Ilium

Aiko

The Dream Land Trilogy

I. Long Distance Voyager

II. Dreams of Future's Past

III. Diaspora

www.ingramcontent.com/pod-product-compliance
Lightning Source LLC
Chambersburg PA
CBHW020340180626
46812CB00001B/276